RECEIV

THE M
PR

BY
CATHERINE MANN

AND

DANTE'S
MARRIAGE PACT
BY
DAY LECLAIRE

"I'm not going away with you."

"This isn't going to die down." He kept his voice even and low, reasonable. The stakes were too important for all of them. "The reporters will swarm you by morning, if not sooner. Your friends will sell photos of the two of us together."

"Then we're through, you and I."

"Do you honestly think anyone's going to believe the breakup is for real? The timing will seem too convenient."

"We ended things last weekend."

Like hell. "Tell that to the papers and see if they believe you. Pleading a breakup isn't going to buy you any kind of freedom from their interest."

She studied him through narrowed eyes. "How do I know you're not just using this as an excuse to get back together?"

Was he? An hour ago, he would have done anything to get into her bed again.

Dear Reader,

Welcome to my world of the "Rich, Rugged & Royal" Medina family! I've always been a fan of fairytales about princes and princesses earning their happily ever after. In deciding to create my own fairytale royal family, I was entranced by the possibility that a prince could be living incognito right next door. From that emerged the deposed royal patriarch, King Enrique Medina (who in my mind looks just like Sean Connery) and his three sons.

In *The Maverick Prince*, you'll meet the youngest Medina heir, Antonio, at just the moment his identity is exposed, much to the surprise of his new lover. I hope you enjoy Antonio and Shannon's passionate journey from Texas to Florida in search of true love. Stay tuned for Duarte Medina's story and Carlos Medina's book next year.

Happy reading!

Catherine Mann

www.catherinemann.com

THE MAVERICK PRINCE

BY
CATHERINE MANN

Published in Great Britain 2011
by Mills & Boon, an imprint of Harlequin (UK) Limited,
Eton House, 18-24 Paradise Road, Richmond, Surrey TW9 1SR

© Catherine Mann 2010

ISBN: 978 0 263 88322 0

51-1111

Harlequin (UK) policy is to use papers that are natural, renewable and recyclable products and made from wood grown in sustainable forests. The logging and manufacturing processes conform to the legal environmental regulations of the country of origin.

Printed and bound in Spain
by Blackprint CPI, Barcelona

USA TODAY bestseller **Catherine Mann** is living out her own fairytale ending on a sunny Florida beach with her Prince Charming husband and their four children. With more than thirty-five books in print in over twenty countries, she has also celebrated wins for both a RITA® Award and a Booksellers' Best Award. Catherine enjoys chatting with readers online—thanks to the wonders of the wireless internet that allows her to cyber-network with her laptop by the water! To learn more about her work, visit her website, www.CatherineMann.com, or reach her by snail mail at PO Box 6065, Navarre, FL 32566, USA.

To my favorite little princesses and princes—Megan, Frances, James and Zach. Thank you for inviting Aunt Cathy to your prince and princess tea parties. The snack cakes and Sprite were absolutely magical!

Prologue

GlobalIntruder.com
Exclusive: For Immediate Release

Royalty Revealed!

Do you have a prince living next door? Quite possibly!

Courtesy of a positive identification made by one of the GlobalIntruder.com's very own photojournalists, we've successfully landed the scoop of the year. The deposed Medina monarchy has not, as was rumored, set up shop in a highly secured fortress in Argentina. The three Medina heirs—with their billions—have been living under assumed names and rubbing elbows with everyday Americans for decades.

We hear the sexy baby of the family, Antonio, is already taken in Texas by his waitress girlfriend

Shannon Crawford. She'd better watch her back now that word is out about her secret shipping magnate!

Meanwhile, never fear, ladies. There are still two single and studly Medina men left. Our sources reveal that Duarte dwells in his plush resort in Martha's Vineyard. Carlos—a surgeon, no less—resides in Tacoma. Wonder if he makes house calls?

No word yet on their father, King Enrique Medina, former ruler of San Rinaldo, an island off the coast of Spain. But our best reporters are hot on the trail.

For the latest update on how to nab a prince, check back in with the GlobalIntruder.com. And remember, you heard it here first!

One

Galveston Bay, Texas

"King takes the queen." Antonio Medina declared his victory and raked in the chips, having bluffed with a simple high-card hand in Texas Hold'Em.

Ignoring an incoming call on his iPhone, he stacked his winnings. He didn't often have time for poker since his fishing charter company went global, but joining backroom games at his pal Vernon's Galveston Bay Grille had become a more frequent occurrence of late. Since Shannon. His gaze snapped to the long skinny windows on either side of the door leading out to the main dining area where she worked.

No sign of Shannon's slim body, winding her way through the brass, crystal and white linen of the five-star restaurant. Disappointment chewed at him in spite of his win.

A cell phone chime cut the air, then a second right

afterward. Not his either time, although the noise still forced his focus back to the private table while two of Vernon Wolfe's cronies pressed the ignore button, cutting the ringing short. Vernon's poker pals were all about forty years senior to Antonio. But the old shrimp-boat captain turned restaurateur had saved Antonio's bacon back when he'd been a teen. So if Vernon beckoned, Antonio did his damnedest to show. The fact that Shannon also worked here provided extra oomph to the request.

Vernon creaked back in the leather chair, also disregarding his cell phone currently crooning "Son of a Sailor" from his belt. "Ballsy move holding with just a king, Tony," he said, his voice perpetually raspy from years of shouting on deck. His face still sported a year-round tan, eyes raccoon ringed from sunglasses. "I thought Glenn had a royal flush with his queen and jack showing."

"I was taught to bluff by the best." Antonio—or Tony Castillo as he was known these days—grinned.

A smile was more disarming than a scowl. He always smiled so nobody knew what he was thinking. Not that even his best grin had gained him forgiveness from Shannon after their fight last weekend.

Resisting the urge to frown, Tony stacked his chips on the scarred wooden table Vernon had pried from his boat before docking himself permanently at the restaurant. "Your pal Glenn needs to bluff better."

Glenn—a coffee addict—chugged his java faster when bluffing. For some reason no one else seemed to notice as the high-priced attorney banged back his third brew laced with Irish whiskey. He then simply shrugged, loosened his silk tie and hooked it on the back of the chair, settling in for the next round.

Vernon swept up the played cards, flipping the king of hearts between his fingers until the cell stopped singing vintage Jimmy Buffett. "Keep winning and they're not going to let me deal you in anymore."

Tony went through the motions of laughing along, but he knew he wasn't going anywhere. This was his world now. He'd built a life of his own and wanted nothing to do with the Medina name. He was Tony Castillo now. His father had honored that. Until recently.

For the past six months, his deposed king of a dad had sent message after message demanding his presence at the secluded island compound off the coast of Florida. Tony had left that gilded prison the second he'd turned eighteen and never looked back. If Enrique was as sick as he claimed, then their problems would have to be sorted out in heaven…or more likely in somewhere hotter even than Texas.

While October meant autumn chills for folks like his two brothers, he preferred the lengthened summers in Galveston Bay. The air conditioner still cranked in the redbrick waterside restaurant in the historic district.

Muffled live music from a flamenco guitarist drifted through the wall along with the drone of dining clientele. Business was booming for Vernon. Tony made sure of that. Vernon had given Antonio a job at eighteen when no one else would trust a kid with sketchy ID. Fourteen years and many millions of dollars later, Tony figured it was only fair some of the proceeds from the shipping business he'd built should buy the aging shrimp-boat captain a retirement plan.

Vernon nudged the deck toward Glenn to cut, then dealt the next hand. Glenn shoved his buzzing BlackBerry beside his spiked coffee and thumbed his cards up for a peek.

Tony reached for his…and stopped…tipping his ear toward the sound from outside the door. A light laugh cut through the clanging dishes and fluttering strum of the

Spanish guitar. *Her* laugh. Finally. The simple sound made him ache after a week without her.

His gaze shot straight to the door again, bracketed by two windows showcasing the dining area. Shannon stepped in view of the left lengthy pane, pausing to punch in an order at the servers' station. She squinted behind her cat-eye glasses, the retros giving her a naughty schoolmarm look that never failed to send his libido surging.

Light from the globed sconces glinted on her pale blond hair. She wore her long locks in a messy updo, as much a part of her work uniform as the knee-length black skirt and form-fitting tuxedo vest. She looked sexy as hell—and exhausted.

Damn it all, he would help her without hesitation. Just last weekend he'd suggested as much when she'd pulled on her clothes after they'd made love at his Bay Shore mansion. She'd shut him down faster than the next heartbeat. In fact, she hadn't spoken to him or returned his calls since.

Stubborn, sexy woman. It wasn't like he'd offered to set her up as his mistress, for crying out loud. He was only trying to help her and her three-year-old son. She always vowed she would do anything for Kolby.

Mentioning that part hadn't gone well for him, either.

Her lips had pursed tight, but her eyes behind those sexy black glasses had told him she wanted to throw his offer back in his face. His ears still rang from the slamming door when she'd walked out. Most women he knew would have jumped at the prospect of money or expensive gifts. Not Shannon. If anything, she seemed put off by his wealth. It had taken him two months to persuade her just to have coffee with him. Then two more months to work his way into bed with her. And after nearly four weeks of mind-bending sex, he was still no closer to understanding her.

Okay, so he'd built a fortune from Galveston Bay being

one of the largest importers of seafood. Luck had played a part by landing him here in the first place. He'd simply been looking for a coastal community that reminded him of home.

His real home, off the coast of Spain. Not the island fortress his father had built off the U.S. The one he'd escaped the day he'd turned eighteen and swapped his last name from Medina to Castillo. The new surname had been plucked from one of the many branches twigging off his regal family tree. Tony *Castillo* had vowed never to return, a vow he'd kept.

And he didn't even want to think about how spooked Shannon would be if she knew the well-kept secret of his royal heritage. Not that the secret was his to share.

Vernon tapped the scarred wooden table in front of him. "Your phone's buzzing again. We can hold off on this hand while you take the call."

Tony thumbed the ignore button on his iPhone without looking. He only disregarded the outside world for two people, Shannon and Vernon. "It's about the Salinas Shrimp deal. They need to sweat for another hour before we settle on the bottom line."

Glenn rolled his coffee mug between his palms. "So when we don't hear back from you, we'll all know you hit the ignore button."

"Never," Tony responded absently, tucking the device back inside his suit coat. More and more he looked forward to Shannon's steady calm at the end of a hectic day.

Vernon's phone chimed again—Good God, what was up with all the interruptions?—this time rumbling with Marvin Gaye's "Let's Get It On."

The grizzled captain slapped down his cards. "That's my wife. Gotta take this one." Bluetooth glowing in his ear, he shot to his feet and tucked into a corner for semiprivacy. "Yeah, sugar?"

Since Vernon had just tied the knot for the first time seven months ago, the guy acted like a twenty-year-old newlywed. Tony walled off flickering thoughts of his own parents' marriage, not too hard since there weren't that many to remember. His mother had died when he was five.

Vernon inhaled sharply. Tony looked up. His old mentor's face paled under a tan so deep it almost seemed tattooed. What the hell?

"Tony." Vernon's voice went beyond raspy, like the guy had swallowed ground glass. "I think you'd better check those missed messages."

"Is something wrong?" he asked, already reaching for his iPhone.

"You'll have to tell us that," Vernon answered without once taking his raccoonlike eyes off Tony. "Actually, you can skip the messages and just head straight for the internet."

"Where?" He tapped through the menu.

"Anywhere." Vernon sank back into his chair like an anchor thudding to the bottom of the ocean floor. "It's headlining everywhere. You won't miss it."

His iPhone connected to the internet and displayed the top stories—

> Royalty Revealed!
> Medina Monarchy Exposed!

Blinking fast, he stared in shock at the last thing he expected, but the outcome his father had always feared most. One heading at a time, his family's cover was peeled away until he settled on the last in the list.

> Meet the Medina Mistress!

The insane speed of viral news... His gaze shot straight to the windows separating him from the waiters' station, where seconds ago he'd seen Shannon.

Sure enough, she still stood with her back to him. He wouldn't have much time. He had to talk to her before she finished tapping in her order or tabulating a bill.

Tony shot to his feet, his chair scraping loudly in the silence as Vernon's friends all checked their messages. Reaching for the brass handle, he kept his eyes locked on the woman who turned him inside out with one touch of her hand on his bare flesh, the simple brush of her hair across his chest until he forgot about staying on guard. Foreboding crept up his spine. His instincts had served him well over the years—steering him through multimillion-dollar business decisions, even warning him of a frayed shrimp net inching closer to snag his feet.

And before all that? The extra sense had powered his stride as he'd raced through the woods, running from rebels overthrowing San Rinaldo's government. Rebels who hadn't thought twice about shooting at kids, even a five-year-old.

Or murdering their mother.

The Medina cover was about more than privacy. It was about safety. While his family had relocated to a U.S. island after the coup, they could never let down their guard. And damn it all, he'd selfishly put Shannon in the crosshairs simply because he had to have her in his bed.

Tony clasped her shoulders and turned her around. Only to stop short.

Her beautiful blue eyes wide with horror said it all. And if he'd been in doubt? The cell phone clutched in Shannon's hand told him the rest.

She already knew.

* * *

She didn't want to know.

The internet rumor her son's babysitter had read over the phone had to be a media mistake. As did the five follow-up articles she'd found in her own ten-second search with her cell's internet service.

The blogosphere could bloom toxic fiction in minutes, right? People could say whatever they wanted, make a fortune off click-throughs and then retract the erroneous story the next day. Tony's touch on her shoulders was so familiar and stirring he simply couldn't be a stranger. Even now her body warmed at the feel of his hands until she swayed.

But then hadn't she made the very same mistake with her dead husband, buying into his facade because she *wanted* it to be true?

Damn it, Tony wasn't Nolan. All of this would be explained away and she could go back to her toe-curling affair with Tony. Except they were already in the middle of a fight over trying to give her money—an offer that made her skin crawl. And if he was actually a prince?

She swallowed hysterical laughter. Well, he'd told her that he had money to burn and it could very well be he'd meant that on a scale far grander than she could have ever imagined.

"Breathe," her ex-lover commanded.

"Okay, okay, okay," she chanted on each gasp of air, tapping her glasses more firmly in place in hopes the dots in front of her eyes would fade. "I'm okay."

Now that her vision cleared she had a better view of her place at the center of the restaurant's attention. And when had Tony started edging her toward the door? Impending doom welled inside her as she realized the local media would soon descend.

"Good, steady now, in and out." His voice didn't sound any different.

But it also didn't sound Texan. Or southern. Or even northern for that matter, as if he'd worked to stamp out any sense of regionality from himself. She tried to focus on the timbre that so thoroughly strummed her senses when they made love.

"Tony, please say we're going to laugh over this misunderstanding later."

He didn't answer. His square jaw was set and serious as he looked over her shoulder, scanning. She found no signs of her carefree lover, even though her fingers carried the memory of how his dark hair curled around her fingers. His wealth and power had been undeniable from the start in his clothes and lifestyle, but most of all in his proud carriage. Now she took new note of his aristocratic jaw and cheekbones. Such a damn handsome and charming man. She'd allowed herself to be wowed. Seduced by his smile.

She'd barely come to grips with dating a rich guy, given all the bad baggage that brought up of her dead husband. A crooked sleaze. She'd been dazzled by Nolan's glitzy world, learning too late it was financed by a Ponzi scheme.

The guilt of those destroyed lives squeezed the breath from her lungs all over again. If not for her son, she might very well have curled inside herself and given up after Nolan took his own life. But she would hold strong for Kolby.

"Answer me," she demanded, hoping.

"This isn't the place to talk."

Not reassuring and, oh God, why did Tony still have the power to hurt her? Anger punched through the pain. "How long does it take to say *damned rumor?*"

He slid an arm around her shoulders, tucking her to his side. "Let's find somewhere more private."

"Tell me now." She pulled back from the lure of his familiar scent, minty patchouli and sandalwood, the smell of exotic pleasures.

Tony—Antonio—Prince Medina—whoever the hell he was—ducked his head closer to hers. "Shannon, do you really want to talk here where anyone can listen? The world's going to intrude on our town soon enough."

Tears burned behind her eyes, the room going blurry even with her glasses on. "Okay, we'll find a quiet place to discuss this."

He backed her toward the kitchen. Her legs and his synched up in step, her hips following his instinctively, as if they'd danced together often…and more. Eyes and whispers followed them the entire way. Did everyone already know? Cell phones sang from pockets and vibrated on tabletops as if Galveston quivered on the verge of an earthquake.

No one approached them outright, but fragments drifted from their huddled discussions.

"Could Tony Castillo be—"

"—Medina—"

"—With that waitress—"

The buzz increased like a swarm of locusts closing in on the Texas landscape. On her life.

Tony growled lowly, "There's nowhere here we can speak privately. I need to get you out of Vernon's."

His muscled arm locked her tighter, guiding her through a swishing door, past a string of chefs all immobile and gawking. He shouldered out a side door and she had no choice but to follow.

Outside, the late-day sun kissed his bronzed face, bringing his deeply tanned features into sharper focus. She'd always known there was something strikingly foreign about him. But she'd believed his story of dead parents, bookkeepers who'd emigrated from South America. Her own parents had died in a car accident before she'd graduated from college. She'd thought they'd at least shared similar childhoods.

Now? She was sure of nothing except how her body still betrayed her with the urge to lean into his hard-muscled strength, to escape into the pleasure she knew he could bring.

"I need to let management know I'm leaving. I can't lose this job." Tips were best in the evening and she needed every penny. She couldn't afford the time it would take to get her teaching credentials current again—if she could even find a music-teaching position with cutbacks in the arts.

And there weren't too many people out there in search of private oboe lessons.

"I know the owner, remember?" He unlocked his car, the remote chirp-chirping.

"Of course. What was I thinking? You have connections." She stifled a fresh bout of hysterical laughter.

Would she even be able to work again if the Medina rumor was true? It had been tough enough finding a job when others associated her with her dead husband. Sure, she'd been cleared of any wrongdoing, but many still believed she must have known about Nolan's illegal schemes.

There hadn't even been a trial for her to state her side. Once her husband had made bail, he'd been dead within twenty-four hours.

Tony cursed low and harsh, sailor-style swearing he usually curbed around her and Kolby. She looked around, saw nothing... Then she heard the thundering footsteps a second before the small cluster of people rounded the corner with cameras and microphones.

Swearing again, Tony yanked open the passenger door to his Escalade. He lifted her inside easily, as if she weighed nothing more than the tray of fried gator appetizers she'd carried earlier.

Seconds later he slid behind the wheel and slammed the door a hair's breadth ahead of the reporters. Fists pounded on the tinted windows. Locks auto-clicked. Shannon sagged in the leather seat with relief.

The hefty SUV rocked from the force of the mob. Her heart rate ramped again. If this was the life of the rich and famous, she wanted no part.

Shifting into Reverse then forward, Tony drove, slow but steady. People peeled away. At least one reporter fell on his butt but everyone appeared unharmed.

So much for playing chicken with Tony. She would be wise to remember that.

He guided the Escalade through the historic district a hint over the speed limit, fast enough to put space between them and the media hounds. Panting in the aftermath, she still braced a hand on the dash, her other gripping the leather seat. Yet Tony hadn't even broken a sweat.

His hands stayed steady on the wheel, his expensive watch glinting from the French cuffs of his shirt. Restored brick buildings zipped by her window. A young couple dressed for an evening out stepped off the curb, then back sharply. While the whole idea of being hunted by the paparazzi scared her to her roots, right here in the SUV with Tony, she felt safe.

Safe enough for the anger and betrayal to come bubbling to the surface. She'd been mad at him since their fight last weekend over his continued insistence on giving her money.

But those feelings were nothing compared to the rage that coursed through her now. "We're alone. Talk to me."

"It's complicated." He glanced in the rearview mirror. Normal traffic tooled along the narrow street. "What do you want to know?"

She forced herself to say the words that would drive a permanent wedge between her and the one man she'd dared let into her life again.

"Are you a part of that lost royal family, the one everybody thought was hiding in Argentina?"

The Cadillac's finely tuned engine hummed in the silence. Lights clicked on automatically with the setting sun, the dash glowing.

His knuckles went white on the steering wheel, his jaw flexing before he nodded tightly. "The rumors on the internet are correct."

And she'd thought her heart couldn't break again.

Her pride had been stung over Tony's offer to give her money, but she would have gotten over it. She would have stuck to her guns about paying her own way, of course. But *this?* It was still too huge to wrap her brain around. She'd slept with a prince, let him into her home, her body, and considered letting him into her heart. His deception burned deep.

How could she have missed the truth so completely, buying into his stories about working on a shrimp boat as a teen? She'd assumed his tattoo and the closed over pierced earlobe were parts of an everyman past that seduced her as fully as his caresses.

"Your name isn't even Tony Castillo." Oh God. She pressed the back of her hand against her mouth, suddenly nauseated because she didn't even know the name of the guy she'd been sleeping with.

"Technically, it could be."

Shannon slammed her fists against the leather seat instead of reaching for him as she ached to do. "I'm not interested in technically. Actually, I'm not interested in people who lie to me. Can I even trust that you're really thirty-two years old?"

"It isn't just my decision to share specific details. I have other family members to consider. But if it's any consolation, I really am thirty-two. Are you really twenty-nine?"

"I'm not in a joking mood." Shivering, she thumbed her bare ring finger where once a three-carat diamond had rested. After Nolan's funeral, she'd taken it off and sold it along with everything else to pay off the mountain of debt. "I should have known you were too good to be true."

"Why do you say that?"

"Who makes millions by thirty-two?"

He cocked an arrogant eyebrow. "Did you just call me a moocher?"

"Well, excuse me if that was rude, but I'm not exactly at my best tonight."

His arms bulged beneath his Italian suit—she'd had to look up the exclusive Garaceni label after she'd seen the coat hanging on his bedpost.

Tony looked even more amazing out of the clothes, his tanned and muscled body eclipsing any high-end wardrobe. And the smiles he brought to her life, his uninhibited laughter were just what she needed most.

How quiet her world had been without him this week. "Sorry to have hurt your feelings, pal. Or should I say, Your Majesty? Since according to some of those stories I'm 'His Majesty's mistress.'"

"Actually, it would be 'Your Highness.'" His signature smile tipped his mouth, but with a bitter edge. "Majesty is for the king."

How could he be so flippant? "Actually, you can take your title and stuff it where the sun—"

"I get the picture." He guided the Escalade over the Galveston Island Causeway, waves moving darkly below. "You'll need time to calm down so we can discuss how to handle this."

"You don't understand. There's no calming down. You lied to me on a fundamental level. Once we made l—" she stumbled over the next word, images of him moving over her, inside her, stealing her words and breath until her stomach churned as fast as the waters below "—after we went to bed together, you should have told me. Unless the sex didn't mean anything special to you. I guess if you had to tell every woman you slept with, there would be no secret."

"Stop!" He sliced the air with his hand. His gleaming Patek Philippe watch contrasted with scarred knuckles, from his sailing days he'd once told her. "That's not true and not the point here. You were safer not knowing."

"Oh, it's for my own good." She wrapped her arms around herself, a shield from the hurt.

"How much do you know about my family's history?"

She bit back the urge to snap at him. Curiosity reined in her temper. "Not much. Just that there was a king of some small country near Spain, I think, before he was overthrown in a coup. His family has been hiding out to avoid the paparazzi hoopla."

"Hoopla? This might suck, but that's the least of my worries. There are people out there who tried to kill my family and succeeded in murdering my mother. There are people who stand to gain a lot in the way of money and power if the Medinas are wiped off the planet."

Her heart ached for all he had lost. Even now, she wanted to press her mouth to his and forget this whole insane mess.

To grasp that shimmering connection she'd discovered with him the first time they'd made love in a frenzied tangle at his Galveston Bay mansion.

"Well, believe it, Shannon. There's a big bad world outside your corner of Texas. Right now, some of the worst will start focusing on me, my family and anyone who's close to us. Whether you like it or not, I'll do whatever it takes to keep you and Kolby protected."

Her son's safety? Perspiration froze on her forehead, chilling her deeper. Why hadn't she thought of that? Of course she'd barely wrapped her brain around Tony... Antonio. "Drive faster. Get me home now."

"I completely agree. I've already sent bodyguards ahead of us."

Bodyguards?

"When?" She'd barely been able to think, much less act. What kind of mother was she not to have considered the impact on Kolby? And what kind of man kept bodyguards on speed dial?

"I texted my people while we were leaving through the kitchen."

Of course he had people. The man was not merely the billionaire shipping magnate she'd assumed, he was also the bearer of a surname generations old and a background of privilege she couldn't begin to fathom.

"I was so distracted I didn't even notice," Shannon whispered, sinking into her seat. She wasn't even safe in her own neighborhood anymore.

She couldn't wish this away any longer. "You really are this Medina guy. You're really from some deposed royal family."

His chin tipped with unmistakable regality. "My name is Antonio Medina. I was born in San Rinaldo, third son of King Enrique and Queen Beatriz."

Her heart drumming in her ears, panic squeezed harder at her rib cage. How could she have foreseen this when she met him five months ago at the restaurant, bringing his supper back to the owner's poker game? Tony had ordered a shrimp po'boy sandwich and a glass of sweet tea.

Poor Boy? How ironic was that?

"This is too weird." And scary.

The whole surreal mess left her too numb to hurt anymore. That would return later, for sure. Her hands shook as she tapped her glasses straight.

She had to stay focused now. "Stuff like this happens in movies or a hundred years ago."

"Or in my life. Now in yours, too."

"Nuh-uh. You and I?" She waggled her hand back and forth between them. "We're history."

He paused at a stop sign, turning to face her fully for the first time since he'd gripped her shoulders at the restaurant. His coal black eyes heated over her, a bold man of uninhibited emotions. "That fast, you're ready to call an end to what we've shared?"

Her heart picked up speed from just the caress of his eyes, the memory of his hands stroking her. She tried to answer but her mouth had gone dry. He skimmed those scarred knuckles down her arm until his hand rested on hers. Such a simple gesture, nothing overtly erotic, but her whole body hummed with awareness and want.

Right here in the middle of the street, in the middle of an upside down situation, her body betrayed her as surely as he had.

Wrong. Wrong. Wrong. She had to be tough. "I already ended things between us last weekend."

"That was a fight, not a breakup." His big hand splayed over hers, eclipsing her with heat.

"Semantics. Not that it matters." She pulled herself

away from him until her spine met the door, not nearly far enough. "I can't be with you anymore."

"That's too damn bad, because we're going to be spending a lot of time together after we pick up your son. There's no way you can stay in your apartment tonight."

"There's no way I can stay with *you*."

"You can't hide from what's been unleashed. Today should tell you that more than anything. It'll find you and your son. I'm sorry for not seeing this coming, but it's here and we have to deal with it."

Fear for her son warred with her anger at Tony. "You had no right," she hissed between clenched teeth, "no right at all to play with our lives this way."

"I agree." He surprised her with that. However, the reprieve was short. "But I'm the only one who can stand between you both and whatever fallout comes from this revelation."

TWO

A bodyguard stood outside the front door of her first-floor apartment. A bodyguard, for heaven's sake, a burly guy in a dark suit who could have passed for a Secret Service employee. She stifled the urge to scream in frustration.

Shannon flung herself out of the Escalade before it came to a complete stop, desperate to see her child, to get inside her tiny apartment in hopes that life would somehow return to normal. Tony couldn't be serious about her packing up to go away with him. He was just using this to try to get back together again.

Although what did a *prince* want with her?

At least there weren't any reporters in the parking lot. The neighbors all seemed to be inside for the evening or out enjoying their own party plans. She'd chosen the large complex for the anonymity it offered. Multiple three-story buildings filled the corner block, making it difficult to tell one apartment from another in the stretches of yellow units with tiny white balconies. At the center of it all, there was a pool and tiny playground, the only luxuries she'd allowed herself. She might not be able to give Kolby a huge yard, but he would have an outdoor place to play.

Now she had to start the search for a haven all over again.

"Here," she said as she thrust her purse toward him, her keys in her hand, "please carry this so I can unlock the door."

He extended his arm, her hobo bag dangling from his big fist. "Uh, sure."

"This is not the time to freak out over holding a woman's purse." She fumbled for the correct key.

"Shannon, I'm here for you. For you and your handbag."

She glanced back sharply. "Don't mock me."

"I thought you enjoyed my sense of humor."

Hadn't she thought just the same thing earlier? How could she say good-bye to Tony—he would never be Antonio to her—forever? Her feet slowed on the walkway between the simple hedges, nowhere near as elaborate as the gardens of her old home with Nolan, but well maintained. The place was clean.

And safe.

Having Tony at her back provided an extra layer of protection, she had to admit. After he'd made his shocking demand that she pack, he'd pulled out his phone and began checking in with his lawyer. From what she could tell hearing one side of the conversation, the news was spreading fast, with no indication of how the Global Intruder's people had cracked his cover. Tony didn't lose his temper or even curse.

But her normally lighthearted lover definitely wasn't smiling.

She ignored the soft note of regret spreading through her for all she would leave behind—this place. *Tony.* He strode alongside her silently, the outside lights casting his shadow over hers intimately, moving, tangling the two together as they walked.

Stopping at her unit three doors down from the corner, Tony exchanged low words with the guard while she slid the key into the lock with shaking hands. She pushed her way inside and ran smack into the babysitter already trying to open up for her. The college senior was majoring in elementary education and lived in the same complex. There might only be seven years between her and the girl in a concert T-shirt, but Shannon couldn't help but feel her own university days spent studying to be a teacher happened eons ago.

Shannon forced herself to stay calm. "Courtney, thanks for calling me. Where's Kolby?"

The sitter studied her with undisguised curiosity—who could blame her?—and pointed down the narrow hall toward the living room. "He's asleep on the couch. I thought it might be better to keep him with me in case any reporters started showing up outside or something." She hitched her bulging backpack onto one shoulder. "I don't think they would stake out his window, but ya never know. Right?"

"Thank you, Courtney. You did exactly the right thing." She angled down the hall to peek in on Kolby.

Her three-year-old son slept curled on the imported leather sofa, one of the few pieces that hadn't been sold to pay off debts. Kolby had poked a hole in the armrest with a fountain pen just before the estate sale. Shannon had strapped duct tape over the tear, grateful for one less piece of furniture to buy to start her new life.

Every penny she earned needed to be tucked away for

emergencies. Kolby counted on her, her sweet baby boy in his favorite Thomas the Tank Engine pj's, matching blanket held up to his nose. His blond hair was tousled and spiking, still damp from his bath. She could almost smell the baby-powder sweetness from across the room.

Sagging against the archway with relief, she turned back to Courtney. "I need to pay you."

Shannon took back her hobo bag from Tony and tunneled through frantically, dropping her wallet. Change clanked on the tile floor.

What would a three-year-old think if he saw his mother's face in some news report? Or Tony's, for that matter? The two had only met briefly a few times, but Kolby knew he was Mama's friend. She scooped the coins into a pile, picking at quarters and dimes.

Tony cupped her shoulder. "I've got it. Go ahead and be with your son."

She glanced up sharply, her nerves too raw to take the reminder of how he'd offered her financial help mere moments after sex last weekend. "I can pay my own way."

Holding up his hands, he backed away.

"Fine, Shannon. I'll sit with Kolby." He cautioned her with a look not to mention their plans to pack and leave.

Duh. Not that she planned to follow all *his* dictates, but the fewer who knew their next move the better for avoiding the press and anyone else who might profit from tracking their moves. Even the best of friends could be bought off.

Speaking of payoffs… "Thank you for calling me so quickly." She peeled off an extra twenty and tried not to wince as she said goodbye to ice cream for the month. She usually traded babysitting with another flat-broke single mom in the building when needed for work and dates.

Courtney was only her backup, which she couldn't—and didn't—use often. "I appreciate your help."

Shaking her head, Courtney took the money and passed back the extra twenty. "You don't need to give me all that, Mrs. Crawford. I was only doing my job. And I'm not gonna talk to the reporters. I'm not the kind of person who would sell your story or something."

"Really," Shannon urged as she folded the cash back into her hand, "I want you to have it."

Tony filled the archway. "The guard outside will walk you home, just to make sure no one bothers you."

"Thanks, Mr. Castillo. Um, I mean…" Courtney stuffed the folded bills into her back pocket, the college coed eyeing him up and down with a new awareness. "Mr. Medina… Sir? I don't what to call you."

"Castillo is fine."

"Right, uh, bye." Her face flushed, she spun on her glitter flip-flops and took off.

Shannon pushed the door closed, sliding the bolt and chain. Locking her inside with Tony in a totally quiet apartment. She slumped back and stared down the hallway, the ten feet shrinking even more with the bulk of his shoulders spanning the arch. Light from the cheap brown lamp glinted off the curl in his black hair.

No wonder Courtney had been flustered. He wasn't just a prince, but a fine-looking, one-hundred-percent *man*. The kind with strong hands that could finesse their way over a woman's body with a sweet tenderness that threatened to buckle her knees from just remembering. Had it only been a week since they'd made love in his mammoth jetted tub? God knows she ached as if she'd been without him for months.

Even acknowledging it was wrong with her mind, her body still wanted him.

* * *

Tony wanted her.

In his arms.

In his bed.

And most of all, he wanted her back in his SUV, heading away from here. He needed to use any methods of persuasion possible and convince her to come to his house. Even if the press located his home address, they wouldn't get past the gates and security. So how to convince Shannon? He stared down the short tiled hallway at her.

Awareness flared in her eyes. The same slam of attraction he felt now and the first time he'd seen her five months ago when he'd stopped by after a call to play cards. Vernon had mentioned hiring a new waitress but Tony hadn't thought much of it—until he met her.

When Tony asked about her, the old guy said he didn't know much about Shannon other than her crook of a husband had committed suicide rather than face a jury. Shannon and her boy had been left behind, flat broke. She'd worked at a small diner for a year and a half before that and Vernon had hired her on a hunch. Vernon and his softie heart.

Tony stared at her now every bit as intently as he had that first time she'd brought him his order. Something about her blue-gray eyes reminded him of the ocean sky just before a storm. Tumultuous. Interesting.

A challenge. He'd been without a challenge for too long. Building a business from nothing had kept him charged up for years. What next?

Then he'd seen her.

He'd spent his life smiling his way through problems and deals, and for the first time he'd found someone who saw past his bull. Was it the puzzle that tugged him? If so, he wasn't any closer to solving the mystery of Shannon.

Every day she confused him more, which made him want her more.

Pushing away from the door, she strode toward him, efficiently, no hip swish, just even, efficient steps. Then she walked out of her shoes, swiping one foot behind her to kick them to rest against the wall. No shoes in the house. She'd told him that the two times he'd been allowed over her threshold for no more than fifteen minutes. Any liaisons between them had been at his bayside mansion or a suite near the restaurant. He didn't really expect anything to happen here with her son around, even asleep.

And given the look on her face, she was more likely to pitch him out. Better to circumvent the boot.

"I'll stay with your son while you pack." He removed his shoes and stepped deeper into her place, not fancy, the sparse generic sort of a furnished space in browns and tan—except for the expensive burgundy leather sofa with a duct-taped *X* on the armrest.

Her lips thinned. "About packing, we need to discuss that further."

"What's to talk about?" He accepted their relationship was still on hold, but the current problems with his identity needed to be addressed. "Your porch will be full by morning."

"I'll check into a hotel."

With the twenty dollars and fifty-two cents she had left in her wallet? He prayed she wasn't foolish enough to use a credit card. Might as well phone in her location to the news stations.

"We can talk about where you'll stay *after* you pack."

"You sound like a broken record, Tony."

"*You*'re calling *me* stubborn?"

Their standoff continued, neither of them touching, but he was all too aware of her scrubbed fresh scent.

Shannon, the whole place, carried an air of some kind of floral cleaner. The aroma somehow calmed and stirred at the same time, calling to mind holding her after a mind-bending night of sex. She never stayed over until morning, but for an hour or so after, she would doze against his chest. He would breathe in the scent of her and him and *them* blended together.

His nose flared.

Her pupils widened.

She stumbled back, her chest rising faster. "I do need to change my clothes. Are you sure you'll be all right with Kolby?"

It was no secret the couple of times he'd met the boy, Kolby hadn't warmed up to him. Nothing seemed to work, not ice cream or magic coin tricks. Tony figured maybe the boy was still missing his father.

That jerk had left Shannon bankrupt and vulnerable. "I can handle it. Take all the time you need."

"Thank you. I'm only going to change clothes though. No packing yet. We'll have to talk more first, Tony—um, Antonio."

"I prefer to be called *Tony*." He liked the sound of it on her tongue.

"Okay...Tony." She spun on her heel and headed toward her bedroom.

Her steps still efficient, albeit faster, were just speedy enough to bring a slight swing to her slim hips in the pencil-straight skirt. Thoughts of peeling it down and off her beautiful body would have to wait until she had the whole Antonio/Tony issue sorted out.

If only she could accept that he'd called himself Tony Castillo almost longer than he'd remembered being Antonio Medina.

He even had the paperwork to back up the Castillo

name. Creating another persona hadn't been that difficult, especially once he'd saved enough to start his first business. From then on, all transactions were shuttled through the company. Umbrella corporations. Living in plain sight. His plan had worked fine until someone, somehow had pierced the new identities he and his brothers had built. In fact, he needed to call his brothers, who he spoke to at most a couple of times a year. But they might have insights.

They needed a plan.

He reached inside his jacket for his iPhone and ducked into the dining area where he could see the child but wouldn't wake him. He thumbed the seven key on his speed dial…and Carlos's voice mail picked up. Tony disconnected without leaving a message and pressed the eight key.

"Speak to me, my brother." Duarte Medina's voice came through the phone. They didn't talk often, but these weren't normal circumstances.

"I assume you know." He toyed with one of Shannon's hair bands on the table.

"Impossible to miss."

"Where's Carlos? He's not picking up." Tony fell back into their clipped shorthand. They'd only had each other growing up and now circumstances insisted they stay apart. Did his brothers have that same feeling, like they'd lost a limb?

"His secretary said he got paged for an emergency surgery. He'll be at least another couple of hours. Apparently Carlos found out as he was scrubbing in, but you know our brother." Duarte, the middle son, tended to play messenger with their father. The three brothers spoke and met when they could, but there were so many crap memories from their childhood, those reunions became further apart.

Tony scooped up the brown band, a lone long strand

of her blond hair catching the light. "When a patient calls…"

"Right."

It could well be hours before they heard from Carlos, given the sort of painstaking reconstructive surgeries he performed on children. "Any idea how this exploded?"

His brother hissed a long angry curse. "The Global Intruder got a side-view picture of me while I was visiting our sister."

Their half sister Eloisa, their father's daughter from an affair shortly after they had escaped to the States. Enrique had still been torn up with grief from losing his wife… not to mention the guilt. But apparently not so torn up and remorseful he couldn't hop into bed with someone else. The woman had gone on to marry another man who'd raised her daughter as his own.

Tony had only met his half sister once as a teen, a few years before he'd left the island compound. She'd only been seven at the time. Now she'd married into a high-profile family jam-packed with political influence and a fat portfolio. Could she be at fault for bringing the media down on their heads for some free PR for her new in-laws? Duarte seemed to think she wanted anonymity as much as the rest of them. But could he have misjudged her?

"Why were you visiting Eloisa?" Tony tucked the band into his pocket.

"Family business. It doesn't matter now. Her in-laws were there. Eloisa's sister-in-law—a senator's wife—slipped on the dock. I kept her from falling into the water. Some damn female reporter in a tree with a telephoto lens caught the mishap. Which shouldn't have mattered, since Senator Landis and his wife were the focus of the picture. I still don't know how the photographer pegged me from a side view, but there it is. And I'm sorry for bringing this crap down on you."

Duarte hadn't done anything wrong. They couldn't live in a bubble. In the back of Tony's mind, he'd always known it was just a matter of time until the cover story blew up in their faces. He'd managed to live away from the island anonymously for fourteen years, his two older brothers even longer.

But there was always the hope that maybe he could stay a step ahead. Be his own man. Succeed on his own merits. "We've all been caught in a picture on occasion. We're not vampires. It's just insane that she was able to make the connection. Perfect storm of bad luck."

"What are your plans for dealing with this perfect storm?"

"Lock down tight while I regroup. Let me know when you hear from Carlos."

Ending the call, Tony strode back into the living room, checked on Kolby—still snoozing hard—and dropped to the end of the sofa to read messages, his in-box already full again. By the time Tony scrolled through emails that told him nothing new, he logged on to the internet for a deeper peek. And winced. Rumors were rampant.

That his father had died of malaria years ago—false.

Supposition that Carlos had plastic surgery—again, false.

Speculation that Duarte had joined a Tibetan monastery—definitely false.

And then there were the stories about him and Shannon, which actually happened to be true. The whole "Monarch's Mistress" was really growing roots out there in cyberspace. Guilt kicked him in the gut that Shannon would suffer this kind of garbage because of him. The media feeding frenzy would only grow, and before long they would stir up all the crap about her thief of a dead husband. He tucked away his phone in disgust.

"That bad?" Shannon asked from the archway.

She'd changed into jeans and a simple blue tank top. Her silky blond hair glided loosely down her shoulders, straight except for a slight crimped ring where she'd bound it up on her head for work. She didn't look much older than the babysitter, except in her weary—wary—eyes.

Leaning back, he extended his legs, leather creaking as he stayed on the sofa so as not to spook her. "The internet is exploding. My lawyers and my brothers' lawyers are all looking into it. Hopefully we'll have the leak plugged soon and start some damage control. But we can't stuff the genie back into the bottle."

"I'm not going away with you." She perched a fist on one shapely hip.

"This isn't going to die down." He kept his voice even and low, reasonable. The stakes were too important for all of them. "The reporters will swarm you by morning, if not sooner. Your babysitter will almost inevitably cave in to one of those gossip rag offers. Your friends will sell photos of the two of us together. There's a chance people could use Kolby to get to me."

"Then we're through, you and I." She reached for her sleeping son on the sofa, smoothing his hair before sliding a hand under his shoulders as if to scoop him up.

Tony touched her arm lightly, stopping her. "Hold on before you settle him into his room." As far as Tony was concerned, they would be back in his Escalade in less than ten minutes. "Do you honestly think anyone's going to believe the breakup is for real? The timing will seem too convenient."

She sagged onto the arm of the sofa, right over the silver *X*. "We ended things last weekend."

Like hell. "Tell that to the papers and see if they believe you. The truth doesn't matter to these people. They probably printed photos of an alien baby last week. Pleading a breakup isn't going to buy you any kind of freedom from their interest."

"I know I need to move away from Galveston." She glanced around her sparsely decorated apartment, two pictures of Kolby the only personal items. "I've accepted that."

There wouldn't be much packing to do.

"They'll find you."

She studied him through narrowed eyes. "How do I know you're not just using this as an excuse to get back together?"

Was he? An hour ago, he would have done anything to get into her bed again. While the attraction hadn't diminished, since his cover was blown, he had other concerns that overshadowed everything else. He needed to determine the best way to inoculate her from the toxic fallout that came from associating with Medinas. One thing for certain, he couldn't risk her striking out on her own.

"You made it clear where we stand last weekend. I get that. You want nothing to do with me or my money." He didn't move closer, wasn't going to crowd her. The draw between them filled the space separating them just fine on its own. "We had sex together. Damn good sex. But that's over now. Neither one of us ever asked for or expected more."

Her gaze locked with his, the room silent but for their breathing and the light snore of the sleeping child. Kolby. Another reminder of why they needed to stay in control.

In fact, holding back made the edge sharper. He skimmed his knuckles along her collarbone, barely touching. A week ago, that pale skin had worn the rasp of his beard. She didn't move closer, but she didn't back away, either.

Shannon blinked first, her long lashes sweeping closed while she swallowed hard. "What am I supposed to do?"

More than anything he wanted to gather her up and tell her everything would be okay. He wouldn't allow anything less. But he also wouldn't make shallow promises.

Twenty-seven years ago, when they'd been leaving San Rinaldo on a moonless night, his father had assured them everything would be fine. They would be reunited soon.

His father had been so very wrong.

Tony focused on what he could assure. "A lot has happened in a few hours. We need to take a step back for damage assessment tonight at my home, where there are security gates, alarms, guards watching and surveillance cameras."

"And after tonight?"

"We'll let the press think we are a couple, still deep in that affair." He indulged himself in one lengthy, heated eye-stroke of her slim, supple body. "Then we'll stage a more public breakup later, on our terms, when we've prepared a backup plan."

She exhaled a shaky breath. "That makes sense."

"Meanwhile, my number one priority is shielding you and Kolby." He sifted through options, eliminating one idea after another until he was left with only a single alternative.

Her hand fell to rest on her sleeping son's head. "How do you intend to do that?"

"By taking you to the safest place I know." A place he'd vowed never to return. "Tomorrow, we're going to visit my father."

Three

"Visit your father?" Shannon asked in total shock. Had Tony lost his mind? "The King of San Rinaldo? You've got to be kidding."

"I'm completely serious." He stared back at her from the far end of the leather sofa, her sleeping son between them.

Resisting Tony had been tough enough this past week just knowing he was in the same town. How much more difficult would it be with him in the same house for one night much less days on end? God, she wanted to run. She bit the inside of her lip to keep from blurting out something she would regret later. Sorting through her options could take more time than they appeared to have.

Kolby wriggled restlessly, hugging his comfort blanket tighter. Needing a moment to collect her thoughts and her resolve, she scooped up her son.

"Tony, we'll have to put this discussion on hold." She

cradled her child closer and angled down the hall, ever aware of a certain looming prince at her back. "Keep the lights off, please."

Shadows playing tag on the ceiling, she lowered Kolby into the red caboose bed they'd picked out together when she moved into the apartment. She'd been trying so hard to make up for all her son had lost. As if there was some way to compensate for the loss of his father, the loss of security. Shannon pressed a kiss to his forehead, inhaling his precious baby-shampoo smell.

When she turned back, she found Tony waiting in the doorway, determination stamped on his square jaw. Well, she could be mighty resolute too, especially when it came to her son. Shannon closed the curtains before she left the room and stepped into the narrow hall.

She shut the door quietly behind her. "You have to know your suggestion is outrageous."

"The whole situation is outrageous, which calls for extraordinary measures."

"Hiding out with a king? That's definitely what I would call extraordinary." She pulled off her glasses and pinched the bridge of her nose.

Before Nolan's death she'd worn contacts, but couldn't afford the extra expense now. How much longer until she would grow accustomed to glasses again?

She stared at Tony, his face clear up close, everything in the distance blurred. "Do you honestly think I would want to expose myself, not to mention Kolby, to more scrutiny by going to your father's? Why not just hide out at your place as we originally discussed?"

God, had she just agreed to stay with him indefinitely?

"My house is secure, up to a point. People will figure out where I live and they'll deduce that you're with me.

There's only one place I can think of where no one can get to us."

Frustration buzzed in her brain. "Seems like their telephoto lenses reach everywhere."

"The press still hasn't located my father's home after years of trying."

But she thought… "Doesn't he live in Argentina?"

He studied her silently, the wheels almost visibly turning in his broad forehead. Finally, he shook his head quickly.

"No. We only stopped off there to reorganize after escaping San Rinaldo." He adjusted his watch, the only nervous habit she'd ever observed in him. "My father did set up a compound there and paid a small, trusted group of individuals to make it look inhabited. Most of them also escaped San Rinaldo with us. People assumed we were there with them."

What extreme lengths and expense their father had gone to. But then wasn't she willing to do anything to protect Kolby? She felt a surprise connection to the old king she'd never met. "Why are you telling me this much if it's such a closely guarded secret?"

He cupped her shoulder, his touch heavy and familiar, *stirring*. "Because it's that important I persuade you."

Resisting the urge to lean into him was tougher with each stroke of his thumb against the sensitive curve of her neck. "Where *does* he live then?"

"I can't tell you that much," he said, still touching and God, it made her mad that she didn't pull away.

"Yet you expect me to just pack up my child and follow you there." She gripped his wrist and moved away his seductive touch.

"I detect a note of skepticism in your voice." He shoved his hands in his pockets.

"A note? Try a whole freaking symphony, Tony." The sense of betrayal swelled inside her again, larger and larger until it pushed bitter words out. "Why should I trust you? Especially now?"

"Because you don't have anyone else or they would have already been helping you."

The reality deflated her. She only had a set of in-laws who didn't want anything to do with her or Kolby since they blamed her for their son's downfall. She was truly alone.

"How long would we be there?"

"Just until my attorneys can arrange for a restraining order against certain media personnel. I realize that restraining orders don't always work, but having one will give us a stronger legal case if we need it. It's one thing to stalk, but it's another to stalk and violate a restraining order. And I'll want to make sure you have top-of-the-line security installed at your new home. That should take about a week, two at the most."

Shannon fidgeted with her glasses. "How would we get there?"

"By plane." He thumbed the face of his watch clean again.

That meant it must be far away. "Forget it. You are not going to isolate me that way, cut me off from the world. It's the equivalent of kidnapping me and my son."

"Not if you agree to go along." He edged closer, the stretch of his hard muscled shoulders blocking out the light filtering from the living area. "People in the military get on planes all the time without knowing their destination."

She tipped her chin upward, their faces inches apart. Close enough to feel his heat. Close enough to kiss.

Too close for her own good. "Last time I checked, I wasn't wearing a uniform." Her voice cracked ever so slightly. "I didn't sign on for this."

"I know, Shanny…." He stroked a lock of her hair intimately. "I *am* sorry for all this is putting you through, and I will do my best to make the next week as easy for you as possible."

The sincerity of his apology soothed the ragged edges of her nerves. It had been a long week without him. She'd been surprised by how much she had missed his spontaneous dates and late-night calls. His bold kisses and intimate caresses. She couldn't lie to herself about how much he affected her on both an emotional and physical level. Otherwise this mess with his revealed past wouldn't hurt her so deeply.

Her hand clenched around her glasses. He gently slid them from her hand and hooked them on the front of her shirt. The familiarity of the gesture kicked her heart rate up a notch.

Swaying toward him, she flattened her hands to his chest, not sure if she wanted to push him away or pull him nearer. Thick longing filled the sliver of space between them. An answering awareness widened his pupils, pushing and thinning the dark brown of his eyes.

He lowered his head closer, closer still until his mouth hovered over hers. Heated breaths washed over her, stirring even hotter memories and warm languid longing. She'd thought the pain of Nolan's deceit had left her numb for life…until she saw Tony.

"Mama?"

The sound of her son calling out from his room jolted her back to reality. And not only her. Tony's face went from seductive to intent in a heartbeat. He pulled the door open just as Kolby ran through and into his mother's arms.

"Mama, Mama, Mama…" He buried his face in her neck. "Monster in my window!"

* * *

Tony shot through the door and toward the window in the child's room, focused, driven and mentally kicking himself for letting himself be distracted.

He barked over his shoulder, "Stay in the hall while I take a look."

It could be nothing, but he'd been taught at a young age the importance of never letting down his guard. Adrenaline firing, he jerked the window open and scanned the tiny patch of yard.

Nothing. Just a Big Wheel lying on its side and a swing dangling lazily from a lone tree.

Maybe it was only a nightmare. This whole blast from the past had him seeing bogeymen from his own childhood, too. Tony pushed the window down again and pulled the curtains together.

Shannon stood in the door, her son tucked against her. "I could have sworn I closed the curtains."

Kolby peeked up. "I opened 'em when I heard-ed the noise."

And maybe this kid's nightmare was every bit as real as his own had been. On the off chance the boy was right, he had to check. "I'm going outside. The guard will stay here with you."

She cupped the back of her child's head. "I already warned the guard. I wasn't leaving you to take care of the 'monster' by yourself."

Dread kinked cold and tight in his gut. What if something had happened to her when she had stepped outside to speak to the guard? He held in the angry words, not wanting to upset her son.

But he became more determined by the second to persuade her and the child to leave Galveston with him.

"Let's hope it was nothing but a tree branch. Right, kiddo?"

Tony started toward the door just as his iPhone rang. He glanced at the ID and saw the guard's number. He thumbed the speaker phone button. "Yes?"

"Got him," the guard said. "A teenager from the next complex over was trying to snap some pictures on his cell phone. I've already called the police."

A sigh shuddered through Shannon, and she hugged her son closer, and God, how Tony wanted to comfort her.

However, the business of taking care of her safety came first. "Keep me posted if there are any red flags when they interview the trespasser. Good work. Thanks."

He tucked his phone back into his jacket, his heart almost hammering out of his chest at the close call. This could have been worse. He knew too well from past experience how bad it could have been.

And apparently so did Shannon. Her wide blue eyes blinked erratically as she looked from corner to corner, searching shadows.

To hell with giving her distance. He wrapped an arm around her shoulders until she leaned on him ever so slightly. The soft press of her against him felt damn right in a day gone wrong.

Then she squeezed her eyes closed and straightened. "Okay, you win."

"Win what?"

"We'll go to your home tonight."

A hollow victory, since fear rather than desire motivated her, but he wasn't going to argue. "And tomorrow?"

"We'll discuss that in morning. Right now, just take us to your house."

* * *

Tony's Galveston house could only be called a mansion.

The imposing size of the three-story structure washed over Shannon every time they drove through the scrolled iron gates. How Kolby could sleep through all of this boggled her mind, but when they'd convinced him the "monster" was gone—thanks to the guard—Kolby had been all yawns again. Once strapped into the car seat in the back of Tony's Escalade, her son had been out like a light in five minutes.

If only her own worries could be as easily shaken off. She had to think logically, but fears for Kolby nagged her. Nolan had stolen so much more than money. He'd robbed her of the ability to feel safe, just before he took the coward's way out.

Two acres of manicured lawn stretched ahead of her in the moonlight. The estate was intimidating during the day, and all the more ominously gothic at night with shadowy edges encroaching. It was one thing to visit the place for a date.

It was another to take shelter here, to pack suitcases and accept his help.

She'd lived in a large house with Nolan, four thousand square feet, but she could have fit two of those homes inside Tony's place. In the courtyard, a concrete horse fountain was illuminated, glowing in front of the burgundy stucco house with brown trim so dark it was almost black. His home showcased the Spanish architecture prevalent in Texas. Knowing his true heritage now, she could see why he would have been drawn to this area.

Silently he guided the SUV into the garage, finally safe and secure from the outside world. For how long?

He unstrapped Kolby from the seat and she didn't argue. Her son was still sleeping anyway. The way Tony's big hands managed the small buckles and shuffled the sleeping child onto his shoulder with such competence touched her heart as firmly as any hothouse full of roses.

Trailing him with a backpack of toy trains and trucks, she dimly registered the house that had grown familiar after their dates to restaurants, movies and the most amazing concerts. Her soul, so starved for music, gobbled up every note.

Her first dinner at his home had been a five-course catered meal with a violinist. She could almost hear the echoing strains bouncing lightly off the high-beamed ceiling, down to the marble floor, swirling along the inlay pattern to twine around her.

Binding her closer to him. They hadn't had sex that night, but she'd known then it was inevitable.

That first time, Tony had been thoughtful enough to send out to a different restaurant than his favored Vernon's, guessing accurately that when a person worked eight hours a day in one eating establishment, the food there lost its allure.

He'd opted for Italian cuisine. The meal and music and elegance had been so far removed from paper plate dinners of nuggets and fries. While she adored her son and treasured every second with him, she couldn't help but be wooed by grown-up time to herself.

Limited time as she'd never spent the night here. Until now.

She followed Tony up the circular staircase, hand on the crafted iron banister. The sight of her son sleeping so limp and relaxed against Tony brought a lump to her throat again.

The tenderness she felt seeing him hold her child reminded her how special this new man in her life was. She'd chosen him so carefully after Nolan had died, seeing

Tony's innate strength and honor. Was she really ready to throw that away?

He stopped at the first bedroom, a suite decorated in hunter green with vintage maps framed on the walls. Striding through the sitting area to the next door, he flipped back the brocade spread and set her son in the middle of the high bed.

Quietly, she put a chair on either side as a makeshift bed rail, then tucked the covers over his shoulders. She kissed his little forehead and inhaled his baby-fresh scent. Her child.

The enormity of how their lives had changed tonight swelled inside her, pushing stinging tears to the surface. Tony's hand fell to rest on her shoulder and she leaned back….

Holy crap.

She jolted away. How easily she fell into old habits around him. "I didn't mean…"

"I know." His hand fell away and tucked into his pocket. "I'll carry up your bags in a minute. I gave the house staff the night off."

She followed him, just to keep their conversation soft, not because she wasn't ready to say good-night. "I thought you trusted them."

"I do. To a point. It's also easier for security to protect the house with fewer people inside." He gestured into the sitting area. "I heard what you said about feeling cut off from the world going to my father's and I understand."

His empathy slipped past her defenses when they were already on shaky ground being here in his house again. Remembering all the times they'd made love under this very roof, she could almost smell the bath salts from last weekend. And with him being so understanding on top of everything else…

He'd lied. She needed to remember that.

"I realize I have to do what's right for Kolby." She sagged onto the striped sofa, her legs folding from an emotional and exhausting night. "It scares the hell out of me how close a random teenager already got to my child, and we're only a couple of hours into this mess. It makes me ill to think about what someone with resources could do."

"My brothers and I have attorneys. They'll look into pressing charges against the teen." He sat beside her with a casual familiarity of lovers.

Remember the fight. Not the bath salts. She inched toward the armrest. "Let me know what the attorneys' fees are, please."

"They're on retainer. Those lawyers also help us communicate with each other. My attorney will know we're going to see my father if you're worried about making sure someone is aware of your plans."

Someone under his employ, all of this bought with Tony's money that she'd rejected a few short days ago. And she couldn't think of any other way. "You trust this man, your lawyer?"

"I have to." The surety in his voice left little room for doubt. "There are some transactions that can't be avoided no matter how much we want to sever ties with the past."

A darker note in his voice niggled at her. "Are you talking about yourself now?"

He shrugged, broad shoulders rippling the fabric of his fine suit.

Nuh-uh. She wasn't giving up that easily. She'd trusted so much of her life to this man, only to find he'd misled her.

Now she needed something tangible, something honest from him to hold on to. Something to let her know if that honor and strength she'd perceived in him was real. "You said you didn't want to break off our relationship. If that's true, this would be a really good time to open up a little."

Angling toward her, Tony's knee pressed against hers, his eyes heating to molten dark. "Are you saying we're good again?"

"I'm saying…" She cleared her throat that had suddenly gone cottony dry. "Maybe I could see my way clear to forgiving you if I knew more about you."

He straightened, his eyes sharp. "What do you want to know?"

"Why Galveston?"

"Do you surf?"

What the hell? She watched the walls come up in his eyes. She could almost feel him distancing himself from her. "Tony, I'm not sure how sharing a *Surf's Up* moment is going to make things all better here."

"But have you ever been surfing?" He gestured, his hands riding imaginary waves. "The Atlantic doesn't offer as wild a ride as the Pacific, but it gets the job done, especially in Spain. Something to do with the atmospheric pressure coming down from the U.K. I still remember the swells tubing." He curled his fingers around into the cresting circle of a wave.

"You're a *surfer?*" She tried to merge the image of the sleek business shark with the vision of him carefree on a board. And instead an image emerged of his abandon when making love. Her breasts tingled and tightened, awash in the sensation of sea spray and Tony all over her skin.

"I've always been fascinated with waves."

"Even when you were in San Rinaldo." The picture of him began to make more sense. "It's an island country, right?"

She'd always thought the nautical art on his walls was tied into his shipping empire. Now she realized the affinity for such pieces came from living on an island. So much about him made sense.

His surfing hand soared to rest on the gold flecked globe beside the sofa. Was it her imagination or was the gloss dimmer over the coast of Spain? As if he'd rubbed his finger along that area more often, taking away the sheen over time.

He spun the globe. "I thought you didn't know much about the Medinas."

"I researched you on Google on my phone while we were driving over." Concrete info had been sparse compared to all the crazy gossip floating about, but there were some basics. Three sons. A monarch father. A mother who'd been killed as they were escaping. Her heart squeezed thinking of him losing a parent so young, not much older than Kolby.

She pulled a faltering smile. "There weren't any surfer pictures among the few images that popped up."

Only a couple of grainy formal family portraits of three young boys with their parents, everyone happy. Some earlier photos of King Enrique looking infinitely regal.

"We scrubbed most pictures after we escaped and regrouped." His lighthearted smile contrasted with the darker hue deepening his eyes. "The internet wasn't active in those days."

The extent of his rebuilding shook her to her shoes. She'd thought she had it rough leaving Louisiana after her husband's arrest and death. How tragic to have your past wiped away. The enormity of what had happened to his family, of how he'd lived since then, threatened to overwhelm her.

How could she not ache over all he'd been through? "I saw that your mother died when I read up on your past. I'm so sorry."

He waved away her sympathy. "When we got to...where my father lives now, things were isolated. But at least we still had the ocean. Out on the waves, I could forget about everything else."

Plowing a hand through his hair, he stared just past her, obviously locked in some deep memories. She sensed she was close, so close to the something she needed to reassure her that placing herself and her son in his care would be wise, even if there weren't gossip seekers sifting through her trash.

She rested her hand on his arm. "What are you thinking?"

"I thought you might like to learn next spring. Unless you're already a pro."

"Not hardly." Spring was a long way off, a huge commitment she wasn't anywhere near ready to make to anyone. The thought of climbing on a wave made her stomach knot almost as much as being together that long. "Thanks for the offer, but I'll pass."

"Scared?" He skimmed his knuckles over her collarbone, and just that fast the sea-spray feel tingled through her again.

"Hell, yes. Scared of getting hurt."

His hand stilled just above her thumping heart. Want crackled in the air. Hers? Or his? She wasn't sure. Probably equal measures from both of them. That had never been in question. And too easily he could draw her in again. Learning more about him wasn't wise after all, not tonight.

She pulled away, her arms jerky, her whole body out of whack. She needed Tony's lightness now. Forget about serious peeks into each other's vulnerable pasts. "No surfing for me. Ever try taking care of a toddler with a broken leg?"

"When did you break your leg?" His eyes narrowed. "Did he hurt you? Your husband?"

How had Tony made that leap so quickly?

"Nolan was a crook and a jerk, but he never raised a hand to me." She shivered, not liking the new direction their conversation had taken at all. This was supposed to teach her more about him. Not the other way around. "Do we have to drag more baggage into this?"

"If it's true."

"I told you. He didn't abuse me." Not physically. "Having a criminal for a husband is no picnic. Knowing I missed the signs… Wondering if I let myself be blind to it because I enjoyed the lifestyle… I don't even know where to start in answering those questions for myself."

She slumped, suddenly exhausted, any residual adrenaline fizzling out. Her head fell back.

"Knowing you as I do, I find it difficult to believe you would ever choose the easy path." Tony thumbed just below her eyes where undoubtedly dark circles were all but tattooed on her face. "It's been a long day. You should get some rest. If you want, I'll tuck you in," he said with a playful wink.

She found the old Tony much easier to deal with than the new. "You're teasing, of course."

"Maybe…" And just that fast the light in his eyes flamed hotter, intense. "Shanny, I would hold you all night if you would let me. I would make sure no one dared threaten you or your son again."

And she wanted to let him do just that. But she'd allowed herself to depend on a man before… "If you hold me, we both know I won't get any rest, and while I'll have pleasure tonight, I'll be sorry tomorrow. Don't you think we have enough wrong between us right now without adding another regret to the mix?"

"Okay...." Tony gave her shoulder a final squeeze and stood. "I'll back off."

Shannon pushed to her feet alongside him, her hands fisted at her sides to keep from reaching for him. "I'm still mad over being kept in the dark, but I appreciate all the damage control."

"I owe you that much and more." He kissed her lightly on the lips without touching her anywhere else, lingering long enough to remind her of the reasons they clicked. Her breath hitched and it was all she could do not to haul him in closer for a firmer, deeper connection.

Pulling back, he started toward the door.

"Tony?" Was that husky voice really hers?

He glanced over his shoulder. So easily she could take the physical comfort waiting only a few feet away in his arms. But she had to keep her head clear. She had to hold strong to carve out an independent life for her and her son and that meant drawing clear boundaries.

"Just because I might be able to forgive you doesn't mean you're welcome in my bed again."

Four

She wasn't in her own bed.

Shannon wrestled with the tenacious grip of her shadowy nightmare, tough as hell to do when she couldn't figure out where she was. The ticking grandfather clock, the feel of the silky blanket around her, none of it was familiar. And then a hint of sandalwood scent teased her nose a second before...

"Hey." Tony's voice rumbled through the dark. "It's okay. I'm here."

Her heart jumped. She bolted upright, the cashmere afghan twisting around her legs and waist. Blinking fast, she struggled to orient herself to the surroundings so different from her apartment, but the world blurred in front of her from the dark and her own crummy eyesight. Shannon pressed her hands to the cushiony softness of a sofa and everything came rushing back. She was at Tony's, in the sitting room outside where Kolby slept.

"It's okay," Tony continued to chant, squeezing her shoulder in his broad hand as he crouched beside the couch.

Swinging her feet to the ground, she gathered the haunting remnants of her nightmare. Shadows smoked through her mind, blending into a darker mass of memories from the night Nolan died, except Tony's face superimposed itself over that of her dead husband.

Nausea burned her throat. She swallowed back the bite of bile and the horror of her dream. "Sorry, if I woke you." Oh, God, her son. "Is Kolby all right?"

"Sleeping soundly."

"Thank goodness. I wouldn't want to frighten him." She took in Tony's mussed hair and hastily hauled on jeans. The top button was open and his chest was bare. Gulp. "I'm sorry for disturbing you."

"I wasn't asleep." He passed her glasses to her.

As she slid them on, his tattoo came into focus, a nautical compass on his arm. Looking closer she realized his hair was wet. She didn't want to think about him in the shower, a tiled spa cubicle they'd shared more than once. "It's been a tough night all around."

"Want to talk about what woke you up?"

"Not really." Not ever. To anyone. "I think my fear for Kolby ran wild in my sleep. Dreams are supposed to help work out problems, but sometimes, it seems they only make everything scarier."

"Ah, damn, Shanny, I'm sorry for this whole mess." He sat on the sofa and slid an arm around her shoulders.

She stiffened, then decided to hell with it all and leaned back against the hard wall of chest. With the nightmare so fresh in her mind, she couldn't scavenge the will to pull away. His arms banded around her in an instant and her head tucked under his chin. Somehow it was easier to accept this comfort when she didn't have to look in his eyes. She'd been alone with her bad dreams for so long. Was it wrong to take just a second's comfort from his arms roped so thick with muscles nothing could break through to her? She would be strong again in a minute.

The grandfather clock ticked away minutes as she stared at his hands linked over her stomach—at the lighter band of skin where his watch usually rested. "Thanks for coming in to check on us, especially so late."

"It can be disconcerting waking in an unfamiliar place alone." His voice vibrated against her back, only her thin nightshirt between them and his bare chest.

Another whiff of his freshly showered scent teased her nose with memories of steam-slicked bodies.

"I've been here at least a dozen times, but never in this room. It's a big house." They'd met five months ago, started dating two months later…had starting sleeping together four weeks ago. "Strange to think we've shared the shower, but I still haven't seen all of your home."

"We tended to get distracted once our feet hit the steps," he said drily.

True enough. They'd stayed downstairs on early dinner dates here, but once they'd ventured upstairs…they'd always headed straight for his suite.

"That first time together—" Shannon remembered was after an opera when her senses had been on overload and her hormones on hyperdrive from holding back "—I was scared to death."

The admission tumbled out before she could think, but somehow it seemed easier to share such vulnerabilities in the dark.

His muscles flexed against her, the bristle of hair on his arms teasing goose bumps along her skin. "The last thing I ever want to do is frighten you."

"It wasn't your fault. That night was a big leap of faith for me." The need to make him understand pushed past walls she'd built around herself. "Being with you then, it was my first time since Nolan."

He went completely still, not even breathing for four ticks of the clock before she felt his neck move with a swallow against her temple. "No one?"

"No one." Not only had Tony been her sole lover since Nolan, he'd been her second lover ever.

Her track record for picking men with secrets sucked.

His gusty sigh ruffled her hair. "I wish you would have told me."

"What would that have changed?"

"I would have been more…careful."

The frenzy of their first time stormed her mind with a barrage of images…their clothes fluttering to carpet the stairs on their way up. By the top of the steps they were naked, moonlight bathing his olive skin and casting shadows along the cut of muscles. Kissing against the wall soon had her legs wrapped around his waist and he was inside her. That one thrust had unfurled the tension into shimmering sensations and before the orgasm finished tingling all the way to the roots of her hair, he'd carried her to his room, her legs still around him. Again, she'd found release in bed with him, then a languid, leisurely completion while showering together.

Just remembering, an ache started low, throbbing between her legs. "You were great that night, and you know it." She swatted his hand lightly. "Now wipe the arrogant grin off your face."

"You can't see me." His voice sounded somber enough.

"Am I right, though?"

"Look at me and see."

She turned around and dared to peer up at him for the first time since he'd settled on the couch behind her. Her intense memories of that evening found an echo in his serious eyes far more moving than any smile.

Right now, it was hard to remember they weren't a couple anymore. "Telling you then would have made the event too serious."

Too important.

His offer to "help" her financially still loomed unresolved between them, stinging her even more than last weekend after the enormous secret he'd kept from her. Why couldn't they be two ordinary people who met at the park outside her apartment complex? What would it have been like to get to know Tony on neutral, normal ground? Would she have been able to see past the pain of her marriage?

She would never know.

"Shannon." His voice came out hoarse and hungry. "Are you okay to go back to sleep now? Because I need to leave."

His words splashed a chill over her heated thoughts. "Of course, you must have a lot to take care of with your family."

"You misunderstand. I *need* to leave, because you're killing me here with how much I've hurt you. And as if that wasn't enough to bring me to my knees, every time you move your head, the feel of your hair against my chest just about sends me over the edge." His eyes burned with a coal-hot determination. "I'll be damned before I do anything to break your trust again."

Before she could unscramble her thoughts, he slid his arms from her and ducked out the door as silently as he'd arrived. Colder than ever without the heat of Tony all around her, she hugged the blanket closer.

No worries about any more nightmares, because she was more than certain she wouldn't be able to go back to sleep.

By morning, Tony hadn't bothered turning down the covers on his bed. After leaving Shannon's room, he'd spent most of the night conferring with his lawyer and a security firm. Working himself into the ground to distract himself from how much he hurt from wanting her.

With a little luck and maneuvering, he could extend his week with her into two weeks. But bottom line, he *would* ensure her safety.

At five, he'd caught a catnap on the library sofa, jolting awake when Vernon called him from the front gate. He'd buzzed the retired sea captain through and rounded up breakfast.

His old friend deserved some answers.

Choosing a less formal dining area outside, he sat at the oval table on the veranda shaded by a lemon tree, Vernon beside him with a plate full of churros. Tony thumbed the edge of the hand-painted stoneware plate—a set he'd picked up from a local craftsman to support the dying art of the region.

Today of all days, he didn't want to think overlong on why he still ate his same childhood breakfast—deep fried strips of potato dough. His mother had always poured a thick rich espresso for herself and mugs of hot chocolate for her three sons, an informal ritual in their centuries-old castle that he now knew was anything but ordinary.

Vernon eyed him over the rim of his coffee cup. "So it's all true, what they're saying in the papers and on the internet?"

Absurd headlines scrolled through his memory, along-side reports that had been right on the money. "My brother's not a Tibetan monk, but the general gist of that first report from the Global Intruder is correct."

"You're a prince." He scrubbed a hand over his dropped jaw. "Well, hot damn. Always knew there was something special about you, boy."

He preferred to think anything "special" about him came from hard work rather than a genetic lottery win. "I hope you understand it wasn't my place to share the details with you."

"You have brothers and a father." He stirred a hefty dollop of milk into his coffee, clinking the spoon against the edges of the stoneware mug. "I get that you need to consider their privacy, as well."

"Thanks, I appreciate that."

He wished Shannon could see as much. He'd hoped bringing her here would remind her of all that had been good between them. Instead those memories had only come back to bite him on the ass when she'd told him that he was her first since her husband died. The revelation still sucker punched the air from his gut.

Where did they go from there? Hell if he knew, but at least he had more time to find out. Soon enough he would have her in his private jet that waited fueled and ready a mile away.

The older man set down his mug. "I respect that you gotta be your own man."

"Thank you again." He'd expected Vernon to be angry over the secrecy, had even been concerned over losing his friendship.

Vernon's respect meant a lot to him, as well as his advice. From day one when Tony had turned in his sparse job application, Vernon had treated him like a son, showing him the ropes. They had a lot of history. And just like fourteen years ago, he offered unconditional acceptance now.

His mentor leaned forward on one elbow. "What does your family have to say about all of this?"

"I've only spoken with my middle brother." He pinched off a piece of a churro drizzled with warm honey. Popping it into his mouth, he chewed and tried not think of how much of his past stayed imprinted on him.

"According to the papers, that would be Duarte. Right?" When Tony nodded, Vernon continued, "Any idea how the story broke after so many years?"

And wasn't that the million-dollar question? He, his brothers and their lawyers were no closer to the answer on that one today than they'd been last night. "Duarte doesn't have any answers yet, other than some photojournalist caught him in a snapshot and managed to track down details. Which is damn strange. None of us look the same since we left San Rinaldo as kids."

"And there are no other pictures of you in the interim?"

"Only a few stray shots after I became Tony. Carlos's face has shown up in a couple of professional magazines." But the image was so posed and sterile, Tony wasn't sure he would recognize his own sibling on the street. For the best.

His father always insisted photos would provide dangerous links, as if he'd been preparing them from the beginning to split up. Or preparing them for his death.

Not the normal way for a kid to live, but they weren't a regular family. He'd grown accustomed to it eventually… until it almost seemed normal. Until he was faced with a regular person's life, like Shannon's treasured photos of her son.

He broke off another inch of a churro. His hand slowed halfway to his mouth as he got that feeling of "being watched." He checked right fast—

Kolby stood in the open doorway, blanket trailing from his fist.

Uh, okay. So now what? He'd only met the child a few times before last night and none had gone particularly well. Tony had chalked it up to Kolby being shy around strangers or clingy. Judging by the thrust of his little jaw and frown now, there was no mistaking it. The boy didn't like him.

That needed to change. "Hey, kiddo. Where's your mom?"

Kolby didn't budge. "Still sleepin'."

Breaking the ice, Vernon tugged out a chair. "Wanna have a seat and join us?"

Never taking his eyes off Tony, Kolby padded across the tile patio and scrambled up to sit on his knees. Silently, he simply blinked and stared with wide blue-gray eyes just like Shannon's, his blond hair spiking every which way.

Vernon wiped his mouth, tossed his linen napkin on the plate and stood. "Thanks for the chow. I need to check on business. No need to see me out."

As his old friend deserted ship, unease crawled around inside Tony's gut. His experience with children was nonexistent, even when he'd been a kid himself. He and his brothers had been tutored on the island. They'd been each other's only playmates.

The island fortress had been staffed with security guards, not the mall cop sort, but more like a small deployed military unit. Cleaning staff, tutors, the chef and groundskeepers were all from San Rinaldo, older supporters of his father who'd lost their families in the coup. They shared a firm bond of loyalty, and a deep-seated need for a safe haven.

Working on the shrimp boat had felt like a vacation, with the wide open spaces and no boundaries. Most of all he enjoyed the people who didn't wear the imprint of painful loss in their eyes.

But still, there weren't any three-year-olds on the shrimp boat.

What did kids need? "Are you hungry?"

"Some of that." Kolby pointed to Tony's plate of churros. "With peanut bubber."

Grateful for action instead of awkward silence, he shoved to his feet. "Peanut butter it is then. Follow me."

Once he figured out where to look. He'd quit cooking for himself about ten years ago and the few years he had, he wasn't whipping up kiddie cuisine.

About seven minutes later he unearthed a jar from the cavernous pantry and smeared a messy trail down a churro before chunking the spoon in the sink.

Kolby pointed to the lid on the granite countertop. "We don't waste."

"Right." Tony twisted the lid on tight. Thinking of Shannon pinching pennies on peanut butter, for crying out loud, he wanted to buy them a lifetime supply.

As he started to pass the plate to Kolby, a stray thought broadsided him. Hell. Was the kid allergic to peanuts? He hadn't even thought to ask. Kolby reached. Tony swallowed another curse.

"Let's wait for your mom."

"Wait for me why?" Her softly melodic voice drifted over his shoulder from across the kitchen.

He glanced back and his heart kicked against his ribs. They'd slept together over the past month but never actually *slept*. And never through the night.

Damn, she made jeans look good, the washed pale fabric clinging to her long legs. Her hair flowed over her shoulders and down her back, still damp from a shower. He remembered well the silky glide of it through his fingers... and so not something he should be thinking about with her son watching.

Tony held up the plate of churros. "Can he eat peanut butter?"

"He's never tried it that way before, but I'm sure he'll like it." She slipped the dish from his grip. "Although, I'm not so certain that breakable stoneware is the best choice for a three-year-old."

"Hey, kiddo, is the plate all right with you?"

"'S okay." Kolby inched toward his mother and wrapped an arm around her leg. "Like trains better. And milk."

"The milk I can handle." He yanked open the door on the stainless steel refrigerator and reached for the jug. "I'll make sure you have the best train plates next time."

"Wait!" Shannon stopped him, digging into an oversized bag on her shoulder and pulling out a cup with a vented lid. "Here's his sippy cup. It's not Waterford, but it works better."

Smoothly, she filled it halfway and scooped up the plate. Kolby held on to his mother all the way back to the patio.

For the first time he wondered why he hadn't spent more time with the boy. Shannon hadn't offered and he hadn't pushed. She sat and pulled Kolby in her lap, plate in front just out of his reach. The whole family breakfast scenario wrapped around him, threatening his focus. He skimmed a finger along his shirt collar— Hell. He stopped short, realizing he wasn't wearing a tie.

She pinched off a bite and passed it to her son. "I had a lot of time to think last night."

So she hadn't slept any better than he had. "What did you think about after I left?"

Her eyes shot up to his, pink flushing her face. "Going to see your father, of course."

"Of course." He nodded, smiling.

"Of course," Kolby echoed.

As the boy licked the peanut butter off the churro, she traced the intricate pattern painted along the edge of the plate, frowning. "I would like to tell Vernon and your lawyer about our plans for the week and then I'll come with you."

He'd won. She would be safe, and he would have more time to sway her. Except it really chapped his hide that she trusted him so little she felt the need to log her travel itinerary. "Not meaning to shoot myself in the foot here, but why Vernon instead of my lawyer? Vernon is my friend. I financed his business."

"You own the restaurant?" Her slim fingers gravitated back to the china. "*You* are responsible for my paychecks? I thought the Grille belonged to Vernon."

"You didn't know?" Probably a good thing or he might well have never talked her into that first date. "Vernon was a friend when I needed one. I'm glad I could return the favor. He's more than delivered on the investment."

"He gave you a job when your past must have seemed spotty," she said intuitively.

"How did you figure that out?"

"He did the same for me when I needed a chance." A bittersweet smile flickered across her face much like how the sunlight filtered through the lemon tree to play in her hair. "That's the reason I trust him."

"You've worked hard for every penny you make there."

"I know, but I appreciate that he was fair. No handouts, and yet he never took advantage of how much I needed that job. He's a good man. Now back to our travel plans." She rested her chin on her son's head. "Just to be sure, I'll also be informing my in-laws—Kolby's grandparents."

His brows slammed upward. She rarely mentioned them, only that they'd cut her out of their lives after their son died. The fact that she would keep such cold fish informed about their grandson spoke of an innate sense of fair play he wasn't sure he would have given in her position.

"Apparently you trust just about everyone more than me."

She dabbed at the corners of her mouth, drawing his attention to the plump curve of her bottom lip. "Apparently so."

Not a ringing endorsement of her faith in him, but he would take the victory and focus forward. Because before sundown, he would return to his father's island home off the coast of Florida.

She was actually in a private plane over...

Somewhere.

Since the window shades were closed, she had no idea whether they were close to land or water. So where were they? Once airborne, she'd felt the plane turn, but quickly lost any sense of whether they were going north or south, east or west. Although north was unlikely given he'd told her to pack for warm weather.

How far had they traveled? Tough to tell since she'd napped and she had no idea how fast this aircraft could travel. She'd been swept away into a world beyond anything she'd experienced, from the discreet impeccable service to the sleeping quarters already made up for her and Kolby on arrival. Questions about her food preferences had resulted in a five-star meal.

Shannon pressed a hand to her jittery stomach. God,

she hoped she'd made the right decision. At least her son seemed oblivious to all the turmoil around them.

The cabin steward guided Kolby toward the galley kitchen with the promise of a snack and a video. As they walked toward the back, he dragged his tiny fingers along the white leather seats. At least his hands were clean.

But she would have to make a point of keeping sharp objects out of Kolby's reach. She shuddered at the image of a silver taped *X* on the luxury upholstery.

Her eyes shifted to the man filling the deep seat across from her couch. Wearing gray pants and a white shirt with the sleeves rolled up, he focused intently on the laptop screen in front of him, seemingly oblivious to anyone around him.

She hated the claustrophobic feeling of needing his help, not to mention all the money hiding out entailed. Dependence made her vulnerable, something she'd sworn would never happen again. Yet here she was, entrusting her whole life to a man, a man who'd lied to her.

However, with her child's well-being at stake, she couldn't afford to say no.

More information would help settle the apprehension plucking at her nerves like heart strings. Any information, since apparently everything she knew about him outside of the bedroom was false. She hadn't even known he owned the restaurant where she worked.

Ugh.

Of course it seemed silly to worry about being branded as the type who sleeps with the boss. Having an affair with a drop-dead sexy prince trumped any other gossip. "How long has it been since you saw your father?"

Tony looked up from his laptop slowly. "I left the island when I was eighteen."

"Island?" Her hand grazed the covered window as she

envisioned water below. "I thought you left San Rinaldo as a young boy."

"We did." He closed the computer and pivoted the chair toward her, stretching his legs until his feet stopped intimately close to hers. "I was five at the time. We relocated to another island about a month after we escaped."

She scrunched her toes in her gym shoes. Her scuffed canvas was worlds away from his polished loafers and a private plane. And regardless of how hot he looked, she wouldn't be seduced by the trappings of his wealth.

Forcing her mind back on his words rather than his body, she drew her legs away from him. Was the island on the east coast or west coast? Provided Enrique Medina's compound was even near the U.S. "Your father chose an island so you and your brothers would feel at home in your new place?"

He looked at her over the white tulips centered on the cherry coffee table. "My father chose an island because it was easier to secure."

Gulp. "Oh. Right."

That took the temperature down more than a few degrees. She picked at the piping on the sofa.

Music drifted from the back of the plane, the sound of a new cartoon starting. She glanced down the walkway. Kolby was buckled into a seat, munching on some kind of crackers while watching the movie, mesmerized. Most likely by the whopping big flat screen.

Back to her questions. "How much of you is real and what's a part of the new identity?"

"My age and birthday are real." He tucked the laptop into an oversized briefcase monogrammed with the Castillo Shipping Corporation logo. "Even my name is technically correct, as I told you before. Castillo comes from my mother's family tree. I took it as my own when I turned eighteen."

Resting her elbow on the back of the sofa, she propped her head in her palm, trying her darnedest to act as casual as he appeared. "What does your father think of all you've accomplished since leaving?"

"I wouldn't know." He reclined, folding his hands over his stomach, drawing her eyes and memories to his rock-hard abs.

Her toes curled again until they cracked inside her canvas sneakers. "What does he think of us coming now?"

"You'll have to ask him." His jaw flexed.

"Did you even tell him about the extra guests?" She resisted the urge to smooth the strain away from the bunched tendons in his neck. How odd to think of comforting him when she still had so many reservations about the trip herself.

"I told his lawyer to inform him. His staff will make preparations. Kolby will have whatever he needs."

Who was this coolly factual man a hand stretch away? She almost wondered if she'd imagined carefree Tony... except he'd told her that he liked to surf. She clung to that everyday image and dug deeper.

"Sounds like you and your father aren't close. Or is that just the way royalty communicates?" If so, how sad was that?

He didn't answer, the drone of the engines mingling with the cartoon and the rush of recycled air through the vents. While she wanted her son to grow up independent with a life of his own, she also planned to forge a bond closer than cold communications exchanged between lawyers and assistants.

"Tony?"

His eyes shifted to the shuttered window beside her

head. "I didn't want to live on a secluded island any longer. So I left. He disagreed. We haven't resolved the issue."

Such simple words for so deep a breach where attorneys handled *all* communiqués between them. The lack of communication went beyond distant to estrangement. This wasn't a family just fractured by location. Something far deeper was wrong.

Tucking back into his line of sight, she pressed ahead. This man had already left such a deep imprint on her life, she knew she wouldn't forget him. "What have your lawyers told your father about Kolby and me? What did they tell your dad about our relationship?"

"Relationship?" He pinned her with his dark eyes, the intensity of his look—of him—reaching past the tulips as tangibly as if he'd taken that broad hand and caressed her. He was such a big man with the gentlest of touches.

And he was thorough. God, how he was thorough.

Her heart pounded in her ear like a tympani solo, hollow and so loud it drowned out the engines.

"Tony?" she asked. She *wanted*.

"I let him know that we're a couple. And that you're a widow with a son."

It was one thing to carry on a secret affair with him. Another to openly acknowledge to people—to family—that they were a couple.

She pressed hard against her collarbone, her pulse pushing a syncopated beat against her fingertips. "Why not tell your father the truth? That we broke up but the press won't believe it."

"Who says it's not the truth? We slept together just a week ago. Seems like less than that to me, because I swear I can still catch a whiff of your scent on my skin." He leaned closer and thumbed her wrist.

Her fingers curled as the heat of his touch spread farther. "But about last weekend—"

"Shanny." He tapped her lips once, then traced her rounded sigh. "We may have argued, but when I'm in the room with you, my hand still gravitates to your back by instinct."

Her heart drummed faster until she couldn't have responded even if she tried. But she wasn't trying, too caught up in the sound of him, the desire in his every word.

"The pull between us is that strong, Shannon, whether I'm deep inside you or just listening to you across a room." A half smile kicked a dimple into one cheek. "Why do you think I call you late at night?"

She glanced quickly at the video area checking to make sure her son and the steward where still engrossed in Disney, then she whispered, "Because you'd finished work?"

"You know better. Just the sound of you on the other end of the line sends me rock—"

"Stop, please." She pressed her fingers to his mouth. "You're only hurting us both."

Nipping her fingers lightly first, he linked his hand with hers. "We have problems, without a doubt, and you have reason to be mad. But the drive to be together hasn't eased one bit. Can you deny it? Because if you can, then that is it. I'll keep my distance."

Opening her mouth, she formed the words that would slice that last tie to the relationship they'd forged over the past few months. She fully intended to tell him they were through.... But nothing came out. Not one word.

Slowly, he pulled back. "We're almost there."

Almost where? Back together? Her mind scrambled to keep up with him, damn tough when he kept jumbling her brain. She was a flipping magna cum laude graduate. She resented feeling like a bimbo at the mercy of her libido. But how her libido sang arias around this man...

He shoved to his feet and walked away. Just like that, he cut their conversation short as if they both hadn't been sinking deep into a sensual awareness that had brought them both such intense pleasure in the past. She tracked the lines of his broad shoulders, down to his trim waist and taut butt showcased so perfectly in tailored pants.

Her fingers dug deep into the sofa with restraint. He stopped by Kolby and slid up the window covering.

"Take a look, kiddo, we're almost there." Tony pointed at the clear glass toward the pristine sky.

Ah. *There.* As in they'd arrived there, at his father's island. She'd been so caught up in the sensual draw of undiluted Tony that she'd temporarily forgotten about flying away to a mystery location.

Scrambling down the sofa, she straightened her glasses and stared out the window, hungry for a peek at their future—temporary—home. And yes, curious as hell about the place where Tony had grown up. Sure enough, an island stretched in the distance, nestled in miles and miles of sparkling ocean. Palm trees spiked from the lush landscape. A dozen or so small outbuildings dotted a semicircle around a larger structure.

The white mansion faced the ocean in a *U* shape, constructed around a large courtyard with a pool. She barely registered Kolby's "oohs" and "aahs" since she was pretty much overwhelmed by the sight herself.

Details were spotty but she would get an up-close view soon enough of the place Tony had called home for most of his youth. Even from a distance she couldn't miss the grand scale of the sprawling estate, the unmistakable sort that housed royalty.

The plane banked, lining up with a thin islet alongside the larger island. A single strip of concrete marked the private runway. As they neared, a ferryboat came into focus. To ride from the airport to the main island? They sure were serious about security.

The intercom system crackled a second before the steward announced, "We're about to begin our descent to our destination. Please return to your seats and secure your lap belts. Thank you, and we hope you had a pleasant flight."

Tony pulled away from the window and smiled at her again. Except now, the grin didn't reach his eyes. Her stomach fluttered, but this time with apprehension rather than arousal.

Would the island hold the answers she needed to put Tony in her past? Or would it only break her heart all over again?

Five

Daylight was fading fast and a silence fourteen years old between him and his father was about to be broken.

Feet braced on the ferry deck, Tony stared out over the rail at the island where he'd spent the bulk of his childhood and teenage years. He hated not being in command of the boat almost as much as he hated returning to this place. Only concern for Shannon and her son could have drawn him back where the memories grew and spread as tenaciously as algae webbing around coral.

Just ahead, a black skimmer glided across the water, dipping its bill into the surface. With each lap of the waves against the hull, Tony closed off insidious emotions before they could take root inside him and focused on the shore.

An osprey circled over its nest. Palm trees lined the beach with only a small white stucco building and a two-lane road. Until you looked closer and saw the guard tower.

When he'd come to this island off the coast of St.
Augustine at five, there were times he'd believed they were
home...that his father had moved them to another part of
San Rinaldo. In the darkest nights, he'd woken in a cold
sweat, certain the soldiers in camouflage were going to
cut through the bars on his windows and take him. Other
nights he imagined they'd already taken him and the bars
locked him in prison.

On the worst of nights, he'd thought his mother was still
alive, only to see her die all over again.

Shannon's hand slid over his elbow, her touch tentative,
her eyes wary. "How long did I sleep on the plane?"

"A while." He smiled to reassure her, but the feeling
didn't come from his gut. Damn, but he wished the past
week had never happened. He would pull her soft body
against him and forget about everything else.

Wind streaked her hair across her face. "Oh, right. If
you tell me, I might get a sense of how far away we are
from Galveston. I might guess where we are. Being cut off
from the world is still freaking me out just a little."

"I understand, and I'll to do my best to set things right as
soon as possible." He wanted nothing more than to get off
this island and return to the life he'd built, the life he chose.
The only thing that made coming back here palatable was
having Shannon by his side. And that rocked the deck
under his feet, realizing she held so much influence over
his life.

"Although, I have to admit," she conceded as she
tucked her son closer, "this place is so much more than I
expected."

Her gaze seemed to track the herons picking their way
along the shore, sea oats bowing at every gust. Her grayish-
blue eyes glinted with the first hints of excitement. She
must not have noticed the security cameras tucked in trees

and the guard on the dock, a gun strapped within easy reach.

Tony gripped the rail tighter. "There's no way to prepare a person."

Kolby squealed, pitching forward in his mother's arms.

"Whoa…" Tony snagged the kid by the back of his striped overalls. "Steady there."

A hand pressed to her chest, Shannon struggled for breath. "Thank God you moved so fast. I can't believe I looked away. There's just so much to see, so many distractions."

The little guy scowled at Tony. "Down."

"Buddy," Tony stated as he shook his head, "sometime you're going to have to like me."

"Name's not buddy," Kolby insisted, bottom lip out.

"You're right. I'm just trying to make friends here." Because he intended to use this time to persuade Shannon breaking up had been a crappy idea. He wondered how much the child understood. Since he didn't know how else to approach him, he opted for straight up honesty. "I like your mom, so it's important that you like me."

Shannon's gasp teased his ear like a fresh trickle of wind off the water. As much as he wanted to turn toward her, he kept his attention on the boy.

Kolby clenched Tony's shirt. "Does you like *me?*"

"Uh, sure." The question caught him off guard. He hadn't thought about it other than knowing it was important to win the son over for Shannon's sake. "What do you like?"

"Not you." He popped his bottom lip back in. "Down, pwease."

Shannon caught her son as he leaned toward her. Confusion puckering her brow, her eyes held Tony's for a second before she pointed over the side. "Is that what you wanted to see, sweetie?"

A dolphin zipped alongside the ferry. The fin sliced through the water, then submerged again.

Clapping his tiny hands, Kolby chanted, "Yes, yes, yes."

Again, Shannon saw beauty. He saw something entirely different. The dolphins provided port security. His father had gotten the idea from his own military service, cutting-edge stuff back then. The island was a minikingdom and money wasn't an object. Except this kingdom had substantially fewer subjects.

Tony wondered again if the secluded surroundings growing up could have played into his lousy track record with relationships as an adult. There hadn't been any teenage dating rituals for practice. And after he left, he'd been careful with relationships, never letting anything get too complicated. Work and a full social life kept him happy.

But the child in front of him made things problematic in a way he hadn't foreseen.

For years he'd been pissed off at his father for the way they'd had to live. And here he was doing the same to Kolby. The kid was entertained for the moment, but that would end fast for sure.

Protectiveness for both the mother and son seared his veins. He wouldn't let anything from the Medina past mark their future. Even if that meant he had to reclaim the very identity he'd worked his entire adulthood to shed.

The ferry slid against the dock. They'd arrived at the island.

And Prince Antonio Medina was back.

What was it like for Tony to come back after so long away? And it wasn't some happy homecoming, given the estrangement and distance in this family that communicated through lawyers.

Shannon wanted to reach across the limousine to him, but Tony had emotionally checked out the moment the ferry docked. Of course he'd been Mr. Manners while leaving the ferry and stepping into the Mercedes limo.

Watch your step... Need help? However, the smiles grew darker by the minute.

Maybe it was her own gloomy thoughts tainting her perceptions. At least Kolby seemed unaffected by their moods, keeping his nose pressed to the window the whole winding way to the pristine mansion.

Who wouldn't stare at the trees and the wildlife and finally, the palatial residence? White stucco with a clay tiled roof, arches and opulence ten times over, the place was the size of some hotels or convention centers. Except no hotel she'd stayed in sported guards armed with machine guns.

What should have made her feel safer only served to remind her money and power didn't come without burdens. To think, Tony had grown up with little or no exposure to the real world. It was a miracle he'd turned out normal.

If you could call a billionaire prince with a penchant for surfing "normal."

The limousine slowed, easing past a towering marble fountain with a "welcome" pineapple on top—and wasn't that ironic in light of all those guards? Once the vehicle stopped, more uniformed security appeared from out of nowhere to open the limo. Some kind of servant—a butler perhaps—stood at the top of the stairs. While Tony had insisted he wanted nothing to do with his birthplace, he seemed completely at ease in this surreal world. For the first time, the truth really sunk in.

The stunningly handsome—stoically silent—man walking beside her had royal blood singing through his veins.

"Tony?" She touched his elbow.

"After you," he said, simply gesturing ahead to the double doors sweeping open.

Scooping Kolby onto her hip, she took comfort in his sturdy little body and forged ahead. Inside. *Whoa.*

The cavernous circular hall sported gold gilded archways leading to open rooms. Two staircases stretched up either side, meeting in the middle. And, uh, stop the world, was that a Picasso on the wall?

Her canvas sneakers squeaked against marble floors as more arches ushered her deeper into the mansion. And while she vowed money didn't matter, she still wished she'd packed different shoes. Shannon straightened the straps on Kolby's favorite striped overalls, the ones he swore choo-choo drivers wore. She'd been so frazzled when she'd tossed clothes into a couple of overnight bags, picking things that would make him happy.

Just ahead, French doors opened on to a veranda that overlooked the ocean. Tony turned at the last minute, guiding her toward what appeared to be a library. Books filled three walls, interspersed with windows and a sliding brass ladder. Mosaic tiles swirled outward on the floor, the ceiling filled with frescos of globes and conquistadors. The smell of fresh citrus hung in the air, and not just because of the open windows. A tall potted orange tree nestled in one corner beneath a wide skylight.

An older man slept in a wingback by the dormant fireplace. Two large brown dogs—some kind of Ridgeback breed, perhaps?—lounged to his left and right.

Tony's father. A no-kidding king.

Either age or illness had taken a toll, dimming the family resemblance. But in spite of his nap, he wasn't going gently into that good night. No slippers and robe for this meeting. He wore a simple black suit with an ascot rather than a tie, his silver hair slicked back. Frailty and his pasty pallor made her want to comfort him.

Then his eyes snapped open. The sharp gleam in his coal dark eyes stopped her short.

Holy Sean Connery, the guy might be old but he hadn't lost his edge.

"Welcome home, *hijo prodigo*." *Prodigal son*.

Enrique Medina spoke in English but his accent was still unmistakably Spanish. And perhaps a bit thick with emotion? Or was that just wishful thinking on her part for Tony's sake?

"Hello, Papa." Tony palmed her back between her shoulder blades. "This is Shannon and her son Kolby."

The aging monarch nodded in her direction. "Welcome, to you and to your son."

"Thank you for your hospitality and your help, sir." She didn't dare wade into the whole *Your Highness* versus *Your Majesty* waters. Simplicity seemed safest.

Toying with a pocket watch in his hand, Enrique continued, "If not for my family, you would not need my assistance."

Tony's fingers twitched against her back. "Hopefully we won't have to impose upon you for long. Shannon and her son only need a place to lay low until this blows over."

"It won't blow over," Enrique said simply.

Ouch. She winced.

Tony didn't. "Poor choice of words. Until things calm down."

"Of course." He nodded regally before shifting his attention her way. "I am glad to have you here, my dear. You brought Tony home, so you have already won favor with me." He smiled and for the first time, she saw the family resemblance clearly.

Kolby wriggled, peeking up from her neck. "Whatsa matter with you?"

"Shhh…Kolby." She pressed a quick silencing kiss to his forehead. "That's a rude question."

"It's an honest question. I do not mind the boy." The king shifted his attention to her son. "I have been ill. My legs are not strong enough to walk."

"I'm sorry." Kolby eyed the wheelchair folded up and tucked discreetly alongside the fireplace. "You musta been bery sick."

"Thank you. I have good doctors."

"You got germs?"

A smile tugged at the stern face. "No, child. You and your mother cannot catch my germs."

"That's good." He stuffed his tiny fists into his pockets. "Don't like washin' my hands."

Enrique laughed low before his hand fell to rest on one dog's head. "Do you like animals?"

"Yep." Kolby squirmed downward until Shannon had no choice but to release him before he pitched out of her arms. "Want a dog."

Such a simple, painfully normal wish and she couldn't afford to supply it. From the pet deposit required at her apartment complex to the vet bills… It was out of her budget. Guilt tweaked again over all she couldn't give her child.

Yet hadn't Tony been denied so much even with such wealth? He'd lost his home, his mother and gained a gilded prison. Whispers of sympathy for a motherless boy growing up isolated from the world softened her heart when she most needed to hold strong.

Enrique motioned Kolby closer. "You may pet my dog.

Come closer and I will introduce you to Benito and Diablo. They are very well trained and will not hurt you."

Kolby didn't even hesitate. Any reservations her son felt about Tony certainly didn't extend to King Enrique—or his dogs. Diablo sniffed the tiny, extended hand.

A cleared throat startled Shannon from her thoughts. She glanced over her shoulder and found a young woman waiting in the archway. In her late twenties, wearing a Chanel suit, she obviously wasn't the housekeeper.

But she was stunning with her black hair sleeked back in a simple clasp. She wore strappy heels instead of sneakers. God, it felt silly to be envious of someone she didn't know, and honestly, she only coveted the pretty red shoes.

"Alys," the older man commanded, "enter. Come meet my son and his guests. This is my assistant, Alys Reyes de la Cortez. She will show you to your quarters."

Shannon resisted the urge to jump to conclusions. It wasn't any of her business who Enrique Medina chose for his staff and she shouldn't judge a person by their appearance. The woman was probably a rocket scientist, and Shannon wouldn't trade one single sticky hug from her son for all the high-end clothes on the planet.

Not that she was jealous of the gorgeous female with immaculate clothes, who fit perfectly into Tony's world. After all, he hadn't spared more than a passing glance at the woman.

Still, she wished she'd packed a pair of pumps.

An hour later, Shannon closed her empty suitcases and rocked back on her bare heels in the doorway of her new quarters.

A suite?

More like a luxury condominium within the mansion. She sunk her toes into the Persian rug until her chipped pink polish disappeared in the apricot and gray pattern. She and Kolby had separate bedrooms off a sitting area with an eating space stocked more fully than most kitchens. The balcony was as large as some yards.

Had the fresh-cut flowers been placed in here just for her? She dipped her face into the crystal vase of lisianthus with blooms that resembled blue roses and softened the gray tones in the decor.

After Alys had walked them up the lengthy stairs to their suite, Kolby had run from room to room for fifteen minutes before winding down and falling asleep in an exhausted heap under the covers. He hadn't even noticed the toy box at the end of his sleigh bed yet, he'd been so curious about their new digs. Tony had given them space while she unpacked, leaving for his quarters with a simple goodbye and another of those smiles that didn't reach his eyes.

The quiet echoed around her, leaving her hyperaware of other sounds…a ticking grandfather clock in the hall… the crashing ocean outside… Trailing her fingers along the camelback sofa, she looked through the double doors, moonlight casting shadows along her balcony. Her feet drew her closer until the shadows took shape into the broad shoulders of a man leaning on the railing.

Tony? He felt like a safe haven in an upside down day. But how had he gotten there without her noticing his arrival?

Their balconies must connect, which meant someone had planned for them to have access to each other's rooms. Had he been waiting for her? Anticipation hummed through her at the notion of having him all to herself.

Shannon unlocked and pushed open the doors to the patio filled with topiaries, ferns and flowering cacti. A swift ocean breeze rolled over her, lifting her hair and fluttering her shirt along her skin in whispery caresses. God, she was tired and emotional and so not in the right frame of mind to be anywhere near Tony. She should go to bed instead of staring at his sinfully sexy body just calling to her to rest her cheek on his back and wrap her arms around his waist. Her fingers fanned against her legs as she remembered the feel of him, so much more intense with his sandalwood scent riding the wind.

Need pooled warm and languid and low, diluting her already fading resistance.

His shoulders bunched under his starched white shirt a second before he glanced over his shoulder, his eyes haunted. Then they cleared. "Is Kolby asleep?"

"Yes, and thank you for all the preparations. The toys, the food…the flowers."

"All a part of the Medina welcome package."

"Perhaps." But she'd noticed a few too many of their favorites for the choices to have been coincidental. She moved forward hesitantly, the tiles cool against the bottoms of her feet. "This is all…something else."

"Leaving San Rinaldo, we had to downsize." He gave her another of those dry smiles.

More sympathy slid over her frustration at his secrets. "Thank you for bringing us here. I know it wasn't easy for you."

"I'm the reason you have to hide out in the first place until we line up protection for you. Seems only fair I should do everything in my power to make this right."

Her husband had never tried to fix any of his mistakes, hadn't even apologized after his arrest in the face of irrefutable evidence. She couldn't help but appreciate the way Tony took responsibility. And he cared enough to smooth the way for her.

"What about you?" She joined him at the swirled iron

railing. "You wouldn't have come here if it weren't for me. What do you hope to accomplish for yourself?"

"Don't worry about me." He leaned back on his elbows, white shirt stretching open at the collar to reveal the strong column of his neck. "I always look out for myself."

"Then what are you gaining?"

"More time with you, at least until the restraining order is in place." The heat of his eyes broadcast his intent just before he reached for her. "I've always been clear about how much I want to be with you, even on that first date when you wouldn't kiss me good-night."

"Is that why you chased me? Because I said no?"

"But you didn't keep saying no and still, here I am turned on as hell by the sound of your voice." He plucked her glasses off, set them aside and cradled her face in his palms. "The feel of your skin."

While he owned an empire with corporate offices that took up a bayside block, his skin still carried the calluses of the dockworker and sailor he'd been during his early adulthood. He was a man who certainly knew how to work with his hands. The rasp as he lightly caressed her cheekbones reminded her of the sweet abrasion when he explored farther.

He combed through along her scalp, strands slithering across his fingers. "The feel of your hair."

A moan slipped past her lips along with his name, "Tony…"

"Antonio," he reminded her. "I want to hear you say my name, know who's here with you."

And in this moment, in his eyes, he was that foreign prince, less accessible than her Tony, but no less exciting and infinitely as irresistible, so she whispered, "Antonio."

His touch was gentle, his mouth firm against hers. She parted her lips under his and invited in the familiar sweep, taste and pure sensation. Clutching his elbows, she swayed, her breasts tingling, pulling tight. Before she could think or stop herself, she brushed slightly from side to side, increasing the sweet pleasure of his hard chest teasing her. His hard thigh between her legs.

She stepped backward.

And tugged him with her.

Toward the open French doors leading into her bedroom, her body overriding her brain as it always seemed to do around Tony. She squeezed her legs together tighter against the firm pressure of his muscled thigh, so close, too close. She wanted, *needed* to feel him move inside her first.

Sinking her fingernails deeper, she ached to ask him to stay with her, to help her forget the worries waiting at home. "Antonio—"

"I know." He eased his mouth from hers, his chin scraping along her jaw as he nuzzled her hair and inhaled. "We need to stop."

Stop? She almost shrieked in frustration. "But I thought… I mean, you're here and usually when we let things go this far, we finish."

"You're ready to resume our affair?"

Affair. Not just one night, one satisfaction, but a relationship with implications and complications. Her brain raced to catch up after being put on idle while her body took over. God, what had she almost done? A few kisses along with a well-placed thigh, and she was ready to throw herself back in his bed.

Planting her hands on his chest, she stepped away. "I can't deny that I miss you and I want you, but I have no desire to be labeled a Medina mistress."

His eyebrows shot up toward his hairline. "Are you saying you want to get married?"

Six

"Married?" Shannon choked on the word, her eyes so wide with shock Tony was almost insulted. "No! No, definitely not."

Her instant and emphatic denial left zero room for doubt. She wasn't expecting a proposal. Good thing, since that hadn't crossed his mind. Until now.

Was he willing to go that far to protect her?

She turned away fast, her hands raised as she raced back into the sitting area. "Tony—Antonio—I can't talk to you, look at you, risk kissing you again. I need to go to bed. To sleep. Alone."

"Then what do you want from me?"

"To end this craziness. To stop thinking about you all the time."

All the time?

He homed in on her words, an obvious slip on her part because while she'd been receptive and enthusiastic in bed, she'd given him precious little encouragement once they had their clothes back on again. Their fight over his simple offer of money still stung. Why did she have to reject his attempt to help?

She paced, restlessly lining up her shoes beside the sofa, scooping Kolby's tiny train from a table, lingering to rearrange the blue flowers. "You've said you feel the same. Who the hell wants to be consumed by this kind of ache all the time? It's damned inconvenient, especially when it can't lead anywhere. It's not like you were looking for marriage."

"That wasn't my intention when we started seeing each other." Yet somehow the thought had popped into his head out there on the patio. Sure, it had shocked the crap out of him at first. Still left him reeling. Although not so much that he was willing to reject the idea outright. "But since you've brought it up—"

Her hands shot up in front of her, between them. "Uh-uh, no sirree. You were the one to mention the *M* word."

"Fine, then. The marriage issue is out there, on the table for discussion. Let's talk it through."

She stopped cold. "This isn't some kind of business merger. We're talking about our lives here, and not just ours. I don't have the luxury of making another mistake. I already screwed up once before, big time. My son's well-being depends on my decisions."

"And I'm a bad choice because?"

"Do not play with my feelings. Damn it, Tony." She jabbed him in the chest with one finger. "You know I'm attracted to you. If you keep this up, I'll probably cave and we'll have sex. We probably would have on the plane if the steward and my son hadn't been around. But I would have been sorry the minute the orgasm chilled and is that really how you want it to be between us? To have me waking up regretting it every time?"

With images of the two of them joining the mile-high club fast-tracking from his brain to his groin, he seriously considered saying to hell with regrets. Let this insanity between them play out, wherever it took them.

Her bed was only a few steps away, offering a clear and tempting place to sink inside her. He would sweep away her clothes and the covers— His gaze hooked on the afghan draped along the end corner of the mattress.

Damn. Who had put that there? Could his father be deliberately jabbing him with reminders of their life as a family in hopes of drawing him back into the fold? Of course Enrique would, manipulative old cuss that he was.

That familiar silver blanket sucker punched him back to reality. He would recognize the one-of-a-kind afghan anywhere. His mother had knitted it for him just before she'd been killed, and he'd kept it with him like a shield during the whole hellish escape from San Rinaldo. Good God, he shouldn't have had to ask her why he was a bad choice. He knew the reason well.

Tony stumbled back, away from the memories and away from this woman who saw too much with her perceptive gray-blue eyes.

"You're right, Shannon. We're both too exhausted to make any more decisions today. Sleep well." His voice as raw as his memory-riddled gut, he left.

Dazed, Shannon stood in the middle of the sitting room wondering what the hell had just happened.

One second she'd been ready to climb back into Tony's arms and bed, the next they'd been talking about marriage.

And didn't that still stun her numb with thoughts of how horribly things had ended with Nolan?

But only seconds after bringing up the marriage issue, Tony had emotionally checked out on her again. At least he'd prevented them from making a mistake. It was a mistake, right?

Eyeing her big—empty—four-poster bed, she suddenly wasn't one bit sleepy. Tony overwhelmed her as much as the wealth. She walked into her bedroom, studying the Picasso over her headboard, this one from the artist's rose period, a harlequin clown in oranges and pinks. She'd counted three works already by this artist alone, including some leggy elephant painting in Kolby's room.

She'd hidden the crayons and markers.

Laughing at the absurdity of it all, she fingered a folded cashmere afghan draped over the corner of the mattress. So whispery soft and strangely worn in the middle of this immaculately opulent decor. The pewter-colored yarn complemented the apricot and gray tones well enough, but she wondered where it had come from. She tugged it from the bed and shook it out.

The blanket rippled in front of her, a little larger than a lap quilt, not quite long enough for a single bed. Turning in a circle she wrapped the filmy cover around her and padded back out to the balcony. She hugged the cashmere wrap tighter and curled up in a padded lounger, letting the ocean wind soothe her face still warm from Tony's touch.

Was it her imagination or could she smell hints of him even on the blanket? Or was he that firmly in her senses as well as her thoughts? What was it about Tony that reached to her in ways Nolan never had? She'd responded to her husband's touch, found completion, content with her life right up to the point of betrayal.

But Tony... Shannon hugged the blanket tighter. She

hadn't been hinting at marriage, damn it. Just the thought of giving over her life so completely again scared her to her toes.

So where did that leave her? Seriously considering becoming exactly what the media labeled her—a monarch's mistress.

Tony heard...the silence.

Finally, Shannon had settled for the night. Thank God. Much longer and his willpower would have given out. He would have gone back into her room and picked up where they'd left off before he'd caught sight of the damn blanket.

This place screwed with his head, so much so he'd actually brought up marriage, for crying out loud. It was like there were rogue waves from his past curling up everywhere and knocking him off balance. The sooner he could take care of business with his father the sooner he could return to Galveston with Shannon, back to familiar ground where he stood a better chance at reconciling with her.

Staying out of her bed for now was definitely the wiser choice. He walked down the corridor, away from her and that blanket full of memories. He needed his focus sharp for the upcoming meeting with his father. This time, he would face the old man alone.

Charging down the hall, he barely registered the familiar antique wooden benches tucked here, a strategic table and guard posted there. Odd how quickly he slid right back into the surroundings even after so long away. And even stranger that his father hadn't changed a thing.

The day had been one helluva ride, and it wasn't over yet. Enrique had been with his nurse for the past hour, but should be ready to receive him now.

Tony rounded the corner and nodded to the sentinel outside the open door to Enrique's personal quarters. The space was made for a man, no feminine touches to soften the room full of browns and tans, leather and wood. Enrique saved his Salvador Dali collection for himself, a trio of the surrealist's "soft watches" melting over landscapes.

The old guy had become more obsessed with history after his had been stolen from him.

Enrique waited in his wheelchair, wearing a heavy blue robe and years of worries.

"Sit," his father ordered, pointing to his old favored chair.

When Tony didn't jump at his command, Enrique sighed heavily and muttered under his breath in Spanish. "Have a seat," he continued in his native tongue. "We need to talk, *mi hijo*."

They did, and Tony had to admit he was curious— concerned—about his father's health. Knowing might not have brought him home sooner, but now that he was here, he couldn't ignore the gaunt angles and sallow pallor. "How sick are you really?" Tony continued in Spanish, having spoken both languages equally once they'd left San Rinaldo. "No sugar coating it. I deserve the truth."

"And you would have heard it earlier if you had returned when I first requested."

His father had never *requested* anything in his life. The stubborn old cuss had been willing to die alone rather than actually admit how ill he was.

Of course Antonio had been just as stubborn about ignoring the demands to show his face on the island. "I am here now."

"You and your brothers have stirred up trouble." A great big *I told you so* was packed into that statement.

"Do you have insights as to how this leaked? How did

that reporter identify Duarte?" His middle brother wasn't exactly a social guy.

"Nobody knows, but my people are still looking into it. I thought you would be the one to expose us," his father said wryly. "You always were the impetuous one. Yet you've behaved decisively and wisely. You have protected those close to you. Well done."

"I am past needing your approval, but I thank you for your help."

"Fair enough, and I'm well aware that you would not have accepted that help if Shannon Crawford was not involved. I would be glad to see one of my sons settled and married before I die."

His gut pitched much like a boat tossed by a wave. "Your illness is that bad?" An uneasy silence settled, his father's rattling breaths growing louder and louder. "Should I call a nurse?"

Or his assistant? He wasn't sure what Alys Reyes de la Cortez was doing here, but she was definitely different from the older staff of San Rinaldo natives Enrique normally hired.

"I may be old and sick, but I don't need to be tucked into bed like a child." His chin tipped.

"I'm not here to fight with you."

"Of course not. You're here for my help."

And he had the feeling his father wasn't going to let him forget it. They'd never gotten along well and apparently that hadn't changed. He started to rise. "If that's all then, I will turn in."

"Wait." His father polished his eighteen-karat gold pocket watch with his thumb. "My assistance comes at a price."

Shocked at the calculating tone, Tony sank back into his chair. "You can't be serious."

"I am. Completely."

He should have suspected and prepared himself. "What do you want?"

"I want you to stay for the month while you wait for the new safety measures to be implemented."

"Here? That's all?" He made it sound offhand but already he could feel the claustrophobia wrap around his throat and tighten. The Dali art mocked him with just how slippery time could be, a life that ended in a flash or a moment that extended forever.

"Is it so strange I want to see what kind of man you have matured into?"

Given Enrique had expected Tony to break their cover, he must not have had high expectations for his youngest son. And that pissed him off. "If I don't agree? You'll do what? Feed Shannon and her son to the lions?"

"Her son can stay. I would never sacrifice a child's safety. The mother will have to go."

He couldn't be serious. Tony studied his father for some sign Enrique was bluffing…but the old guy didn't have a "tell." And his father hadn't hesitated to trust his own wife's safety to others. What would stop him from sending Shannon off with a guard and a good-luck wish?

"She would never leave without her child." Like his mother. Tony restrained a wince.

"That is not my problem. Are you truly that unwilling to spend a month here?"

"What if the restraining order comes through sooner?"

"I would ask you to stay as a thanks for my assistance. I have risked a lot for you in granting her access to the island."

True enough, or so it would feel to Enrique with his near agoraphobic need to stay isolated from the world.

"And there are no other conditions?"

A salt and pepper eyebrow arched. "Do you want a contract?"

"Do you? If Shannon decides to leave by the weekend, I could simply go, too. What's the worst you can do? Cut me out of the will?" He hadn't taken a penny of his father's money.

"You always were the most amusing of my sons. I have missed that."

"I'm not laughing."

His father's smile faded and he tucked the watch into a pocket, chain jingling to a rest. "Your word is sufficient. You may not want any part of me and my little world here, but you are a Medina. You are my son. Your honor is not in question."

"Fair enough. If you're willing to accept my word, then a month it is." Now that the decision was made, he wondered why his father had chosen that length of time. "What's your prognosis?"

"My liver is failing," Enrique said simply without any hint of self-pity. "Because of the living conditions when I was on the run, I caught hepatitis. It has taken a toll over the years."

Thinking back, Tony tried to remember if his father had been sick when they'd reunited in South America before relocating to the island...but he only recalled his father being coolly determined. "I didn't know. I'm sorry."

"You were a child. You did not need to be informed of everything."

He hadn't been told much of *anything* in those days, but even if he had, he wasn't sure he would have heard. His grief for his mother had been deep and dark. That, he remembered well. "How much longer do you have?"

"I am not going to kick off in the next thirty days."

"That isn't what I meant."

"I know." His father smiled, creases digging deep. "I have a sense of humor, too."

What had his father been like before this place? Before the coup? Tony would never know because time was melting away like images in the Dali paintings on the wall.

While he had some memories of his mother from that time, he had almost none of his father until Enrique had met up with them in South America. The strongest memory he had of Enrique in San Rinaldo? When his father gathered his family to discuss the evacuation plan. Enrique had pressed his pocket watch into Tony's hands and promised to reclaim it. But even at five, Tony had known his father was saying goodbye for what could have been the last time. Now, Enrique wanted him back to say goodbye for the last time again.

How damned ironic. He'd brought Shannon to this place because she needed him. And now he could only think of how much he needed to be with her.

Seven

Where was Tony?

The next day after lunch, Shannon stood alone on her balcony overlooking the ocean. Seagulls swooped on the horizon while long legged blue herons stalked prey on the rocks. Kolby was napping. A pot of steeped herbal tea waited on a tiny table along with dried fruits and nuts.

How strange to have such complete panoramic peace during such a tumultuous time. The balcony offered an unending view of the sea, unlike the other side with barrier islands. The temperature felt much the same as in Galveston, humid and in the seventies.

She should make the most of the quiet to regain her footing. Instead, she kept looking at the door leading into Tony's suite and wondering why she hadn't seen him yet.

Her morning had been hectic and more than a little overwhelming learning her way around the mansion with Alys. As much as she needed to resist Tony, she'd missed having his big comforting presence at her side while she explored the never-ending rooms packed nonchalantly with priceless art and antiques.

And they'd only toured half of the home and grounds.

Afterward, Alys had introduced two women on hand for sitter and nanny duties. Shannon had been taken aback by the notion of turning her son over to total strangers, although she had to confess, the guard assigned to shadow Kolby reassured her. She'd been shown letters of recommendation and résumés for each individual. Still, Shannon had spent the rest of the morning getting to know each person in case she needed to call on their help.

Interestingly, none of the king's employees gave away the island's location despite subtle questions about traveling back to their homes. Everyone on Enrique's payroll seemed to understand the importance of discretion, as well as seeing to her every need. Including delivering a closet full of clothes that just happened to fit. Not that she'd caved to temptation yet and tried any of it on. A gust rolling off the ocean teased the well-washed cotton of her sundress around her legs as she stood on the balcony.

The click of double doors opening one suite down snapped her from her reverie. She didn't even need to look over her shoulder to verify who'd stepped outside. She knew the sound of his footsteps, recognized the scent of him on the breeze.

"Hello, Tony."

His Italian loafers stopped alongside her feet in simple pink and brown striped flip-flops. *Hers.* Not ones from the new stash.

Leaning into her line of sight, he rested his elbows on the iron rail. "Sorry not to have checked in on you sooner. My father and I spent the morning troubleshooting on a conference call with my brothers and our attorneys."

Of course. That made sense. "Any news?"

"More of the same. Hopefully we can start damage control with some valid info leaked to the press to turn the tide. There's just so much out there." He shook his head sharply then forced a smile. "Enough of that. I missed you at lunch."

"Kolby and I ate in our suite." The scent of Tony's sandalwood aftershave had her curling her toes. "His table manners aren't up to royal standards."

"You don't have to hide in your rooms. There's no court or ceremony here." Still, he wore khakis and a monogrammed blue button-down rolled up at the sleeves rather than the jeans and shorts most everyday folks would wear on a beach vacation.

And he looked mighty fine in every starched inch of fabric.

"Formality or not, there are priceless antiques and art all easily within a child's reach." She trailed her fingers along the iron balustrade. "This place is a lot to absorb. We need time. Although I hope life returns to normal sooner rather than later."

Could she simply pick up where she'd left off? Things hadn't been so great then, given her nearly bankrupt account and her fight with Tony over more than money, over her very independence. Yet hadn't she been considering resuming the affair just last night?

Sometimes it was tough to tell if her hormones or her heart had control these days.

He extended his hand. "You're right. Let's slow things down. Would you like to go for a walk?"

"But Kolby might wake up and ask for m—"

"One of the nannies can watch over him and call us the second his eyes open. Come on. I'll update you on the wackiest of the internet buzz." A half grin tipped one side of his tanned face. "Apparently one source thinks the Medinas have a space station and I've taken you to the mother ship."

Laughter bubbled, surprising her, and she just let it roll free with the wind tearing in from the shore. God, how she needed it after the stressful past couple of days—a stressful week for that matter, since she had broken off her relationship with Tony. "Lead the way, my alien lover."

His smile widened, reaching his eyes for the first time since their ferry had pulled up to the island. The power outshone the world around her until she barely noticed the opulent surroundings on their way through the mansion to the beach.

The October sun high in the sky was blinding and warm, hotter than when she'd been on the balcony, inching up toward eighty degrees perhaps. Her mind started churning with possible locations. Could they be in Mexico or South America? Or were they still in the States? California or—

"We're off the coast of Florida."

Glancing up sharply, she swallowed hard, not realizing until that moment how deeply the secrecy had weighed on her. "Thank you."

He waved aside her gratitude. "You would have figured it out on your own in a couple of days."

Maybe, but given the secrecy of Enrique's employees, she wasn't as certain. "So, what about more of those wacky internet rumors?"

"Do you really want to discuss that?"

"I guess not." She slid off her flip-flops and curled her toes in the warm sand. "Thank you for all the clothes for me and for Kolby, the toys, too. We'll enjoy them while we're here. But you know we can't keep them."

"Don't be a buzz kill." He tapped her nose just below the

bridge of her glasses. "My father's staff ordered everything. I had nothing to do with it. If it'll make you happy, we'll donate the lot to Goodwill after you leave."

"How did he get everything here so fast?" She strode into the tide, her shoes dangling from her fingers.

"Does it matter?" He slid off his shoes and socks and joined her, just into the water's reach.

With the more casual and familiar Tony returning, some of the tension left her shoulders. "I guess not. The toys are awesome, of course, but Kolby enjoys the dogs most. They seem incredibly well trained."

"They are. My father will have his trainers working with the dogs to bond with your son so they will protect him as well if need be while you are here."

She shivered in spite of the bold beams of sunshine overhead. "Can't a dog just be a pet?"

"Things aren't that simple for us." He looked away, down the coast at an osprey spreading its wings and diving downward.

How many times had he watched the birds as a child and wanted to fly away, too? She understood well the need to escape a golden cage. "I'm sorry."

"Don't be." He rejected her sympathy outright.

Pride iced his clipped words, and she searched for a safer subject.

Her eyes settled on the rippling crests of foam frosting the gray-blue shore. "Is this where you used to surf?"

"Actually, the cove is pretty calm." He pointed ahead to an outcropping packed with palm trees. "The best spot is about a mile and a half down. Or at least it was. Who knows after so many years?"

"You really had free rein to run around the island." She stepped onto a sandbar that fingered out into the water. As a mother, she had a tough time picturing her child exploring this junglelike beach at will.

"Once I was a teenager, pretty much. After I was through with schooling for the day, of course." A green turtle popped his head from the water, legs poking from the shell as he swam out and slapped up the beach. "Although sometimes we even had class out here."

"A field trip to the beach? What fun teachers you had."

"Tutors."

"Of course." The stark difference in their upbringings wrapped around her like seaweed lapping at her ankles. She tried to shake free of the clammy negativity. "Surfing was your P.E.?"

"Technically, we had what you would call phys ed, but it was more of a health class with martial arts training."

During her couple of years teaching high school band and chorus before she'd met Nolan, some of her students went to karate lessons. But they'd gone to a gym full of other students, rather than attending in seclusion with only two brothers for company. "It's so surreal to think you never went to prom, or had an after-school job or played on a basketball team."

"We had games here…but you're right in that there was no stadium of classmates and parents. No cheerleaders." He winked and smiled, but she sensed he was using levity as a diversion.

How often had he done that in the past and she'd missed out hearing his real thoughts or feelings because she wanted things to be uncomplicated?

Shannon squeezed his bulging forearm. "You would have been a good football player with your size."

"Soccer." His bicep twitched under her touch. "I'm from Europe, remember?"

"Of course." Unlikely she would ever forget his roots now that she knew. And she wanted to learn more about this strong-jawed man who thought to order a miniature motorized Jeep for her son—and then give credit to his father.

She tucked her hand into the crook of his arm as she swished through the ebbs and flow of the tidewaters. "So you still think of yourself as being from Europe? Even though you were only five when you came to the U.S.?"

His eyebrows pinched together. "I never really thought of this as the U.S. even though I know how close we are."

"I can understand that. Everything here is such a mix of cultures." While the staff spoke English to her, she'd heard Spanish spoken by some. Books and magazines and even instructions on labels were a mix of English, Spanish and some French. "You mentioned thinking this was still San Rinaldo when you got here."

"Only at first. My father told us otherwise."

What difficult conversations those must have been between father and sons. So much to learn and adjust to so young. "We've both lost a lot, you and I. I wonder if I sensed that on some level, if that's what drew us to each other."

He slid an arm around her shoulders and pulled her closer while they kicked through the surf. "Don't kid yourself. I was attracted to how hot you looked walking away in that slim black skirt. And then when you glanced over your shoulder with those prim glasses and do-me eyes." He whistled long and low. "I was toast from the get-go."

Trying not to smile, her skin heating all the same, she elbowed him lightly. "Cro-Magnon."

"Hey, I'm a red-blooded male and you're sexy." He traced the cat-eye edge of her glasses. "You're also entirely too serious at the moment. Life will kick us in the ass all on its own soon enough. We're going to just enjoy the moment, remember? No more buzz kills."

"You're right." Who knew how much longer she would have with Tony before this mess blew up in her face? "Let's go back to talking about surfing and high school dances. You so would have been the bad boy."

"And I'll bet you were a good girl. Did you wear those studious glasses even then?"

"Since I was in the eighth grade." She'd hated how her nose would sweat in the heat when she'd marched during football games. "I was a dedicated musician with no time for boys."

"And now?"

"I want to enjoy this beautiful ocean and a day with absolutely nothing to do." She bolted ahead, kicking through the tide, not sure how to balance her impulsive need for Tony with her practical side that demanded she stay on guard.

Footsteps splashed behind her a second before Tony scooped her up. And she let him.

The warm heat of his shoulder under her cheek, the steady pump of his heart against her side had her curling her arms around his neck. "You're getting us all wet."

His eyes fell to her shirt. His heart thumped faster. "Are you having fun?"

"Yes, I am." She toyed with the springy curls at the nape of his neck. "You always make sure of that, whether it's an opera or a walk by the beach."

"You deserve to have more fun in your life." He held her against his chest with a familiarity she couldn't deny. "I would make things easier for you. You know that."

"And you know where I stand on that subject." She cupped his face, his stubble so dark and thick that he wore a perpetual five o'clock shadow. "This—your protection, the trip, the clothes and toys—it's already much more than I'm comfortable taking."

She needed to be clear on that before she even considered letting him closer again.

He eased her to her feet with a lingering glide of her body down his. "We should go back."

The desire in his eyes glinted unmistakably in the afternoon sun. Yet, he pulled away.

Her lips hungered and her breasts ached—and *he* was walking away again, in spite of all he'd said about how much he wanted her. This man confused the hell out of her.

Five days later, Shannon lounged on the downstairs lanai and watched her son drive along the beach in his miniature Jeep, dogs romping alongside. This was the first time she'd been left to her own devices in days. She'd never been romanced so thoroughly in her life. True to his word, over the past week Tony had been at his most charming.

Could her time here already be almost over?

Sipping freshly squeezed lemonade—although the drink tasted far too amazing for such a simple name—she savored the tart taste. Of course everything seemed sharper, crisper as tension seeped from her bones. The concerns of the world felt forever away while the sun warmed her skin and the waves provided a soothing sound track to her days.

And she had Tony to thank for it all. She'd never known there were so many entertainment options on an island. Of course Enrique Medina had spared no expense in building his compound.

A movie screening room with all the latest films piped in for private viewing.

Three different dining rooms for everything from family style to white-tie.

Rec room, gym, indoor and outdoor swimming pools.

She could still hear Kolby's squeal of delight over the stable of horses and ponies.

Throughout it all, Tony had been at her side with tantalizing brushes of his strong body against hers. All the while his rich chocolate brown eyes reminded Shannon that the next move was up to her. Not that they stood a chance at finding privacy today. The grounds buzzed with activity, and today, no sign of Tony.

Behind her, the doors snicked open. Tony? Her heart stuttered a quick syncopation as she glanced back.

Alys walked toward her, high heels clicking on the tiled veranda as she angled past two guards comparing notes on their twin BlackBerry phones. Shannon forced herself to keep the smile in place. It would be rude to frown in disappointment, especially after how helpful the woman had been.

Too bad the disappointment wasn't as easy to hide from herself. No doubt about it, Tony was working his way back into her life.

The king's assistant stopped at the fully stocked outdoor bar and poured a glass of lemonade from the crystal pitcher.

Shannon thumbed the condensation on the cold glass. "Is there something you need?"

"Antonio wanted me to find you, and I have." She tapped her silver BlackBerry attached to the waistband of her linen skirt. Ever crisp with her power suit and French manicure. As usual the elegant woman didn't have a wrinkle in sight, much less wince over working in heels all day. "He'll be out shortly. He's finishing up a meeting with his father."

"I should get Kolby." She swung her feet to the side.

How silly to be glad she'd caved and used some of the new clothes. She had worn everything she brought with her twice and while the laundry service easily kept up with her limited wardrobe, she'd begun to feel a little ungrateful not to wear at least a few of the things that someone had gone to a lot of trouble to provide. Shannon smoothed the de la Renta scoop-necked dress, the fabric so decadently soft it caressed her skin with every move.

"No need to stop the boy's fun just yet. Antonio is on his way." Alys perched on the edge of the lounger, glass on her knee.

Shannon rubbed the hem of her dress between two fingers much like Kolby with his blanket when he needed soothing. "I hear you're the one who ordered all the new clothes. Thank you."

Alys saw to everything else in this smoothly run place. "No need for thanks. It's my job."

"You have excellent taste." She tugged the hem back over her knees.

"I saw your photo online and chose things that would flatter your frame and coloring. It's fun to shop on someone else's dime."

More than a dime had gone into this wardrobe. Her closet sported new additions each morning. Everything from casual jeans and designer blouses to silky dresses and heels to wear for dinner. An assortment of bathing suits to choose from….

And the lingerie. A decadent shiver slid down her spine at the feel of the fine silks and satins against her skin. Although it made her uncomfortable to think of this woman choosing everything.

Alys turned her glass around and around on her knee. "The expense you worry about is nothing to them. They can afford the finest. It would bother them to see you struggling. Now you fit in and that gives the king less to worry about."

God forbid her tennis shoes should make the king uncomfortable. But saying as much would make her sound ungrateful, so she toyed with her glasses, pulling them off and cleaning them with her napkin even though they were already crystal clear. The dynamics of this place went beyond any household she'd ever seen. Alys seemed more comfortable here than Tony.

Shannon slid her glasses back on. "If you don't mind my asking, how long have you been working for the king?"

"Only three months."

How long did she intend to stay? The island was luxurious, but in more of a vacation kind of way. It was so cut off from the world, time seemed to stand still. What kind of life could the woman build in this place?

Abruptly, Alys leaped to her feet. "Here is Antonio now."

He charged confidently through the door, eyes locked on Shannon. "Thank you for finding her, Alys."

The assistant backed away. "Of course." Alys stepped out of hearing range, giving them some privacy.

Forking a hand through his hair—messing up the precise combing from his conference with his father—Tony wore a suit without a tie. The jacket perhaps a nod toward meeting with his father? His smile was carefree, but his shoulders bore the extra tension she'd come to realize accompanied time he had spent with the king.

"How did your meeting go?"

"Don't want to talk about that." Tony plucked a lily from the vase on the bar, snapped the stem off and tucked the bloom behind her ear. "Would much rather enjoy the view. The flower is almost as gorgeous as you are."

The lush perfume filled each breath. "All the fresh flowers are positively decadent."

"I wish I could take credit, but there's a hothouse with a supply that's virtually unlimited."

Yet another amenity she wouldn't have guessed, although it certainly explained all the fresh-cut flowers. "Still," she repeated as she touched the lily tucked in her hair, "I appreciate the gesture."

"I would make love to you on a bed of flowers if you let me." He thumbed her earlobe lightly before skimming his knuckles along her collarbone.

How easy it would be to give over to the delicious seduction of his words and his world. Except she'd allowed herself to fall into that trap before.

And of course there was that little technicality that *he* had been the one holding back all week. "What about thorns?"

He laughed, his hand falling away from her skin and palming her back. "Come on, my practical love. We're going out."

Love? She swallowed to dampen her suddenly cottony mouth. "To lunch?"

"To the airstrip."

Her stomach lurched. This slice of time away was over already? "We're leaving?"

"Not that lucky, I'm afraid. Your apartment is still staked out with the press and curious royalty groupie types. You may want to consider a gated community on top of the added security measures. I know the cost freaks you out, but give my lawyer another couple of days to work on those restraining orders and we can take it from there. As for where we're going today, we're greeting guests and I'd like you to come along."

They weren't leaving. Relief sang through her so intensely it gave her pause.

Tony cocked his head to the side. "Would you like to come with me?"

"Uh, yes, I think so." She struggled to gather her scrambled thoughts and composure. "I just need to settle Kolby."

Alys cleared her throat a few feet away. "I've already notified Miss Delgado, the younger nanny. She's ordering a picnic lunch and bringing sand toys. Then of course she will watch over him during his naptime if needed. I assume that's acceptable to you?"

Her son would enjoy that more than a car ride and waiting around for the flight. She was growing quite spoiled having afternoons completely free while Kolby napped safely under a nanny's watchful care. "Of course. That sounds perfect."

Shannon smiled her thanks and reached out to touch the woman's arm. Except Alys wasn't looking at her. The king's assistant had her eyes firmly planted elsewhere.

On Tony.

Shock nailed her feet to the tiles. Then a fierce jealousy vibrated through her, a feeling that was most definitely ugly and not her style. She'd thought herself above such a primitive emotion, not to mention Tony hadn't given the woman any encouragement.

Still, Shannon fought the urge to link her arm with his in a great big "mine" statement. In that unguarded moment, Alys revealed clearly what she hoped to gain from living here.

Alys wanted a Medina man.

Eight

Tony guided the Porsche Cayenne four-wheel drive along the island road toward the airstrip, glad Shannon was with him to ease the edge on the upcoming meeting. Although having her with him brought a special torment all its own.

The past week working his way back into her good graces had been a painful pleasure, sharpening the razor edge on his need to have her in his bed again. Spending time with her had only shown him more reasons to want her. She mesmerized him with the simplest things.

When she sat on the pool edge and kicked her feet through the water, he thought of those long legs wrapped around him.

Seeing her sip a glass of lemonade made him ache to taste the tart fruit on her lips.

The way she cleaned her glasses with a gust of breath

fogging the frames made him think of her panting in his ear as he brought her to completion.

Romancing his way back into her good graces was easier said than done. And the goal of it all made each day on this island easier to bear.

And after they returned to Galveston? He would face that then. Right now, he had more of his father's past to deal with.

"Tony?" Bracing her hand against the dash as the rutted road challenged even the quality shock absorbers, she looked so right sitting in the seat next to him. "You still haven't told me who we're picking up. Your brothers, perhaps?"

Steering the SUV under the arch of palm trees lining both sides of the road, he searched for the right words to prepare Shannon for something he'd never shared with a soul. "You're on the right track." His hands gripped the steering wheel tighter. "My sister. Half sister, actually. Eloisa."

"A sister? I didn't know...."

"Neither does the press." His half sister had stayed under the radar, growing up with her mother and stepfather in Pensacola, Florida. Only recently had Eloisa reestablished contact with their father. "She's coming here to regroup, troubleshoot. Prepare. Now that the Medina secret is out, her story will also be revealed soon enough."

"May I ask what that story might be?"

"Of course." He focused on the two-lane road, a convenient excuse to make sure she didn't see any anger pushing past his boundaries. "My father had a relationship with her mother after arriving in the U.S., which resulted in Eloisa. She's in her mid-twenties now."

Shannon's eyes went wide behind her glasses.

"Yeah, I know." Turning, he drove from the jungle road

onto a waterside route leading to the ferry station. "That's a tight timeline between when we left San Rinaldo and the hookup." Tight timeline in regard to his mother's death.

"That must have been confusing for you. Kolby barely remembers his father and it's been tough for him to accept you. And we haven't had to deal with adding another child to the mix."

A child? With Shannon? An image of a dark-haired baby—his baby—in her arms blindsided him, derailing his thoughts away from his father in a flash. His foot slid off the accelerator. Shaking free of the image was easier said than done as it grew roots in his mind—Kolby stepping into the picture until a family portrait took shape.

God, just last week he'd been thinking how he knew nothing about kids. She was the one hinting at marriage, not him. Although she said the opposite until he didn't know what was up.

Things with Shannon weren't as simple as he'd planned at the outset. "My father's affair was his own business."

"Okay, then." She pulled her glasses off and fogged them with her breath. She dried them with the hem of her dress. "Do you and your sister get along?"

He hauled his eyes from Shannon's glasses before he swerved off onto the beach. Or pulled onto the nearest side road and to hell with making it to the airstrip on time.

"I've only met her once before." When Tony was a teenager. His father had gone all out on that lone visit with his seven-year-old daughter. Tony didn't resent Eloisa. It wasn't her fault, after all. In fact, he grew even more pissed off at his father. Enrique had responsibilities to his daughter. If he wanted to stay out of her life, then fine. Do so. But half measures were bull.

Yet wasn't that what he'd been offering Shannon? Half measures?

Self-realization sucked. "She's come here on her own since then. She and Duarte have even met up a few times, which in a roundabout way brought on the media mess."

"How so?" She slid her glasses back in place.

"Our sister married into a high-profile family. Eloisa's husband is the son of an ambassador and brother to a senator. He's a Landis."

She sat up straighter at the mention of America's political royalty. Talk about irony.

Tony slowed for a fuel truck to pass. "The Landis name naturally comes with media attention." He accelerated into the parking lot alongside the ferry station, the boat already close to shore. An airplane was parked on the distant airstrip. "Her husband—Jonah—likes to keep a low profile, but that's just not possible."

"What happened?"

"Duarte was delivering one of our father's messages, which put him on a collision course with a press camera. We're still trying to figure out how the Global Intruder made the connection. Although, it's a moot point now. Every stray photo of all of us has been unearthed, every detail of our pasts."

"Of my past?" Her face drained of color.

"I'm afraid so."

All the more reason for her to stay on the island. Her husband's illegal dealings, even his suicide, had hit the headlines again this morning, thanks to muckrakers looking for more scandal connected to the Medina story. He would only be able to shield Shannon from that for so long. She had a right to know.

"I've grown complacent this week." She pressed a hand to her stomach. "My poor in-laws."

The SUV idled in the parking spot, the ferry already

preparing to dock. He didn't have much time left alone with her.

Tony skimmed back her silky blond hair. "I'm sorry all this has come up again. And I hate it that I can't do more to fix things for you."

Turning toward his touch, she rested her face in his hand. "You've helped this week."

He wanted to kiss her, burned to recline the seats and explore the hint of cleavage in her scoop-necked dress. And damned if that wasn't exactly what he planned to do.

Slanting his mouth over her, he caught her gasp and took full advantage of her parted lips with a determined sweep of his tongue. Need for her pumped through his veins, fast-tracked blood from his head to his groin until he could only feel, smell, taste undiluted *Shannon*. Her gasp quickly turned to a sigh as she melted against him, the curves of her breasts pressed to his chest, her fingernails digging deeply into his forearms as she urged him closer.

He was more than happy to accommodate.

It had been so long, too long since they'd had sex before their argument over his damned money. Nearly fourteen days that seemed like fourteen years since he'd had his hands on her this way, fully and unrestrained, tunneling under her clothes, reacquainting himself with the perfection of her soft skin and perfect curves. She fit against him with a rightness he knew extended even further with their clothes off. A hitch in her throat, the flush rising on the exposed curve of her breasts keyed him in to her rising need, as if he couldn't already tell by the way she nearly crawled across the seat to get closer.

Shannon wanted sex with him every bit as much as he wanted her. But that required privacy, not a parking lot in clear view of the approaching ferry.

Holding back now was the right move, even if it was killing him.

"Come on. Time to meet my sister." He slid out of her arms and the SUV and around to her door before she could shuffle her purse from her lap to her shoulder.

He opened the door and she smiled her thanks without speaking, yet another thing he appreciated about her. She sensed when he didn't want to talk anymore. He'd shared things with women over the years, but until her, he'd never found one with whom he could share silence.

The lapping waves, the squawk of gulls, the endless stretch of water centered him, steadying his steps and reminding him how to keep his balance in a rocky world.

Resting his head on Shannon's back, he waited while the ferry finished docking. His sister and her husband stood at the railing. Eloisa's husband hooked an arm around her shoulders, the couple talking intently.

Eloisa might not be a carbon copy of their father, but she carried an air of something unmistakably Medina about her. His father had once said she looked like their grandmother. Tony wouldn't know, since he couldn't remember his grandparents who'd all died before he was born.

The loudspeaker blared with the boat captain announcing their arrival. Disembarking, the couple stayed close together, his brother-in-law broadcasting a protective air. Jonah was the unconventional Landis, according to the papers. If so, they should get along just fine.

The couple stepped from the boat to the dock, and up close Eloisa didn't appear nearly as calm as from a distance. Lines of strain showed in her eyes.

"Welcome," Tony said. "Eloisa, Jonah, this is Shannon Crawford, and I'm—"

"Antonio, I know." His sister spoke softly, reserved. "I recognize you both from the papers."

He'd met Eloisa once as a child when she'd visited the island. She'd come back recently, but he'd been long gone by then.

They were strangers and relatives. Awkward, to say the least.

Jonah Landis stepped up. "Glad you could accommodate our request for a visit so quickly."

"Damage control is important."

Eloisa simply took his hand, searching his face. "How's our father?"

"Not well." Had Shannon just stepped closer to him? Tony kept his eyes forward, knowing in his gut he would see sympathy in her eyes. "He says his doctors are doing all they can."

Blinking back tears, Eloisa stood straighter with a willowy strength. "I barely know him, but I can't envision a world without him in it. Sounds crazy, I'm sure."

He understood too well. Making peace was hard as hell, yet somehow she seemed to have managed.

Jonah clapped him on the back. "Well, my new bro, I need to grab Eloisa's bags and meet you at the car."

A Landis who carried his own luggage? Tony liked the unpretentious guy already.

And wasn't that one of the things he liked most about Shannon? Her down-to-earth ways in spite of her wealthy lifestyle with her husband. She seemed completely unimpressed with the Medina money, much less his defunct title.

For the first time he considered she might be right. She may be better off without the strain of his messed-up family.

Which made him a selfish bastard for pursuing her. But

he couldn't seem to pull back now when his world had been rocked on its foundation. The sailor in him recognized the only port in the storm, and right now, only a de la Renta dress separated him from what he wanted—needed—more than anything.

However, he needed to choose his time and place carefully with the private island growing more crowded by the minute.

The next afternoon, Shannon sat beside Tony in the Porsche four-wheel drive on the way to the beach. He'd left her a note to put on her bathing suit and meet him during Kolby's naptime. She'd been taken aback at the leap of excitement in her stomach over spending time alone with him.

The beach road took them all the way to the edge of the shoreline. He shifted the car in Park, his legs flexing in black board shorts as he left the car silently. He'd been quiet for the whole drive, and she didn't feel the need to fill the moment with aimless babbling. Being together and quiet had an appeal all its own.

Tugging on the edge of the white cover-up, she eyed the secluded stretch of beach. Could this be the end of the "romancing" and the shift back to intimacy? Her stomach fluttered faster.

She stepped from the car before he could open her door. Wind ruffled his hair and whipped his shorts, low slung on his hips. She knew his body well but still the muscled hardness hitched her breath in her throat. Bronzed and toned—smart, rich and royal to boot. Life had handed him an amazing hand, and yet he still chose to work insane hours. In fact, she'd spent more time with him this past week than during the months they'd dated in Galveston.

And everything she learned confused her more than solving questions.

She jammed her hands in the pockets of her cover-up. "Are you going to tell me why we're here?"

"Over there." He pointed to a cluster of palm trees with surfboards propped and waiting.

"You're kidding, right? Tony, I don't surf, and the water must be cold."

"You'll warm up. The waves aren't high enough today for surfing. But there're still some things even a beginner can do." He peeled off his T-shirt and she realized she was staring, damn it. "You won't break anything. Trust me."

He extended a hand.

Trust? Easier said than done. She eyed the boards and looked back at him. They were on the island, she reminded herself, removed from real life. And bottom line, while she wasn't sure she trusted him with her heart, she totally trusted him with her body. He wouldn't let anything happen to her.

Decision made, she whipped her cover-up over her head, revealing her crocheted swimsuit. His eyes flamed over her before he took her cover-up and tossed it in the SUV along with his T-shirt. He closed his hands around hers in a warm steady grip and started toward the boards.

She eyed the pair propped against trees—obviously set up in advance for their outing. One shiny and new, bright white with tropical flowers around the edges. The other was simpler, just yellow, faded from time and use. She looked at the water again, starting to have second—

"Hey." He squeezed her hand. "We're just going to paddle out. Nothing too adventurous today, but I think you're going to find even slow and steady has some unexpected thrills."

And didn't that send her heart double timing?

Thank goodness he moved quickly. Mere minutes later she was on her stomach, on the board, paddling away from shore to…nowhere. Nothing but aqua blue waters blending into a paler sky. Mild waves rolled beneath her but somehow never lifted her high enough to be scary, more of a gentle rocking. The chilly water turned to a neutral sluice over her body, soothing her into becoming one with the ocean.

One stroke at a time she let go of goals and racing to the finish line. Her life had been on fast-paced frenetic since Nolan died. Now, for the first time in longer than she could remember, she was able to unwind, almost hypnotized by the dip, dip, dip of her hands and Tony's into the water.

Tension she hadn't even realized kinked her muscles began to ease. Somehow, Tony must have known. She turned her head to thank him and found him staring back at her.

She threaded her fingers through the water, sun baking her back. "It's so quiet out here."

"I thought you would appreciate the time away."

"You were right." She slowed her paddling and just floated. "You've given over a lot of your time to make sure Kolby and I stayed entertained. Don't you need to get back to work?"

"I work from the island using my computer and telecoms." His hair, even darker when wet, was slicked back from his face, his damp skin glinting in the sun. "More and more of business is being conducted that way."

"Do you ever sleep?"

"Not so much lately, but that has nothing to do with work." He held her with his eyes locked on her face, no suggestive body sweep, just intense, undiluted Tony.

And she couldn't help but wonder why he went to so much trouble when they weren't sleeping together anymore.

If his conscience bothered him, he could have assigned guards to watch over her and she wouldn't have argued for Kolby's sake. Yet here he was. With her.

"What do you see in me?" She rested her cheek on her folded hands. "I'm not fishing for compliments, honest to God, it's just we seem so wrong for each other on so many levels. Is it just the challenge, like building your business?"

"Shanny, you take *challenge* to a whole 'nother level."

She flicked water in his face. "I'm being serious here. No joking around, please."

"Seriously?" He stared out at the horizon for a second as if gathering his thoughts. "Since you brought up the business analogy, let's run with that. At work you would be someone I want on my team. Your tenacity, your refusal to give up—even your frustrating rejection of my help— impress the hell out of me. You're an amazing woman, so much so that sometimes I can't even look away."

He made her feel strong and special with a few words. After feeling guilty for so long, of wondering if she could hold it all together for Kolby, she welcomed the reassurance coursing through her veins as surely as the current underneath her.

Tony slid from his board and ducked under. She watched through the clear surface as he freed the ankle leash attaching him to his board.

Resurfacing beside her, he stroked the line of her back. "Sit up for a minute."

"What?" She'd barely heard him, too focused on the feel of his hand low on her waist.

"Sit up on the board and swing your legs over the side." He held the edge. "I won't let you fall."

"But your board's drifting." She watched the faded yellow inch away.

"I'll get it later. Come on." He palmed her back, helping her balance as finally, she wriggled her way upright.

She bobbled. Stifled a squeal. Then realized what was the worst that could happen? She would be in the water. Big deal. And suddenly the surfboard steadied a little, still rocking but not out of control. The waters lapped around her legs, cool, exciting.

"I did it." She laughed, sending her voice out into that endlessness.

"Perfect. Now hold still," he said and somehow slid effortlessly behind her.

Her balance went haywire again for a second, the horizon tilting until she was sure they would both topple over.

"Relax," he said against her ear. "Out here, it's not about fighting, it's the one place you can totally let go."

The one place *he* could let go? And suddenly she realized this was about more than getting her to relax. He was sharing something about himself with her. Even a man as driven and successful as himself needed a break from the demands of everyday life. Perhaps because of moments like these he kept it all together rather than letting the tension tighten until it snapped.

She fit herself against him, his legs behind hers as they drifted. Her muscles slowly melted until she leaned into him. The waves curled underneath, his chest wet and bristly against her skin. A new tension coiled inside her, deep in her belly. Her swimsuit suddenly felt too tight against her breasts that swelled and yearned for the brush of the air and Tony's mouth.

His palms rested on her thighs. His thumbs circled a light massage, close, so close. Water ebbed and flowed over her heated core, waves sweeping tantalizing caresses on her aching flesh. Her head sagged onto his shoulder.

With each undulation of the board, he rocked against her, stirring, growing harder until he pressed fully erect along her spine. Every roll of the board rubbing their bodies against each other had to be as torturous for him as it was for her. His hands moved higher on her legs, nearer to what she needed. Silently. Just as in tune with each other as when they'd been paddling out.

She worried at first that someone might see, but with their backs to the shore and water…she could lose herself in the moment. Already his breaths grew heavier against her ear, nearly as fast as her own.

They could both let go and find completion right here without ever moving. Simply feeling his arousal against her stirred Shannon to a bittersweet edge. And good God, that scared the hell out of her.

The wind chilled, and she recognized the sting of fear all too well. She'd thought she could ride the wave, so to speak, and just have an affair with Tony.

But this utter abandon, the loss of control, the way they were together, it was anything but simple, something she wasn't sure she was ready to risk.

Scavenging every bit of her quickly dwindling willpower, she grabbed his wrists, moved his hands away…

And dived off the side of the board.

Nine

Tony propped his surfboard against a tree and turned to take Shannon's. The wariness in her eyes frustrated the hell out of him. He could have sworn she was just as into the moment out there as he was—an amazing moment that had been seconds away from getting even better.

And then she'd vaulted off the board and into the water.

Staying well clear of him, she'd said she was ready to return to shore. She hadn't spoken another word since. Had he blown a whole week's worth of working past her boundaries only to wreck it in one afternoon? Problem was, he still didn't know what had set her off.

She stroked a smudge of sand from his faded yellow board. "Is it all right to leave them here so far from where we started?"

They'd drifted at least a mile from the SUV. "I'll buy new ones. I'm a filthy rich prince, remember?"

Yeah, sexual frustration was making him a little cranky, and he suspected no amount of walking would take the edge off. Worse yet, she didn't even rise to the bait of his crabby words full of reminders of why they'd broken up in the first place.

Fine. Who the hell knew what she needed?

He started west and she glided alongside him. The wind picked up, rustling the trees and sweeping a layer of sand around his ankles.

Shannon gasped.

"What?" Tony looked fast. "Did you step on something? Are you getting chilly?"

Shaking her head, she pointed toward the trees, branches and leaves sweeping apart to reveal the small stone chapel. "Why didn't I notice that when we drove here?"

"We approached the beach from a different angle."

"It's gorgeous." Her eyes were wide and curious.

"No need to look so surprised. I told you that we lived here 24/7. My father outfitted the island with everything we would need, from a small medical clinic to that church." He took in the white stone church, mission bell over the front doors. It wasn't large, but big enough to accommodate everyone here. His older brother had told him once it was the only thing on the island built to resemble a part of their old life.

"Were you an altar server?"

Her voice pulled him back to the present.

"With a short-lived tenure." He glanced down at her, so damn glad she was talking to him again. "I couldn't sit still and the priest frowned on an altar server bringing a bag of books and Legos to keep himself entertained during the service."

"Legos?" She started walking again. "Really?"

"Every Sunday as I sat out in the congregation. I would

have brought more, but the nanny confiscated my squirt gun."

"Don't be giving Kolby any ideas." She elbowed him lightly, then as if realizing what she'd done, picked up her pace.

Hell no, he wasn't losing ground that fast. "The nanny didn't find my knife though."

Her mouth dropped open. "You brought a knife to church?"

"I carved my initials under the pew. Wanna go see if they're still there?"

She eyed the church, then shook her head. "What's all this about today? The surfing and then stories about Legos?"

Why? He hadn't stopped to consider the reasons, just acting on instinct to keep up with the crazy, out-of-control relationship with Shannon. But he didn't do things without a reason.

His gut had pointed him in this direction because... "So that you remember there's a man in here." He thumped his chest. "As well as a filthy rich prince."

But no matter what he said or how far he got from this place, the Medina heritage coursed through his veins. Regardless of how many times he changed his name or started over, he was still Antonio Medina. And Shannon had made it clear time and time again, she didn't want that kind of life. Finally, he heard her.

Several hours later, Shannon shoved her head deeper into the industrial sized refrigerator in search of a midnight snack. A glass of warm milk just wasn't going to cut it.

Eyeing the plate of *trufas con cognac* and small cups of *crema catalana,* she debated whether to go for the brandy truffles or cold custard with caramel on top…. She picked one of each and dropped into a seat at the steel table.

Silence bounced and echoed in the cavernous kitchen. She was sleepy and cranky and edgy. And it was all Tony's fault for tormenting her with charming stories and sexy encounters on the water—then shutting her out. She nipped an edge of the liqueur-flavored chocolate. Amazing. Sighing, she sagged back in the chair.

Since returning from their surfing outing, he'd kept his distance. She'd thought they were getting closer on a deeper level when he'd shared about his sister and even the Lego, then, wham. He'd turned into the perfect—distant—host at the stilted family dinner.

Not that she'd been able to eat a bite.

Now, she was hungry, in spite of the fact she'd finished off the truffle. She spooned a scoop of custard into her mouth, although she suspected no amount of gourmet pastries would satisfy the craving gnawing her inside.

When she'd started dating Tony, she'd taken a careful, calculated risk because her hormones had been hollering for him and she'd been a long, long time without sex. Okay, so her hormones hadn't been shouting for just any man. Only Tony. A problem that didn't seem to have abated in the least.

"Ah, hell." Tony's low curse startled her upright in her seat.

Filling the archway, he studied her cautiously. He wore jeans and an open button-down that appeared hastily tossed on. He fastened two buttons in the middle, slowly shielding the cut of his six-pack abs.

Cool custard melted in her mouth, her senses singing. But her heart was aching and confused. She toyed with the neck of her robe nervously. The blue peignoir set covered her from neck to toes, but the loose-fitting chiffon and lace brushed sensual decadence against her skin. The froufrou little kitten heels to match had seemed over-the-top in her room, but now felt sexy and fun.

Her hands shook. She pressed them against the steel topped table. "Don't mind me. I'm just indulging in a midnight feeding frenzy. I highly recommend the custard cups in the back right corner of the refrigerator."

He hesitated in the archway as if making up his mind, then walked deeper into the kitchen, passing her without touching. "I was thinking in terms of something more substantial, like a sandwich."

"Are princes allowed to make their own snacks?"

"Who's going to tell me no?" He kicked the fridge closed, his hands full of deli meat, cheese and lettuce, a jar of spread tucked under his elbow.

"Good point." She swirled another spoonful. "I hope the cook doesn't mind I've been foraging around. I actually used the stove, too, when I cooked a late night snack for Kolby. He woke up hungry."

Tony glanced over from his sandwich prep. "Is he okay?"

"Just a little homesick." Her eyes took in the sight of the Tony she remembered, a man who wore jeans low-slung on his hips. And rumpled hair…she enjoyed the disobedient swirls in his hair most.

"I'm sorry for that." His shoulders tensed under the loose chambray.

"Don't get me wrong, I appreciate how everyone has gone out of their way for him. The gourmet kid cuisine makes meals an adventure. I wish I had thought to tell him rolled tortillas are snakes and caterpillars." Pasta was called worms or a nest. "I'm even becoming addicted to Nutella crepes. But sometimes, a kid just needs the familiar feel of home."

"I understand." His sandwich piled high on a plate, he took a seat—across from her rather than beside as he would have in the past.

"Of course you do." She clenched her hands together to keep from reaching out to him. "Well, I'll have to make sure the cook knows I tried to put everything back where I found it."

"He's more likely to be upset that you called him a cook rather than a chef."

"Ah, a chef. Right. All those nuances between your world and mine." How surreal to be having a conversation with a prince over a totally plebian hoagie.

Tony swiped at his mouth with a linen napkin and draped it over his knee again. "You ran in a pretty high-finance world with your husband."

Her husband's dirty money.

She shoved away the custard bowl. Thoughts of the media regurgitating that mess for public consumption made her nauseated. She wasn't close to her in-laws, but they would suffer hearing their precious son's reputation smeared again.

And God help them all if her own secrets were somehow discovered.

Best to lie low and keep to herself. Although she was finding it increasingly difficult to imagine how she would restart her life. Even if she was able to renew her teaching credentials, who was going to want to hire the infamous Medina Mistress who'd once been married to a crook? When this mess was over, she would have to dig deep to figure out how to recreate a life for herself and Kolby.

Could Tony be having second thoughts about their relationship? His strict code of honor would dictate he take care of her until the media storm passed, but she didn't want to be his duty.

They'd dated. They'd had sex. But she only just realized how much of their relationship had been superficial as they both dodged discussing deeper, darker parts of their past.

Still, she wasn't ready to plunge into the murkiest of waters that made up her life with Nolan. She wasn't even sure right now if Tony would want to hear.

But regardless of how things turned out between them, she needed him to understand the real her. "I didn't grow up with all those trappings of Nolan's world. My dad was a high school science teacher and a coach. My mom was the elementary school secretary. We had enough money, but we were by no means wealthy." She hesitated, realizing… "You probably already know all of that."

"Why would you think so?" he asked, although he hadn't denied what she said.

"If you've had to be so worried about security and your identity, it makes sense you or your lawyer or some security team you've hired would vet people in your life."

"That would be the wise thing to do."

"And you're a smart man."

"I haven't always acted wisely around you."

"You've been a perfect gentleman this week and you know it," she said, as close as she could come to hinting that she ached for his touch, his mouth on her body, the familiar rise of pleasure and release he could bring.

Tony shrugged and tore into his sandwich again, a grandfather clock tolling once in the background.

"Kolby thinks we're on vacation."

"Good." He finished chewing, tendons in his strong neck flexing. "That's how he should remember this time in his life."

"It's unreal how you and your father have shielded him from the tension in your relationship."

"Obviously not well enough to fool you." His boldly handsome face gave nothing away.

"I know some about your history, and it's tough to miss how little the two of you talk. Your father's an interesting man." She'd enjoyed after-dinner discussions with Enrique and Eloisa about current events and the latest book they'd read.

The old king may have isolated himself from the world, but he'd certainly stayed abreast with the latest news. The discussions had been enlightening on a number of levels, such as how the old king wasn't as clipped and curt with his daughter as he was with Tony.

Tony stared at the last half of his snack, tucking a straggly piece of lettuce back inside. "What did you make for Kolby?"

His question surprised her, but if it kept him talking…

"French toast. It's one of his favorite comfort foods. He likes for me to cut the toast into slices so he can dip it into the syrup. Independence means a lot, even to a three-year-old." It meant a lot to adults. She reached for her bowl to scrape the final taste of custard and licked the spoon clean. The caramel taste exploded into her starving senses like music in her mouth.

Pupils widening with awareness until they nearly pushed away his brown irises, Tony stared back at her across the table, intense, aroused. Her body recognized the signs in him well even if he didn't move so much as an inch closer.

She set the spoon down, the tiny clink echoing in the empty kitchen. "Tony, why are you still awake?"

"I'm a night owl. Some might call me an insomniac."

"An insomniac? I didn't know that." She laughed darkly. "Although how could I since we've never spent an entire night together? Have you had the problem long?"

"I've always been this way." He turned the plate around on the table. "My mother tried everything from warm milk to a 'magic' blanket before just letting me stay up. She used to cook for me too, late at night."

"Your mother, the queen, cooked?" She inched to the edge of her chair, leaning on her elbows, hoping to hold his attention and keep him talking.

"She may have been royalty even before she married my father, but there are plenty in Europe with blue blood and little money." Shadows chased each other across his eyes. "My mother grew up learning the basics of managing her own house. She insisted we boys have run of the kitchen. There were so many everyday places that were off-limits to us for safety reasons, she wanted us to have the normalcy of popping in and out of the kitchen for snacks."

Like any other child. A child who happened to live in a sixteenth-century castle. She liked his mother, a woman she would never meet but felt so very close to at the moment. "What did she cook for you?"

"A Cyclops."

"Excuse me?"

"It's a fried egg with a buttered piece of bread on top." He swirled his hand over his plate as if he could spin an image into reality. "The bread has a hole pinched out of the middle so the egg yolk peeks out like a—"

"Like a Cyclops. I see. My mom called it a Popeye." And with the memory of a simple egg dish, she felt the connection to Tony spin and gain strength again.

He glanced up, a half smile kicking into his one cheek. "Cyclops appealed to the bloodthirsty little boy in me. Just like Kolby and the caterpillar and snake pasta."

To hell with distance and waiting for him to reach out, she covered his hand with hers. "Your mother sounds wonderful."

He nodded briefly. "I believe she was."

"Believe?"

"I have very few memories of her before she…died." He turned his hand over and stroked hers with his thumb. "The beach. A blanket. Food."

"Scents do tend to anchor our memories more firmly."

More shadows drifted through his eyes, darker this time, like storm clouds. *Died* seemed such a benign word to describe the assassination of a young mother, killed because she'd married a king. A vein pulsed visibly in Tony's temple, faster by the second. He'd dealt with such devastating circumstances in life honorably, while her husband had turned to stealing and finally, to taking the ultimate coward's way out.

She held herself very still, unthreatening. Her heart ached for him on a whole new and intense level. "What do you remember about when she died? About leaving San Rinaldo?"

"Not much really." He stayed focused on their connected hands, tracing the veins on her wrist with exaggerated concentration. "I was only five."

So he'd told her before. But she wasn't buying his nonchalance. "Traumatic events seem to stick more firmly in our memory. I recall a car accident when I couldn't have been more than two." She wouldn't back down now, not when she was so close to understanding the man behind the smiles and bold gestures. "I still remember the bright red of the Volkswagen bug."

"You probably saw pictures of the car later," he said dismissively, then looked up sharply, aggressively full of bravado. The storm clouds churned faster with each throb of the vein on his temple. He stroked up her arm with unmistakable sensual intent. "How much longer are you going to wait before you ask me to kiss you again? Because right now, I'm so on fire for you, I want to test out the sturdiness of that table."

"Tony, can you even hear yourself?" she asked, frustrated and even a bit insulted by the way he was jerking her around. "One minute you're Prince Romance and Restraint, the next you're ignoring me over dinner. Then you're spilling your guts. Now, you proposition me—and not too suavely, I might add. Quite frankly, you're giving me emotional whiplash."

His arms twitched, thick roped muscles bulging against his sleeves with restrained power. "Make no mistake, I have wanted you every second of every day. It's all I can do not to haul you against me right now and to hell with the dozens of people that might walk in. But today on the water and tonight here, I'm just not sure this crazy life of mine is good enough for you."

Her body burned in response to his words even as her mind blared a warning. Tony had felt the increasing connection too, and it scared him. So he'd tried to run her off with the crude offer of sex on the table.

Well too damn bad for him, she wasn't backing down. She'd wanted this, *him,* for too long to turn away.

Ten

He'd wanted Shannon back in his bed, but somewhere between making a sandwich and talking about eggs, she'd peeled away walls, exposing thoughts and memories that were better forgotten. They distracted. Hurt. Served no damn purpose.

Anger grated his raw insides. "So? What'll it be? Sex here or in your room?"

She didn't flinch and she didn't leave. Her soft hand stayed on top of his as she looked at him with sad eyes behind her glasses. "Is that what this week has been about?"

He let his gaze linger on the vee of her frothy nightgown set. Lace along the neckline traced into the curve of her breasts the way his hands ached to explore. "I've been clear from the start about what I want."

"Are you so sure about that?"

"What the hell is that supposed to mean?" he snapped.

Sliding from her chair, she circled the table toward him, her heels clicking against the tile. She stopped beside him, the hem of her nightgown set swirling against his leg. "Don't confuse me with your mother."

"Good God, there's not a chance of that." He toppled her into his lap and lowered his head, determined to prove it to her.

"Wait." She stopped him with a hand flattened to his chest just above the two closed buttons. Her palm cooled his overheated skin, calming and stirring, but then she'd always been a mix of contradictions. "You suffered a horrible trauma as a child. No one should lose a parent, especially in such an awful way. I wish you could have been spared that."

"I wish my *mother* had been spared." His hands clenched in her robe, his fists against her back.

"And I can't help but wonder if you helping me—a mother with a young child—is a way to put her ghost to rest. Putting your own ghosts to rest in the process."

Given the crap that had shaken down in his past, he'd done a fine job turning his life around. Frustration poured acid on his burning gut. "You've spent a lot of time thinking about this."

"What you told me this afternoon and tonight brought things into focus."

"Well, thanks for the psychoanalysis." His words came out harsh, but right now he needed her to walk away. "I would offer to pay you for the services, but I wouldn't want to start another fight."

"Sounds to me like you're spoiling for one now." Her eyes softened with more of that concern that grated along his insides. "I'm sorry if I overstepped and hit a nerve."

A nerve? She'd performed a root canal on his emotions. His brain echoed with the retort of gunfire stuttering, aimed at him, his brothers. His mother. He searched for what to say to shut down this conversation, but he wasn't sure of anything other than his need for a serious, body-draining jog on the beach. Problem was? The beach circled right back around to this place.

Easing from his lap, she stood and he tamped down the swift kick of disappointment. Except she didn't leave. She extended her hand and linked her fingers with his.

Just a simple connection, but since he was raw to the core, her touch fired deep.

"Shannon," he said between teeth clenched tight with restraint, "I'm about a second from snapping here. So unless you want me buried heart deep inside you in the next two minutes, you need to go back to your room."

Her hold stayed firm, cool and steady.

"Shannon, damn it all, you don't know what you're doing. You don't want any part of the mood I'm in." Her probing may have brought on the mood, but he wouldn't let it contaminate her.

Angling down with slow precision, she pressed her lips to his. Not moving. Only their mouths and hands linked.

He wanted—needed—to move her away gently. But his fingers curled around the softness of her arm.

"Shanny," he whispered against her mouth, "tell me to leave."

"Not a chance. I only have one question."

"Go ahead." He braced himself for another emotional root canal.

She brought his hand to her chest, pressing his palm against her breast. "Do you have a condom?"

Relief splashed over him like a tidal wave. "Hell, yes, I have one, two in fact, in my wallet. Because even when we're not talking, I know the way we are together could combust at any second. And I will always, always make sure you're protected and safe."

Standing, he scooped her into his arms. Purring her approval, she hooked her hands behind his neck and tipped her face for a full kiss. The soft cushion of her breasts against his chest sent his libido into overdrive. He throbbed against the sweet curve of her hip. At the sweep of tongue, the taste of caramel and *her,* he fought the urge to follow through on the impulse to have her here, now, on the table.

He sketched his mouth along her jaw, down to her collarbone, the scent of her lavender body wash reminding him of shared showers at his place. "We need to go upstairs."

"The pantry is closer." She nipped his bottom lip. "And empty. We can lock the door. I need you now."

"Are you su—?"

"Don't even say it." She dipped her hands into the neckline of his loose shirt, her fingernails sinking insistently deep. "I want you. No waiting."

Her words closed down arguments and rational thought. He made a sure-footed beeline across the tiled floor toward the pantry. Shannon nuzzled his neck, kissed along his jaw, all the while murmuring disjointed words of need that stoked him higher—made his feet move faster. As he walked, her silky blond hair and whispery robe trailed, her sexy little heels dangling from her toes.

Dipping at the door, he flipped the handle and shouldered inside the pantry, a food storage area the size of a small bedroom. The scent of hanging dried herbs coated the air, the smell earthy. He slid her glasses from her face and set them aside on a shelf next to rows of bottled water.

As the door eased closed, the space darkened and his

other senses increased. She reached for the light switch and he clasped her wrist, stopping her.

"I don't need light to see you. Your beautiful body is fired into my memory." His fingers crawled up her leg, bunching the frothy gown along her soft thigh, farther still to just under the curve of her buttocks. "Just the feel of you is about more than my willpower can take."

"I don't want your willpower. I'm fed up with your restraint. Give me the uninhibited old Tony back." Her husky voice filled the room with unmistakable desire.

Pressing her hips closer, he tasted down her neck, charting his way to her breasts. An easy swipe cleared the fabric from her shoulders and he found a taut nipple. Damn straight he didn't need light. He knew her body, knew just how to lave and tease the taut peak until she tore at his shirt with frantic hands.

His buttons popped and cool air blanketed his back, warm Shannon writhing against his front. Hooking a finger along the rim of her bikini panties, he stroked her silky smooth stomach. Tugging lightly, he started the scrap of fabric downward until she shimmied them the rest of the way off.

Stepping closer, the silky gown bunched between them, she flattened her hand to the fly of his jeans. He went harder against the pleasure of her touch. Shannon. Just Shannon.

She unzipped his pants and freed his arousal. Clasping him in her fist, she stroked once, and again, her thumb working over his head with each glide. His eyes slammed shut.

Her other hand slipped into his back pocket and pulled out his wallet. A light crackle sounded as she tore into the packet. Her deft fingers rolled the sheath down the length of him with torturous precision.

"Now," she demanded softly against his neck. "Here. On the stepstool or against the door, I don't care as long as you're inside me."

Gnawing need chewed through the last of his restraint. She wanted this. He craved her. No more waiting. Tony backed her against the solid panel of the door, her fingernails digging into his shoulders, his back, lower as she tucked her hand inside his jeans and boxers.

Arching, urging, she hooked her leg around his, opening for him. Her shoe clattered to the floor but she didn't seem to notice or care. He nudged at her core, so damp and ready for him. He throbbed—and thrust.

Velvet heat clamped around him, drew him deeper, sent sparks shooting behind his eyelids. In the darkened room, the pure essence of Shannon went beyond anything he'd experienced. And the importance of that expanded inside him, threatening to drive him to his knees.

So he focused on her, searching with his hands and mouth, moving inside and stroking outside to make sure she was every bit as encompassed by the mind-numbing ecstasy. She rocked faster against him. Her sighs came quicker, her moans of pleasure higher and louder until he captured the sound, kissing her and thrusting with his tongue and body. He explored the soft inside of her mouth, savoring the soft clamp of her gripping him with spasms he knew signaled her approaching orgasm.

Teeth gritted, he held back his own finish. Her face pressed to his neck. Her chants of *yes, yes, yes* synced with his pulse and pounding. Still, he held back, determined to take her there once more. She bowed away from the door, into him, again and again until her teeth sunk into his shoulder on a stifled cry of pleasure.

The scent of her, of slick sex and *them* mixed with the already earthy air.

Finally—*finally*—he could let go. The wave of pleasure pulsing through him built higher, roaring louder in his ears. He'd been too long without her. The wave crested. Release crashed over him. Rippling through him. Shifting the ground under his feet until his forehead thumped against the door.

Hauling her against his chest, heart still galloping, as they both came back down to earth in the pantry.

The pantry, for God's sake?

His chances of staying away from Shannon again were slim. That path didn't work for either of them. But if they were going to be together, he would make sure their next encounter was total fantasy material.

Sun glinting along the crystal clear pool, Shannon tugged Kolby's T-shirt over his head and slid his feet into tiny Italian leather sandals. She'd spent the morning splashing with her son and Tony's sister, and she wasn't close to working off pent-up energy. Even the soothing ripple of the heated waters down the fountain rock wall hadn't stilled the jangling inside her.

After making love in the pantry, she and Tony had locked themselves in her room where he'd made intense and thorough love to her. Her skin remembered the rasp of his beard against her breasts, her stomach, the insides of her thighs. How could she still crave even more from him? She should be in search of a good nap rather than wondering when she could get Tony alone again.

Of course she would have to find him first.

He'd left via her balcony just as the morning sun peeked over the horizon. Now that big orange glow was directly overhead and no word from him. She deflated her son's water wings. The hissing air and the maternal ritual reminded her of Tony's revelations just before they'd ended up in the closet.

Could he be avoiding her to dodge talking further? He'd made no secret of using sex to skirt the painful topic. She couldn't even blame him when she'd been guilty of the same during their affair. What did this do to their deadline to return home?

Kolby yanked the hem of her cover-up. "Want another movie."

"We'll see, sweetie." Kolby was entranced by the large home theater, but then what child wouldn't be?

Tony's half sister shaded her eyes in the lounger next to them, an open paperback in her other hand. "I can take him in if you want to stay outside. Truly, I don't mind." She toyed with her silver shell necklace, straightening the conch charm.

"But you're reading. And aren't you leaving this afternoon? I don't want to keep you from your packing."

"Do you honestly think any guest of Enrique Medina is bothered by packing their own suitcases? Get real." She snorted lightly. "I have plenty of time. Besides, I've been wanting to check out the new Disney movie for my library's collection."

She'd learned Eloisa was a librarian, which explained the satchel of books she'd brought along. Her husband was an architect who specialized in restoring historic landmarks. They were an unpretentious couple caught up in a maelstrom. "What if the screening room doesn't have the movie you w—" She stopped short. "Of course they have whatever you're looking for on file."

"A bit intimidating, isn't it?" Eloisa pulled on her wraparound cover-up, tugging her silver necklace out so the conch charm was visible. "I didn't grow up with all of this and I suspect you didn't, either."

Shannon rubbed her arms, shivering in spite of the eighty-degree day. "How do you keep from letting it over-whelm you?"

"I wish I could offer you reassurance or answers, but honestly I'm still figuring out how to deal with all of this myself. I had only begun to get to know my birth father a few months ago." She looked back at the mission-style mansion, her eyebrows pinching together. "Now the whole royal angle has gone public. They haven't figured out about me. Yet. That's why we're here this week, to talk with Enrique and his attorneys, to set up some preemptive strikes."

"I'm sorry."

Thank God Eloisa had the support of her husband. And Tony had been there for her. Who was there for him? Even his brothers hadn't shown up beyond sterile conference calls.

"You have nothing to apologize for, Shannon. I'm only saying it's okay to feel overwhelmed. Cut yourself some slack and do what you can to stay level. Let me watch a movie with your son while you swim or enjoy a bubble bath or take a nap. It's okay."

Indecision warred inside her. These past couple of weeks she'd had more help with Kolby than since he was born. Guilt tweaked her maternal instincts.

"Please, Mama?" Kolby sidled closer to Eloisa. "I like Leesa."

Ah, and just like that, her maternal guilt worried in another direction, making her fret that she hadn't given her son enough play dates or socialization. Funny how a mother worried no matter what.

Shannon nodded to Tony's sister. "If you're absolutely sure."

"He's a cutie, and I'm guessing he will be asleep before

the halfway point. Enjoy the pool a while longer. It'll be good practice for me to spend time with him." She smiled whimsically as she ruffled his damp hair. "Jonah and I are hoping to have a few of our own someday."

"Thank you. I accept gratefully." Shannon remembered well what it felt like to be young and in love and hopeful for the future. She couldn't bring herself to regret Nolan since he'd given her Kolby. "I hope we'll have the chance to speak again before you leave this afternoon?"

"Don't worry." Eloisa winked. "I imagine we'll see each other again."

With a smile, Shannon hugged her little boy close, inhaling his baby fresh scent with a hint of chlorine.

He squirmed, his cheeks puffed with a wide smile. "Wanna go."

She pressed a quick kiss to his forehead. "Be good for Mrs. Landis."

Eloisa took his hand. "We'll be fine."

Kolby waved over his shoulder without a backward glance.

Too restless for a bath or nap, she eyed the pool and whipped off her cover-up. Laps sounded like the wisest option. Diving in, she stared through the chlorinated depths until her eyes burned, forcing her to squeeze them shut. She lost herself in the rhythm of slicing her arms through the heated water, no responsibilities, no outside world. Just the *thump, thump, thump* of her heart mingling with the roar of the water passing over her ears.

Five laps later, she flipped underwater and resurfaced face up for a backstroke. She opened her eyes and, oh my, the view had changed. Tony stood by the waterfall in black board shorts.

Whoa. Her stomach lurched into a swan dive. Tony's bronzed chest sprinkled with hair brought memories of their night together, senses on overload from the darkened herb-scented pantry, later in the brightly lighted luxury of her bedroom. Who would have thought dried oregano and rosemary could be aphrodisiacs?

His eyes hooked on her crocheted two piece with thorough and unmistakable admiration. He knew every inch of her body and made his appreciation clear whether she wore high-end garb or her simple black waitress uniform, wilted from a full shift. God, how he was working his way into her heart as well as her life.

She swam toward the edge with wide lazy strokes. "Is Kolby okay?"

"Enjoying the movie and popcorn." He knelt by the edge, his elbow on one knee drawing her eye to the nautical compass tattooed on his bicep. "Although with the way his head is drooping, chances are he'll be asleep anytime now."

"Thank you for checking on him." She resisted the urge to ask Tony what *he*'d been doing since he left her early this morning.

"Not a problem." His fingers played through the water in front of her without touching but so close the swirls caressed her breasts. "I said I intended to romance you and I got sidetracked. I apologize for that. The woman I'm with should be treated like a princess."

His *princess?* Shock loosened her hold on the edge of the pool. Tony caught her arm quickly and eased her from the water to sit next to him. His gaze swept her from soaking wet hair to dripping toes. Appreciation smoked, darkening his eyes to molten heat she recognized well.

He tipped her chin with a knuckle scarred from handling sailing lines. "Are you ready to be royally romanced?"

Eleven

A five-minute walk later, Tony flattened his palm to Shannon's back and guided her down the stone path leading from the mansion to the greenhouse. Her skin, warmed from the sun, heated through her thin cover-up. Soon, he hoped to see and feel every inch of her without barriers.

He'd spent the morning arranging a romantic backdrop for their next encounter. Finding privacy was easier said than done on this island, but he was persistent and creative. Anticipation ramped inside him.

He was going to make things right with her. She deserved to be treated like a princess, and he had the resources to follow through. His mind leaped ahead to all the ways he could romance her back on the mainland now that he understood her better—once he fulfilled the remaining weeks he'd promised his father.

A kink started in his neck.

Squeezing his hand lightly, she followed him along the

rocky path, the mansion smaller on the horizon. Few trees stood between them and the glass building ahead. Early on, Enrique had cleared away foliage for security purposes.

"Where are we going?"

"You'll see soon."

Farther from shore, a sprawling oak had been saved. The mammoth trunk declared it well over a hundred years old. As a kid, he'd begged to keep this one for climbing. His father had gruffly agreed. The memory kicked over him, itchy and ill timed.

He brushed aside a branch, releasing a flock of butterflies soaring toward the conservatory, complete with two wings branching off the main structure. "This is the greenhouse I told you about. It also has a café style room."

Enrique had done his damnedest to give his sons a "normal" childhood, as much as he could while never letting them off the island. Tony had undergone some serious culture shock after he'd left. At least working on a shrimper had given him time to absorb the mainland in small bites. Back then, he'd even opted to rent a sailboat for a home rather than an apartment.

As they walked past a glass gazebo, Shannon tipped her face to his. Sunlight streaked through the trees, bathing her face. "Is that why the movie room has more of a theater feel?"

Nodding, he continued, "There's a deli at the ferry station and an ice cream parlor at the creamery. I thought we could take Kolby there."

He hoped she heard his intent to try with her son as well, to give this relationship a real chance at working.

"Kolby likes strawberry flavored best," she said simply.

"I'll remember that," he assured her. And he meant it.

"We also have a small dental clinic. And of course there's the chapel."

"They've thought of everything." Her mouth oohed over a birdbath with doves drinking along the edge.

"My father always said a monarch's job was to see to the needs of his people. This island became his minikingdom. Because of the isolation, he needed to make accommodations, try to create a sense of normalcy." Clouds whispered overhead and Tony guided her faster through the garden. "He's started a new round of renovations. A number of his staff members have died of old age. That presents a new set of challenges as he replaces them with employees who aren't on the run, people who have options."

"Like Alys."

"Exactly," he said, just as the skies opened up with an afternoon shower. "Now, may I take you to lunch? I know this great little out-of-the-way place with kick-ass fresh flowers."

"Lead on." Shannon tugged up the hood on her cover-up and raced alongside him.

As the rain pelted faster, he charged up the stone steps leading to the conservatory entrance. Tony threw open the double doors, startling a sparrow into flight around the high glass ceiling in the otherwise deserted building. A quick glance around assured him that yes, everything was exactly as he'd ordered.

"Ohmigod, Tony!" Shannon gasped, taking in the floral feast for her eyes as well as her nose. "This is breathtaking."

Flipping the hood from her head, she plunged deeper into the spacious greenhouse where a riot of scents and colors waited. Classical music piped lowly from hidden speakers. Ferns dangled overhead. Unlike crowded nurseries she'd visited in the past, this space sprawled more like an indoor floral park.

An Italian marble fountain trickled below a skylight, water spilling softly from a carved snake's mouth as it curled around some reclining Roman god. Wrought iron screens sported hydrangeas and morning glories twining throughout, benches in front for reading or meditation. Potted palms and cacti added height to the interior landscape. Tiered racks of florist's buckets with cut flowers stretched along a far wall. She spun under the skylight, immersing herself in the thick perfume, sunbeams and Debussy's *Nocturnes*.

While she could understand Tony's point about not wanting to be isolated here indefinitely, she appreciated the allure of the magical retreat Enrique had created. Even the rain *tap, tap, tapping* overhead offered nature's lyrical accent to the soft music.

Slowing her spin, she found Tony staring at her with undeniable arousal. Tony, and only Tony because the space appeared otherwise deserted. Her skin prickled with awareness at the muscular display of him in nothing but board shorts and deck shoes.

"Are we alone?" she asked.

"Completely," he answered, gesturing toward a little round table set for two, with wine and finger foods. "Help yourself. There are stuffed mussels, fried squid, vegetable skewers, cold olives and cheese."

She strode past him, without touching but so close a magnetic field seemed to activate, urging her to seal her body to his.

"It's been so wonderful here indulging in grown-up food after so many meals of chicken nuggets and pizza." She broke off a corner of ripe white cheese and popped it in her mouth.

"Then you're going to love the beverage selection." Tony scooped up a bottle from the middle of the table. "Red wine from Basque country or sherry from southern Spain?"

"Red, please. But can we wait a moment on the food? I want to see everything here first."

"I was hoping you would say that." He passed her a crystal glass, half full.

She sipped, staring at him over the rim. "Perfect."

"And there's still more." His fingers linked with hers, he led her past an iron screen to a secluded corner.

Vines grew tangled and dense over the windows, the sun through the glass roof muted by rivulets of rain. A chaise longue was tucked in a corner. Flower petals speckled the furniture and floor. Everything was so perfect, so beautiful, it brought tears to her eyes. God, it still scared her how much she wanted to trust her feelings, trust the signals coming from Tony.

To hide her eyes until she could regain control, she rushed to the crystal vase of mixed flowers on the end table and buried her face in the bouquet. "What a unique blend of fragrances."

"It's a specially ordered arrangement. Each flower was selected for you because of its meaning."

Touched by the detailed thought he'd put into the encounter, she pivoted to face him. "You told me once you wanted to wrap me in flowers."

"That's the idea here." His arms banded around her waist. "And I was careful to make sure there will be no thorns. Only pleasure."

If only life could be that simple. With their time here running out, she couldn't resist.

"You're sure we won't be interrupted?" She set her wine glass on the end table and linked her fingers behind his neck. "No surveillance cameras or telephoto lenses?"

"Completely certain. There are security cameras outside, but none inside. I've given the staff the afternoon off and our guards are not Peeping Toms. We are totally and completely alone." He anchored her against him, the rigid length of his arousal pressing into her stomach with a hefty promise.

"You prepared for this." And she wanted this, wanted him. But… "I'm not sure I like being so predictable."

"You are anything but predictable. I've never met a more confusing person in my life." He tugged a damp lock of her hair. "Any more questions?"

She inhaled deeply, letting the scents fill her with courage. "Who can take off faster the other person's clothes?"

"Now there's a challenge I can't resist." He bunched her cover-up in his hands and peeled the soft cotton over her head.

Shaking her hair free, she leaned into him just as he slanted his mouth over hers. His fingers made fast work of the ties to her bathing suit top. The crocheted triangles fell away, baring her to the steamy greenhouse air.

She nipped his ear where a single dot-shaped scar stayed from a healed-over piercing. A teenage rebellion, he'd told her once. She could envision him on a Spanish galleon, a swarthy and buffed pirate king.

For a moment, for *this* moment, she let herself indulge in foolish fantasies, no fears. She would allow the experience to sweep her away as smoothly as she brushed off his board shorts. She pushed aside the sterner responsible voice inside her that insisted she remember past mistakes and tread cautiously.

"It's been too damn long." He thumbed off her swimsuit bottom.

"Uh, hello?" She kicked the last fabric barrier away and

prayed other barriers could be as easily discarded. "It's been less than eight hours since you left my room."

"Too long."

She played her fingers along the cut of his sculpted chest, down the flat plane of his washboard stomach. Pressing her lips to his shoulder, she kissed her way toward his arm until she grazed the different texture of his tattooed flesh—inked with a black nautical compass. "I've always wanted to ask why you chose this particular tattoo."

His muscles bunched and twitched. "It symbolizes being able to find my way home."

"There's still so much I don't know about you." Concerns trickled through her like the rain trying to find its way inside.

"Hey, we're here to escape. All that can wait." He slipped her glasses from her face and placed them on the end table.

Parting through the floral arrangement to the middle, he slipped out an orchid and pinched off the flower. He trailed the bloom along her nose, her cheekbones and jaw in a silky scented swirl. "For magnificence."

Her knees went wobbly and she sat on the edge of the chaise, tapestry fabric rough on the backs on her thighs, rose-petal smooth. He tucked the orchid behind her ear, easing her back until she reclined.

Returning to the vase, he tugged free a long stalk with indigo buds and explored the length of her arm, then one finger at a time. Then over her stomach to her other hand and back up again in a shivery path that left her breathless.

"Blue salvia," he said, "because I think of you night and day."

His words stirred her as much as the glide of the flower

over her shoulder. Then he placed it on the tiny pillow under her head.

A pearly calla lily chosen next, he traced her collarbone before lightly dipping between her breasts.

"Shannon," he declared hoarsely, "I chose this lily because you are a majestic beauty."

Detouring, he sketched the underside of her breast and looped round again and again, each circle smaller until he teased the dusky tip. Her body pulled tight and tingly. Her back arched into the sweet sensation and he transferred his attention to her other breast, repeating the delicious pattern.

Reaching for him, she clutched his shoulders, aching to urge him closer. "Tony…"

Gently, he clasped her wrists and tucked them at her sides. "No touching or I'll stop."

"Really?"

"Probably not, because I can't resist you." He left the lily in her open palm. "But how about you play along anyway? I guarantee you'll like the results."

Dark eyes glinting with an inner light, Tony eased free… "A coral rose for passion."

His words raspy, his face intense, he skimmed the bud across her stomach, lower. Lower still. Her head fell back, her eyes closed as she wondered just how far he would dare go.

The silky teasing continued from her hip inward, daring more and even more. A husky moan escaped between her clenched lips.

Still, he continued until the rose caressed…oh my. Her knee draped to the side giving him, giving the flower, fuller access as he teased her. Gooseflesh sprinkled her skin. Her body focused on the feelings and perfumes stoking desire higher.

A warm breath steamed over her stomach with only a second's warning before his mouth replaced the flower. Her fingers twitched into a fist, crushing the lily and releasing a fresh burst of perfume. A flick of his tongue, alternated with gentle suckles, caressed and coaxed her toward completion.

Her head thrashed as she chased her release. He took her to the brink, then retreated, drawing out the pleasure until the pressure inside her swelled and throbbed...

And bloomed.

A cry of pleasure burst free and she didn't bother holding it back. She rode the sensation, gasping in floral-tinged breaths.

His bold hands stroked upward as he slid over her, blanketing her with his hard, honed body. She hooked a languid leg over his hip. Her arm draped his shoulders as she drew him toward her, encouraging him to press inside.

The smell of crushed flowers clung to his skin as she kissed her way along his chest, back up his neck. He filled her, stretched her, moved inside her. She was surprised to feel desire rising again to a fevered pitch. Writhing, she lost herself in the barrage of sensations. The bristle of his chest hair against her breasts. The silky softness of flower petals against her back.

And the scents—she gasped in the perfect blend of musk and sex and earthy greenhouse. She raked his back, broad and strong and yet so surprisingly gentle, too.

He was working his way not only into her body but into her heart. When had she ever stood a chance at resisting him? As much as she tried to tell herself it was only physical, only an affair, she knew this man had come to mean so much more to her. He reached her in ways no one ever had before.

She grappled at the hard planes of his back, completion so close all over again.

"Let go and I'll catch you," he vowed against her ear and she believed him.

For the first time in so long, she totally trusted.

The magnitude exploded inside her, blasting through barriers. Pleasure filled every niche. Muscles knotted in Tony's back as he tensed over her and growled his own hoarse completion against her ear.

Staring up at the rain-splattered skylight, tears burning her eyes again, she held Tony close. She felt utterly bare and unable to hide any longer. She'd trusted him with her body.

Now the time had come to trust him with her secrets.

Twelve

Tony watched Shannon on his iPhone as she talked to Kolby. She'd assured him that she wanted to stay longer in their greenhouse getaway, once she checked on her son.

Raindrops pattered slowly on the skylight, the afternoon shower coming to an end. Sunshine refracted off the moisture, casting prisms throughout the indoor garden.

He had Shannon back in his bed and in his life and he intended to do anything it took to keep her there. The chemistry between them, the connection—it was one of a kind. The way she'd calmly handled his bizarre family set-up, keeping her down-to-earth ways in the face of so much wealth… Finally, he'd found a woman he could trust, a woman he could spend his life with. Coming back to the island had been a good thing after all, since it had made him realize how unaffected she was by the trappings. In a compass, she would be the magnet, a grounding center.

And he owed her so much better than he'd delivered thus

far. He'd wrecked Shannon's life. It was up to him to fix it. Here, alone with her in the bright light of day, he couldn't avoid the truth.

They would get married.

The decision settled inside him with a clean fit, so much so he wondered why he hadn't decided so resolutely before now. His feelings for her ran deep. He knew she cared for him, too. And marrying each other would solve her problems.

They were making progress. He could tell she'd been swayed by the flowers, the ambience.

A plan formed in his mind. Later tonight he would take her to the chapel, lit with candles, and he would propose, while the lovemaking they'd shared here was still fresh in her memory.

Now he just had to figure out the best way to persuade her to say yes.

Thumbing the off button, she disconnected her call. "The nanny says Kolby has only just woken up and she's feeding him a snack." She passed his phone to him and curled against his side on the chaise. "Thanks for not teasing me about being overprotective. I can't help but worry when I'm not with him."

"I would too, if he was mine," he said. Then her surprised expression prompted him to continue, "Why do you look shocked?"

"No offense meant." She smoothed a hand along his chest. "It's just obvious you and he haven't connected."

Something he would need to rectify in order to be a part of Shannon's life. "I will never let you or him down the way his father did."

She winced and he could feel her drawing back into herself. He wanted all barriers gone between them as fully as they'd tossed aside their clothes.

"Hey, Shannon, stay with me here." He cupped her bare hip. "I asked you before if your husband hit you and you said no. Did you lie about that?"

Sitting up abruptly, she gathered her swimsuit off the floor.

"Let's get dressed and then we can talk." She yanked on the suit bottom briskly.

Waiting, he slid on his board shorts. She tied the bikini strings behind her neck with exaggerated effort, all the while staring at the floor. A curtain of tousled blond locks covered her face. Just when he'd begun to give up on getting an answer, she straightened, shaking her hair back over her shoulders.

"I was telling the truth when I said Nolan never laid a hand on me. But there are things I need to explain in order for you to understand why it's so difficult for me to accept help." Determination creased her face. "Nolan was always a driven man. His perfectionism made him successful in business. And I'd been brought up to believe marriage is forever. How could I leave a man because he didn't like the way I hung clothes in the closet?"

He forced his hands to stay loose on his knees, keeping his body language as unthreatening as possible when he already sensed he would want to beat the hell out of Nolan Crawford by the end of this conversation—if he wasn't already dead.

Plucking a flower petal from her hair, she rubbed the coral-colored patch between two fingers. "Do you know how many people laughed at me because I was upset that he didn't want me to work? He said he wanted us to have more time together. Somehow any plans I made with others were disrupted. After a while I lost contact with my friends."

The picture of isolation came together in his head with startling clarity. He understood the claustrophobic feeling of being cut off from the rest of the world. Although he couldn't help but think his father's need to protect his children differed from an obsessive—abusive—husband dominating his wife. Rage simmered, ready to boil.

She scooped her cover-up from the floor and clutched it to her stomach. "Then I got pregnant. Splitting up became more complicated."

Hating like hell the helpless feeling, he passed her glasses back to her. It was damn little, but all he could see her accepting from him right now.

With a wobbly smile, she slid them on her face and seemed to take strength from them. "When Kolby was about thirteen months old, he spiked a scary high fever while I was alone with him. Nolan had always gone with us to pediatric check-ups. At the ER, I was a mess trying to give the insurance information. I had no idea what to tell them, because Nolan had insisted I not 'worry' about such things as medical finances. That day triggered something in me. I needed to take care of my son."

He took her too-cold hand and rubbed it between his.

"Looking back now I see the signs were there. Nolan's computer and cell phone were password protected. He considered it an invasion of privacy if I asked who he was speaking to. I thought he was cheating. I never considered…"

He squeezed her hand in silent encouragement.

"So I decided to learn more about the finances, because if I needed to leave him, I had to make sure my son's future was protected and not spirited away to some Cayman account." She fidgeted, her fingers landing on the blue salvia—*I think of you often* took on a darker meaning. "I was lucky enough to figure out his computer password."

"*You* discovered the Ponzi scheme?" Good God,

what kind of strength would it take to turn in her own husband?

"It was the hardest thing I've ever done, but I handed over the evidence to the police. He'd stolen so much from so many people, I couldn't stay silent. His parents posted bail, and I wasn't given warning." She spun the stem between her thumb and forefinger. "When he walked back into the house, he had a gun."

Shock nailed him harder than a sail boom to the gut.

"My God, Shannon. I knew he'd committed suicide but I had no idea you were there. I'm so damn sorry."

"That's not all, though. For once the media didn't uncover everything." She drew herself up straight. "Nolan said he was going to kill me, then Kolby and then himself."

Her words iced the perspiration on his brow. This was so much worse than he'd foreseen. He cupped an arm around her shoulders and pulled her close. She trembled and kept twirling the flower, but she didn't stop speaking.

"His parents pulled up in the driveway." A shuddering sigh racked her body, her profile pained. "He realized he wouldn't have time to carry out his original plan. Thank God he locked himself in his office before he pulled the trigger and killed himself."

"Shannon." Horror threatened to steal his breath, but for her, he would hold steady. "I don't even know what to say to fix the hell you were put through."

"I didn't tell his parents what he'd planned. They'd lost their son and he'd been labeled a criminal." She held up the blue salvia. "I couldn't see causing them more grief when they thought of him."

Her eyes were filled with tears and regret. Tony kissed her forehead, then pulled her against his chest. "You were generous to the memory of a man who didn't deserve it."

"I didn't do it for him. No matter what, he's the father

of my child." She pressed her cheek harder against him and hugged him tightly. "Kolby will have to live with the knowledge that his dad was a crook, but I'll be damned before I'll let my son know his own father tried to kill him."

"You've fought hard for your son." He stroked her back. "You're a good mother and a strong woman."

She reminded him of a distant memory, of his own mother wrapping him in a silver blanket as they left San Rinaldo and telling him the shield would keep him safe. She'd been right. If only he could have protected her, as well.

Easing away, Shannon scrubbed her damp cheeks. "Thank God for Vernon. I'd sold off everything to pay Nolan's debts, even my piano and my oboe. The first waitressing job I landed in Louisiana didn't cover expenses. We were running out of options when Vernon hired me. Everyone else treated me like a pariah. Even Nolan's parents didn't want anything to do with either of us. So many people insisted I must have known what he was doing. That I must have tucked away money for myself. The gossip and the rumors were hell."

Realization, understanding spewed inside him like the abrupt shower of the sprinklers misting over the potted plants. He'd finally found a woman he could trust enough to propose marriage.

Only to find a husband was likely the last thing she ever wanted again.

Three hours later, Shannon sat on the floor in her suite with Kolby, rolling wooden trains along a ridged track. An ocean breeze spiraled through the open balcony door. She craved the peace of that boundless horizon. Never again would she allow herself to be hedged in as she'd been in her marriage.

After she'd finished dredging up her past, she'd needed to see her son. Tony had been understanding, although she could sense he wanted to talk longer. Once she'd returned to her suite, she'd showered and changed—and had been with her son ever since.

The past twenty-four hours had been emotionally charged on so many levels. Tony had been supportive and understanding, while giving her space. He'd also been a tender—thorough—lover.

Could she risk giving their relationship another try once they returned to the mainland? Was it possible for her to be a part of a normal couple?

A tug on her shirt yanked her attention back to the moment. Kolby looked up at her with wide blue eyes. "I'm hungry."

"Of course, sweetie. We'll go down to the kitchen and see what we can find." Hopefully the cook—the *chef*—wouldn't object since he must be right in the middle of supper prep. "We just need to clean up the toys first."

As she reached for the train set's storage bin, she heard a throat clear behind her and jerked around to find her on-again lover standing in the balcony doorway.

Her stomach fluttered with awareness, and she pressed her sweaty palms to her jeans. "How long have you been there?"

"Not long." Tony had showered and changed as well, wearing khakis and a button-down. "I can make his snack."

Whoa, Tony was seeking time with her son? That signaled a definite shift in their relationship. Although she'd seen him make his own breakfast in the past, she couldn't miss the significance of this moment and his efforts to try.

Turning him away would mean taking a step back. "Are you sure?"

Because God knows, she still had a boatload of fears.

"Positive," he said, his voice as steady as the man.

"Okay then." She pressed a hand over her stomach full of butterflies. "I'll just clean up here—"

"We've got it, don't we, pal?"

Kolby eyed him warily but he didn't turn away, probably because Tony kept his distance. He wasn't pushing. Maybe they'd both learned a lot these past couple of weeks.

"Okay, then." She stood, looking around the room, unsure what to do next. "I'll just, uh…"

Tony touched her hand lightly. "You mentioned selling your piano and I couldn't miss the regret in your voice. There's a Steinway Grand in the east wing. Alys or one of the guards can show you where if you would like to play."

Would she? Her fingers twitched. She'd closed off so much of her old life, including the good parts. Her music had been a beautiful bright spot in those solitary years of her life with Nolan. How kind of Tony to see beyond the surface of the harrowing final moments that had tainted her whole marriage. In the same way he'd chosen flowers based on facets of her personality, he'd detected the creativity she'd all but forgotten, honoring it in a small, simple offer.

Nodding her head was tougher than she thought. Her body went a little jerky before she could manage a response. "I would like that. Thank you for thinking of it and for spending time with Kolby."

He was a man who saw beyond her material needs…a man to treasure.

Her throat clogging with emotion, she backed from the room, watching the tableau of Tony with her son. Antonio Medina, a prince and billionaire, knelt on the floor with Kolby, cleaning up a wooden train set.

Tony chunked the caboose in the bin. "Has your mom ever cooked you a Cyclops?"

"What's a cycle-ops?" His face was intent with interest.

"The sooner we clean up the trains, the sooner I can show you."

She pressed a hand to her swelling heart. Tony was handling Kolby with ease. Her son would be fine.

After getting directions from Alys, Shannon found the east wing and finally the music room. What a simple way to describe such an awe-inspiring space. More of a circular ballroom, wooden floors stretched across, with a coffered ceiling that added texture as well as sound control. Crystal chandeliers and sconces glittered in the late afternoon sun.

And the instruments… Her feet drew her deeper into the room, closer to the gold gilded harp and a Steinway grand piano. She stroked the ivory keys reverently, then zipped through a scale. Pure magic.

She perched on the bench, her hands poised. Unease skittered up her spine like a double-timed scale, a sense of being watched. Pivoting around, she searched the expansive room….

Seated in a tapestry wingback, Enrique Medina stared back at her from beside a stained glass window. Even with his ill health, the deposed monarch radiated power and charisma. His dogs asleep on either side, he wore a simple dark suit with an ascot, perfectly creased although loose fitting. He'd lost even more weight since her arrival.

Enrique thumbed a gold pocket watch absently. "Do not mind me."

Had Tony sent her to this room on purpose, knowing his father would be here? She didn't think so, given the stilted relationship between the two men. "I don't want to disturb you."

"Not at all. We have not had a chance to speak alone, you and I," he said with a hint of an accent.

The musicality was pleasing to the ear. Every now and then, a lilt in certain words reminded her of how Tony spoke, small habits that she hadn't discerned as being raised with a foreign language. But she could hear the similarity more clearly when listening to his father.

While she'd seen the king daily during her two weeks on the island, those encounters had been mostly during meals. He'd spent the majority of his time with his daughter. But since Eloisa and her husband had left this afternoon, Enrique must be at loose ends. Shannon envied them that connection, and missed her own parents all the more. How much different her life might have been if they hadn't died. Her mother had shared a love of music.

She stroked the keyboard longingly. "Who plays the piano?"

"My sons took lessons as a part of the curriculum outlined by their tutors."

"Of course, I should have realized," she said. "Tony can play?"

Laughter rattled around inside his chest. "That would be a stretch. My youngest son can read music, but he did not enjoy sitting still. Antonio rushed through lessons so he could go outside."

"I can picture that."

"You know him well then." His sharp brown eyes took in everything. "Now my middle boy, Duarte, is more disciplined, quite the martial arts expert. But with music?" Enrique waved dismissively. "He performs like a robot."

Her curiosity tweaked for more details on Tony's family. Over the past couple of weeks, their relationship had deepened, and she needed more insights to still the fears churning her gut. "And your oldest son, Carlos? How did he fare with the piano lessons?"

A dark shadow crossed Enrique's face before he schooled his regal features again. "He had a gift. He's a surgeon now, using that touch in other ways."

"I can see how the two careers could tap into the same skill," she said, brushing her fingers over the gleaming keys.

Perhaps she could try again to find a career that tapped into her love of music. What a gift it would be to bring joy deeper into her life again.

Enrique tucked one hand into his pocket. "Do you have feelings for my son?"

His blunt question blindsided her, but she should have realized this cunning man never chatted just for conversation's sake. "That is a personal question."

"And I may not have time to wait around for you to feel comfortable answering."

"You're playing the death card? That's a bit cold, don't you think, sir?"

He laughed, hard and full-out like Tony did—or like he used to. "You have a spine. Good. You are a fine match for my stubborn youngest."

Her irritation over his probing questions eased. What parent didn't want to see their children settled and happy? "I appreciate your opening your home to me and my son and giving us a chance to get to know you."

"Diplomatically said, my dear. You are wise to proceed thoughtfully. Regrets are a terrible thing," he said somberly. "I should have sent my family out of San Rinaldo sooner. I waited too long and Beatriz paid the price."

The darker turn of the conversation stilled her. She'd wanted more insights into Tony's life, yet this was going so much deeper than she had anticipated.

Enrique continued, "It was such chaos that day when the coup began. We had planned for my family to take one escape route and I would use another." His jaw flexed sharply in his gaunt face. "I made it out, and the rebels found my family. Carlos was injured trying to save his mother."

The picture of violence and terror he painted sounded like something from a movie, so unreal, yet they'd lived it. "Tony and your other sons witnessed the attack on their mother?"

"Antonio had nightmares for a year, and then he became obsessed with the beach and surfing. From that day on, he lived to leave the island."

She'd known the bare bones details of their escape. But the horror they'd lived through, the massive losses rolled over her with a new vividness. Tony's need to help her had more to do with caring than control. He didn't want to isolate her or smother her by managing everything the way her husband had. Tony tried to help her because he'd failed to save someone else he cared about.

Somehow, knowing this made it easier for her to open her heart. To take a chance beyond their weeks here.

Without question, he would have to understand her need for independence, but she also had to appreciate how he'd been hurt, how those hurts had shaped him. And as Antonio Medina and Tony Castillo merged in her mind, she couldn't ignore the truth any longer.

She loved him.

Approaching footsteps startled her, drawing her focus from the past and toward the arched entry. Tony stepped into view just when her defenses were at their lowest. No doubt her heart was in her eyes. She started toward him, only to realize *his* eyes held no tender feelings.

The harsh angles of his face blared a forewarning before he announced, "There's been a security breach."

Thirteen

Shock jolted through Shannon, followed closely by fear. "A security breach? Where's Kolby?"

She shot to her feet and ran across the music room to Tony. The ailing king reached for his cane, his dogs waking instantly, beating her there by a footstep. Enrique steadied himself with a hand against the wall, but he was up and moving. "What happened?"

"Kolby is fine. No one has been hurt, but we have taken another hit in the media."

Enrique asked, "Have they located the island?"

"No," Tony said as Alys slid into view behind him. "It happened at the airport when Eloisa and Jonah's flight landed in South Carolina. The press was waiting, along with crowds of everyday people wanting a picture to sell for an easy buck."

Shannon's stomach lurched at another assault in the

news. "Could the frenzy have to do with the Landis family connections?"

"No," Tony said curtly. "The questions were all about their vacation with Eloisa's father the king."

Alys angled past Tony with a wheelchair. "Your Majesty, I'll take you to your office so you can speak to security directly."

The king dropped into the wheelchair heavily. "Thank you, Alys." His dogs loped into place alongside him. "I am ready."

Nerves jangled, Shannon started to follow, but Tony extended a hand to stop her.

"We need to talk."

His chilly voice stilled her feet faster than any arm across the entranceway. Had he been holding back because of concerns for his father's health? "What's wrong? What haven't you told me?"

She stepped closer for comfort. He crossed his arms over his chest.

"The leak came from this house. There was a call placed from here this afternoon—at just the right time—to an unlisted cell number."

"Here? But your father's security has been top notch." No wonder he was so concerned.

Tony unclipped his iPhone from his waistband. "We have security footage of the call being made."

Thumbing the controls, he filled the screen with a still image of a woman on the phone, a woman in a white swimsuit cover-up, hood pulled over her head.

A cover-up just like hers? "I don't understand. You think this is *me*? Why would I tip off the media?"

His mouth stayed tight-lipped and closed, and his eyes… Oh God, she recognized well that condemning look from the days following Nolan's arrest and then his death.

Steady. Steady. She reminded herself Tony wasn't Nolan or the other people who'd betrayed her, and he had good reasons to be wary. She drew in a shuddering breath.

"I understand that Enrique brought you up to be unusually cautious about the people in your life. And he had cause after what happened to your mother." Thoughts of Tony as a small child watching his mother's murder brushed sympathy over her own hurt. "But you have to see there's nothing about me that would hint at this kind of behavior."

"I know you would do anything to secure your son's future. Whoever sold this information received a hefty pay-off." He stared back at her with cold eyes and unswerving surety.

In a sense he was right. She would do anything for Kolby. But again, Tony had made a mistake. He'd offered her money before, assuming that would equate security to her. She had deeper values she wanted to relay to her son, like the importance of earning a living honorably. Tony had needed to prove that himself in leaving the island. Why was it so difficult to understand she felt the same way?

Her sympathy for him could only stretch so far.

"You actually believe I betrayed you? That I placed everyone here at risk for a few dollars?" Anger frothed higher and higher inside her. "I never wanted any of this. My son and I can get by just fine without you and your movie theater." She swatted his arm. "Answer me, damn you."

"I don't know what to think." He pinched the bridge of his nose. "Tell me it was an accident. You called a friend just to shoot the breeze because you were homesick and that friend sold you out."

Except as she'd already told him and he must remember, she didn't have friends, not anymore. Apparently she didn't even have Tony. "I'm not going to defend myself to you. Either you trust me or you don't."

He gripped her shoulders, his touch careful, his eyes more tumultuous. "I want a future with you. God, Shannon, I was going to ask you to marry me later tonight. I planned to take you back to the chapel, go inside this time and propose."

Her heart squeezed tight at the image he painted. If this security nightmare hadn't occurred, she would have been swept off her feet. She would have been celebrating her engagement with him tonight, because by God, she would have said yes. Now, that wasn't possible.

"You honestly thought we could get married when you have so little faith in me?" The betrayal burned deep. And hadn't she sworn she'd never again put herself in a position to feel that sting from someone she cared about? "You should have included some azaleas in the bouquet you chose for us. I hear they mean fragile passion."

She shrugged free of his too tempting touch. The hole inside her widened, ached.

"Damn it all, Shannon, we're talking." He started toward her.

"Stop." She held up a hand. "Don't come near me. Not now. Not ever."

"Where are you going?" He kept his distance this time. "I need to know you're safe."

"Has the new security system been installed at my apartment?"

His mouth tight, he nodded. "But we're still working on the restraining orders. Given the renewed frenzy because of Eloisa's identity—"

"The new locks and alarms will do for now."

"Damn it, Shannon—"

"I have to find Alys so she can make the arrangements."

She held her chin high. Pride and her child were all she had left now that her heart was shattered to pieces. "Kolby and I are returning to Texas."

"Where are Shannon and her son?"

His father's question hammered Tony's already pounding head. In his father's study, he poured himself three fingers of cognac, bypassing the Basque wine and the memories it evoked. Shannon wrapped around him, the scent of lilies in her hair. "You know full well where she is. Nothing slips past you here."

They'd spent the past two hours assessing the repercussions of the leak. The media feeding frenzy had been rekindled with fresh fuel about Eloisa's connection to the family. Inevitable, yet still frustrating. It gnawed at his gut to think Shannon had something to do with this, although he reassured himself it must have been an accident.

And if she'd simply slipped up and made a mistake, he could forgive her. She hadn't lived the Medina way since the cradle. Remembering all the intricacies involved in maintaining such a high level of security was difficult. If she would just admit what happened, they could move on.

His father rolled back from the computer desk, his large dogs tracking his every move from in front of the fireplace. "Apparently I do not know everything happening under my roof, because somebody placed a call putting Eloisa's flight at risk. I trusted someone I shouldn't have."

"You trusted me and my judgment." He scratched his tightening rib cage.

His father snorted with impatience. "Do not be an impulsive jackass. Think with your brain and not your heart."

"Like you've always done?" Tony snapped, his patience for his father's cryptic games growing short. "No thank you."

Once he finished his one-month obligation, he wouldn't set foot on this godforsaken island again. If memories of his life here before were unhappy, now they were gut-wrenching. His father should come to the mainland anyway for medical treatment. Even Enrique's deep coffers couldn't outfit the island with unlimited hospital options.

Enrique poured himself a drink and downed it swiftly. "I let my heart guide me when I left San Rinaldo. I was so terrified something would happen to my wife and sons that I did not think through our escape plan properly."

Invincible Enrique was admitting a mistake? Tony let that settle inside him for a second before speaking.

"You set yourself up as a diversion. Sounds pretty self-less to me." He'd never doubted his father's bravery or cool head.

"I did not think it through." He refilled his glass and stared into the amber liquid, signs of regret etched deep in his forehead. Illness had never made the king appear weak, but at this moment, the ghosts of an old past showed a vulnerability Tony had never seen before. "If I had, I would have taken into account the way Carlos would react if things went to hell. I arrogantly considered my plan foolproof. Again, I thought with my emotions and those assassins knew exactly how to target my weakness."

Tony set aside his glass without touching a drop. Empathy for his father seared him more fully than alcohol. Understanding how it felt to have his feelings ripped up through his throat because of a woman gave him insights to his father he'd never expected. "You did your best at the time."

Could he say the same when it came to Shannon?

"I tried to make that right with this island. I did everything in my power to create a safe haven for my sons."

"But we all three left the protection of this place."

"That doesn't matter to me. My only goal was keeping you safe until adulthood. By the time you departed, you took with you the skills to protect yourself, to make your way in the world. That never would have been possible if you'd grown up with obligations to a kingdom. For that, I'm proud."

Enrique's simply spoken words enveloped him. Even though his father wasn't telling him anything he didn't already know, something different took root in him. An understanding. Just as his mother had made the silver security blanket as a "shield," to make him feel protected, his father had been doing the same. His methods may not have been perfect, but their situation had been far from normal. They'd all been scrambling to patch together their lives.

Some of his understanding must have shown on his face, because his father smiled approvingly.

"Now, son, think about Shannon logically rather than acting like a love-sick boy."

Love-sick boy? Now that stung more than a little. And the reason? Because it was true. He did love her, and that had clouded his thinking.

He loved her. And he'd let his gut drive his conclusions rather than logic. He forced his slugging heart to slow and collected what he knew about Shannon. "She's a naturally cautious woman who wouldn't do anything to place her son at risk. If she had a call to make, she would check with you or I to make sure the call was safe. She wouldn't have relied on anyone else's word when it comes to Kolby."

"What conclusion does that lead you to?"

"We never saw the caller's face. I made an assumption

based on a female in a bathing suit cover-up. The caller must have been someone with detailed knowledge of our security systems in order to keep her face shielded. A woman of similar build. A person with something to gain and little loyalty to the Medinas…" His brain settled on… "Alys?"

"I would bet money on it." The thunderous anger Enrique now revealed didn't bode well for the assistant who'd used her family connections to take advantage of an ailing king with an aging staff. "She was even the one to order Shannon's clothes. It would be easy to make sure she had the right garb…."

Shannon had done nothing wrong.

"God, I wonder if Alys could have even been responsible for tipping off the Global Intruder about that photo of Duarte when it first ran, before he was identified." The magnitude of how badly he'd screwed up threatened to kick his knees out from under him. He braced a hand on his father's shoulder, touching his dad for the first time in fourteen years. "Where the hell is Alys?"

Enrique swallowed hard. He clapped his hand over Tony's for a charged second before clearing his throat.

"Leave Alys to me." His royal roots showed through again as he assumed command. "Don't you have a more pressing engagement?"

Tony checked his watch. He had five minutes until the ferry pulled away for the airstrip. No doubt his father would secure the proof of Alys's deception soon, but Shannon needed—hell, she deserved—to know that he'd trusted in her innocence without evidence.

He had a narrow, five-minute window to prove just how much he loved and trusted her.

* * *

The ferry horn wailed, signaling they were disconnecting from the dock. The crew was stationed at their posts, lost in the ritual of work.

Kolby on her hip, Shannon looked at the exotic island for the last time. This was hard, so much harder than she'd expected. How would she ever survive going back to Galveston where even more memories of Tony waited? She couldn't. She would have to start over somewhere new and totally different.

Except there was no place she could run now that would be free of Medina reminders. The grocery store aisles would sport gossip rags. Channel surfing could prove hazardous. And she didn't even want to think of how often she would be confronted with Tony's face peering back at her from an internet headline, reminding her of how little faith he'd had in her. As much as she wanted to say to hell with it all and accept whatever he offered, she wouldn't settle for half measures ever again.

Tears blurred the exotic shoreline, sea oats dotting the last bit of sand as they pulled away. She squeezed her eyes closed, tears cool on her heated cheeks.

"Mommy?" Kolby patted her face.

She scavenged a wobbly smile and focused on his precious face. "I'm okay, sweetie. Everything's going to be fine. Let's look for a dolphin."

"Nu-uh," he said. "Why's Tony running? Can he come wif us, pretty pwease?"

What? She followed the path of her son's pointing finger....

Tony sprinted down the dock, his mouth moving but his words swallowed up by the roar of the engines and churning water behind the ferry. Her heart pumped in time with his long-legged strides. She almost didn't dare hope, but then Tony had always delivered the unexpected.

Lowering Kolby to the deck with one arm, she leaned over the rail, straining to hear what he said. Still, the wind whipped his words as the ferry inched away. Disappointment pinched as she realized she would have to wait for the ferry to travel back again to speak to him. So silly to be impatient, but her heart had broken a lifetime's worth in one day.

Just as she'd resigned herself to waiting, Tony didn't stop running. Oh my God, he couldn't actually be planning to—

Jump.

Her heart lodged in her throat for an expanded second as he was airborne. Then he landed on deck with the surefooted ease of an experienced boater. Tony strode toward her with even, determined steps, the crew parting to make way.

He extended his hand, his fist closed around a clump of sea oats, still dripping from where he'd yanked them up. "You'll have to use your imagination here because I didn't have much time." He passed her one stalk. "Imagine this is a purple hyacinth, the 'forgive me' flower. I hope you will accept it, along with my apology."

"Go ahead. I'm listening." Although she didn't take his pretend hyacinth. He had a bit more talking to do after what he'd put her through.

Kolby patted his leg for attention. Winking down at the boy, Tony passed him one of the sea oats, which her son promptly waved like a flag. With Kolby settled, Tony shifted his attention back to Shannon.

"I've been an idiot," he said. Sea spray dampened his hair, increasing the rebellious curls. "I should have known you wouldn't do anything to put Kolby or my family at risk.

And if you'd done so inadvertently, you would have been upfront about it." He told her all the things she'd hoped to hear earlier.

While she appreciated the romanticism of his gesture, a part of her still ached that he'd needed proof. Trust was such a fragile thing, but crucial in any relationship.

"What brought about this sudden insight to my character? Did you find some new surveillance tape that proves my innocence?"

"I spoke to my father. He challenged me, made me think with my head instead of my scared-as-hell heart. And thank God he did, because once I looked deeper I realized Alys must have made the call. I can't help but wonder if she's the one who made the initial leak to the press. We don't have proof yet, but we'll find it."

Alys? Shannon mulled over that possibility, remembering the way the assistant had stared at Tony with such hunger. She'd sensed the woman wanted to be a Medina. Perhaps Alys had also wanted all the public princess perks to go with it rather than a life spent in hiding.

Tony extended his hand with the sea oats again, tickling them across Kolby's chin lightly before locking eyes with Shannon. "But none of that matters if you don't trust me."

Touching the cottony white tops of the sea oats, she weighed her words carefully. This moment could define the rest of her life. "I realize the way you've grown up has left marks on you…what happened with your mother… living in seclusion here. But I can't always worry when that's going to make you push me away again just because you're afraid I'll betray you."

Her fingers closed around his. "I've had so many people turn away from me. I can't—I won't—spend my life proving myself to you."

"And I don't expect you to." He clasped both hands around hers, his skin callused and tough, a little rough around the edges like her impetuous lover. "You're absolutely right. I was wrong. What I feel for you, it's scary stuff. But the thought of losing you is a helluva lot scarier than any alternative."

"What exactly are you saying?" She needed him to spell it out, every word, every promise.

"My life is complicated and comes with a lot more cons than pros. There's nothing to stop Alys from spilling everything she knows, and if so, it's really going to hit the fan. A life with me won't be easy. To the world, I am a Medina. And I hope you will consent to be a Medina, too."

He knelt in front of her with those sea oats—officially now her favorite plant.

"Shannon, will you be my bride? Let me be your husband and a father to Kolby." He paused to ruffle the boy's hair, eliciting a giant smile from her son. "As well as any other children we may have together. I can't promise I won't be a jackass again. I can almost guarantee that I will. But I vow to stick with it, stick with us, because you mean too much to me for me to ever mess this up again."

Sinking to her knees, she fell into his arms, her son enclosed in the circle. "Yes, I'll marry you and build a family and future with you. Tony Castillo, Antonio Medina, and any other name you go by, I love you, too. You've stolen my heart for life."

"Thank God." He gathered her closer, his arms trembling just a hint.

She lost track of how long they knelt that way until Kolby squirmed between them, and she heard the crew applauding and cheering. Together, she and Tony stood as the ferry captain shouted orders to turn the boat around.

Standing at the deck with Tony, she stared at the approaching island, a place she knew they would visit over the years. She clasped his arm, her cheek against his compass tattoo. Tony rested his chin on her head.

His breath caressed her hair. "The legend about the compass is true. I've found my way home."

Surprised, she glanced up at him. "Back to the island?"

Shaking his head, he tucked a knuckle under her chin and brushed a kiss across her mouth. "Ah, Shanny, *you* are my home."

* * * * *

That's when he made his mistake. Before she could escape, he reached out and caught her hand in his.

It hit with all the heat and power of a lightning bolt, stunning him. The sizzle, the inner sparks, the arc of want and desire, like someone had forced his entire body into a light socket and then amped up the juice. It all cascaded through him in an unending torrent. It wasn't that it hurt, it just surprised him. Worse, it horrified him because he had a hideous feeling he knew what caused it. He'd heard the stories over the years. Watched as one by one, cousin and brother had fallen to its insidious influence.

Shayla pulled back from him. "What was that?" she demanded, her brows snapping together. "What did you just do to me?"

"Son of a—" He shook his head to clear it. "I think I just Infernoed you."

Dear Reader,

One of the fun parts of writing stories about the Dantes—
stories that stand alone or can be enjoyed as part of
the whole—is building family relationships. I love the
various roles each member plays, mainly because I come
from a large family. I've always been fascinated by the
interaction and dynamics that result when such different
and individual people are thrown into the same mixing
bowl. Often times it's chaos!

For instance, one family member is known as Queen of
the Universe. Another as The Rebel. Still another as Mr
Organization. During my teen years, my brother dubbed
me The Girl Who Lives Upstairs because I liked to hide
out in my room and read and write. I think that what
has made the Dantes such a joy is that I can explore
each aspect of these very different men and women and
uncover their unique role in the family.

This story, *Dante's Marriage Pact*, starts at the very same
glittering affair as the last book, *Dante's Temporary
Fiancée*. It's a Dante reception that doesn't ignite just
one Inferno match, but two. Read on to discover how
Draco, the troublemaker of the group, learns the true
meaning of trouble when a one-night stand turns into
something far deeper and more lasting. And I hope you
notice the small Dante bombshell that's dropped in the
last chapter!

All the best,

Day Leclaire

DANTE'S
MARRIAGE PACT

BY
DAY LECLAIRE

Published in Great Britain 2011
by Mills & Boon, an imprint of Harlequin (UK) Limited,
Eton House, 18-24 Paradise Road, Richmond, Surrey TW9 1SR

© Day Totton Smith 2010

ISBN: 978 0 263 88322 0

51-1111

Harlequin (UK) policy is to use papers that are natural, renewable and
recyclable products and made from wood grown in sustainable forests. The
logging and manufacturing processes conform to the legal environmental
regulations of the country of origin.

Printed and bound in Spain
by Blackprint CPI, Barcelona

To Carolyn Greene, who holds my hand
through the best and the worst.

One

She was a nervous wreck.

Shayla Charleston stood in the luxurious bathroom at the San Francisco headquarters of Dantes, one of the world's premier jewelry empires, and regarded herself in the mirror. To her relief her nerves didn't show, and once she got through tonight this would all be over. Not only that, but tomorrow she'd turn twenty-five and maybe, just maybe, fulfill each of the three goals she had set for herself.

Goal number one: Pay back her grandmother. Shayla had worked like a dog these past three years to reimburse Grandmother Charleston for the cost of her college education, an education her grandmother had scrimped and saved for, even at the risk of allowing their home to decay around their ears. Though her grandmother had hoped Shayla would resurrect the family business, she hadn't inherited the talent or the ability. But she could and would represent the family interests when she met with members of the

Dante clan tomorrow. If she were very lucky, that meeting would provide her grandmother with badly needed financial security, something Shayla would do anything to ensure, no matter how difficult.

Goal number two: Get the job of her dreams. Shayla smiled broadly. Check, check and double check. The minute she escaped her meeting with the Dantes, she'd climb on a plane headed straight for Europe, where she'd begin her job as a translator for the highly reclusive international businessman, Derek Algier. The job would take her to some of the most beautiful and exotic countries in the world and she flat-out could not wait.

Goal number three: Tomorrow, before she assumed her new responsibilities, Shayla wanted to be swept off her feet and experience a mad, impetuous romance. Just this once. One night of passion before she reverted to her more reserved, dependable nature. Was that too much to ask?

She pressed an anxious hand to her stomach. But first, she had a party to crash.

The door to the restroom opened and several women entered. Everyone exchanged polite smiles and one of the women gave Shayla's gown an envious glance. It relieved her mind since it confirmed that the alterations she'd made to her mother's designer gown—one left over from the Charlestons' glory days—were invisible to even the most discerning eye.

Even better, a quick, assessing glance in the mirror assured her that her makeup looked exactly right, as did her hair. Considering the lighting conditions and scratched mirror in the cheap little motel room she'd rented, all she could afford at this point, it was a miracle that she'd managed to pull it together as well as she had. No question about it, she exuded wealth and privilege, something the Charlestons hadn't experienced in a full decade thanks to the Dantes.

Now to do a little reconnaissance in anticipation of tomorrow's meeting. If she could get a feel for some of the prime players, she just might gain an edge in their negotiations, something she badly needed considering how out of her depth she was. She reached for her vintage beaded handbag and the list buried inside, dismayed to discover that the clasp had once again popped open when she'd set it on the counter.

The bag had also been her mother's, another echo from the past that whispered of genteel elegance and casual prosperity. She wouldn't have minded the broken clasp except for one not-so-minor detail.

The items she carried inside were worth millions.

She couldn't afford to lose the precious bundle. Unlike her college education, she'd never be able to repay her grandmother for the loss. Reaching inside, Shayla tucked the leather pouch into the deepest corner of the bag—not that it was terribly deep. Then she extracted the list her grandmother had given her and scanned the names one last time, committing them to memory.

Primo Dante, the family patriarch and founder of the Dantes jewelry empire, now retired. Severo Dante, CEO and chairman of the board. Then there were the twins. Marco handled international sales and relations. She doubted she'd meet him. Lazzaro was their chief financial officer. Guaranteed he'd sit in on the meeting. That was the best intel her grandmother had to offer and that her own research could turn up, which would have to do.

Satisfied that she had the names down pat, Shayla refolded the paper and tucked it into her handbag. She double-checked to make certain she secured the clasp good and tight. Taking a deep breath, she examined her appearance one final time and nodded. She could only hope she'd fit in.

Exiting the restroom, she scanned the guests waiting in the foyer outside of the reception. This would be the most difficult part, and most traumatic for someone of her nature. Security stood at the doorway collecting invitations. She waited until a large, laughing crowd descended and attached herself to one side, slipping past during the momentary confusion. And just like that, she crashed the Dantes' reception. She hastened across the threshold and focused. First business. Check out the Dantes on her list.

Then maybe she'd find the perfect man, a man who'd make tonight the most special of her life.

Draco Dante noticed her the instant she stepped into the room. Noticed her, and wanted her with a fierceness that nearly brought him to his knees. He felt the visceral tug of attraction and didn't resist. Of course, at that point he didn't fully appreciate the ramifications of what was happening. Or if he did, he assumed on some level that he could fight free from its hold whenever he wanted. He didn't realize The Inferno had set its hooks in him and was reeling him toward his doom. He still believed himself in control of his own destiny.

Until that night he'd never believed in The Inferno. Never believed in the family legend—or curse, as some considered it. In his opinion it was ludicrous to think that a man could identify his soul mate with a simple touch. Ridiculous to believe that there even were such things as soul mates. Resisted with all his might the possibility that there was one woman out there meant just for him…and only one. He'd heard the stories over the years. Watched as one by one, cousin and brother had fallen to its insidious influence. But whatever this was, whatever hit him when he first set eyes on this woman stole every thought from his head save one.

Take the woman.

At a guess she stood a full five foot eight and had a wealth of hair knotted at her nape, the ebony color a perfect complement to her ink-blotch eyes. Though her curves weren't voluptuous they were impressive enough to capture the attention of most of the men in the room. Or maybe it was the way she displayed them, in a ruby-red halter dress that hugged her breasts and nipped in at her narrow waist before pouring over shapely hips and a deliciously rounded backside.

She stepped across the threshold and moved with graceful purpose toward a corner display out of the main flow of traffic.

He headed toward her, cutting off the competition with a neat sidestep. She stood in front of one of the Eternity wedding band displays, riveted by the rings, her full attention focused on them. "Beautiful, aren't they?" he said.

She continued to study the display, effectively ignoring him. "Stunning," she murmured.

"I believe this is the part where we're supposed to introduce ourselves," he prompted with a smile.

"No, thanks," she said with a quick, reserved glance and shifted to move around him.

That's when he made his mistake. Before she could escape, he reached out and caught her hand in his. "Wait—"

It hit with all the heat and power of a lightning bolt, stunning him. The sizzle, the inner sparks, the arc of want and desire, like someone had forced his entire body into a light socket and then amped up the juice. It all cascaded through him in an unending torrent. It wasn't that it hurt, it just surprised him. Worse, it horrified him because he had a hideous feeling he'd just confirmed his worst suspicions.

She pulled back from him. "What was that?" she demanded, her brows snapping together. "What did you just do to me?"

"Son of a—" He shook his head to clear it. "I think I just Infernoed you."

"Well, don't do it again. I didn't like it." With that, she turned her back on him and disappeared into the crowd.

It took Draco an instant to react. Not certain whether to swear or laugh—maybe both—he went after the woman. He caught up with her near another display.

He stood at her side, not that she took any notice. "Are you telling me that you only felt a shock when we touched? It wasn't anything more than that?"

Her attention remained fixed on the gems as though they held the answer to all of life's mysteries. "Was I supposed to feel something more?"

"The way I've heard it…yes."

She turned her head and regarded him with a curious stare. Her eyes were large and tilted at the edges, and filled with something sad and ageless. They were also stunning in their ability to convey her every emotion. And right now they conveyed a clear message: Go. Away. "I have no idea what you're talking about."

Why was it that the one woman he wanted more than any other wouldn't give him the time of day? If it weren't so frustrating, it would be funny. "Maybe we could start over. I'm—"

She whirled to confront him, the skirt of her dress flaring around her, the hem catching at his legs as though eager to embrace him. She pressed her fingertips to his lips. "No names," she whispered urgently. "I'm crashing the party and if I get caught, you can honestly say you don't know who I am. That way you won't get into trouble, too."

Aw, hell. He didn't dare admit he was a Dante now. "Are you here to steal something?"

Astonishment mingled with shock. No way could she have faked that look. "No, of course not."

"That's good." Very good. "How about first names? People do exchange them, you know, even when they're crashing parties." Because of his position as Dantes' head gemologist, he was extremely careful to keep his rather unusual name out of the spotlight, so she shouldn't connect it with the Dante family.

She caught her lower lip between her teeth and the top of his head almost came off. More than anything he wanted that sweet, succulent lip captured between his own teeth. "I guess that can't hurt," she conceded. "I'm Shayla."

"Draco," he said. "Draco-with-no-last-name."

"Oh, dear." She offered a teasing smile. "Did your parents dislike you?"

"What, Draco?" He returned her smile with a rueful one of his own. "It's a family name. My mother's maiden name. I also had it long before *Harry Potter* came out, in case you were wondering."

"It means dragon, doesn't it?"

"Afraid so."

A hint of hesitation flowed across her expression. "And are you?"

"A dragon?" He pondered the idea. "I can be when it's important to me. If someone takes what I consider mine."

"Then I'll have to make sure I avoid taking anything you value."

"Always a wise move."

He decided to experiment and shifted closer to see how Shayla would respond. Her reaction was so subtle, he almost missed it. But it was there. It was definitely there. The thick fringe of her eyelashes flickered ever so slightly and tension swept across her shoulders. It didn't make sense to him. Why hide it? If it were anything similar to what he felt right this minute, she should be falling all over him.

The Inferno—assuming it really was The Inferno, and he still had his doubts about that—clouded rational thought, driving a man to find a way to touch the woman he craved, to inhale her. To carry her off and bury himself in her until neither of them could move or think or breathe.

"Why are you fighting it?" he asked in an undertone.

"Fighting what?"

This time she couldn't hide the lie and he didn't waste time arguing. Before she realized his intention, he caught her hand in his. Heat flared between them, more intense this time, pouring into his veins like effervescent champagne. Every beat of his heart drove it further and deeper, strengthening the connection until it threatened to overpower him.

"Shayla…"

He whispered her name into the few inches of space separating them, filling the sound with every ounce of the desire he felt. Her lips parted and her breathing quickened. She swayed, yielding ever so slightly. He caught the subtle fragrance of her perfume, crisp and spicy with a dash of sultry thrown in. Somehow he suspected the scent epitomized the woman.

"What have you done to me?"

She asked the question with such bewilderment that he flinched. "I'm sorry. It isn't something I can control."

"I don't have time for this right now. Make it stop."

Draco didn't insult her with prevarication. "I wouldn't even if I could. I want you, sweetheart. And I think you want me, too."

She closed her eyes and he wondered if she were fighting the tug, that relentless, unyielding pull. Not that she could win this particular battle. At least… No one ever had. "I have something else I need to take care of first," she whispered.

He moved in, erasing those few inches that separated them, just close enough so hips and thighs brushed. Just enough so he felt the soft crush of her breasts against his chest. Just enough so his mouth hovered within a whisper of her lips. "Whatever you're here for can wait. This can't."

She looked at him, enchanting him with an open display of pleasure and desire. She utterly captivated him. She was swift to smile, swifter to laugh, her movements like quicksilver, filled with energy, yet as graceful as a dancer's. He wanted all that grace and energy in his bed. Wanted that magical sparkle for himself. Like a dragon hoarding his treasure, came the whimsical thought. "I've never done this before. Never lost control or acted so impulsively," she admitted.

"I'm wish I could say the same. Tell me you're not going to fight what we're feeling."

Her mouth quivered on the verge of a smile. "I'm not sure I could."

He bent his head and feathered a kiss along her jawline. "That makes two of us. So, instead of crashing this very boring party, why don't you sneak away with me? I promise I won't bore you."

She shuddered in reaction. Then her smile blossomed and the soft sound of her laughter made it clear that whatever connection they'd forged during these brief moments together had won out. The day had already been an interesting one. First, he'd received a phone call from his brother's ex-investigator, Juice, with news that another fire diamond had been found…the fourth of six that had been stolen from Draco in a clever swindle a full decade before. This new information gave him one more opportunity to find the person behind the con.

And now the most beautiful woman Draco had ever seen had walked into the reception and blew his earlier convictions about The Inferno straight out of the water. Or, maybe it wasn't The Inferno. Maybe it was just a bad case of lust or a sexual lightning bolt of some kind.

"What is this?" she asked. Her voice, though low, carried a wealth of passion flavored with a sweet Southern warmth. Georgia? Or perhaps South Carolina. "And why you and not some other man here?" She gestured to indicate the milling crowd. "I don't understand what's happening."

The thought of Shayla giving herself to someone else filled Draco with a ferocity that he could barely wrestle into submission. "I don't know how or why we formed this connection," he admitted. "Not exactly. But if it makes you feel any better, it's the same for me."

He couldn't resist. He had to touch her. He skimmed the tips of his fingers along the inside of her forearm from elbow to wrist in a silent demand. *Come with me.* It was like touching a silken thread of fire. She shivered in response and swayed toward him, giving him an equally silent answer. Sliding his arm around her waist, he drew her through the doorway of the reception area and down a long corridor toward a bank of private elevators. He used his key to access the car and the minute the doors parted, they stepped inside. He inserted his key again to access the top floor, which housed four private penthouse suites.

She frowned when she realized which button he'd pushed. "Where are we going?"

"Up." The single-word answer didn't satisfy her, but right now it took every ounce of focus and determination to keep his hands off her.

"And what is up there?"

"Dantes maintains suites for visiting clients from out of town who are anxious to exchange their millions for one of Dantes' premier collections. I'm staying in one temporarily." For some reason the information caused her to relax ever so slightly. "It also gives us a place where we can discuss our situation without the risk of interruption."

"Just discuss?"

He gave it to her straight. "That depends."

She tilted her head to one side. "On what?"

"On what we want to do about this." He took her hand in his, lacing their fingers together in order to make his point.

She drew in a sharp breath, her dark eyes flaming with desire. "What is that?" she asked unevenly. "And this time I expect an answer. A straight answer, if you don't mind."

Fortunately, the doors parted before he had to try to put it into words. The instant they stepped off the elevator, he tugged at her hand, drawing her across the foyer to a door leading to his penthouse suite. His stay there was a temporary situation during the planning and building stages of his new home. Only one of the other three suites was currently occupied, housing the King and Queen of Verdonia, rulers of the country that supplied Dantes with the most beautiful amethysts in the world. Many of the Eternity rings on display this evening featured their gemstones.

Fumbling with his keys, Draco found the correct one. He shoved it into the lock, and managed to get the door open and the appropriate alarm code entered before sweeping her into his arms and carrying her across the threshold. He didn't bother to analyze the symbolism of his actions. His main concern was to lock the two of them away while he coaxed her into the nearest bed. Assuming he lasted long enough to find his bed.

He carried her through to the expansive living room, one that offered views of both the city and the bay. Setting her on her feet, he took her clutch purse and tossed it in the general direction of the couch. It bounced on the cushion and then somersaulted onto the floor.

She started in alarm. "No, wait. My purse—"

"—will be there in the morning."

He reached for her, but she held up a hand before he could pull her back into his arms. She shot an uneasy glance in the direction her purse had taken. She must have decided it was safe enough for the time being because she returned her focus to him.

"Just wait a moment, Draco." He loved the way her voice caressed his name, drawing it out and layering a soft Southern hitch onto the two syllables. "You said you would explain what caused that spark when we first touched. Before this goes any further, I want to know how you did that."

"I'm sorry if I hurt you." He spoke with utter sincerity. "It wasn't deliberate."

She stared at her hand, rubbing her palm with her thumb, before eyeing him warily. "It hasn't gone away."

"It will." He hoped.

She lifted an eyebrow. "And what, exactly, is *it?*"

"Our family calls it The Inferno," he reluctantly admitted, deliberately not using his last name in case it scared her off. "When we're intensely attracted to certain women, it causes that sort of reaction."

"Certain women?" She wavered between outrage and curiosity. "What do you mean by that?"

He hesitated, aware that a deep pit yawned in front of him. He chose his words with care, hoping they'd help him skirt disaster. "Women we want. Women we're intensely attracted to. At least, I'm assuming that's what generated the sparks between us. To be honest, it's never happened to me before."

"Got it." Her mouth twitched. "It's your version of a mating call."

It was his turn to feel a flash of outrage, though it was edged with amusement. "Hell, at least I'm not bugling and pawing the ground," he muttered.

"You just roar and breathe fire?" she suggested with a teasing laugh.

"Only with you." If the words contained a growling hint

of that roar, there was nothing he could do to prevent it. She'd just have to be grateful he didn't spew flames.

He waited. All the while the want flared higher and stronger than ever before. She was right. If he could roar and breathe fire, he'd do it. Hell, if it meant winning her for his mate, he'd sprout wings and carry her off to the nearest lair, assuming such a thing existed.

He saw her soften and realized he'd avoided the trap. Better yet, she came into his arms as though she belonged, which on some level she did. Maybe on every level.

It was his last rational thought for a long time.

He cupped her face and then paused to appreciate the moment. Her lips parted in anticipation, damp and full, while desire openly shaped her expression. No pretense. No hesitation. Just pure passion freely offered. She was beyond lovely. And yet, even as he studied her, a hint of bewilderment filled her eyes with a sooty darkness.

"Are you having second thoughts?" she asked.

"Not a single one."

"Oh." Her expression revealed a heart-wrenching vulnerability. "I thought you were going to kiss me now that we have that Inferno problem out of the way. But you haven't."

"Ah, but this is a first kiss."

She considered his words. "And that makes a difference?"

"It makes a huge difference." He continued to scrutinize her face. "A first kiss… You remember that one. It makes an indelible impression. It deserves the proper amount of thought and consideration. For instance, are you the sort of woman who likes a slow, leisurely exploration? Should I sample your mouth the way I would taste a new dish, in small cautious bites?"

"That's a definite possibility," she agreed.

He tilted his head to one side and shook his head. "But

not quite right for you. Maybe this hunger between us needs to be fed fast. Attacked. Wrestled into submission with hard, explosive kisses."

The breath shivered from her lungs. "Tempting..." The word escaped on a sigh of longing.

"More tempting than you can imagine," he admitted. "But still not right for a first kiss. Hard and fast will come later."

A hint of amusement mingled with her longing. "But it will come?"

"Without question."

"And for our first kiss?" A thread of urgency spun through her question.

"Kissing you will be like sampling a rare wine." He leaned in, so close their lips almost touched. "First, there's the appearance. The color and sparkle. The deep, rich ebony of your eyes. The way they glitter against your pale skin." He swept his thumbs across her cheeks. "The hint of roses." His breath caressed her lips. "The blaze of rubies."

"Funny. I see emeralds and gold." Her smile blossomed, filled with enchantment. "And just a hint of amber."

Is that how his eyes appeared to her? He lowered his head to the silken joining of shoulder and throat, warming it with his breath. "And next comes the scent, that delicious bouquet of flower and fruit and spice that floods the senses and drives the anticipation. And you do, sweetheart. You flood my senses."

Her eyes fluttered closed as she breathed him in. "You smell like a forest, cedar mixed with an undertone of something earthy and highly masculine."

His body clenched at the undisguised need rippling through her comment. "Do you like it?"

"Very much." The words sighed from her, making it almost impossible to continue.

All he wanted was to take her—here and now—but he

fought the urge, fought to seduce her inch by agonizing inch. "And then there's that first taste," he managed to say. He brushed his lips across hers, just the lightest of touches before drawing back. "A mere sample, to tease and delight."

She followed where he led, lifting toward him, trembling in her urgency. "Taste me again, Draco. Now."

This time he didn't resist. He took her mouth, the taking firm and thorough, revealing a hint of the intense desire that drove him to the brink of insanity. She tasted sweet, honey-sweet and warm, her hunger a perfect mirror of his own. Her lips were plump and soft and giving. And her skin... Heaven help him, he'd never touched anything so soft.

He cupped her shoulders, bared by the halter top, and tripped his fingertips along her collarbones. She shivered, her mouth parting on a moan. It was a clear offer to deepen the kiss, and he did just that, giving her a hint of hard and explosive. She returned his kiss with a passion he'd only sus-pected—and hoped—she possessed.

Her arms wrapped around his neck and she threaded her fingers through his hair, tugging him closer so she could give back with an intensity that practically brought him to his knees. The scent of her twined around him, while her mouth tempted and tantalized, dipping inward in brief enticing forays. He let her take the lead. For now. He wanted her to familiarize herself with him—his scent, his taste, his touch.

His possession.

Long minutes slid by while she satisfied that first wave of desire. Then she pulled back just enough to draw in a deep breath. She stared up at him and shook her head in disbelief. "I don't understand any of this. I've never done this before. I mean *never*."

"In that case, I appreciate being the first."

"I'm glad I chose you." Her expression turned impish.

"After all, how often will I have a chance to sample such an excellent vintage?"

She made the comment with such grace and humor that it utterly endeared her to him. She returned to his arms and the quality of their embrace changed, this time becoming more certain in the melding of male to female. More familiar with how their mouths fit together and how their bodies moved one against the other.

But it still wasn't enough. It wouldn't be enough until he had her in his bed, with nothing between them but hot, willing flesh, their bodies joined as man was meant to be joined with his woman.

And in that moment Draco knew. Knew beyond a shadow of a doubt.

Shayla was his Inferno mate.

Two

Draco cupped Shayla's face, tilting it so he could enhance their kiss, sliding from passionate to tender, from tender to demanding, from demanding to teasing. Her heart hammered in time with his own and he absorbed the helpless shudder she gave. His hands shifted, dropping from her face and circling her neck to the clasp hidden beneath the intricate knot of her hair. A quick flick of his fingers released it and the silk poured from her shoulders, baring her breasts.

For a split second his heart and lungs forgot how to function. Never before had he seen such perfection. Slowly he reached for her, drawing out the moment until it was bowstring-taut. Gently, oh, so gently, he sculpted her with his fingertips. She trembled in reaction and her nipples pearled into tight, deep rosy peaks.

"Draco…" His name shuddered in the air, filled with a bittersweet yearning. "Please."

"Don't ask me to rush this." He barely recognized the

low, gruff tenor of his voice, filled with dark hunger. "I can't. I won't. I want it to be perfect, not some fast, awkward tumble."

A smile flirted with her mouth, a mouth still full and red from his kisses. "Just out of curiosity, are you even capable of a fast, awkward tumble?"

"I hope not." Dear heaven, he hoped not. "But everything about you makes me lose control."

Her smile grew. "Everything?"

He leaned in and inhaled her unique perfume. "Your scent." He circled the areola of her nipple with his index finger. "The silky feel of your skin. Your taste…"

He drew the tip of her breast into his mouth, nipping at the sensitive bud. Her breath caught. Held. Released on a cry of urgent demand. It was an irresistible siren's call.

He had only a vague memory of their transition from the living room to the bedroom. Leaving the lights off, he touched a panel just inside the doorway that activated the window treatments. They opened with a soft swish, silvering the room with starlight and brightening it with the hint of a rising moon.

He eased back, allowing the cool air to momentarily relieve the relentless burn of their passion and enable him to regain some modicum of control. When it came to the current situation, he needed every ounce of that control. He ripped his bow tie from around his neck and, one by one, removed the studs from his shirt front and cuffs. All the while Shayla stood swallowed in shadows, watching his every move with a gaze almost impossible to read.

He tossed his shirt aside and approached. The moonlight brought an unworldly sheen to her skin. She made a stunning palette of soft pearl and glittering jet misted with silver. Only her lips and the gown that clung to her hips added any color, a deep, dense ruby. He considered himself somewhat of a connoisseur of beauty, perhaps because of his occupation. When it came to gemstones, he was an expert—on their grading, their purity, their color and value. And yet, he didn't think he'd ever seen anything or anyone more beautiful than this woman.

She waited for him, unmoving, allowing his touch. Allowing him to slowly lower the zip of her gown. It pooled at her feet and he lifted her free of it.

"We're going to make love now, aren't we?" she asked.

"Yes."

"Will it be like our first kiss?"

He couldn't help smiling. "Better, I hope."

She flashed him a sparkling look, filled with feminine mystery and earthy desire. "Prove it," she whispered.

He lifted an eyebrow. "A challenge?"

"Are you up to it?" Shayla teased.

Oh, hell, yes. "Ask me that again in an hour, though I suspect you'll know the answer yourself by then."

He reached for her, but instead of touching her, he plucked one of the clips from her hair. The heavy mass loosened, edging downward toward her shoulders. He removed the next two and her hair uncoiled, cascading like an ebony waterfall over her shoulders and down her back. He fisted his hand in the strands, surprised by the thickness and weight of it. It seemed too much for her slender neck to bear. And yet, she did.

Gently, he tipped her back onto the bed. She lifted her leg and braced her high-heeled shoe against his abdomen. The tip of her stiletto scraped across the sensitive skin. "Do you mind?"

"Careful," he warned. "You wouldn't want to cut our evening short."

She laughed, soft and low. "No, I wouldn't want that."

He slid her shoe from her foot before lifting her other leg

and repeating the process. Her stockings followed. Finally, he eased away the remaining few scraps of silk and lace, baring her to his gaze. She epitomized everything he'd heard about women from the South. She was all velvet softness and stunning feminine curves. But beneath he could see the shapely sweep of well-toned muscle and sinew. Strength concealed beneath silk. Did the dichotomy also represent the true nature of the woman?

His own clothing followed the same path as hers, and then he was beside her, drawing her into his arms. She slid beneath him and wrapped herself around him. Draco could feel the hammer of her heart against his, hear the hitch of her breath and feel the flush that seemed to flow from her very core. He cupped her, cupped the quickening warmth, and slowly stoked the fire until it threatened to consume them both.

"Draco," she cried, surging toward him, opening to him, nearly sending him straight over the edge.

"I'm right here, sweetheart. Hang on a moment longer." He protected himself before settling between her thighs and moistening himself in her heat. "I don't think I can wait. Fast and furious this first time. Slow and teasing next."

She stiffened ever so slightly. "Maybe we should go with slow this first time. Very slow."

A short, hard laugh exploded from him. "Not sure that's possible."

She held him off with a delicate hand that possessed surprising strength. "You don't understand. Earlier when I said I'd never done this before, I meant that I've never done *any* of this before. If you'd be so kind, I'd really prefer slow until I get the hang of this."

He froze. "You're a virgin?"

She smiled, that enchanting smile that seemed to befuddle every thought in his head. "Not for much longer."

Draco fought for control. Fought to pull away. Fought to

shoehorn honor ahead of desire. He lifted onto his forearms. "Why?" he groaned. "Why me?"

Humor flashed through her dark gaze. "How could I not?" She gathered up his hand, laced it with her fingers so their palms joined. "When you seduced me with one touch."

His amusement matched hers. "*I* seduced *you?* I'm beginning to think it was the other way around." The last few seconds of conversation had helped him regain his control enough to ask one final question, at the very least to slow things down. "Are you sure?"

She pulled him back into her arms, looping her arms around his neck. "Positive."

"But no pressure, right?"

Her soft laugh arrowed through him, leaving him teetering on a knife-sharp precipice. "None."

"I'm relieved to hear it."

No matter what it took, he'd make this night one of the most special of her life. He drew out the preliminaries, stroking the softness of her breasts and belly. Tracing leisurely circles from her toes to her upper thighs. Sketching kisses from hip to hip before tenderly finding the heart of her. Urging her up and up and up until she hovered just within reach of the peak.

Satisfied that her pleasure was at its highest point, he carefully mated his body to hers, easing into her. Teasing and tempting as he penetrated. Moving. Then thrusting. Finally, driving. Edging her closer and closer to that tantalizing moment of climax. She matched his rhythm like a woman born to the dance. Her skin acquired a pearlescent sheen, flushed with passion. And when she gazed up at him, her eyes were ocean-deep, midnight-black and filled with the wonder of newfound desire.

He watched her climb, watched her climax knot the muscles of her body and burn in her eyes. Heard the pleasure of it ripped from her throat as she bowed backward, helpless beneath the onslaught. And he followed her over, one with her in the ultimate melding of male to female. Never had it been like this with any other woman. And he knew—knew beyond doubt and to the very core—that it never would be again. Only with this woman would he experience a bond that took him to such heights.

The aftermath hit and they collapsed into each other's arms. A long moment passed where neither of them had the breath or energy to speak, a moment out of time. A moment where, as a Dante, Draco recognized the power of The Inferno and surrendered to it.

He didn't understand how it had happened or why, but this woman was his soul mate, their destinies woven together in a tapestry just beginning. He had no idea what shape the final picture would take, only that they were bound together from this time forward. He couldn't help but wonder how Shayla would react when she discovered the extent of their bond.

Gently, he rolled to one side and tucked her close. One thing he knew for certain, it would take time to claim this woman. She was quicksilver, impossible to pin down, held only through desire and temptation. She would have to come to him, be coaxed into his arms, his bed and his life through patience—not something he excelled at. But win her he would and before she knew it she'd wake up with a ring on her finger and a husband at her side.

He thought they slept for a short time because when he moved again it felt as though the night had deepened. With a groan, he levered onto an elbow and forked his fingers into her hair. She blinked sleepily at him, her smile filled with sweet delight.

"Hello, there," she murmured.

"I believe you had a question a while ago," he said in a

low, husky voice. "Something about whether our lovemaking would be as good as our kisses. Care to offer an opinion?"

"That's right. I did wonder about that." She wrinkled her brow, pretending to give it serious consideration. "Your kisses are definitely superb. I had serious doubts that anything could surpass them."

"Well, hell," he grumbled. "Now you have me worried."

"As for your lovemaking…"

"Seriously worried."

"…and taking into consideration that I don't have a basis for comparison…"

"Duly noted."

Her teasing expression faded, replaced by a satisfaction he couldn't mistake. "It was beyond imagination, Draco." Remnants of their shared passion underscored her comment. "I never realized it could be so wonderful."

He kissed the tip of her nose. "So you admit that we Dantes—or at least this Dante—is talented in more arenas than just the jewelry business?"

The instant the question left his mouth she stiffened beneath him, staring in shocked disbelief. "*What* did you say?" The question came out low and furious and filled with feminine outrage.

He froze. "What's wrong?" Because, clearly, something was. It must have been something he said. It sure as hell couldn't have been anything he'd done. That had been as close to perfection as he'd ever experienced. "Shayla?"

Her breathing came swift and shallow, almost panicked. "You never told me your last name. Remember, we agreed? When we first met, you just said Draco."

He stared blankly. "What does that matter now? We're not at the reception and I promise I won't tell the rest of my relatives that you crashed the party."

She shoved at his chest. "But you're a Dante."

He kept her pinned in place, determined to have this out, suspecting she'd run if he let her go. "I brought you up here in a private elevator. I used a key, for crying out loud. Who the hell would have access to this floor and this suite if not a Dante?"

"You told me the apartments were reserved for clients. I assumed you were a client of the Dantes." She thumped his chest with her fist. He reluctantly shifted back. The instant he did she squirmed out from beneath him and snatched the sheet against her chest, putting as much distance between them as the bed allowed. "So, it's true? You…you're a *Dante?*"

He glared at her, offended. "You say that as though it were a dirty word. What the hell's wrong with being a Dante?"

Shayla scooped up the wings of her hair and hooked them behind her ears. How could this have happened? How could she not have realized? The one time, the very first time, she allowed passion to override common sense *this* happened. She'd given her virginity to the one man she should have avoided at all costs, whose family had destroyed her own and left them utterly destitute. The family who, according to her grandmother, were responsible for the death of Shayla's parents. How was that possible? *Why wasn't Draco on the list?* If it had been she'd have instantly made the connection and none of this would have happened.

She fought to keep from weeping. In a blink of the eye, something so spectacularly right had turned hideously wrong. It was as though the fates were conspiring against her. What next? Would her proposal to the Dantes also end in disaster because of her foolishness this night? Would Derek Algier call and tell her he'd changed his mind about hiring her? Would her precious chance at freedom evaporate with the coming of the morning sun?

Draco continued to wait for Shayla to answer his question,

looking hard and fierce and dangerously male, epitomizing the nature of his name. She moistened her lips, scrambling to come up with an excuse he'd buy.

"I guess there's nothing wrong with being a Dante," she conceded. Okay, lied. "I just… I didn't know and—"

He slowly relaxed, sliding back into his role of lover. "Got it. You're intimidated."

"Intimidated!" More than anything she wanted to escape the bed, but considering she'd be confronting the cocky bastard totally nude, she forced herself to stay put. She struggled to keep any hint of insult from her voice. "I'm not intimidated," she corrected with a calm she was far from feeling.

His hazel eyes narrowed, the gold flecks glittering a clear warning. "But for some reason, my being a Dante makes a difference."

She faltered, not quite certain how to respond, other than to use one small tidbit her grandmother had mentioned in passing. "The Dante men have something of a…reputation, shall we say?" Based on what just happened, a well-deserved reputation, she grudgingly admitted to herself. So, maybe he wasn't being cocky so much as honest.

"And you think that because I'm a Dante all I'm after is a one-night stand?"

It was a tad like the pot calling the kettle black, considering she'd been after just that, herself. Even so, she met his gaze unflinchingly. "Yes."

He shrugged. "Time will prove otherwise," he alarmed her by saying.

Dear heaven. He couldn't mean that, could he? But searching his expression she realized he meant precisely that. She crouched in a silken nest of rumpled sheets, at a total loss. What did she do now? How did she gracefully extricate herself from the situation? She wasn't interested in continuing a relationship with him after this one night, though caution dictated she not risk the loss of her fingers by feeding him that particular piece of information. She was also at a serious disadvantage since she was new to this type of situation. Maybe if she were more sexually experienced she could figure a way to soothe his male ego while she slipped out the door.

Before she had a chance to devise a plan, he caught her hand in his and tugged. Unmistakable want fired in his eyes. "Any other objections, sweetheart, or can we move on?"

More objections than she could possibly express. She needed to make a decision and fast, before he seduced her options right out of her. Either she left now, the smartest choice available to her, or she returned to his arms and allowed him to prove yet again what he did better—kiss or make love.

The first time with him she could rationalize. She hadn't known who he was. And then there had been that overpowering attraction. She stirred uneasily, aware that the warm throbbing in her palm hadn't diminished. Clearly, that attraction hadn't dissipated, despite discovering his full name. But she knew his identity now. His family had deliberately ruined hers, a fact that—according to Grandmother Charleston—had indirectly led to the death of her parents. Whatever the actual truth, the bankruptcy of her family's business had changed her life forever.

"Shayla?" Draco studied her expression. "Apparently you still have concerns. Maybe this will help."

Before she had time to protest, he leaned in, his passionate kiss the first taking. Then his hands took possession of her. He'd learned a lot about her during the few hours they'd been together, how to arouse her with a few clever strokes. And finally he took her under with his words, a tender suggestion that melted her resistance and made her hungry to experience his lovemaking again. Just one more time.

If she left now it wouldn't change anything. What was done was done. She couldn't regain what she'd given him even if she wanted to, any more than she could change how it would affect her meeting with his relatives. Tomorrow she'd turn twenty-five and wing her way out of the country. And truth be told, the memories of this night would linger in her thoughts for the rest of her life. Would it be so terrible to add to those memories, to stack up a few more to take with her when she left? To be mad and impetuous one last time? Who would know that she'd given herself to a Dante, other than herself? Well, and Draco.

Did she leave…or enjoy his lovemaking one more time? It was an easy decision to make.

Shayla surrendered with a sigh. The instant she reached for him and pulled him closer, heat ignited between them, dampening any lingering doubts. She'd spent a lifetime living according to her grandmother's dictates, focused first on her studies, then on making as much money as quickly as possible in order to repay her college expenses.

Come morning she'd complete her familial obligations by stepping into the role of family negotiator while she bartered with the Dantes. Once through, she'd bid Draco a fond farewell and claim her freedom. But tonight would be hers. An indulgence. The one-night stand she'd accused him of wanting and another step toward her independence.

Draco drew her under him and mated his body to hers in one swift move. She gasped as intense pleasure ripped her apart and scattered the pieces. She wrapped her legs around his waist and moved with him. Soared with him. Shot straight through the clouds and winged toward the searing heart of the sun, all within his arms. She heard the low rumble echo through his chest as his climax approached. Knowing she drove him so hard and high so quickly sent her tumbling up, teetering on a peak that had her gasping for breath, before launching into thin air in a delicious freefall.

"Draco…!" His name burst from her lungs in a half sob.

"I know, I know, I know," he chanted.

He drove home, losing himself in her heat. His head reared back and his throat convulsed. Then he said one single word. *Shayla*. He stamped it with such passion and possessiveness, it was as though he laid claim to her, changing the meaning so that it would forevermore be linked to him. Just as her body was linked to his. Just as her heart had become linked to his.

No. Oh, no, no, *no*.

She struggled to deny the possibility of it, scrambled for some other explanation. She was being foolish, caught up in the newness of their lovemaking, lost in a moment of intense desire. There was no connection, nothing to this Inferno that burned in her palm. Their joining was only temporary. Come morning she was leaving, and this night with Draco would fade to a fond and distant memory.

But even as she fought, sleep settled over her, just as she settled into the warmth of Draco's arms, accepting his possession. Accepting the rightness of his protective hold. She reached for him, cleaved to him. And with a tiny sigh of surrender, she linked her hand with his, palm to palm, cementing their bond.

When Shayla awoke she felt the morning through the darkness swathing the room and discovered Draco missing from the bed. She glanced toward the windows. They were tightly shuttered once again, delaying the advent of a new day—her birthday.

She stretched sore, abused muscles and sat up, shoving her hair from her face. Time to get up and leave. She had a lot to accomplish in the next few hours. But part of her regretted. Regretted the need to leave both the bed and the man. Regretted that she couldn't squeeze in one more day and night of pleasure. Before she could escape the bed, Draco returned to the room. It took only one look to realize something was terribly wrong. It also stripped her emotions bare. Acutely self-conscious, she covered herself with the sheet.

"Draco?" She despised the hint of nervousness that tripped through her voice and slithered down her spine. "Is there a problem?"

"Why don't we start with this?" Her beaded bag dangled from one hand. In the other he held the leather pouch.

Shayla stiffened in alarm. How could she have been so careless? Even more damning, how could she have let her purse and its precious contents out of her sight for even one short minute? She must have lost her mind. *Had* lost her mind the instant Draco had put his hands on her. His mouth on her. Had taken possession of her, body and soul.

He took a step toward her, moving from the shadows that enshrouded the outer edges of the room to a position beneath the recessed spotlights in his bedroom ceiling. The light haloed him, giving him the appearance of a dark angel bent on vengeance. Or maybe he'd transformed himself into the dragon for which he'd been named.

"That's my purse, as you well know." She held out her hand. "If you don't mind?"

"Oh, but I do mind." He untied the leather pouch, extracted one of the six parcel papers from inside and unfolded it. A diamond tumbled into his palm, burning with brilliance. "This is a fire diamond," he said.

Or was it an accusation? An odd roughness crisped the edges of his voice, something bitter-hot and laden with long-ago pain, the words overflowing with a subtext she couldn't begin to understand. But it was definitely there.

"How dare you rifle through my purse?" Her response escaped in heavily accented Southern affront. "You have no right—"

"These are all fire diamonds," he stated, more forcefully this time, the statement slicing like honed steel.

The overhead light gathered up the unmistakable sparkle captured within his palm and reflected the brilliance, seeming to fill the room with a fiery glitter—a glitter echoed in the equally fiery gold of Draco's eyes. What an idiot she'd been. This was no ordinary man. Those eyes. The hair. The stunning good looks and charm, a charm now eclipsed by a tough, ruthless edge. It all screamed Dante, even the ruthlessness, a quality her grandmother had long warned was endemic to his family. How terrifyingly ironic that she was now in a position to confirm that firsthand.

Shayla fought to speak past a throat gone bone-dry. "Yes," she finally said. "I do believe they are fire diamonds."

"What the *hell* are you doing with them?"

She escaped from the bed with as much dignity as she could muster, winding the sheet tightly around herself in order to preserve some shred of modesty. Ridiculous considering what they'd been busy doing all night and how many times and ways they'd done it. "They're mine. Give them back this minute."

His eyes narrowed. "Bull. Dantes doesn't sell loose fire diamonds. The only way to purchase them is set in jewelry. So, unless you were foolish enough to pry the diamonds out of their setting…?" He lifted an eyebrow in silent demand.

"I don't owe you an explanation. The diamonds belong to me and unless you can prove otherwise, I suggest you return them to where you found them."

She held out her hand and fixed him with an implacable

gaze. He didn't argue, which surprised her, but folded the diamond back into the blue-and-white parcel paper and returned it to the leather drawstring bag. Jerking the strings closed, he tucked it into her beaded purse and lobbed it toward her.

"You might want to get the clasp on that bag fixed. Everything fell out when I tossed your purse onto the couch last night."

"I'll get right on that." Relief flooded through her now that she had her handbag back in her possession, a very short-lived relief.

"And what about this?" He flipped up his index and middle fingers, a folded piece of paper tucked between them, a very damning piece of paper that listed the main Dante players and their job positions. "Care to explain this?"

How could she have forgotten the list? And of more urgent interest, why wasn't his name on it? Why hadn't he been mentioned in any of the Dante literature or internet research she and her grandmother had done? This morning just kept getting better and better. Gathering the shreds of her dignity, Shayla lifted her chin. "It's none of your business."

His expression iced over, assuming a merciless aspect. "When it comes to the Dantes, it's very much my business." He stepped closer. "You claimed you didn't know me. A lie, sweetheart?"

She refused to back down. "Did you see your name on that list?"

"Damn it, Shayla. What the *hell* is going on?"

"Nothing illicit," she retorted, stung. "It just happens that I have a meeting with certain members of your family today and I was dismayed when I discovered your identity because I didn't want a—" she almost said *one-night stand* and snatched back the words at the last possible second "—an intimate relationship with one Dante to affect my meeting with the others. That's why I crashed the reception last night. I wanted to get a look at who I'd be meeting today." Not that she'd managed even that. Instead, she'd allowed desire to get in the way of her promise to her grandmother. Shame filled her. "Just out of curiosity, why *wasn't* your name on my list?"

"I handle gemstones on a regular basis. Sometimes I carry them. For security reasons I prefer to remain off the grid. Now, about this meeting. Who, what and why, Shayla?" He snapped out the questions. "Not to mention, when?"

At the reminder, she inhaled sharply. "What time is it?"

"Nine."

"Oh, dear heaven." She scooped up her crumpled clothes from the floor and made a beeline for the bathroom. "I have to go. Now."

He caught her arm before she could escape the room. "Not until you explain what's going on."

Desire sizzled through her at his touch, a desire she fought to ignore with only limited success. "I'm not at liberty to explain. Nor do I owe you an explanation."

"Even after last night?"

She forced herself to meet his furious gaze, to cling to every ounce of self-control at her disposal. "Even after last night. One has nothing to do with the other."

"I disagree."

If only he weren't touching her. If only he'd let her go. "Please, Draco," she whispered. "I have to leave. Perhaps we could talk after the meeting."

He continued to hold her and she could tell he waged an inner debate, though she didn't have a clue what he was thinking. Last night he'd been so open and giving, so generous in the way he'd made love to her. In the space of a few minutes he'd gone from the man with whom she'd shared unbearable emotional intimacy to someone hard and ferocious. She shivered. A dragon in fact, as well as name.

"Get dressed." He released her arm, but for some reason the desire didn't ebb as she expected. "Then I'll see you out."

She flinched. Without another word she crossed to the bathroom and shut the door with a decisive click. After a quick shower, she pulled on her gown from the previous night, struggling against a wave of humiliation at wearing an evening dress during daylight hours. She'd return to her dingy little motel room in the previous night's finery, looking like…

Color swept into her face and she deliberately clamped down on every stray thought and emotion. She used Draco's comb to yank the tangles from her hair. Without her clips she couldn't put it up and she most certainly wasn't going out there and scramble around on the floor looking for them. Shoving her feet into her heels, she exited the bathroom.

Draco stood at the threshold leading to the hallway, leaning a shoulder against the doorjamb. He'd used the time she'd been in the bathroom to dress, though in far more casual clothes than what she had available. He'd also chosen unrelieved black; the only color the hard gold glitter of his eyes.

"Would you mind calling me a cab?" she asked with a calm she was far from feeling.

"Already done." He swept a hand in the general direction of the living room and—hallelujah—the exit. "After you."

She hesitated a split second, then led with her chin. Crossing the room, she paused in the doorway, waiting for him to move out of her path. He didn't. He simply watched and waited, no doubt curious to see what she'd do. Well, her grandmother hadn't raised a coward. Shayla might have made some improper choices the night before, but by God she'd own them and take the consequences.

Without a word, she pressed past him. Just that brief contact stirred a storm of emotion. Memories of their night together spun through her, making her dizzy with the sensations they roused. The way Draco had caressed her. The lingering kisses he'd feathered across every inch of her body. The strength of his hold. The way he'd taken her, easing her passage, managing to be powerful and tender and giving all at the same time.

She'd never forget how it had been with him, nor the fact that he was the first man to make love to her. He'd changed her, indelibly branding her. He was part of her and always would be. The thought filled her with anxiety and she tucked it away for some future time when she could take it out and analyze it with the attention it deserved.

Draco shifted and the moment passed, even if the remnants still clung. He called for the elevator and keyed it in for the garage level. At her startled glance, he lifted a shoulder. "Even though it's Saturday, I didn't think you'd appreciate making the Walk of Shame through the main reception area for Dantes' corporate offices, especially if you have a meeting with Sev and Primo later today. You never know who you may run into."

Oh, God, please don't let her cry at his thoughtfulness. "Thank you," she whispered. "I appreciate your consideration."

"I arranged for the cab to meet us at the side entrance. With luck no one will know you spent the night with me. Although…"

She glanced up at him in alarm. "Although?"

"My grandfather, Primo, has a knack for hearing what you'd like to keep quiet."

"My grandmother is the same way." Though she couldn't

imagine how Leticia Charleston might possibly discover that Shayla had slept with the enemy. "I'd prefer it if this could be our secret."

The doors slid open and Draco stepped in front of her, preventing her escape. "Just out of curiosity, would you have slept with me if I'd told you from the start that I was a Dante?"

She didn't bother to sugarcoat it. "No."

Draco's expression hardened and he gave a curt nod. "Thought so. Unfortunately, you've neglected to take into consideration one small detail."

Escape. She just wanted to escape. She stared longingly over his shoulder toward the exit. "What's that?"

He startled her by taking her hand in his, allowing the heat to pulse between them. "The Inferno has other plans for you."

Releasing her, they exited the elevator. He escorted her across the concrete garage toward a steel door that opened onto a side street. Her stiletto heels echoed with every step while the throb centered in her palm matched the rhythmic tempo. A cab stood waiting. Ever the gentleman, Draco held the door for her and helped her in.

"Where to?" he asked.

Until that moment, it hadn't occurred to her that she might have to tell him the name of her motel. But it made perfect sense. He'd want to know where to track her down. One glance at his set expression warned that he hadn't finished saying all he intended to about their night together. Since she couldn't bring herself to mention the fleabag where she'd booked her room, she chose the only other viable option. She lied.

"I'm staying at the Mark Hopkins," she said.

Leaning into the front passenger window, Draco handed the driver a couple of folded bills. "The Mark," he repeated.

And then he stepped back, his gaze fixed on her. This time she didn't have a bit of trouble reading his expression. Both threat and promise were implicit in his hazel eyes.

Three

The minute the cab pulled away and vanished around a corner, Draco reached into his pocket and palmed the diamond concealed there.

The stone pressed into his skin, hard and cold, and yet brimming with fire. He pulled it out and studied the flash of color. No question that it was a fire diamond, though something about it looked different. Off. Until he could analyze it in the lab he wouldn't be able to say what. Nor would he be able to tell if it was one of the six he'd been swindled out of all those years ago. Stones he'd spent a solid decade tracking down, diamond by damnable diamond, until only two were still missing.

One thing he knew beyond a shadow of a doubt. If this diamond had anything to do with Shayla's appointment at Dantes, he intended to be there. In fact, if Primo and Sev had known about the diamonds, they'd have insisted he attend. In the meantime, he'd analyze the stone before he crashed the party, and see if the information he gained wouldn't give them some small advantage in whatever negotiations were imminent.

He stopped by the receptionist's desk on the way to the lab. The company always arranged for someone to man the station over the weekend since many Dantes events occurred then. Or they often had guests in one or more of the penthouse suites who might require assistance during their stay.

"'Morning, Laura."

She greeted him with a friendly smile. "Hello, Mr. Dante. What can I do for you?"

"What time are Primo and Sev arriving for the meeting with Shayla?" He paused. "Damn. Forgot her last name."

"Hang on. I have it here." She called up a calendar on her computer with a punch of a button. "Charleston. Shayla Charleston. The meeting is scheduled to begin at ten-thirty. They'll be using the Jade conference room."

Perfect. An hour would give him just enough time to prepare. "Give me a call when Ms. Charleston arrives, will you? I'll be in the lab."

"Certainly, Mr. Dante."

As it turned out, it didn't take long for the preliminary assessment. What he discovered stunned him. He was fairly certain it would also stun his grandfather, Primo, and his cousin, Sev. Shortly after Laura alerted him to everyone's arrival, Draco entered the conference room through a side door.

Shayla sat in profile. She had presence, he'd give her that, capturing everyone's attention without even trying. She'd once again swept her mass of dark hair into an elegant knot and wore a crisp, tailored skirt and jacket, the lemony color adding a ray of sunshine in contrast to the more somber suits and ties. He couldn't place the designer, but it was definitely a high-priced label, just as her evening gown had been.

He caught Sev's eye and gave him a signal indicating he wanted to sit in on the meeting. His cousin nodded and Draco took a chair at the opposite end of the table from Shayla, beside his grandfather. He suppressed a smile when she studiously avoided looking his way, a fact noted by several of his relatives.

If she wanted to keep their relationship a secret, she was going about it the exact wrong way. She should have acknowledged him. By ignoring him, she might as well have put up a huge sign saying, "We slept together, but I don't want anyone to figure it out." And his sign would say, "Too late. They just have and Primo is *not* happy."

As though to bring home his point, Primo placed a hand on Draco's shoulder, and growled in Italian, "Why must you always be the troublemaker? Explain this to me."

Draco didn't bother trying to explain it. How could he explain something that came as naturally as breathing? Answering in Italian, he simply stated, "She's mine."

Primo's shaggy gray brows shot upward and his hard gold eyes widened. "So Rafe was not the only one Inferno-struck last night."

Draco kept his expression bland. Apparently his brother had taken his suggestion and faked a run-in with The Inferno with Larkin Thatcher. That would prove interesting. "I guess not." He shoved back his chair and stood. "If you'll excuse me, Primo?"

Since it was readily apparent to everyone at the table that he and Shayla were involved, there was no point in pretending. He circled the table and took the chair next to her.

"What are you doing?" she murmured beneath her breath. Alarm rippled through the question. "Get away from me."

"They already know."

"I'm well aware of that fact. Primo made it abundantly clear. But you don't have to rub it in their faces."

She'd caught him by surprise. "You speak Italian?"

"And several other languages, as well." She continued to avoid meeting his gaze. "What I don't understand is why you felt the need to tell them about last night."

"I didn't. You did."

A blush mounted her cheeks. "I most certainly did not." Her Southern accent deepened, blurring her words. "I never said a blessed thing."

"You didn't have to say anything. Let's just say you have an expressive face."

She started to say something, then broke off and snatched a quick breath. "Okay, fine. I'll just have to deal with the embarrassment and stay focused on business."

Embarrassment? For some reason the word irritated the hell out of him. He struggled to keep his voice pitched low. "Why does it embarrass you that we were together last night?" He gathered her hand in his, feeling the flare of The Inferno when their fingers collided and meshed and their palms bumped together. "For that matter, why does it matter what my family suspects? Unless one of us confirms it, they won't know for certain."

"You're touching me. Mix that with whispering and you get a bucket load of guilt."

"Odd. I don't feel the least guilty. Or embarrassed."

He leaned on the final word, hoping for a reaction. And got one. She made the mistake of looking directly at him and he felt that look arrow straight to his groin. It was a wonder the air didn't combust between them. She must have read his reaction in his expression.

"Darn it, Draco. Cut that out. Go sit somewhere else."

"Can't." It was the God's honest truth. No way in hell was he going to stand and provide proof of his attraction for her.

Comprehension had her color deepening. "Why are you

at this meeting?" she asked in despair. "Why couldn't you have had the decency to stay away?"

"Maybe I would have if it hadn't been for this…"

He opened his hand, revealing the diamond he'd taken from her. He'd put it in a protective Lucite box and sent the box shooting toward the center of the conference table. It spun dead center, the diamond inside spitting out shards of brilliant color, igniting the fire buried in its depth.

"It would seem Ms. Charleston has something interesting to show us," Draco informed his family.

Sev snatched up the case and studied it. "Son of a— It's a fire diamond." His gaze narrowed on Shayla, filled with suspicion. "Where did you get this?"

"It's not one of ours," Draco offered helpfully.

Dead silence greeted his comment. "What do you mean it is not ours?" Primo finally demanded. "How is this possible?"

"It is, indeed, a fire diamond," Draco confirmed. "But it doesn't come from one of our mines. Which begs the question…" He swiveled his chair so it faced Shayla. "Where the hell did it come from?"

She'd put the few minutes he'd given her to good use, wrapping herself in an artificial calm. "That diamond, as well as the others in my possession, came from a Charleston mine."

Lazz, the family's CFO, frowned. "I thought your mines were played out years ago."

And that's when it clicked. Draco stiffened. Charleston. Shayla Charleston. As in…Charlestons, the now-defunct jewelry empire. They'd been in direct competition with Dantes decades ago until poor management and the inability to compete against Dantes' fire diamonds had driven them out of business.

"We also thought the mines were played out. A recent

survey has proven that not only aren't they depleted, but they contain fire diamonds." She leaned forward to emphasize her point. "Fire diamonds superior to the Dantes'."

"That's not possible," Sev objected.

She set the leather bag on the table in front of her. "This is a small sample of what we've extracted. Let me repeat that—a *small* sample. You're welcome to examine them at your leisure. I realize it'll take time."

Primo waved his hand toward Draco, indicating he should take care of the analysis and grading. "So." He leaned back in his chair and folded his arms across his chest. "Letty has her own supply of fire diamonds. I am surprised she is giving us advance warning of her intentions. Or is it more in the nature of a threat?"

He tilted his head to one side, and fixed the power of his gaze on Shayla. Draco had seen men of immense power and position crumble beneath that gaze. But not Shayla. She met him look for look.

"It's not a warning, Mr. Dante, or a threat." Her smile flickered to life. Draco considered it one of her most potent weapons. "It's a proposition. My grandmother is offering you the exclusive opportunity to lease our mines."

Sev focused his gaze on Shayla as well, one identical to his grandfather's. "Why?"

"It's quite simple. We're not in the business anymore. My parents, who probably could have revitalized Charlestons, are dead and I have neither the interest nor the ability to run the company," she admitted with endearing candor. "To be blunt, we simply aren't in the position to mine the stones or cut them—other than this initial lot—let alone create jewelry with them. You are."

Primo weighed the information for a long moment before speaking. "There are others who would pay your grandmother a fortune for the mining rights. Competitors of Dantes. Considering she has always blamed us for putting Charlestons out of business and it is in her nature to exact revenge…" He spread his hands wide and shrugged. "Why does she not use this opportunity to her advantage?"

"My grandmother is older now. Losing my parents hit her hard."

Primo nodded. "I heard about the accident. Having lost one of my own sons, along with his wife, I can sympathize with Letty. But it is your loss that grieves me most."

Tears welled in her eyes and she blinked them back, impressing the hell out of Draco with her control. "Thank you."

Primo inclined his head. "Would you be offended if we discuss the situation in Italian?"

"Not at all." She sent him a charming smile. "Would you be offended if I listened in?"

Primo stilled. "You speak Italian?"

"*Parlo italiano fluente*," she admitted.

"Fluently and with an excellent accent," Draco murmured. Then he raised his voice. "In that case… Shayla, would you mind waiting in my office while my family and I discuss the situation?"

She slid back her chair and stood. "Not at all."

Draco escorted her from the conference room and down the hallway to his office. "Help yourself to coffee," he offered. "I made a fresh pot a short time ago."

Before she could guess his intentions he leaned in for a swift kiss. Their lips joined, parted, then met again for a slower, more thorough exploration. Her breath sighed from her lungs, filled with hunger, yet shaded with regret. He wished there were time for more than a swift, stolen kiss. But his family waited and he didn't doubt for a minute that if he delayed any longer they'd guess why.

"I have to go," he reluctantly informed her.

She drew back. "And we shouldn't be mixing business with pleasure, anyway."

"We'll have plenty of time for pleasure later," he reassured her. "Once this is settled."

She turned abruptly. "I look forward to hearing your family's decision," she said.

Her formality amused him, given what they'd been doing a few short hours earlier. "It shouldn't take long."

He returned to the conference room, interrupting a heated exchange between his cousins, who debated Leticia Charleston's motivations for her offer. No one commented on the delay, though Primo pulled out a cigar and swept him with a quick, encompassing stare as he lit up, breaking more California laws and codes than Draco cared to consider.

While the debate continued to rage, Draco leaned back in his chair and took it all in. He wished he remembered more of the history between the Dantes and the Charlestons and made a point of researching the facts as soon as possible. But one small detail captured his full attention.

Primo described Leticia Charleston as a vengeful woman.

Draco understood that quality. Possessed that quality. Intended to exercise his thirst for vengeance to the fullest when he found the person responsible for swindling him out of a half dozen of Dantes' finest and rarest fire diamonds, an event that had taken place a full decade before. He'd been all of twenty at the time and overinflated with his own self-importance, eager to prove himself. That single mistake had changed him.

Permanently.

Primo often referred to him as the Dante troublemaker, but that wasn't quite accurate. Draco was possibly the most deceptive of the Dantes since he hid certain elements of his personality behind a congenial, mischievous mask. But he found he could easily slip into Leticia's shoes and consider the matter from her point of view. Analyze how best she might go about destroying the Dantes.

Conversation wafted over him while his family discussed their options. Once Draco satisfied himself that he'd weighed all the possibilities, he lifted a finger. Silence descended.

Primo waved his cigar in Draco's direction. Smoke sketched the path his hand had taken. "Speak."

"Let's start with what we know," he suggested. "First off, Leticia Charleston wants to alert us to the fact that she now owns a supply of fire diamonds. Based on an admittedly quick examination, I'm forced to concur with what Shayla told us. At first blush, they appear superior to ours."

"But they're real? They haven't been treated?"

"Yes, they're real," Draco said in response to Sev's questions. "And no, they haven't been treated. Unfortunately, I can't give you more specifics until I've had time to run them through a full analysis other than to say that, with a few rare exceptions, they're better than what we have."

Ferocious denial exploded around him. Sev's voice cut across them all. "You can't be serious."

"I'm dead serious," Draco replied. Since he was the expert, there wasn't much they could say to refute the claim, though they wanted to. Badly. "Second. She's offering us first refusal to lease her mines. Why?" He fixed his gaze on his grandfather. "There's bad blood between us. And you described her as a vengeful woman."

Primo took his time blowing out a stream of aromatic smoke. "Cold. Bitter. A nasty creature."

Coming from Primo it was a damning condemnation. Draco nodded. "As mentioned, she could easily peddle her diamonds to any of our competitors. But the best I can figure, she came to us for one reason."

"Which is?" Lazz asked impatiently.

"This gives her a sword to hold over our heads. If we don't dance to her tune, she drops the sword and sells her stones elsewhere. The power and control are hers to wield. For as long as her mines cough up diamonds that trump our own, she can name her price and we'll pay it. Otherwise Dantes loses its status as the only jewelry empire in the world to possess fire diamonds. Worse, if she eventually chooses to sell to our competitors, to all our competitors *except* us," he emphasized, "we'll have a lower grade of diamonds than everyone else possesses. Our fall from grace will be abrupt and hard—"

"—and no doubt be met with tears of joy from jewelers around the world," Sev said sourly.

Lazz nodded in agreement. "Ultimately, it could put us in a very precarious position, business-wise."

"It is logical," Primo agreed.

"If we don't nail the Charleston woman to an ironclad contract, she'll screw us over," Sev stated. "She'll play her game until it bores her and then sell elsewhere."

Primo sighed wearily. "I am forced to admit, it would be in keeping with her nature."

"Then we agree to lease her mines?"

Lazz shook his head. "We agree to examine the stones and insist on our own survey of the mines. We investigate the offer top-to-bottom and then push for the best possible terms."

Sev grimaced. "I suspect the best possible is going to be damn poor."

Draco didn't disagree. "So, we take it one step at a time and see if we can't figure out a way to beat the Charleston woman at her own game."

"And what about Shayla?" Primo's question dropped like a boulder onto a mirror-calm lake, sending out huge, disruptive waves. He studied the tip of his glowing cigar. "I am forced to wonder…what is her purpose in all this? Letty has always blamed us for the death of her son. Does the granddaughter also blame us? Does Shayla have the same thirst for vengeance as her grandmother?"

Draco turned on his grandfather. "Are we responsible for her father's death?"

Primo shook his head. "No more than we are responsible for the depletion of the Charleston mines. But there is much you do not know, much I can explain at a more appropriate time." He flicked ash from his cigar toward an ashtray. "But that does not mean that Shayla does not blame, that she has not been taught to blame. We must give serious consideration to her role in this chess match."

"Shayla's role is quite simple. She's mine." The words escaped before Draco could control them. But he meant every one of them. "She has nothing to do with this."

"She has everything to do with this," Lazz insisted. "She's the one who approached us, not Leticia. How do you know she didn't seduce you as part of her grandmother's plan?"

Primo grimaced. "This troubles me, as well. Though my instinct says Shayla is a good person, we do not yet know her nature well enough to judge whether she hides a thirst for revenge behind the congenial mask she wears."

Draco literally saw red, the heat of it blurring the edges of his vision. It took every ounce of self-control to keep from vaulting across the table and decking someone. "She isn't hiding behind a mask," he rasped out in reply. "She's not like that."

"You've only known her one night!" Lazz snapped.

Draco held out his hand, palm up. "We were chosen for each other."

Sev interrupted, stemming Lazz's simmering retort. "We have to consider every possibility, Draco. Surely you must see that? From what Primo has said, I wouldn't put anything past

Leticia Charleston. Until we see how this plays out, Shayla is suspect. At the very least it puts the two of you on opposite sides of an intensely adversarial business deal."

"Then we'll keep business separate from our personal relationship," Draco shot back.

"I've been there with Francesca and, trust me, it wasn't pretty," his cousin replied, referring to his own experiences when he and his wife first met. "My situation was bad enough. What you're dealing with will be far worse."

Draco shrugged. "So I'll deal."

"And if we have to take the Charlestons down?" Lazz asked. "How will Shayla react to that? For that matter, how will you?"

Draco didn't hesitate. "You know my first loyalty is to my family. When Shayla becomes my wife, her loyalty will be to me, which means to the Dantes."

Lazz snorted, and he and Sev exchanged ironic glances. "You don't know women very well, do you?"

"I know Shayla that well."

"After just one night?" Sev asked skeptically.

Draco climbed to his feet and confronted his cousins. "How long did it take you and Francesca, Sev? I seem to remember it was all of one night." His gaze switched to Lazz. "What about you and Ariana? You may have resisted longer and harder, but in the end you still fell."

Lazz blew out a sigh. "You're that certain?"

Draco didn't hesitate. "Yes."

Sev nodded, though he didn't look happy. "I guess the real question is…does Shayla feel the same way?"

Once again, Draco didn't hesitate. "If she doesn't now, she will in time, once she's had a chance to come to terms with what's happened." He lifted an eyebrow. "Unless you're saying The Inferno doesn't work."

Sev released a humorless laugh. "Oh, it works. You'll

discover just how well soon enough. My concern is whether she's about to become a pawn in this battle, trapped between her loyalty to her grandmother and her feelings for you."

Draco had already considered that possibility. "If she is, she'll be the first piece I capture," he stated firmly. "Whatever it takes to remove her from the playing field. But I *will* protect what's mine."

The meeting didn't last much longer. They invited Shayla back into the conference room and assured her of their interest in pursuing her grandmother's proposition. They requested another survey of the mines, which she readily agreed to. They asked for time to examine the diamonds. Since she'd already suggested as much, she didn't argue that, either. Finally, they asked for a copy of the proposed lease along with any conditions pertaining to it and Shayla promised that her grandmother's lawyer would fax it to them within the week.

To Draco's amusement he watched Shayla charm the men, his grandfather and cousins falling, one by one, beneath the enchantment of her smile and her sunny personality. It wasn't a deliberate maneuver on her part. He'd have caught it if she'd been playing them. He suspected Primo would have, as well. In fact, his grandfather watched Shayla with an eagle eye, careful to reassure himself that this particular apple had fallen well away from the poisoned tree of her grandmother.

The instant the meeting wrapped, Draco whisked Shayla off to his office. "Why don't you come upstairs and have lunch with me," he suggested the moment they were safely closeted inside.

"Not a chance," she said with a small grin. "I have a feeling 'come upstairs and have lunch' is your code for 'come upstairs and take your clothes off.'"

"Well… We could do that, too. I wouldn't mind eating

lunch naked, so long as it's with you." He approached, snagging the lapels of her lemony suit jacket and reeling her in. "Of course, we can also get naked right here in my office. You'll find my couch is extremely comfortable."

She shook her head, unable to suppress a laugh. "As tempting as your offer is, I'll pass." Her amusement faded, replaced by a bittersweet longing. "I'm really sorry, Draco, but I have to go."

"Time to report in to your grandmother?" He tried to keep the edge from his voice with only limited success.

She must have picked up on it, because she met his look dead-on, a hint of defiance glittering in the darkness. "Among other things, yes."

He let it go, determined to tip them over that line from business straight into pleasure, and keep them there. "Why don't we have dinner together?" he suggested. "Somewhere ridiculously expensive and romantic. We'll celebrate a new alliance between the Charlestons and the Dantes."

She avoided his gaze. "A little premature to celebrate an alliance, don't you think?" she asked. "There's a lot of work to accomplish before a lease is signed."

He meant them and their relationship, not the lease, though there didn't seem any point in explaining that fact. Instead, he schooled himself to patience. She didn't understand about The Inferno and what was happening between them. Not yet. Until she did, until she accepted, he needed to take it slow.

"We can fight the past, or accept it and move on." Coming from him, that particular philosophy was almost funny, since he'd spent ten endless years fighting to right a single long-ago wrong. "What happens in the future is up to you. To us."

She released her breath in a drawn-out sigh. "You're right." She turned with a smile, though it didn't contain her usual cheerfulness. He could still see regret lurking around the edges. "Where and when do you want to meet?"

"I'll pick you up at the Mark."

She shook her head. "I'd rather meet you at the restaurant." Her expression turned provocative. "But if you promise not to behave yourself, I'll let you take me home."

His eyebrows winged upward. "*Not* to behave myself?"

She simply looked at him and waited.

Hell, he could do that. He was an expert at not behaving. "Done," he agreed. He didn't get it then. He should have. But he was so desperate to have her again, the little cues went right over his head. "There's a terrific seafood place in North Beach. Do you know where North Beach is?"

"Between Fisherman's Wharf and Chinatown," she answered promptly.

"I'm impressed."

She shrugged it off. "Don't be. I did some exploring before the reception. It's a wonder I could squeeze my poor abused feet into those heels considering how much walking I did."

"Well, I'm glad you managed, since I had such fun taking them off. In fact, I had fun taking off all of your bits and pieces." He couldn't resist touching her again. Kissing her. Gathering her into his arms, where she belonged. She didn't resist, but snuggled in, returning his kiss as though they'd been parted for months, instead of hours. "Meet me at Cocina at eight," he said, when they finally came up for air.

"Draco…"

Somehow her hair had come loose again and he filled his hands with it, allowing it to trickle through his fingers. "Stay," he murmured against her mouth.

"I wish…" She broke off and pulled free of his embrace. Putting some distance between them, she shook her head. "I can't."

He caught an odd emotion rippling across her expression. "Shayla?" Something wasn't right, but he couldn't quite put his finger on it. "What is it, sweetheart?"

She gathered herself with a visible effort. "I'm sorry. I really have to go."

If only he'd pushed a little harder. If only he'd been paying closer attention. But he hadn't. Didn't. And so the moment passed. "I understand." He checked his watch. "Hell, it's hours before I'll see you again. Are you sure you don't want to meet up sooner?"

"Yes." She closed her eyes with a soft exclamation. "I'd love to, but I can't. Draco, you have to let me go. I'll see you at eight."

She darted forward and wrapped her arms around his neck and kissed him, kissed him with a desperate passion. Clung like she'd never let him go. Sighed like a woman in love. He went under with her, losing himself in an embrace that promised everything, but still left him empty-handed when she slipped away and, without another word, exited the room.

The day stretched long and lonely, inching toward the appointed time they'd agreed to meet. He arrived a full fifteen minutes early. Shayla was running late. More than eight months late, as it turned out. But Draco didn't know that then.

After a full hour of pulverizing breadsticks, he was forced to face facts. She wasn't coming. He threw down a wad of cash and headed for the Mark, where the snooty reservationist on duty informed him that there was no Shayla Charleston staying with them. Had never been a Shayla Charleston staying with them. And could he please step aside so that *paying* customers might be assisted.

Next, Draco placed a call to Leticia Charleston, who claimed she had no knowledge of her granddaughter's whereabouts and no, she couldn't be bothered to pass on a message. She ended the conversation by informing him that any further contact should be through her attorney...unless, of course, the Dantes were no longer interested in leasing her mines.

Draco's final call was to Juice, a former associate of his brother, Luc. Juice specialized in background checks, finding what others didn't want found, and all things stored in cyberspace. "I have a job for you," Draco informed him the instant the call went through.

"What is it with you Dantes?" Juice's deep bass voice rumbled in his ear. "You don't know how to say, 'Hello'? Even a quick, 'How ya doin'?' But, no. It's always, 'I need some info and I need it yesterday.' First your brother, Rafe, hits me up last night, now you tonight."

Draco fought for patience. "Hello. How ya doin'? I need some info and I need it yesterday. I want you to dig up everything you can on a Shayla Charleston. Then I want you to find her for me."

"I'm not sure I like the way you say 'find her,' my man."

It had been an endless night and Draco's control finally snapped. "What's the way I said it have to do with anything?" he snarled.

"That depends. First, you best remember you're the one asking for a favor." He let that sink in.

Draco swore. "I'm sorry, Juice. She's…" She's what? His Inferno mate? Apparently not since she'd walked away from what they'd had. "She's important."

"Inferno, important?"

Draco didn't bother to deny it. "Yeah."

"Well, okay then. That brings us to my second question. What happens to the girl once I track her down?"

Hell. "Either I put a wedding ring on her finger or she's going to wish we'd never met."

"Huh. Sounds to me like you're tempted to do both."

"That's a distinct possibility," Draco growled.

"I'll have her for you within the week," Juice promised.

"But if you don't mind me saying, I suggest you seriously consider pursuing option one, rather than option two."

Draco glared down at the phone. "And why is that?"

"Because you and I would have to have a serious conversation if you decide on option two. And trust me, you don't want that to happen."

With that, the phone went dead. Draco closed his eyes and swore again, more virulently this time. He'd never hurt Shayla, not when he was honor-bound to protect her. She was his mate. He was worried. Concerned. He needed to find her, discover why she'd stood him up. Was it because of her grandmother? Because he was a Dante? Or something else… something worse? Until he found her, he'd never know.

But all the while, Lazz's question ran through his mind like a broken recording. *How do you know she didn't seduce you as part of her grandmother's plan?* Draco shook his head. No. It couldn't have been a setup. She didn't know who he was when they'd met. The others, sure. But not him. His name hadn't been on the list. She'd been patently shocked when he told her he was a Dante.

But… What if he was wrong? What if history was repeating itself and he'd once again fallen for a clever con?

Damn it to hell!

Draco's palm throbbed and he rubbed it with his thumb. He'd thought The Inferno had forged a permanent connection between them. Now he wondered. Maybe it had worked, but only on him. Maybe his Inferno connector was on the fritz. Maybe he'd be the first to find his soul mate, only to discover that she didn't feel the same way.

Perfect. Draco Dante, the only member of his entire family to screw up The Inferno. *Porca vacca!* He really was trouble.

Four

Nine months later...

Draco had lost Shayla in the fading glory of summer and found her again in the burgeoning promise of a fertile spring. But he did find her, though it had taken Juice far longer than the week he'd anticipated. How ironic that it was here, hiding out in her family home, where he'd started his search.

The Charleston house stood at the end of a long drive, an ancient antebellum mansion best seen from a kind distance. The closer Draco came, the more apparent the ravages of time, despite the flowering trees and perennials that attempted to disguise the slow decline into rot. The mansion stood exposed, shimmering through the humidity beneath a merciless and unforgiving sun. He didn't understand it. The handful of diamonds Shayla had shown him could have more than transformed the place. So, why hadn't they put the money the Dantes had paid for them to good use?

An ancient housekeeper opened the door and shuffled him along to a shabby parlor, where he was formally announced. Leticia Charleston responded by leveling a glare at the housekeeper, no doubt because she'd had the effrontery to permit a Dante across her precious threshold. Caving to the inevitable, Leticia waved Draco toward a high-backed chair decorated in faded damask. He ignored the invitation to sit.

"As I've informed you each time you've phoned, Mr. Dante, Shayla is not here."

As badly as he wanted to call her a liar, his family continued to do business with the woman, though now they were locked in fierce negotiations to purchase the mines, rather than to lease them. Ticking her off was not in Dantes' best interest. Unfortunately, he wasn't the most charming of Primo's grandchildren. That honor went to his cousin, Marco.

Worse, after so many months of searching, Draco's temper was worn down to a small, jagged nub. The least wrong word caused him to shoot first, talk later. Unfortunately once the hapless transgressor went down in flames it didn't leave a lot of room for discussion. And as appealing as the image of Shayla's grandmother being turned to a pile of ash was, he needed to try for a more diplomatic approach.

"She's here," he nearly growled.

So much for diplomacy.

Leticia lifted a perfectly drawn eyebrow a shade darker than her perfectly styled, deep gold hair. Now he could tell where her funds had been channeled. For a woman in her early seventies, she looked spectacular on the outside, even if the inner corrosion ran strong and deep. It would seem the decayed exterior of the house reflected the personality of its mistress.

"Are you calling me a liar?" she demanded.

He glared at her, dragon to dragon. "I believe if you'll

take a look in one of those half-dozen bedrooms upstairs, you'll find your missing granddaughter." He shot a grim look around the cavernous room. "Considering the size of this place I can understand you accidentally misplacing her. But if you need me to help look…?" He lifted his own eyebrow, one as black as soot.

"A *half*-dozen? I'll have you know there are a *full* dozen bedrooms upstairs, none of which contain my granddaughter. Shayla is not some princess I'm keeping locked away in a tower, despite what you clearly believe. And you are most certainly not a prince, but some ill-mannered creature possessing not an ounce of civilized behavior." Leticia shot to her feet and gestured toward the door leading to the hallway… and the way out. "Now, if you don't mind?"

"Here's the problem." He planted his feet firmly atop a handmade Tabriz carpet that still carried a whiff of lost elegance. Then he folded his arms across his chest. "I do mind. I mind very much."

Leticia stuck out a chin identical to her granddaughter's, fire burning in eyes as blue as Shayla's were black. Her only show of nerves was the way she gripped a ring dangling from a gold chain strung around her neck. Based on the glitter of diamonds, he suspected it was her wedding ring, though why she wore it around her neck instead of on her finger he couldn't begin to guess. Maybe widows in the South did it that way.

"She's not here," Leticia informed him. As though aware she'd exposed her anxiety, she tucked her ring away beneath her elegant silk blouse.

Draco met her, chin for jaw, putting a spark of fire in his own hazel-gold eyes. "Yes, she is."

He didn't know who would have caved first if a voice hadn't interrupted the standoff. "Grandmother? I need your opinion." The sound of her came like a sip of water to a parched and desperate desert. Painfully slow footsteps crossed the cypress floorboards of the foyer, heading straight for the parlor and sounding like the ring of destiny. "Oh, I'm sorry. I didn't realize you had company."

Leticia fell back into her chair with a word that had Draco's brows shooting skyward, while her expression soured, threatening to destroy all the hard work of her plastic surgeon. "Why, it's a miracle. My beloved granddaughter has appeared out of thin air after all these long months." She bit off each word as if it was acid in her mouth and drummed her synthetic nails against the armrest of her chair. "Hallelujah and kill the fatted calf."

Draco spared her a sardonic look before turning. "Hello, Shayla."

He heard the sharp catch of her breath the instant she realized who he was. "Draco."

His name escaped on a current of emotions, only a few of which he could identify. Disbelief. Wonder. An underscoring of pain. He could understand the disbelief since she'd run so long and hard to escape him. But the other two left him bewildered.

She stood a few steps inside the parlor, as though poised to vanish as unexpectedly as she'd appeared. She held two small, crocheted blankets clutched to her chest, one a bright and cheerful yellow, the other a tumble of rainbow colors. She looked different than he remembered, softer. More country casual than city chic. Sweet and oh, so not-so innocent.

Maybe it was her hair, which she wore pulled back from her face and fastened with two clips so it sheeted down her back in an inky waterfall. Or maybe it was her dress, at least what he could see of it around the blankets she held. It was simple ivory, pleated at the neckline and flowing, long and loose, to her calves.

None of the differences mattered, he knew that much for

certain. All that mattered was the hard joyous thrum of The Inferno and the relentless kick of desire, the intensity building to a fever pitch now that he was finally face-to-face with her. He'd have snatched her in his arms, except for one small detail.

In the past months he'd come to the conclusion that Lazz was right. His Inferno mate had screwed him over—literally and figuratively—no doubt at the behest of her grandmother.

"Hello, Shayla." There were so many things he wanted to say to her. So many things he planned to get off his chest once he found her. But standing there, staring at her, he couldn't think of one damn word of his entire speech. "It's been a while."

"I guess you're here to talk to my grandmother about the purchase contracts." She took a swift step backward. "I'll leave you to it."

"I'm not here to see your grandmother." He approached, not the least surprised by the alarm building in her dark gaze. It had been a long, difficult chase, but she'd just been trapped and he didn't intend to release her anytime soon. "I'm here to talk to you."

"This really isn't a good time," she began, taking another swift step backward.

She clutched the blankets in a white-knuckle grip, holding them almost protectively against her chest. It was her profound nervousness, bordering on fear, that finally gave her away. He looked at her this time. Really looked. And then it was his turn for his breath to hitch. His turn to stare in stunned disbelief.

"You're pregnant." The words escaped, part statement, part accusation.

From behind him, he heard Leticia moan. "Shayla,

you're *pregnant*? Why didn't you tell your poor, dear grand-mamma?"

Shayla's confused gaze darted from him to her grandmother and back again. "Yes, I'm pregnant. I guess that means there's cause for celebration all around. I understand you're married, Draco. Congratulations."

Married? "Who the hell told you that?" he snarled, though he could guess.

"My grandmother."

He suspected that if she'd thought first she might not have given him an honest answer. "Did she?"

Naturally, the old woman continued to brazen it out. "That's what I heard." She rolled her eyes. "But what do I know? You Dantes breed like rabbits. With so many to choose from, it's possible I got the name of the groom wrong."

"That tears it." He shot her a blistering glare that had her shrinking back against the cushions of her chair. "I don't care if this is your house, I want you out of this room right now."

"Well, I never!" Leticia said, playing the affronted grand dame to the hilt.

"Then it's about time you did," Draco shot back. He stabbed a finger in the direction of the door. "Excuse us. Please." He nearly choked on that final word, before switching his attention to Shayla. She'd run if given half the chance, though considering the extent of her pregnancy he had a reasonable shot at catching her this time round. And it wouldn't take nine months, either. "Shayla and I have a lot to talk about."

Leticia didn't want to leave, he could see the resistance in every line of her whip-thin body. "Very well, I'll go." Her eyes narrowed on Draco, the soft baby blues bright with malice. "But I'll be back."

"Yeah, that's what all villains say," he muttered.

Shayla must have heard because she glanced out the

window, biting her lip. He wondered if it was to hold back laughter or to keep herself from tearing him a new one. The door closed behind Leticia, just shy of a slam, leaving them in murky silence. Draco didn't hesitate. Most of his questions could be answered with one easy move.

Before she realized his intent, he swept her into his arms and kissed her. It was a hard, ruthless kiss, one that gave no quarter, but demanded a response, a definitive answer to months' worth of questions. He put every bit of the loss and hunger, anger and pain, hope and despair into that melding of lips.

He felt her resistance, her initial panic. Her hands pressed against his chest, attempting to hold him at bay. And then it all changed. A soft moan caught in her throat, a moan of intense longing and desire. Where before her hands pushed, now they lifted and tangled in his hair. Tugged to bring him closer. Her lips parted and she deepened the kiss, easing it from hard to generous, ruthless to eager, filling it with a joyful welcome.

She felt good in his arms. Right. Her scent swirled around him, a uniquely familiar one that he connected with on some deep, primal level. And her taste… Her sweet taste and fervent touch caused The Inferno to burn with a blistering intensity. She was his. Had been his from the moment they touched.

A soft kick impacted against his abdomen, coming from the tight mound of Shayla's belly. He broke off the embrace and took a swift step back, staring in shock. "Are you all right? The baby? I think I hurt it."

"Not at all." She smiled, a soft, radiant smile that knocked first at his heart, then at his legs, threatening to send him straight to his knees. "He or she must have felt left out and given you a little kick to say hello."

Draco closed his eyes in relief. Great. *Great way to start, Dante.* He hesitated, not quite certain how to go from there.

He wasn't accustomed to being indecisive and it irritated him. Okay, fine. The hell with starting out by getting his feet wet. He'd just dive right in.

Dragging in a deep breath, he pinned Shayla with his gaze. "Is the baby mine?"

"Are you married?" she countered. "You never actually said. Earlier, I mean."

"No. I'm not married."

"Engaged?" she persisted.

He ran a hand through his hair, reaching deep for the patience he'd lost eight-plus endless months ago. "I'm not married. Not engaged. Not seeing anyone. Not interested in seeing anyone," he asserted. "With one exception. You."

An emotion swept across her elegant features, so fast he couldn't quite identify it. Hurt, maybe? "Then why have you waited so long to come and see me?"

Okay, definitely hurt. He approached, deliberately stepping into a bright patch of sunlight. It cut hot and sharp across his face, giving her a clear view of both his expression and his eyes. "Let me make this crystal clear. I have been searching for you since the moment you disappeared. When you didn't show up for dinner, I stopped by the Mark—who, incidentally had never heard of you. Next, I called your grandmother—who professed ignorance. I won't bother to comment on that."

This time Shayla allowed the smallest of smiles to curve her mouth before bringing it under swift control. "Since I was on a plane, technically she didn't know my precise location."

"If you say so." They'd discuss her departure from San Francisco soon enough. Guaranteed, it would be long and unpleasant. But it would happen. "My third call was to Juice."

Her brow wrinkled in bewilderment. "Who's Juice?"

"He worked for my brother's security firm years ago and after the business closed down, he went independent. Let's just say he's an expert at finding what's lost and recovering it."

Shayla stilled. "You asked him to recover me?" she asked.

"Hell, yes, I asked him to recover you."

She crossed to a window seat overlooking the expansive grounds at the rear of the mansion. Taking a seat, her restless hands folded and refolded the blankets she held. They were handmade baby blankets Draco now realized. "He must not be very good at his job if it took him all this time to find me."

Not quite knowing what to do with himself, Draco paced in front of her. "Maybe if you hadn't spent most of that time trying to dodge me, he'd have had an easier time of it."

"I wasn't dodging you," she corrected. "I had a job that involved extensive travel."

"Yeah, right." He didn't bother to conceal his skepticism. "Regardless, Juice tracked you all over Europe. Maybe if your employer, Algier, weren't such a recluse who keeps his schedule top secret, I would have managed to catch you. I almost pulled it off in Copenhagen." Disgust ripped through his voice. "We probably passed each other at the airport. After that, you fell off the grid."

"I came home," she said simply.

"That was three months ago." Three months. Three impossibly long months and she'd been here all along. Son of a— "I've called your grandmother weekly since you left me high and dry in San Francisco, asking whether you'd been in touch. She categorically denied being in contact with you."

Shayla lifted a shoulder in a shrug that caused her dress to swirl across the surface of her rounded belly. More than anything he wanted to touch her burgeoning flesh, to feel again the impatient kick of the baby tucked safe within her womb. "I asked her not to."

"Got it." A wintry bitterness descended. More and more it would seem Lazz was right. "Was seducing me part of your grandmother's plan in order to gather inside information on the Dantes?"

She froze. "Is that what you think?"

His temper escaped his grasp. "What the hell am I supposed to think, Shayla? We spent one incredible night together. You acted as though it meant as much to you as it did to me. But it was all a lie, wasn't it? You made a date with me, planning all the while to stand me up. You left without a word of explanation, not so much as a note or phone call. Then you went abroad with Derek Algier. Personally, I think you were running like you had the devil at your heels." He allowed nine months of fury to underscore his words. "And you would have been right. I was behind you almost every step of the way, hell-bound to find you."

Other than a telltale trace of color sweeping across her cheekbones, she remained remarkably composed. "If you found out I worked for Derek, then you must know I wasn't running from you."

"I think that job turned out to be a very convenient way of avoiding me." He cut her off before she could slam him with a heated reply. "And if it wasn't, why else would you keep running?" He tried to keep the bite out of the question and failed miserably. "Why else would you have kept your pregnancy a secret?"

"Because you're married."

It took every ounce of self-control not to roar like his namesake. "For the last time, I am *not* married."

"Well, no. But I thought you were." She sighed. "I'll have

to remember to check my facts when it comes to my grand-mother."

"How many years have you known her, and you're only just now coming to that conclusion?" He waved that aside. "Never mind. Answer me this, Shayla. What would you have done if you'd been told the truth from the start? If that—" He swallowed the epithet he was about to use to describe Leticia so he wouldn't offend Shayla. It went down like a bitter pill. "If your grandmother hadn't lied and told you I was married, what would you have done?"

She fell silent for an endless moment. With the light at her back, he couldn't read the expression in her dark eyes. Couldn't tell what she thought or how she felt, and it was killing him inch by torturous inch. Finally, she spoke. "I would have called you to tell you I was pregnant with your baby."

The simple statement hit like a blow to the solar plexus. It took endless seconds to regain use of his lungs and limbs. Once he had, he approached and sank onto the padded bench beside her. The sunshine streamed in through the window and warmed his back like a blessing. Ever so gently he reached out and slid his hand across her abdomen. The Inferno burned hot against his palm, hot against the life cupped beneath.

"Our baby," he murmured.

To his surprise, Shayla leaned into him and allowed her head to fall against his shoulder. It struck him that if he'd been wrong about his suspicions—that going to bed with him had not been part of some Machiavellian plot forged by Leticia Charleston—then Shayla had probably spent the past nine months standing strong, all on her own. Granted, she had the Wicked Witch to assist her, but that couldn't have been much help. Not when her grandmother had a hidden agenda she was clearly running, play by dangerous play.

The best he could tell, there were two options. Either

Leticia and Shayla had devised a plan of revenge to even the score with the Dantes for long-past transgressions, and sleeping with him was somehow part of it. Or Shayla was an innocent bystander. He was absolutely certain about one thing. Leticia was up to something. The Dantes just hadn't uncovered the how-and-when portion of the slowly unfolding play. But guaranteed, the instant the curtain fell on the final act, it would be with a dagger in their collective backs.

It was also clear to him that Leticia wanted to keep him well away from Shayla and their baby. The question was…why? Was the baby somehow part of her plot, or an unexpected wrinkle? And how much did Shayla know? How involved was she in all this? Only time would tell. Until then, first things first.

"Why would your grandmother go out of her way to keep us apart?" he demanded. "Wouldn't she want the baby to have a name?"

Shayla stiffened. "The baby will have a name. My name. The Charleston name."

"Our baby is a Dante," he corrected implacably. "He'll have the Dante name. We'll marry as soon as it can be arranged."

Where some women would have gotten angry and obstinate, Shayla simply smiled. "You can't force me to the altar, Draco. I've lived almost my entire life with Grandmother Charleston. She's spent the past seventy-two years learning how to operate a steamroller and she's one of the best at it I've ever seen. I've lived my entire life sidestepping her. If she can't force me in the direction she wants me to go, what makes you think you'll have any better success?"

Shayla was like moonbeams and stardust, filled with magic but impossible to pin down. But that didn't mean he wouldn't try. "Because you want what's best for our child. And staying here, raising a child as a single mother, having your grandmother as a strong influence in your baby's life is not in our child's best interest."

"But you are?"

"I'm his father," Draco stated simply.

"His?" she repeated.

"Chances are it's a boy. The Dantes have never quite gotten the hang of producing daughters, despite the occasional error in judgment." He grinned to let her know he was teasing about his sister, Gianna. "Regardless of the sex, I intend to be there for our child on a daily basis. Not for the occasional, flying visit, but every single day of his or her life."

"I see."

She appeared troubled, which disturbed him more than he cared to admit. After all, what had she expected him to say? "Good luck and goodbye"? Or… "Here's the monthly check, don't call me, I'll call you"? He tilted his head to one side. "You have a problem with my being involved?"

"Not exactly."

He pushed. "Then what exactly?"

She fussed with the blankets some more, though the best he could tell they weren't going to fold any neater. "I gather that this daily contact is supposed to take place in San Francisco?"

"I'd be willing to move here," he conceded. "But there's another important point you should take into consideration before deciding where we live. If you and the baby join me in San Francisco, you'll both be surrounded by the love and support of my family. Our son will have grandparents who'll adore him and be an intricate part of his life. And he'll have more aunts and uncles and cousins than he can count."

"I grew up without all of that," she countered. "I've done just fine."

That was open to debate. Fortunately, he retained sufficient discretion not to point that out. "The Dantes all get together at least once a week at Primo's. We vacation together during the summer at our lake house. The wives all support each other and help with babysitting duties. Granted, considering your background you may find all the intermingling a bit overwhelming at first, everybody in everybody else's business. But would you deny our son the opportunity to be part of such a large, close-knit family? Be honest, Shayla. Didn't you miss that growing up? Which is the better lifestyle, here or there?"

"If I decide that moving to San Francisco is a better option, why does it have to involve marriage?" she asked in a reasonable voice. "Marriage is a huge commitment. And it's not like we're in love with each other."

He forced himself to remain silent, to choose his words as though they were the most precious of commodities. "I come from an old-world, extremely traditional Italian family, one in which premarital sex doesn't happen."

She blinked. "Then what did we have?"

He smiled. "Premarital sex." His smile faded. "But for my grandparents it doesn't exist, and therefore, didn't happen."

"Boy, are they going to be in for a surprise in a couple weeks," she murmured.

He didn't want to think about that, couldn't be distracted by it. But he wanted her to understand who he was and where he'd come from. "If you were to have our baby outside of wedlock, I would shame Primo and Nonna because I didn't marry you and provide our son with the Dante name. They would never get over it."

Distress filled her eyes, turning them black as midnight. "They'd disown you, wouldn't they?"

"Once upon a time, perhaps, when the line was blacker and more rigidly drawn. But they lost their son and daughter-in-law—my uncle and his wife—in a sailing accident. It changed my grandparents, made them hold tighter to those of us who were left. So, no. They wouldn't disown me. Even if that were a possibility, I wouldn't try to force you to marry me because of it."

"But your relationship with them will never be the same if I don't marry you." When he remained silent, she pressed. "Will it?"

He hadn't expected her to be so shrewd. "It would change," he conceded.

"And if we married? Even if it's only weeks before our baby is born?"

"I'd make it clear that I moved heaven and earth these past months searching for you, intent on finding and marrying you. That even if I'd known you were pregnant I couldn't have done any more in order to track you down. I'll also make it clear that you didn't contact me because you were operating under the mistaken impression that I was already married. Primo would have words with me, no question there. But since you and the baby would bear the Dante name, it would go a long way toward smoothing everything over."

"Why, Draco?" she asked in bewilderment. "Why have you been looking for me all this time?"

"You know why."

He laced her hand with his, pressing palm against palm, Inferno against Inferno. He watched her weigh the options, watched while his entire future hung in the balance. She almost tipped, when suddenly she grimaced. She slipped her hand from his to rest it low on her back and press, the gesture one of supreme weariness. He'd been around enough pregnant women in recent months to understand the source of her discomfort and take a fairly accurate stab at how to relieve it.

"Let me help," he offered.

Gently he shifted her on the window seat so he could get to her back. Running his hands down her spine, he cautiously pressed until he found the bundle of knots just above her buttocks. Then he sank the heel of his palm into the source of her pain and worked at it. Her low moan had him clenching, building a number of knots of his own to replace the ones he relieved in her back.

"How did you learn to do that?" she marveled.

"Watching my cousins and brothers with their wives."

He rested his jaw alongside her temple. He wished he could sit like this for hours, absorbing the soft texture of her skin against his, inhaling her sweet scent with each breath he took, feeling the quiet joy of having her in his arms. He didn't care what it required or what sacrifices he needed to make. This woman was his and he refused to let her go. Not again. Not ever.

"Shayla…"

She stiffened, pulled away from him. "Don't pressure me, Draco. I'm not going to marry you because I'm pregnant with our child, or because of Primo and Nonna, or even for Alessandro and Elia." The use of his parents' names had him shooting her a questioning look. "I've made a point of acquiring a genealogy of your family," she explained.

"Why?"

"Because the baby will need to know who his family is." Her response registered on some deep, elemental level, but before he could comment, she continued. "I can't make any decisions until I speak to Grandmother Charleston. I want to know why she told me you were married."

He could take several wild guesses, but kept them to himself. At least, for now. It wouldn't help his cause to go after Shayla's sole remaining family member. A hideous thought occurred to him and he closed his eyes, wincing. Hell. If he and Shayla married, he'd be related to the old bat through marriage. She'd be his grandmonster-in-law.

And the hits just kept on coming.

As though waiting for her cue to return, Leticia swept into the room and shot off her opening volley. "If you've settled your business with my granddaughter, Mr. Dante, you may feel free to vacate my home."

Draco folded his arms across his chest. "I'm not leaving without Shayla."

"We'll just see about that. One phone call and I can have you removed, by force if necessary. My second phone call will be to my lawyer telling him to tear up the contract authorizing the sale of the Charleston mines to your family."

Shayla waded into the fray. "If everyone is finished making idle threats, we all have some decisions to make."

Leticia sat down abruptly. "I can't begin to imagine what you're talking about. What decisions?"

"For one, whether or not I'm going to marry Draco and move to San Francisco with him."

The words were barely out of Shayla's mouth before Leticia shot to her feet again. "I forbid it! I absolutely, unequivocally forbid it."

Draco was so grateful, he was tempted to kiss the hideous old woman on her narrow, cotton candy-pink mouth. She couldn't have picked a worse comment to make if she'd tried, or one more guaranteed to drive her granddaughter in the exact opposite direction of the one she wanted.

Sure enough, Shayla's eyes narrowed. "You forbid?" she repeated softly.

Draco had to hand it to her. Despite her advanced years, the old broad could still do a fast backtrack. "Perhaps the word *forbid* was ill-advised," she graciously conceded. "But, darling, you must think about what's best for the baby. And flying in your condition could prove dangerous. I'm certain your obstetrician would never agree to it. I suggest you wait until after the baby is born. Then you can go out and visit the Dantes with your—" she lifted her eyes heavenward, a pained expression painted across her face "—little bundle of joy."

It was the look that must have decided Shayla, a look that warned that Leticia Charleston would never forgive her granddaughter for having the temerity to give birth to a child half Dante. It also provided answers to several of Draco's questions, such as whether or not sleeping with him was part of a Charleston plot. Clearly, it wasn't.

Shayla turned to Draco, the pain in her gaze threatening to rip him apart. Though he rejoiced that Leticia had tipped the scales in his favor, he hated that she'd hurt Shayla in the process.

"When can we leave?" she whispered, her breath catching in a slight hiccup.

"That depends. How fast can you pack?"

"Wait!" Leticia aimed for entreaty and still hit demand. "Please, wait, Shayla. I don't want you to leave."

"I understand, Grandmother," she replied gently. "But you've said it yourself. I have to do what's best for my baby."

"But you're the last Charleston in our family. You could have a son." Leticia directed a fulminating glare at Draco. "Dantes have a history of shooting out sons like gumballs from a nickel machine. If you had a boy, he'd be a Charleston. Our name, our line, would continue."

Shayla gasped in disbelief. "Is *that* why you told me Draco was married? Why you worked so hard to keep him from finding me and discovering I was pregnant? So I'd produce a Charleston heir?"

Leticia lifted a shoulder, somehow managing to imbue the gesture with a wealth of exasperation. "That might be one of the reasons on my list. It's not the first item, but it's on there, somewhere. I don't normally approve of illegitimacy, although considering the current benefits to our line, I am willing to make a one-time exception. Even if the boy will be half Dante."

"Very gracious of you," Draco said carefully.

She turned on him like the viper she was. "Oh, get over it," she snapped. "You found out in the nick of time, didn't you? You Dantes always find a way to win the day. So, go ahead and fly her out to California. Your family probably owns a fleet of private planes. Wave your hand and make one of them appear. With any luck the flight will force her into premature labor before you can drag her to the altar. And I'll still get my way…assuming the baby survives."

"Why, you—"

"That's enough." Shayla never raised her voice, yet sheer steel shot through her words, making them all the more powerful. "Grandmother has a point. Before I leave I should visit Dr. Dorling and have him determine the best way for us to get to California." She fixed her grandmother with an unyielding stare. "But I am leaving. I will do what's best for my baby and right now that's Draco."

"And if I refuse to sell the Dantes our mine?" Leticia stalked in Draco's direction though she was smart enough to stay well out of his reach. She gripped her wedding ring, tugging at the chain so hard he wondered if it would snap. "If I threaten to sell it to one of your competitors if you marry my granddaughter? What then?"

There was only one response to her threat, a response—given the circumstances—Draco couldn't resist using. "Frankly, my dear, I don't give a damn."

Five

"How are you feeling?"

Shayla sighed. It must have been at least the twentieth time Draco had asked that question. From the moment they went wheels up, he'd watched her with all the ferocity of a fire-breathing dragon, as though he were guarding a treasure more precious than gold.

"I'm fine," she assured both him and Dr. Dorling. How Draco had convinced her obstetrician to join them on the flight, she had no idea. No doubt it involved a sizable amount of money since the doctor had dropped everything to make the trip. "I feel great."

Dr. Dorling checked the monitors and nodded toward Draco. "Everything is perfect, Mr. Dante. Good oxygen. Excellent heart rate for both mother and baby. Blood pressure right where it should be."

Draco didn't appear the least relieved. Though he didn't pace, Shayla could feel his worry electrifying the space within the luxurious confines of the Dantes' jet. "We should arrive in another two hours," he muttered, digging his thumb into his palm. His Infernoed palm, she noted. "Not long now."

"Draco…"

"It's all right, sweetheart," he attempted to soothe in a voice overflowing with grit and tension. "The pilot has the coordinates for all the landing strips close to hospitals along our flight path."

"Draco." She waited until he gave her his undivided attention. "Would you please relax? The flight isn't making me nervous. The baby isn't making me nervous. The doctor and his machines aren't making me nervous. *You* are."

He blew out a sigh, then smiled, two deep grooves denting his cheeks. It was the smile that did her in. But then, it was his smile that had coaxed her into his bed in the first place. His smile. The burn of his touch. That odd sizzle and jolt when they'd first touched, a sensation that refused to go away, even after more than nine impossibly long months.

He crossed to join her, sliding in beside her and tucking her close. She closed her eyes, absorbing his warmth and allowing the steady beat of his heart and quiet movement of air in and out of his lungs to lull her toward a peaceful limbo. These days she lived in a haze of exhaustion, not to mention feeling uncomfortable and awkward, able to nap at any given moment, though with the constant kicks from the baby, never for long. Her life had changed in monumental ways, and all because of the man who held her safe and secure within his arms.

Years before she'd formulated a plan for her life, one she finally implemented during her stay in San Francisco. She'd been so excited beforehand, seen the possibilities so clearly, without anticipating how her impulsive actions the night she met Draco would ultimately change her life. That had been brought home during those first two months in Europe when her longing for him had been keen and sharp. Months during which pain and loss outweighed the thrill of achieving her ideal job.

Oh, she loved translating for Derek. Adored her employer, one of the kindest, most understanding men she'd ever met. When she'd realized she was pregnant, he'd kept her on as long as he could. But eventually the whispers and suspicion that he'd fathered her baby had interfered with his business negotiations. Plus, the first five months of her pregnancy had been rough, her morning sickness closer to all-day sickness. Finally, she'd decided it simply wasn't safe or healthy to be globe-trotting around Europe during her pregnancy. So, she'd returned home.

She refused to regret the sharp turn her life had taken thanks to that one night with Draco. Regrets weren't part of her nature. And now, once again due to the man who held her so securely in his arms, her life was about to take another acute turn, one she didn't think she could handle.

Draco tucked a lock of her hair behind her ear and she shivered at the touch. "What are you thinking about?" he murmured close to her ear.

"About what will happen when we reach San Francisco," she replied readily enough.

"Nothing very dramatic. I'll take you home once Dr. Dorling is satisfied that you're stable. And then you'll rest."

She made a face. "That's not what I meant."

"We can discuss any other concerns tonight. There's no hurry."

"Yes, there is and you know it." She rubbed her belly, felt the tautness. Knew the baby had dropped low in her womb, eager to escape the safety of its nest. "This cake is just about baked."

She felt his chuckle against her cheek. "Did you just call our baby a cake?"

A reluctant laugh sighed from her. "I guess I did."

He bent down and kissed her. Maybe if the kiss had been like before, hard and hungry and filled with a desperate edge, she'd have been able to resist. But it wasn't. He soothed her with his taking, calmed her with gentleness, roused her with tenderness, branded her with a kiss that caused all others to pale in comparison.

"Well, that got her heart rate and blood pressure up," Dr. Dorling observed. "You might want to save that until after we land."

Reluctantly, Draco pulled back. His tawny eyes glittered like antique gold, filled with a want that echoed her own. "You think there's a lot we need to resolve," he told her in an intimate undertone, low enough that the doctor couldn't overhear. "But that kiss tells me there isn't as much to discuss as you might think."

When she opened her mouth to argue, he shook his head. "Close your eyes, Shayla. Let go and sleep. We'll worry about the future later."

"We?" she murmured.

Naturally, he got the last word, something that she was beginning to realize he excelled at. "Since it's our future, it concerns the both of us."

The quiet beep of the machines joined in tempo with the reassuring beat of Draco's heart. It proved the perfect sedative, sending her off into an easy sleep filled with the most romantic of dreams about a dragon and a princess and sweet rescue. But it vanished like fairy dust the instant the pitch of the jet engines changed. She opened her eyes, blinking in confusion.

"We're starting our descent," Draco informed her. "We should be home in a little over an hour, depending on traffic."

Home.

She assumed he meant his home and wondered how she'd

feel about staying there. Like a guest? Like an intruder? She'd
wanted her own place for more years than she could count,
a nest she could burrow into and feather with the bits and
pieces that would make it distinctly hers. Now that possibility
grew less and less likely.

The minute they touched down at a small regional airport
outside of the city, Dr. Dorling gave her a final examination.
As soon as he cleared her, she thanked him for all his time
and assistance. He gave her the name of a colleague who
agreed to take over her care from this point forward and was
expecting her visit bright and early the next morning.

Draco handed the obstetrician a first-class ticket that
would return him to Atlanta on a commercial flight and
they all exited the plane. While the doctor headed off to
San Francisco International Airport in one car, another car,
complete with driver, awaited to take them home—wherever
that was.

"Sausalito," Draco said, as though reading her mind. "Not
far from Primo and Nonna."

"I thought you lived in the suite where we—"

She broke off abruptly. Where they'd made love. Where
she'd conceived their child, though she hadn't known it at the
time. Where she'd created a connection that continued even
after all this time, gaining in strength with each passing day.
But she couldn't say any of those things aloud, not when the
driver might overhear them.

"I don't live at the suite," he explained. "I just stayed at
Dantes while my house was under construction. The designer
put the last few touches on the place yesterday, so I haven't
seen the final product." He smiled at her. "We'll get to do
that together."

"I'll enjoy that." She hesitated. "Do they know about
me?" she whispered, sparing the driver another uneasy
glance.

Draco must have picked up on her concern because he leaned forward to give the driver directions to his house, then engaged the privacy screen. "It's soundproof," he reassured before picking up the conversational thread again. "I assume you mean, does my family know about you? No, not yet. I didn't want to say anything until we've had time to discuss our options and make decisions about the future."

"I guess you won't be able to keep me hidden for long." She touched her belly to include the existence of their baby. "Not if your family is as close-knit as you say."

He appeared remarkably unconcerned. "I'm hoping it won't take us long to decide what's best for the three of us."

"You think that's marriage." No question there. He'd made that fact abundantly clear.

He lifted a shoulder in a casual shrug. "What can I say? It's how I was raised."

She glanced out the tinted window. She couldn't argue the point. It was how she'd been raised, too. "There's one serious problem with your plan."

"Name it and I'll see if I can't solve it," he replied promptly.

"Solve it," she repeated. She swiveled to face him. "Fixing problems. Finding a way to make sure the roadblocks are removed so you can get from Point A to Point B. That's a core part of your personality, isn't it?"

He didn't deny it. "It's one aspect, yes. I also protect what's mine and do whatever is necessary to recover what's taken from me, whether that takes months…" A darkness flitted through his gaze. "Or years."

She shivered, his expression shooting a chill of dread down her spine. "Is that what I am to you? A possession to be recovered?"

His voice deepened, roughened. "Recovering you is like

recovering a missing piece of myself. Without you, I'm empty. And I suspect you are, as well."

Her throat closed over and she stared at him mutely.

He cupped her face and feathered a kiss across her mouth. "More important, I'll do everything within my power to protect you and our baby. To protect you, provide for you, to try to make you happy."

Shayla snatched a deep breath. "And what about the roadblocks that are in our way?" To her relief, her voice sounded fairly normal, not revealing a trace of the hunger and longing that shot through her.

"What roadblocks?"

"Marriage, for one." She steeled herself, then gave it to him straight. "How do you clear the roadblocks so that we fall in love with each other? Because that's the only reason I'll marry you."

He froze, every scrap of emotion wiped from his expression. He didn't reply. He simply reached for her hand and interlaced it with his, allowing The Inferno to speak for him. And speak it did.

The want roared through her, blistering hot and filled with urgent demand. It didn't matter that she was heavy with his child or that they'd been parted since last summer. Whatever connected them, whether lust or something more, something she couldn't bring herself to recognize, it hadn't dimmed over time. She longed for him on every level, felt the tug at her heart and fought against the emotions that threatened to entrap it. Whatever this feeling, it wasn't love. After so short a time together that would be impossible.

"It's just physical," she insisted beneath her breath. "It isn't real."

"It's a start," Draco replied implacably. "For the sake of our child, we should give it a chance."

She closed her eyes, exhaustion and worry sapping her energy. "You don't understand."

"Then explain it to me."

She hated to strip bare the more painful details of her life, to allow someone to poke and prod indiscriminately at what she preferred to keep private. But Draco deserved that much. She focused on him, her emotions seeping free of her self-control.

"You've met my grandmother, so you can probably imagine how long and hard I've had to fight just to maintain my own identity, to keep from turning into her image of who Shayla Charleston should be."

"It must have been difficult for you."

She could see the bitter comments piling up behind that single, curt observation and appreciated his restraint. "Almost impossible," she confirmed. "I couldn't give an inch or she'd take the proverbial mile."

"Sounds like Leticia."

"Yes, well…" She twisted her hands together. "I lived at home while attending college. It wasn't ideal since my grandmother knew my schedule and expected me to adhere to it."

To her relief, he read between the lines. It wouldn't have been difficult considering she'd been a virgin when he took her to his bed. "I imagine that had a serious impact on your social life."

"I had no social life," she admitted. "Living at home—or rather, with my grandmother—prevented me from enjoying the full college experience."

"Then why do it that way?"

Shayla shrugged. "Because it was cheaper," she said simply. "As a result, I formulated a series of goals for my future that helped get me through college. I couldn't implement them right away, but at least I had them. They were like shiny

Christmas presents waiting for the right time and place to be unwrapped."

He regarded her curiously. "Why couldn't you unwrap them right away?"

Shayla sighed. "Grandmother spent the last of her money on sending me to college. She had dreams of her own. Dreams for rebuilding Charlestons and our chain of jewelry stores. I don't know how she planned to finance it, since she hadn't discovered the fire diamonds at that point. But I was supposed to run the business."

"I gather that didn't appeal to you?"

She shook her head. "That wasn't the real issue. After everything she'd done for me, I'd have stepped up. I took the courses she requested so I'd know enough to tell a good stone from a bad and recognize a fake. Accounting and business courses, as well. But, I don't have the temperament for either, let alone management. And I have zero artistic flare. In other words, I'd be utterly useless helping to rebuild Charlestons. We'd have only ended up bankrupt again. It took a long time before my grandmother came to terms with that fact. To be honest, I'm not fully convinced she has even now."

"What did you want to do instead?"

"I have a natural facility for languages, along with a desire to see other countries and experience their cultures. So, I made a trade with Grandmother. For every course she wanted me to take, I enrolled in one I wanted. My ultimate dream has always been to get a job overseas as a translator."

"That would have taken you out from under Leticia's thumb." Draco pinpointed the problem with typical perceptiveness. "I assume she didn't react well to the idea?"

"She exploded when I told her." Shayla shrugged. "I can understand. After all, there's only the two of us left. Considering everything she's been through, it made it all the more imperative that I find a way to support us. She just objected to how I chose to go about it."

His eyes narrowed. "Knowing your grandmother, she must have found a way to bring pressure to bear. Trowel on the guilt, good and thick." He tilted his head to one side, analyzing, then smiled grimly. "She paid for your education. Used every last dime to her name. She'd lose the mansion if you didn't succeed as a translator. How am I doing so far? Close?"

"You are really good," Shayla marveled. "That's exactly what she said. So I spent the next three years working nonstop in order to pay her back. And I postponed my own plans. When she announced that our diamond mines weren't depleted after all, that a surveyor had not only discovered more, but even better, they contained fire diamonds, I saw my opportunity to pursue the career I always wanted."

"A serious miscalculation on Leticia's part. That's not like her."

Shayla smiled. "She did raise the idea of reopening Charlestons with me once again until I forced her to accept the futility of her plan. I'm simply not competent to run the business. Approaching Dantes was the compromise. It would provide her with the money to revitalize the mansion and keep her comfortable for her remaining years. And it would allow me to find the job of my dreams, which I promptly did."

"All of this went down before we met?"

Shayla nodded. "I updated my passport and applied for a number of positions that offered travel abroad. I was thrilled when the one I wanted the most panned out. Derek needed someone who could leave the country almost immediately. I told my grandmother about it right before I boarded the plane for San Francisco."

"When were you scheduled to leave the country?" he asked in a neutral voice.

She forced herself to meet his gaze, even though she'd have preferred to look anywhere but. "The same evening as our date."

"Why?" He ground out the question, anger reverberating through that single word.

She didn't prevaricate, but told him the truth. "Because I didn't want you to try to stop me."

"Could I have?"

Lord, give her strength. She closed her eyes against the demand in his. Could he have stopped her? Without question. All it would have taken was a single kiss. Kiss? A single look. A single touch, Inferno to Inferno. When it came to Draco Dante, she had zero self-control.

He was waiting for her response and she gathered herself sufficiently to give it to him. "Suffice to say, I wasn't willing to risk the possibility," she replied, neatly sidestepping the issue. "By the time you realized I was gone, I'd be on my way to Barcelona with Derek." He wouldn't like this other part, either. "There's more."

He grimaced. "Might as well put it all out there."

She twisted her hands together, aware that when she finished he wouldn't press for marriage any longer. In fact, she'd be lucky if he didn't just pitch her out of the car, altogether. "My plan contained three parts, goals I wanted to achieve before I turned twenty-five. The first was to find the job of my dreams."

"Enter Derek. Check."

"The second was to provide for my grandmother by offering your family the lease to our mines."

"Meet with the Dantes. Double check." His eyes narrowed, amber hard. "And the third?"

"I turned twenty-five the morning after we met," she began

before trailing off. She wanted to just say it, to get it out there and over with, but she found that she couldn't. Her breath escaped in a slow sigh.

It only took Draco a moment to catch on. "*That's* why you slept with me?" Outrage underscored the question. "You planned to lose your virginity before you turned twenty-five?"

She shook her head. "No!" She flinched. "Well, yes. But not the way you think."

"And I was the lucky guy you chose?"

Did he have to make it sound so lurid? "You don't understand," she tried again. "It wasn't about losing my virginity." How did she explain? "I wanted, just once, to experience a wild, passionate affair. To be swept off my feet and have a single night of pure romance."

"In other words, it could have been any man at the reception that night, even one of my relatives. I was simply the luck of the draw." A muscle leaped along his jaw, warning that he held on to his temper by a mere thread. "It had nothing to do with The Inferno or who I was as a person. You just wanted to sleep with someone before jetting off with good ol' Derek."

A wave of humiliation sent heat streaking across her cheeks while tears pricked her eyes. She fought them back, fought for composure. During the planning stages, having a one-night stand had sounded intrepid, romantic even. Something so out-of-character that she hadn't dared consider it while living in her grandmother's home. Unfortunately, she'd become the poster child for the consequences of illicit sex, even with protection. They might as well slap a photo of her, along with her giant belly, on all the high school walls in the country as a warning. *This could be you!*

"To be fair, I don't think you were too concerned about

who I was as a person, either," she pointed out. "Not at first."

"In other words, if you'd known I was a Dante beforehand, you'd have tumbled into some other man's bed that night."

The tears she'd been holding back through sheer force of will overflowed. "I'm sorry. I don't know what else to say. I wanted to be honest with you so you'd understand why marriage is out of the question. You don't love me anymore than I love you."

He swore. "Don't cry. Please, don't cry, Shayla. It can't be good for either you or the baby."

"I'm not a damn water tap," she managed to protest through her tears. "It's not like I can turn it off with a twist of a knob."

For some reason that made his mouth twitch and a second later she was laughing and crying all at the same time. He opened her purse, found a packet of tissues and pulled one out. He dabbed at her cheeks and eyes and nose.

"Listen to me, sweetheart," he said. "You're tired. I'm tired. We probably could have picked a better time for this conversation."

"I needed to be honest with you."

"I got that. Maybe all that honesty should have come at a slower pace and after a good night's sleep." He gave it further consideration. "And maybe accompanied by several shots of Johnnie Walker."

"Okay." She leaned back against the leather seat and closed her eyes. Exhaustion rolled across her like fog across the bay. "I'm trying, Draco. I've moved out here so our baby will be close to you and the rest of the Dantes. But that's as far as I'm willing to go. I'm not sure I can handle marriage on top of everything else."

"Why?" The question exploded from him, hanging in the air.

It took an unbelievable amount of effort just to open a single eye. "I don't suppose there's any Johnnie Walker stashed in here somewhere?"

"Am I going to need it?"

"Probably."

"Hell." He gave an irritable shrug. "You might as well get it all out. I can't deal with it if I don't know what the problem is."

"That's what you said last time," she muttered.

"Go on. Hit me."

"Okay, here it is… I worked for four long years to carve out the sort of life I wanted. It only took me one night to put an end to that dream." She splayed her hand across her extended abdomen, gave it a gentle rub. "Don't misunderstand. I'll love our baby. I'll never regret having him." She shook her head in exasperation. "*Him?* Now you have me doing it."

"Trust me. It's going to be a boy."

"Fine." She dismissed that with a flick of her fingers. "The point is… Those few months abroad were the best of my life. I was unchained and independent. Until then, I'd never experienced that level of freedom before. Now you want me to marry you. To move in with you. To forcibly create a family. It's going to be tough enough that I'm here in a strange city with a newborn. I'm not sure I can handle marriage on top of everything else. To be honest, I don't want to lose any more of my independence."

Draco was silent for a long time and she wondered if she'd offended him again. "You don't have to handle marriage," he finally said. "There's another option."

Hope blossomed. "What option?"

"We'll make a premarital agreement…a marriage pact, if that works for you. We marry to give the baby the Dante name, but we don't have to live together, if you'd rather not." She caught a certain grimness in his voice, a stoic quality that disturbed her. "It'll be your choice. If and when you want a real marriage, we can reconsider that possibility."

"You'd be willing to do that?" she asked in surprise. "Wouldn't your family notice?"

"It's none of their business."

She gave a short laugh. "That might be your opinion and it might be mine, as well, but I've discovered that it's never the opinion of the rest of the family. They always think they have the right to interfere."

"There's only one person's opinion that matters to me and that's yours. As for my family... Don't worry about them. I'll keep them off your back."

She could feel herself softening. She probably should have insisted on revisiting the discussion in the morning when she'd had time to rest and consider. But instead, she found herself nodding. "Okay, I agree."

He stilled. "You'll marry me?"

"Yes," she found herself saying. Clearly, she'd lost her mind.

"Tomorrow?"

Her eyebrows winged upward. "Can we get married that fast?"

"Absolutely. I'll make the arrangements as soon as we get home."

Panic built in the pit of her stomach and more than anything she wanted to change her mind. Instead, she nodded. "It's a deal."

He gathered her up in his arms. "Since we can't toast our agreement with champagne, we'll seal the deal with another time-honored tradition."

She had a split second to prepare herself before he lowered his head and kissed her, kissed her with a thoroughness that drove every other thought from her head. Their kiss yesterday had been filled with hunger and demand. The one on the plane a gentle benediction. This one was sheer temptation, as though he were reminding her of that wonderfully illicit evening nine months ago when passion had ruled the night and she'd unknowingly surrendered to the ultimate temptation.

Now Draco's kiss stormed her senses, making her forget everything but this man and this moment. For a brief instant she even forgot the baby tucked safely beneath her heart, a baby who'd been the result of that surrender. A baby born from passion and who would know the love of both parents, as well as countless family members.

For her baby's sake, marrying Draco was the smart choice. The only choice. But for her own sake…?

Before she could consider the question, he reluctantly released her and glanced outside. Shayla suddenly realized they'd arrived. While the driver unloaded their bags, Draco helped her from the car, a process that became more difficult with each passing day. A tip passed from his hand to the chauffer's and then they were alone.

She took a moment to study his home while she attempted to unknot the muscles in her back. The house stood wide and proud, a stunning multilevel wood-and-glass structure perched high on the hillside with an incredible view of the bay.

"It's gorgeous," she murmured.

"Wait until you see the inside."

He guided her along the walkway to the front door, stuck his key in the lock and flung open the door. Gently, carefully, tenderly, he lifted her in his arms and carried her across the threshold. "Welcome home," he said.

At the same moment an endless crowd of people jumped out from doorways and closets and from behind furniture, all shouting, "Surprise!"

The instant they realized Draco wasn't alone, silence descended. All eyes locked on Shayla…or more specifically,

Shayla's belly. Primo stood front and center in the middle of the throng, his golden gaze taking in the situation in a single fierce glance.

"Well," he said after a long, awkward moment. "It would seem the surprise is on us, eh?"

Six

Draco watched his wife-to-be take one look at Primo and start babbling. In Italian, no less.

"We're getting married, I swear. First thing in the morning. Well, not first thing. I have a doctor's appointment that I don't think Draco will let me miss. But right after that we're going straight to a justice of the peace and tying the knot. And don't blame your grandson. It's not his fault. He didn't know I was pregnant and he's been looking for me for nine months and would have insisted we marry even if I weren't." She paused long enough to snatch a quick breath. "Pregnant, I mean."

Draco gently eased Shayla onto her feet. "So, what's *your* surprise?" he asked his family.

Primo locked eyes with Draco, a wealth of information passing between them without a single word being spoken. "Your home. It is finished," his grandfather announced at last. "We are giving you a surprise hothouse party. The women, they say it is tradition."

It took Draco a split second to realize that hothouse meant housewarming. "Thank you. I appreciate it. Maybe we can also make it a pre-wedding celebration?"

His gaze swept his relatives, taking in the various reactions ranging from shock to bemusement to out-and-out laughter. Then they closed ranks. After all, they were Dantes and Dantes protected their own. They swept up Shayla, carried her off and eased her onto a couch, building pillows around her for added comfort. One by one, family members approached and introduced themselves while they plied her with food and friendly get-to-know-you questions.

Primo jerked his head toward the outside deck and Draco released a sigh of regret that he wasn't also being pillowed and fed—and wouldn't be anytime in the near future. Once they were outside Primo fumbled in his pocket for the cigar he always carried there, much to Nonna's annoyance, not to mention his physician's. He offered a second to Draco, who knew better than to refuse, given the current circumstances. The two men took their time with the trimming and lighting.

Then Primo devastated Draco with a single look. "You did this to her?"

The words, the look, all had him flinching. "The baby is mine, yes. I'm sorry, Primo. This isn't the way I'd planned things."

"I am unaware of the fact that you plan at all."

The comment stung. Once upon a time it might have been true. But he'd worked long and hard the past decade to prove himself. To overcome the shame of losing the fire diamonds at a time his family teetered on the brink of financial ruin.

Draco fought for patience. "You know The Inferno hit the night of the Eternity reception. And you know Shayla disappeared the next day after we met to discuss leasing the Charleston mines." He paced to the railing and studied the spectacular view through eyes blinded by the past rather than focused on the present. "I've been searching for her ever since she left. Two days ago I finally found her."

"You marry tomorrow?"

"Yes."

"Not by this justice of the peace, *istigatore*."

Draco's mouth tightened. He'd always been considered a troublemaker by his grandfather. Only time would change that. Or maybe, once labeled, it would never change. "How, when and where?"

"I will provide you with the place. My place." Primo stabbed his cigar in Draco's direction. "A small backyard wedding, yes? With the family. And no city official, but a priest. If we can arrange this for tomorrow, *buon*. If not, *presto*. Very soon." He fixed his grandson with a calculating gaze. "My math, it is good. I can add how many months and weeks have slipped by since the reception. The baby, he will not wait much longer."

"No, he won't."

"And your Nonna, she will cry if *il bambino* comes into the world without the Dante name to protect him. You know what I do to any man who makes my *bellezza* weep?" Primo's eyes glittered with threat and promise. "Would you care to guess, *nipote?*"

Draco's mouth settled into grim lines. The same thing he'd do to any man who made Shayla weep. Beat the living crap out of him. "I have a pretty good idea. Trust me, I won't allow that to happen."

"Buon, buon." Primo clapped his hand on Draco's shoulder. "I know you have searched for your Inferno mate these many months. Luc tells me you asked Juice to help find her the very night you lost her. You have done right in this. But you should not have taken her to your bed without first putting

your ring on her finger. To do so dishonors the two of you, not to mention your family. You know this now, yes?"

"*Sì*, Primo. *Sono spiacente*," he apologized.

A smoke trail swept in the direction of the relatives clustered in the living room. "Your family, we will all stay a short while longer, then leave you and Shayla. She needs rest so she does not have the baby before the priest blesses your union. As for the preparations for the ceremony, Nonna and I will take care of these."

Draco inclined his head. "*Grazie*. Shayla and I will arrange for a license tomorrow."

Primo proved himself as good as his word. Within the hour, everyone pitched in to sweep the house clean of clutter and debris. Leftover food disappeared into Draco's cavernous refrigerator, neatly wrapped and labeled. Hugs and kisses were freely dispensed. Then, one by one, the Dantes departed.

An abrupt silence crashed down around Draco and Shayla, strumming to life an unexpected awkwardness. "Why don't I show you the house," he suggested in an effort to break the intensity of the moment.

Shayla seized on the suggestion with patent relief. "I'd like that. I feel like I've been sitting forever."

He took her through the house, pleased by her sincere pleasure and delight at the vaulted ceilings, open spaces and endless windows that offered spectacular views of Angel Island, Belvedere and the bay. The instant he realized exhaustion had replaced enjoyment, he urged her upstairs, where he intended to tuck her into bed as soon as possible.

He opened the door to the master bedroom. "You're welcome to join me in here." One look at her face gave him the unwelcome answer to that suggestion. "But perhaps you'd be more comfortable in this room."

He led her past a tightly closed door toward a bedroom at

the far end of the house from the master suite. She paused outside of the middle room. "What's in here?" she asked.

"Another bedroom," he said dismissively. "It doesn't have a private bath, so—" He attempted to urge her past, but she didn't budge from her position.

Pulling free of his arm, she opened the door and stepped inside. Her breath caught. He'd hoped to inspect the room before showing it to Shayla since he'd only given the decorator and his cousin's wife, Ariana, two days to complete it and hadn't been certain whether their efforts had met with success.

Draco entered behind Shayla and discovered that his demands had not just been met, but exceeded. Whimsy ruled. Silly abounded. Wondrous had ventured into the nursery and nestled in to stay. Shayla wandered deeper into the room, touching the lace-edged changing table with its silly mobile hanging above it. Real and imaginary creatures dangled in every imaginable position from the strings. Some clung for dear life, others hung by wings or toes, one by its tail, each with comical expressions.

The walls were the only part of the room left incomplete, he noted, and blessed Ariana for what she'd been able to finish. Three were painted to resemble a magical forest, rife with playful fairies and trolls and other fantastical creatures. Anyone who saw them would instantly identify them as the work of Ariana's alter ego—Mrs. Pennywinkle, children's book author and illustrator. But the one behind the crib remained notably blank.

Oh, well. He'd tried. And he could guarantee that she had, as well. Considering how surprised the family had been by Shayla's pregnancy, it was clear that Ariana had acceded to his wishes and remained mum about his request for a nursery, even from her husband, Lazz. His mouth curved into a wry smile. Though she hadn't warned him about the housewarming party, no doubt her way to balance the scales.

For the rest of the room, Draco had recommended yellow as the overriding color since it echoed one of the blankets Shayla had made for the baby. The crib was simple and sturdy and rated the safest on the market, the rocking chair positioned adjacent to it the most comfortable money could buy. A baby monitor stood at the ready.

She crossed to the dresser and opened a few of the drawers to reveal garments so tiny it made Draco nervous to imagine their having a baby who could fit into them. Last of all, she opened the louvered closet doors to reveal colorful containers overflowing with toys.

He shifted in place. "I might have gotten carried away."

She glanced over her shoulder and lifted an eyebrow. "Might?"

He blew out his breath. "Did." He shot an uneasy glance around the room, striving to see it through Shayla's eyes. "I guess I should have waited so you could have some input."

She turned to regard him through watchful eyes. "How much input did you have? You only found out about my pregnancy, what? Two days ago?"

Was she upset because he hadn't included her in the decision making? He shrugged. "I wish we could have chosen everything ourselves, but I wasn't sure there'd be time before the baby was born." His mouth quirked into a smile. "I did some research and explained to the decorator what I wanted, I gather at greater length and with more detail than any other room in the house. At least, that's what he finally told me."

Shayla approached. To his surprise, she folded her arms around his neck and tugged him down for a slow, sweet kiss. "Thank you. This is amazing. It's also absolutely perfect."

He rested his forehead against hers. "I know you want

your own place. But maybe for the first few months it would work best to stay here where I can help."

She surprised him again by nodding. "That sounds reasonable. I don't have a problem living with you for the time being so long as you stick to our pact and I can move into my own place when I'm ready."

It wasn't a total surrender, but it gave him time. Time to convince her to turn "for the time being" into plain old forever. To create a real marriage together and a real family. Maybe he could prove that he'd never confine her, but would give her the freedom she craved to accomplish new goals. Craft new dreams. Better dreams. Somehow, someway, he needed to provide her with all the things she lacked so she'd stay instead of run.

Slow down, Dante. First things first, and patience would be at the top of his to-do list, even though it was in seriously short supply these days. He inclined his head toward the door. "Why don't I show you your room?" he offered with an easy smile.

He ushered her into the room next to the nursery. It was smaller than his but with a private bath, small sitting area and cantilevered redwood deck that wrapped around the house and connected with his bedroom. He'd considered having a door cut into the nursery so it accessed the deck, as well, but decided against it for safety reasons.

"We can move the crib and rocker in here temporarily if that would be easier for you," he offered.

She nodded and he caught a flash of exhaustion buried in her eyes. "Thank you. I'd prefer that."

He swept back the bedcovers with one hand and gathered her up with the other. "We can decide all that later. Right now, you need sleep. Dr. Dorling would be furious if he knew we hadn't tucked you in the instant we arrived."

He didn't give her a chance to protest, but eased her onto

the mattress. Kneeling, he removed her shoes. "Do you want to strip down or will you be comfortable enough like this?"

"I'm too tired to strip down," she confessed.

"Then sleep. I'll bring the bags up in a little while along with some dinner and you can change then. You can even indulge yourself and eat in bed."

She yawned, half smothering her reply. "After that meal your relatives prepared, I don't think I'll be able to eat again for a week."

He helped settle her in bed and arranged the pillows for added comfort and support. "Some soup, then?"

Shayla's eyes drooped and she sighed in pleasure. "Some of that minestrone your grandfather made? I've never tasted anything so delicious."

"Absolutely."

He doubted she heard his response. She fell sound asleep on her last word. He checked on her periodically, not the least surprised when she didn't stir. Long after the sun set and evening had deepened into night, he slipped into the room once again. It was clear she wouldn't wake until morning and he gently unbuttoned her dress, easing it off. He debated stripping away all her clothing, but decided she might feel self-conscious about his seeing her naked so late in her pregnancy.

Personally, he thought her unbelievably beautiful. She was softer than before, rounder, her curves lush with impending motherhood. There was also an ethereal radiance about her, an otherworldliness that made him hesitant to touch her, as though she'd magically vanish if he dared lay a hand on her. Vanish like one of the mystical creatures decorating the nursery walls. The mere thought of her disappearing again caused his heart to give a painful lurch.

Soon she'd be both wife and mother, just as he'd be husband

and father. How odd that two short days before he'd been neither of those things, hadn't even known that one reckless night with this woman had created a child. But he found himself fiercely glad that it had happened, that a new life had been breathed into existence from a moment of perfect passion.

He knelt beside the bed and rested his hand against the baby Shayla held safely tucked within her. The Inferno hummed as though recognizing its connection to what snuggled beneath. Draco closed his eyes, realizing he'd fallen and fallen hard. For mother. For child. And then he pressed his cheek to that restless mound, whispered to his son and made promises he'd do everything within his power to keep.

Shayla woke with the sun and sighed in pleasure. It had become more and more difficult to find a comfortable position while her pregnancy came closer and closer to term. But somehow, Draco's spare bed offered the sort of support and relaxation she hadn't experienced in months. She stretched, only then discovering the muscular arm cradling her belly, felt the warm male body spooning her own and buttressing her back and legs.

"This is nice. I could get used to this," Draco rumbled sleepily.

"Easy for you to say. You're not currently a blimp." But it *was* nice, Shayla privately conceded. And she could absolutely get used to it. She shot him a wry look over her shoulder. "Just out of curiosity, what are you doing in my bed?"

"Getting acquainted with our son." He nuzzled the curve of her neck with a raspy cheek. "Getting reacquainted with his mother, too."

She took a quick peek beneath the covers, relieved to see that she still wore two scraps of silk and lace, not that they offered much protection considering how thin they were.

Or how they failed to conceal the dramatic changes to her shape. "And—also just out of curiosity—what happened to my clothes?"

"Gone."

"I see that. Did you gone them?"

"Yup. Would have goned the rest of them but I figured you'd be a tad upset."

She smothered a laugh, which faded when she thought of him seeing her asleep and almost naked...and a full thirty-nine weeks pregnant. "I've lost my figure," she informed him self-consciously, just in case he hadn't noticed.

"No, you haven't. It's right here." His fingers splayed across her stomach while satisfaction rippled through his statement. "And it's even more beautiful than before."

Tears pricked her eyes, tears that never seemed far away. "You don't mind?"

He turned her in his arms so they faced each other. Gently he traced the curve of her cheek, then lower to the painful fullness of her breasts, overflowing from the royal blue cups of her bra, then lower still to the swell of her belly. "How can you ask such a thing? Hell, no, I don't mind. You're a goddess."

It was a lie, but one she could live with. She smiled through her tears. "Does that make you a god?"

"Nope. Just a man. A very lucky, very humble man."

Draco lifted onto one elbow and cupped her face. Leaning in he kissed her wide-awake and she discovered another delightful fact about him. Her husband-to-be was very thorough in the morning. Very. Thorough.

With a reluctant groan, he pulled back. "Hungry? For food, I mean."

"Starving." And not just for food. She eyed him hopefully. "I vaguely remember you saying something about minestrone soup. I don't suppose the offer still stands?"

He grinned. "For breakfast?"

"Why not?" she asked with a shrug. "It's healthier than pickles and ice cream."

A chuckle broke free. "You've been craving pickles and ice cream?"

"No, but I could have," she explained with the sweeping logic of late pregnancy. "Instead it's Primo's minestrone soup."

"He'll be thrilled to hear it. Would you like it served in bed?"

She considered, then made a face and shook her head. "No, thanks. I'll come down right after I shower and dress."

Draco's expression turned wicked. "Need help?"

"I think I can manage," she replied drily.

He levered himself out of bed with an ease Shayla could only envy. These days she felt like an upended turtle, rolling around on its shell. Without her saying a word, he gave her a hand, helping to free her from the nest of mattress, covers and pillows. And he accomplished it with an innate courtesy, as though he'd done the same thing every day for the past half-dozen months. She realized then that his gallantry came naturally, without conscious thought or premeditated intent. It was just who he was.

"You know, you might want to shower in the master suite," he suggested. "The one in here is a combination shower/tub and might be more difficult for you right now. Mine is a free-standing shower. There should be towels in the closet in my bathroom. Give a shout if they're not there. In the meantime, I'll head down and start the soup."

She simply stared at him, helplessly, hopelessly, impossibly drawn to him. But not in love. No, definitely not that. Falling in love would be foolish. It would be dangerous. Worst of all, it would steal away her one shot at freedom. So, why did her heart stutter and pitch at the thought of walking away from him?

"What?" he demanded in response to the look.

She shook her head, ending the moment. "Nothing." She smiled at him, allowing her gratitude to show. "I mean, thank you. I appreciate the offer."

But it wasn't nothing. All the while she stood beneath the soothing spray of the shower she tried to convince herself that their marriage pact would work. She'd stay with him in this beautiful home for the first several weeks after the baby was born—though she wouldn't share a bed with him again. It was too dangerous a risk. She'd put a swift stop to that right now before she grew too attached to having him beside her. Then once she got the hang of being a mother, she'd insist on finding her own place. She'd regain her independence. She'd be free, or at least as free as she could get with the weighty responsibilities of a newborn.

But even as she set new goals for herself and created new dreams she knew deep in her heart that she'd never be free. She and Draco were bound, tied tightly together by the baby she carried. She'd tried running once, telling herself she was chasing her dream. In the end she'd been caught. Fettered tight. And she doubted she'd escape again.

The thought filled her with panic, which receded over the next several hours, though never quite vanished as it continued to disturb the even tenor of her thoughts. While she ate, Draco finalized the details to obtain their marriage license.

"Four weeks for an appointment, my Aunt Fanny," he grumbled.

"We have to wait four weeks?" Shayla asked in alarm.

"I had to pull a few strings, call in several favors, but we can get it done this afternoon." He checked his watch. "That should allow us to fit in your doctor's appointment and lunch beforehand."

She didn't bother to conceal her relief. "Oh. Oh, well, all right, then. You had me worried there."

"You were worried?" he shot back. "I had images of dragging you to Vegas and having you gasp out your 'I dos' while I timed your labor pains."

She grinned. "That would have been quite a story to tell our son." She groaned. "See? I did it again."

Draco leaned a hip against the counter while mainlining caffeine in the form of a very fine Costa Rican coffee. "Dr. Dorling didn't mention whether or not it was a boy? I'd have thought he could have told by the ultrasound."

"I didn't want to know." She patted her belly. "Everything else about this baby has been a surprise. I figured that should be, too."

"Oh, we'll be surprised, all right. If it's a girl, we'll all be downright shocked."

"Is it really that unusual?"

Draco shrugged. "Nonna has the eye, and she said only one girl among this newest generation. Ariana and Lazz already have a lock on that. Their daughter, Amata, was born three months ago."

"Oh, I remember her." Shayla grinned in delight. "She was the one with all the ringlets."

"That's our Amata." He checked his watch. "We'd better get going. We have a busy day ahead of us."

Their first stop was the doctor's office. Both she and Draco instantly took to the new obstetrician, a friendly, outgoing woman who warned them that, based on her examination, Shayla could go into labor at any time. Before they left the office, Dr. Henderly gave them a checklist of items to deal with in preparation for an early delivery. It covered everything from obtaining a car seat suitable for a newborn to preregistering at the hospital.

Since they had a couple of hours to spare, they worked their way through the list before collapsing at a restaurant near the courthouse. While they waited for their meal, Draco pulled Shayla's feet onto his lap. Beneath the linen tablecloth and hidden from the view of the other diners, he gave her a bone-melting massage from calf to toe. Her luncheon massage was followed by a pleasantly quick stop at the registrar's office, where they obtained a marriage license. Then, exhausted, Shayla slept the entire drive home. The instant they arrived at the house, Draco insisted she rest, much to her displeasure.

"I rested in the car," she protested. "And I'm tired of being treated like an invalid."

"Primo called," he explained as he corralled her up the steps. "My grandfather never ceases to amaze with the amount of pull he possesses. He's arranged for a priest to perform the marriage ceremony tonight, at his place, no less."

"So soon?" she made the mistake of asking.

Draco's expression closed over and he retreated behind a cool, polite mask. "Since the doctor suggested you were likely to deliver sooner rather than later, I don't think there's any time to waste. Do you?"

Great. Pregnancy had made her about as tactful as her grandmother. "No, of course not. You're right." Her reassurance only partially mollified him. "What time?"

"Eight. Just before sunset."

It was a sweet gesture on Primo's part. A romantic gesture. "That sounds lovely," she said, then gazed at Draco in distress as a horrifying thought occurred. "I can't take a nap. There's no time. Not if we're getting married tonight."

"Because…?" Impatience rippled through the single word.

"Because I don't have a thing to wear, at least nothing

suitable for a wedding dress." She attempted to push past him toward the stairs. "We have to go back to the city right now so I can find something."

He caught her close and urged her toward her bedroom. "No."

"You don't understand—"

"I do understand, but that doesn't change my answer." Before she could argue further, he lifted a hand to stem the flood. "Don't panic. You're a Dante now. Or will be in a few short hours."

She planted her hands on her hips, or rather, what she could find of her hips, and glared at him. It was either that or cry. "What has my being a Dante got to do with anything?"

He actually had the nerve to laugh at her, sending her temper soaring. "Right, right. Sorry. Forgot you never had the benefit of a big family." He dropped a finger to her lips to hold her silent. "See, this is how it works. I put out the alarm. The phone calls fly and every Dante goes on alert status."

"You're kidding," she said around his finger.

"Not even a little. Since three of my cousins' wives have had babies recently, one of them is bound to own a dress they wore during their pregnancy that you can use for a wedding gown." He replaced his finger with his mouth, stealing a swift, blistering kiss. "Just one phone call and I guarantee, suitable attire will be waiting for you at Primo's in time for the ceremony."

She had her doubts, but they were swiftly laid to rest the instant she arrived at Primo and Nonna's. The women all descended on her and swept her off to one of the bedrooms, where a gown hung from the closet door. One glance warned it wasn't borrowed, but a maternity wedding gown that had been newly purchased for her benefit.

She stood and stared at the gown in disbelief. This time she didn't even try to hold back the tears. The off-the-shoulder sleeves were wisps of puckered ivory tulle, framing a softly ruched bodice. From beneath the pearl-seeded bodice flowed a series of chiffon pleats that would drape loosely over her abdomen. A veil hung nearby, stealing Shayla's breath. Tiny fire diamonds and seed pearls created a delicate tiara complete with a flowing cascade of tulle veiling. It was a beautifully preserved piece.

Shayla touched the veil with trembling fingers. "It's the most gorgeous thing I've ever seen."

Draco's mother, Elia, embraced her. "I wore it at my wedding. It pleases me to have you wear it at yours."

Next on the agenda was hair and makeup. Laughter abounded and Shayla allowed herself to drift along on a current of pleasure, refusing to consider the ramifications of her marriage to Draco—what it meant and how it promised to change her life. She sat patiently beneath the ministrations of the Dante women, Gianna wielding a curling iron, Larkin and Téa taking turns with the makeup case. Once everyone was satisfied, they all stepped back so Shayla could see the results.

"Oh," she murmured. "You've made me beautiful."

"No crying," Gianna warned. "You'll ruin everyone's hard work."

Larkin and Téa had employed subtlety when it came to the makeup, emphasizing the high arch of Shayla's cheekbones and giving depth and definition to her dark eyes. Her mouth appeared softer, rosier and just-kissed moist. Gianna had also worked magic, pulling Shayla's hair away from her face and coaxing the sheet of ebony into a cascade of soft curls.

"Now it is my turn," Nonna announced. Carefully she studded the curls with jasmine blossoms, their sweet scent filling the air.

Shayla stroked one of the ivory petals. "They're absolutely lovely."

"They are from Primo's garden," Nonna explained. "He picked them himself. He thought it might remind you of home."

And it did. Jasmine bloomed yearly in the ruins of her grandmother's garden, its heady scent a welcome advent each May. Elia signaled that the time to dress had arrived. It didn't take long, not with so many women helping. Though Shayla didn't have a hope of disguising her pregnancy, the drapes and folds floated around her, making it far less obvious. Next came the veil. Elia did the honors there. The final touch came when Gianna handed Shayla a bouquet of trailing jasmine to match the flowers in her hair.

Gianna stepped back with a trembling smile. "The veil is something old and borrowed. The dress something new," she explained. She indicated the ribbon they'd used to tie the bouquet together. "And there's your something blue."

Finding herself unable to utter a word, Shayla hugged her sister-to-be, then Elia and Nonna. Three generations of Dante women and soon she'd be one of them. "Thank you so much," she finally managed to say. Her gaze swept the other women in the room. "Thank you all."

From that moment forward the evening passed in a haze. She joined Draco in front of the priest in a garden filled with beds of colorful flowers and overflowing with the warmth of family. Just as the last ray of sunshine touched the gathering in a golden benediction, the priest pronounced them husband and wife.

Draco lifted the single layer of tulle away from her eyes and mouth and cupped her face in a gesture as endearing as it was familiar. "My wife," he announced, his words ripe with possession and stamped with satisfaction.

And then he kissed her. The kiss stripped away nerves and hesitation, crashed through barriers and conflict. In its place it gave hope. Passion. More than that, it offered a promise fraught with possibility.

If only…came the stray notion as resistance slipped away and she succumbed to the embrace. If only this were real. If only they were in love. If only the baby kicking impatiently for freedom weren't responsible for their marriage.

If only they loved each other.

No sooner had the thought been born, than the first star fired to life in the velvety sky overhead. It glittered bright and steady in the heavens, then flashed like the heart of a fire diamond. The Inferno burned within her palm, as though in confirmation, as though it were somehow connected to the star.

A first wish made…

…a first wish granted.

Seven

She was his.

His wife. His woman. His Inferno mate. And soon she would be the mother of his child.

He kissed his wife for the first time, while fading sunlight haloed her. When he lifted his head to gaze down at his bride, the sun had set and the glow of torchlight gave her a wild, mysterious beauty. Eyes deep with endless hope gleamed up at him. And yet the kiss they'd shared, one meant to seal the vows they'd just committed to, felt like far more than mere hope. It felt like a wish. A promise. A door opening toward possibility.

Her arms slid from around his neck until her palms rested against his chest. She stared at the ring he'd put on her finger, no doubt getting her first good look at it. It was one of the Eternity wedding sets showcased at that long-ago reception where they'd originally met.

The central fire diamond was from a Dante mine, and in

Draco's opinion, one of the finest he'd ever seen, equal if not superior to the ones he'd lost. He'd had the smaller diamonds on either side replaced with Charleston fire diamonds as a symbolic bonding of the two families. He didn't doubt she'd catch the significance.

"The Eternity rings all have names, don't they?" she murmured, and glanced up, pinning him with darkness. "What's this one called?"

"Eternally Bound."

A troubled frown touched her brow. "Is that what we are? Eternally bound?"

"If you believe in the legend of The Inferno, yes."

"And if I don't?" A touch of urgency underscored the question. Or maybe it was panic. "What then?"

He tucked a curl behind her ear, keeping his voice low and reassuring, as though soothing a wild creature who'd just discovered itself snared by a hunter. "Then it's just a legend, and just a ring."

"But it's a legend you believe in, isn't it?" she insisted. "A ring that *does* bind us from this point forward."

He'd made two vows to Shayla since he'd found her, heavy with his child. With the first he'd promised to set her free, while the one made only moments ago committed him to love and protect her for the rest of their lives. Somehow, someway, he'd honor both, no matter how difficult. Even though she was right about his wanting to bind her to him in every way possible, he wouldn't hold back what struggled so desperately for release.

The words came with difficulty, but he forced himself to speak them. "What I do or don't believe doesn't change our pact. Once the baby is born and you have time to adjust to motherhood and your transition from Atlanta, you can decide how you want your future to go from there. I won't interfere with that."

He'd opened the door to freedom. Now it was up to her whether she stepped through it, or realized that she was just as free if she chose to stay. She gave a quick nod and a slow smile. Then she gathered his face in her soft hands in a gesture that duplicated their first kiss as husband and wife. And she kissed him with such sweetness that it almost brought him to his knees.

His relatives looked on with broad grins and Draco couldn't help but wonder how long those grins would last if they knew that just minutes after making his vows, he'd promised his wife he'd let her go. He returned the kiss, tamping down on the temptation to pull her closer and kiss her with the sort of passion that had gotten them into their current predicament. If she resisted, it would upset his family and embarrass them both. And if she responded he'd never know if it was because of their audience or because she wanted him.

With a breathless laugh, she stepped back. Before he could catch her again, she disappeared into the clutches of his family and he was forced to let her go. *Relax, Dante.* In a few hours they'd return home and he'd once again hold her while she slept. He could wait until then.

He blew out a sigh. Maybe.

Someone turned on music, filling the air with a weeping aria. Draco headed over to a tub of ice beside a table groaning with food and helped himself to one of Primo's stash of homemade beer. Popping the cap, he glanced around the yard, impressed. He didn't know how his family had pulled together the wedding so quickly, especially on the heels of his housewarming party, but it couldn't have been more beautiful if they'd planned it for months.

An evening breeze poured off the water and kept the temperatures moderate, even a little on the cool side. But all the bodies and movement and activity staved off the chill. He caught sight of Shayla with his sister, Gianna. The two had clearly hit it off. And he noticed that Téa and Larkin joined their small group in the sort of female-bonding ceremony that left him both perplexed and vaguely alarmed. Larkin's head bent close to Shayla's, creating a striking contrast of icy pale against dusky richness, and it suddenly occurred to him that each of the women in the group had been at the same Eternity reception nine months ago. Had they met, even casually? Did they remember one another, if only on some subconscious level? Were they even now comparing notes and making the connection?

Before he could consider the potential ramifications of that bit of speculation, Rafe clapped a hand on his shoulder. "Odd to think that we both met our Inferno brides the same night," he said, his comment an eerie echo of Draco's thoughts from only a few minutes before. Rafe's gaze fixed on Larkin, brimming with the strength of his love. "Or that you were the one responsible for bringing us together."

Draco shrugged. "You were drawn to her long before I arranged that little run-in."

"But I might not have acted on it if you hadn't suggested I fake The Inferno by hiring her as my soul mate." Rafe turned to him. "Seriously, bro, I owe you for that."

"Good. I like having people in my debt."

Rafe chuckled. "Then I'll offer this small piece of advice to help settle my debt. Give Shayla time to adjust. Just be patient and let The Inferno work its magic on her."

Draco tilted his head to one side in consideration, before shaking his head. "Nope. Already came to that conclusion on my own, so you still owe me."

Rafe's eyebrows shot up. "I thought you didn't believe in The Inferno."

"I didn't." Draco's focus returned to his wife. "Until Shayla." And with that he walked away from his brother and toward his future.

The women made room for him when he approached, allowing him to settle in beside his wife and tuck her close. Gradually their circle widened and the two newlyweds sat together for a long time listening while the various Dante relatives told stories, each attempting to top the other. Many of them involved The Inferno and how they met their Inferno mates.

"Did none of you believe in The Inferno? Did you all resist it?" Shayla asked in amazement.

"Primo believed," Rafe conceded. "And Marco. That's about it."

"You forgot Draco. He believed, too," Shayla insisted. "When we first touched and I asked him what he'd done to me he said he'd Infernoed me."

"Draco?" Gianna scoffed. "He's always been a total skeptic. In fact, the night you two met he tried to help Rafe avoid everyone's matchmaking attempts by pretending to experience The Inferno with—" Her eyes widened in alarm the instant she realized how her tongue had gotten away from her. She carefully set her wineglass on the table beside her chair and pushed it well out of reach. Then her gaze shot first to her parents, then to her grandparents. She smiled weakly. "That is… I mean…"

"We know what you mean," her father replied in a crisp voice. "Fortunately, it worked out for all involved."

Rafe shot his sister a grim look. "Nice going, *chiacchierona*."

"I am *not* a chatterbox."

Primo put an end to the imminent sibling spat by holding up his bottle of beer. "*Salute!* To Shayla and *l'istigatore. Cento anni di salute e felicità.*" A hundred years of health and happiness. "And now it is my turn to tell the story of how my beloved Nonna and I became Inferno-struck."

Everyone settled back in their chairs while the family

patriarch offered up the familiar and the bittersweet, a tale of the long-ago time when he and Nonna had first set eyes on one another. Those born to the Dante name had heard it chronicled many times before, but welcomed the retelling for the benefit of the newer additions to the family who hadn't heard the story.

"I had just returned from Florence after completing my studies in jewelry design and manufacturing," he began, patting his pockets for his cigar. At Nonna's narrow-eyed look, he sighed with regret and reached instead for his bottle of homemade beer. Decades worth of memories haunted his striking gold eyes.

"That night was the engagement party for *mio amico*. No," he hastened to correct. "Not just my friend. My *best* friend. Tito stood tall and proud beneath a stand of orange trees. It was June and the blossoms were at their peak, early bloomers dusting the ground like snowflakes while those still clinging to the trees filled the air with such a fragrance…"

Primo shook his head, immersed in events long gone, his gaze steeped in nostalgia. "Never have I smelled anything sweeter." He focused on Nonna, still partially enmeshed in the past, his expression overflowing with nearly sixty years of passion. "Never have I seen anyone more beautiful. My sweet Nonna was all of eighteen to my twenty, orange blossoms clinging to her hair like tiny white stars. And that hair." He put a hand to his chest and gusted out a deep sigh. "I swear it must have been every shade of brown one could imagine. The little ringlets, they tumbled down her back all the way to the tiniest waist I have ever seen."

"And you," Nonna replied with loving tartness. "Looking at me like a wolf does a sheep."

"Not a sheep, *bellezza*. A lamb. I took your hand in mine and that is when The Inferno struck." He offered a smile filled with both pleasure and regret. "Our village, it was a small, traditional place where they took a betrothal as seriously as a wedding. I dishonored my family and my best friend by taking what did not belong to me." He lifted a shoulder in a shrug that spoke volumes. "But when The Inferno strikes, there is no option given, no choice but one."

"So, we left," Nonna said, continuing the story, her voice husky with emotion. "Left our friends and our family and sailed on the first boat to America."

"Did you ever make up with your friend?" Shayla couldn't resist asking.

"I did. One year, not so long ago, when Nonna and I were visiting our families, I went to him, hat in hand. Tito actually thanked me, can you believe? He had married another girl from the village, one who adored him and whom he came to love even more than my Nonna." He grinned broadly. "Though how such a thing is possible, I cannot say. And look at us now, eh?"

He flung his arms wide to indicate the four generations present. Children, grandchildren, and now great-grand-children. "This is the richness and bounty God has granted us. This is how The Inferno rewards us when we are clever enough to follow where it leads."

A shadow drifted across Nonna's expression and Draco suspected it was due to the reminder that her eldest son, Dominic, had chosen a different wife than the one The Inferno selected for him. And though Sev, Nicolò, Marco and Lazz were the products of that union, they were all aware from letters they'd found after their parents' death that Dominic's heart had belonged elsewhere, with a jewelry designer named Cara Moretti.

Unable to bear such sadness at his wedding, Draco gave Nonna a smacking kiss on her cheek and pulled her to her feet. The music had transitioned from arias to a more lively beat and he swung his grandmother into his arms and across the patio. Primo followed suit with Shayla, though at a more sedate pace due to her advanced pregnancy. Soon all the relatives were dancing, bright voices and laughter filling the air. At some point midway through the song his grandparents switched partners so Draco could dance with his wife.

He pulled her close and breathed her in. "If I'd been in Primo's position, I'd have stolen you away, as well."

She wrinkled her nose at him, and teased, "I believe you were in Primo's position and did steal me away. Flew me straight off to your dragon's lair."

He considered. "Your grandmother rather than a fiancé? I suppose you're right." The music washed over and through him. "Now that you've heard all the stories, how do you feel about our family blessing? Or perhaps you consider it a curse."

"Not a curse," she instantly objected. "How could I think that after all those lovely stories?"

"But?"

"But… You don't believe in it, do you?" She searched his face intently. "I mean, really believe in it. It's just convenient to claim because I'm pregnant and it makes our marriage more acceptable to your family, right?"

"You heard them. You saw how they were with each other." His hand tightened on hers, The Inferno throbbing with a passionate beat, singing from one palm to the other. "You feel what I feel. Is this pretense or reality? Will it fade or is it forever?"

A troubled expression edged across her face. "I…I don't know."

He snapped his barriers in place, unwilling to chase her away now that she was finally edging closer—the beauty overcoming her fear of the beast. "Maybe someday you will," he replied lightly.

"You never answered my question," she pointed out. "Do you believe in The Inferno?"

He chose his words with care. "I never did," he admitted. Until he met Shayla.

He didn't give her the opportunity to ask any more questions, but spun her in a dizzying circle that left her breathless and laughing. At the end of the song, he guided her away from his family and toward the gate leading to the driveway.

"Shouldn't we say goodbye?" she asked as he bundled her into the car.

"Eventually they'll notice we're gone," he assured her. "And then they'll all smile knowingly before continuing with the celebration."

It only took a few minutes to make the short drive from Primo's to home. Once there, Draco helped Shayla inside and up the steps. Swinging her into his arms he carried her into his bedroom, with her protesting all the way.

"This is our wedding night," he informed her implacably before setting her on her feet. "We may have an arrangement to live separate lives a month or so from now. But tonight we sleep as husband and wife."

"It's because of The Inferno stories everyone told," she argued. "You're hoping we'll end up like them."

"I think we'll find our own way, either together or apart."

"Regardless of The Inferno?"

He turned her so she faced away from him. "I think we have more important considerations than that damn Inferno." He made short work of the laces holding her dress in place. The bodice sagged and she held it protectively against her breasts. "We have a baby due any day. Why don't we agree to focus on that and let The Inferno take care of itself?"

She turned and he didn't think he'd ever seen a more beautiful sight. Her shoulders and the upper curves of her breasts were bared, the veil she still wore framing them. More than anything he wanted to see her in that veil…and nothing else. He backed her toward the bed until she had no choice but to sit on the edge. Reaching beneath the voluminous skirts of her gown, he removed her shoes, followed by her thigh-high stockings. It amused him to no end to discover that she also wore a pretty little garter decorated in lace, seed pearls and tied with a sassy red bow. She acknowledged his raised eyebrow with a smile every bit as sassy.

Next, he coaxed her out of her gown, leaving her bared to his gaze except for two small scraps of ivory. He waited, waited for the hesitation, for the reluctance for him to proceed any further. But it never came. Taking it as tacit permission, he removed her bra and panties. Then, he rocked back on his heels, studying her with a warm smile.

"You are a picture, *mia adorata*. But I have to say the veil is the perfect touch."

For some reason, either his use of the Italian endearment or his gentle humor, she relaxed. She even managed a flirtatious expression. "Do you want me to wear it to bed?"

The fact that she'd accepted that they would be sleeping together caused something deep and powerful to seize him by the throat. "Not tonight," he replied gruffly.

Draco removed the veil and set it safely aside. Then, one by one he plucked the pearl-tipped pins from her hair so that the curls tumbled down across her shoulders and back. He eased her against the pillows, while gardenia petals scattered across the crisp cotton linens, releasing their sweet scent into the air.

His woman. His wife. Mother of his child. He leaned in and stole a kiss, a soft, easy caress. Then he took another, a more passionate one this time. She returned the first. But she dove into the second, nipping at his lower lip. Tugging at it.

Then her tongue mated with his in a dance he hoped would never end.

Unable to resist, he cupped her breast, tracing the sensitive nipple and swallowing her moan of pleasure. He lowered his head and caressed the tip of one with tongue and teeth, then the other, pleased when they swelled and peaked, signaling the desperate want that flowed through her.

"Draco," she moaned. "We shouldn't."

But he didn't stop, couldn't stop, and her protest drifted into a sigh of pure bliss. Lifting toward his seeking mouth, she offered herself to him. He dined on her as though she were the most succulent of morsels, a banquet of delicious textures and flavors. He found his way to the taut mound of her belly and tickled the baby, getting a rapid series of kicks in response. He drew back in surprise, unable to conceal his delight.

"He's feisty," Draco said.

"You should have seen what happened when I rested my teacup and saucer on my belly. He must have thought it was too hot because he kicked it right off."

Draco covered his child with a widespread hand before kissing his wife again, allowing her to taste his joy. It felt like three hearts linked into one thundering beat. Perhaps they weren't quite in synch. Not yet, anyway. But their rhythm would join together before much longer and the song would be beyond compare.

He deepened their kiss and Shayla shifted beneath him, her breath quickening, filling the air with the sweetest of moans. It wasn't enough, not nearly enough, but he didn't dare make love to her the way he longed to, even though the doctor had given them permission. Despite that, he was determined to make the night as romantic as possible.

Gently, oh, so gently, he cupped the source of her pleasure. He breached the soft folds and scraped his fingers over and in, offering her teasing forays and tempting swirls and dips. She shuddered in reaction and her breath hitched, then gave. With each new touch the breath sobbed from her lungs and she lifted herself toward him, urging him on.

It ended all too soon. She stiffened within his hold and cried out as her release tore through her. Draco gathered her close, just holding her. He felt her tears through his dress shirt and murmured ridiculous reassurances in both English and Italian.

"Shh, now. It's all going to work out."

She opened her eyes, and he could see the dazed satisfaction mingling with her tears. "I didn't think I wanted you to make love to me. But I did. I do. It's just been so long since…" She broke off with a shiver of pleasure.

He couldn't dispute it. In fact, he could tell her right down to the day and hour just how long it had been. But her concession gave him hope. "You're right. It has been a long time. I'm sorry I didn't find you sooner, Shayla."

She relaxed against him and he watched as exhaustion overcame passion and sleep slipped across her face and into her body. No matter how hard she fought to hold it at bay, it waged a war she couldn't win. Little by little it stole the tension from her so she melted into his arms as though she belonged. Which, of course, she did, even if she didn't realize it yet.

Her eyes fluttered open before falling closed again. "Draco?" she murmured.

"I'm right here, sweetheart."

"Don't leave me."

"Never. You might disappear if I do and I don't think I could survive losing you again," he teased, though he could hear an element of raw honesty underscoring the words.

"I don't want to leave you."

He closed his eyes and faced facts. "But you're afraid to

stay. Afraid you'll be trapped in the dragon's lair and never be free again."

She didn't answer.

But then, there *was* no answer, just an undeniable truth that cut him to the very core.

He never knew what woke him. One minute he was sound asleep and the next, painfully alert. He groped for his wife, aware on some level that it was a futile effort. She wasn't in the bed.

He shot upright. "Shayla?" Her name escaped sharp as a report.

"I'm here." He vaguely made out her shape somewhere between the bed and the bathroom. He caught the fear in her voice, a fear mingled with some other emotion. Excitement? "Draco, I think my water just broke."

He shot out of bed and reached her side in two running strides. "Okay, take it easy." He gripped her arms, supporting her. "Aren't we supposed to go to the hospital when that happens?"

"No." She broke off with a quick gasp. "Oh. Oh, my."

He hung on tight, fighting to gather up every ounce of self-control he possessed in order to keep his voice low and even. "Labor pain?"

It took her a full half minute to answer. "Yes."

He debated the safety of releasing her long enough to flip on the overhead light. Decided to chance it. He made it to the door and back in two seconds flat and wrapped a supportive arm around her. "Do you need help dressing?"

She blinked at him in bewilderment. "Why should I get dressed? I just need a nightie."

Maybe labor affected normal brain processes. "You're going to wear a nightie to the hospital?" he questioned with impressive restraint.

She smiled, ridiculously tranquil given the circumstances. "Relax, Draco. It's not like the baby's going to pop out onto the bedroom floor."

Somehow she'd read his mind, considering he'd been thinking just that. He also wanted to believe her, but... "Better safe than sorry. We should go *now*."

"Don't you remember what Dr. Henderly said? We don't leave for the hospital until I'm in active labor." She escaped his grasp and crossed the room. "What I plan to do is go change and then climb back into bed for another hour or two while we time the contractions. Once I'm certain I'm actually in labor, we'll call the doctor."

He vaguely remembered Henderly saying something similar at their appointment—hell, was it only yesterday? He beat back the overwhelming urge to sweep his wife up in his arms and cart her off to the hospital, regardless of protocol. He needed to act, not laze around in bed.

But over the next two hours, that's precisely what they did. Just when he was on the brink of insanity, Shayla agreed to call the doctor and alert her to recent events. He could have roared in relief. Then Shayla proceeded to get up and dress as though it were any other day of the week.

All through the morning he watched his wife like a hawk while going silently mad. Finally, unable to stand it for another second, he slipped out onto the deck—while Shayla mopped a perfectly clean kitchen floor—and called Sev.

He didn't bother with a greeting. "She's in labor and won't go to the hospital," he announced.

"Have you called the doctor?"

"Of course I've called the doctor!" he snapped. "Do you think I'm an imbecile?"

Dead silence met his question, then Sev chuckled. "A subject in need of long and serious debate. But perhaps we should save that for a more convenient time and stick to the issue at hand. How far apart are her contractions?"

"Every twenty minutes or so."

"She's in early labor," Sev explained. Maybe Draco would have taken it better if he hadn't heard the exact same thing from Shayla at least a dozen times over the course of the last several hours. "You never know how long that's going to last with a first baby. When she gets to four or five an hour for a couple hours straight, load her into the car whether she's ready to leave or not."

Finally. An action plan. "Okay. Now you're talking. I can do that."

"So is she vacuuming or dusting?"

Draco shot a hand through his hair, standing it on end. "She's mopping the damn floor! I mean, what's *with* that?"

Sev chuckled. "Yeah, I drew the line when Francesca decided to scrub the bathtub."

"Got it. No bathtubs," he muttered. "I'm telling you, Sev, they need manuals for this stuff. And by that I mean *man*-uals."

"Tell me about it. Francesca was the first to give birth, remember? I didn't have anyone I could call." After filling Draco's head with that horrifying image, Sev added, "Why don't I alert the troops for you?"

He hesitated. "Are they likely to come over?"

"The women will, for sure."

Draco shuddered. Not a chance in hell. "Wait until we leave for the hospital. I'll give you a call on the way and you can send out the alert."

"No problem."

Snapping closed his cell phone, Draco returned inside. He found his wife bent low over the kitchen counter, her hands fisted on the edge in a white-knuckled grip. He instantly came up behind her and rubbed her back, gently talking her through the contraction.

The instant it eased, he asked, "How many is that in the past hour?"

She checked the notebook she'd been using to keep track. "Five."

Son of a bitch! Five? They were at three just a short time ago. What the hell happened to four? At this rate she really would pop their son out onto the floor. Maybe that explained the mopping.

"Time to go," he insisted. "Better to be too early than too late, and with tourists overrunning the city this time of year, traffic is always bad."

To his relief, she didn't argue, though she tested his last shred of sanity by insisting on putting away the various and sundry cleaning products she'd pulled out. The next few hours passed in a haze. He vaguely remembered the drive to the hospital, followed by the check-in procedure. Then a nurse showed up and asked ridiculous questions in order to determine his wife's status. Couldn't she just look at Shayla and see she was in labor? Did they really need to sit there and play twenty thousand questions?

But that wasn't the worst part. Hell, no. The worst part was the endless hours of witnessing Shayla's progression from those early contractions to the ones that had her moaning in agony and clutching his hand in a bone-cracking grip while he watched on, utterly helpless. Of watching the monitors that peaked with each contraction and never came down so that he ended up flat-out lying to her, telling her it had stopped and to rest before the next one hit. By that time she was so far gone, she couldn't even tell the difference between pain and the absence of it. All the while, he told her how and when to breathe, mopped her brow with a damp washcloth and practically drove his fist through her spine because she wanted him to massage her lower back longer and harder.

"Back pain," the nurse murmured sympathetically.

When the doctor finally decided Shayla could start pushing, Draco wanted to fall on his knees and offer hosannas...right up until he saw firsthand the struggle it took her to push something the size of a Hummer through an opening no larger than the eye of a needle. Somehow, though, she did it. And it wasn't a Hummer that slid into the world, but his son who emerged with a squall loud enough to crack plaster.

"Oh, Draco, he's beautiful," Shayla murmured. For some reason, she counted tiny fingers and toes, then counted them again as though she might have gotten it wrong the first time round. "He's the most gorgeous baby in the entire world."

Gently, the nurse transferred the newborn from mother to father, showing Draco how to support a tiny head covered in a tuft of black hair. He stared at his son and felt his heart swell with a love so overpowering, he didn't think he could contain it. His gaze met Shayla's, sharing the moment with her.

His wife. His son.

It didn't matter what it took or what he'd have to do. He'd find a way to keep and protect them, to love and provide for them. He closed his eyes. And, ultimately, he'd set them free.

Draco joined his relatives in the waiting room, endless Dantes overflowing the area. "It's a boy," he announced. "We have a son. Eight pounds, two and a half ounces."

"And the lungs of an opera singer. A miniature *Lucianone*," Rafe joked, using the affectionate name for Pavarotti. "We heard him all the way out here."

Sev approached and slapped Draco on the shoulder. "Congratulations. We're all thrilled for you. With a mother as beautiful as Shayla, you'll be beating the girls off with a stick before you know it."

"Yeah, about that," Draco muttered. He snagged his cousin's shirt and yanked him off to one side where they couldn't be overheard. "There's a problem."

Sev's golden gaze flashed in alarm. "Is something wrong with the baby?"

"I think so." Draco glanced uneasily in the direction of the delivery area. "I think… I think I may have broken him."

Sev blinked. "Broken him. *Broken the baby?*"

"Keep it down, will you?" Draco swallowed—hard—before continuing in a low rush. "When I first found Shayla in Atlanta, I hugged her really tight and the baby kicked, like I'd squeezed him too tight. Then during delivery, she kept begging me to rub her back, you know, as hard as I could." He scrubbed his hands over his face, forcing out his confession. "I think I smushed him."

"Smushed," Sev repeated.

"You heard me," Draco growled. "Shayla kept talking about how beautiful he is. But I gotta tell you, Sev, that baby is the ugliest thing I've ever seen. It's like someone made this beautiful face out of clay and then smacked a fist into it. And…and I think it was *my* fist."

"Smush."

Draco stabbed a finger in his cousin's chest. "Exactly. Smush. I smushed his face either when I hugged her or when I was giving her a back massage. But nobody in the delivery room seemed to notice."

Sev burst out laughing, the sound ringing across the room. Then he locked his arm around Draco's neck and knuckled the top of his head. "Idiot."

Draco fought free, offended. "Why am I an idiot?"

"All babies come out smushed. How great do you think you'd look if you'd just been squeezed out like toothpaste from a tube? Hell, when little Lorenzo was born, he looked like the son of Godzilla. But everything popped back into place after a few weeks. Fortunately for the human race, even when they look like the spawn of Satan, all mothers think their precious newborns are the most beautiful creatures ever born to mankind."

Relief threatened to send Draco to his knees. "So, I didn't…"

"Nope. Now, fair warning… If the kid's seriously ugly after a couple weeks, then you can blame yourself."

Draco felt himself pale.

"Because then you'll know the poor kid takes after you." Sev grinned. "And you have to be the most butt-ugly of all the Dantes."

Eight

As far as Draco was concerned, the next few weeks would have been absolutely perfect if Leticia Charleston hadn't blown into town on her broomstick, accompanied by her flying monkeys—aka her lawyers. Ostensibly, she arrived to sign the final documents selling the Charleston diamond mines to the Dantes, an endless, foot-dragging nine-month process from negotiating the original leasing of the mines to the final sale. At least, that's what she claimed when she landed on their doorstep.

"Would you deny me the opportunity to see my only grandchild now that the Charleston mines are about to become the Dantes?" she demanded. She glared when he hesitated. "Well?"

"I'm thinking."

"Draco?" Shayla's voice came from behind him. "Is that the door?"

He swore beneath his breath. "I've got it."

"Who—" She cradled the baby against her shoulder and peeked around his shoulder. "Grandmother!"

With a long-suffering sigh, Draco stepped back and allowed Leticia across the threshold. "Come on in."

"Gracious as ever," she snapped as she sailed into the house. She paused to study the tiny bundle Shayla held. Something moved across her expression, something that replaced the coldness with an almost human warmth and longing. And then it vanished. "I assume from the excess of blue the poor child is wearing that it's a boy?"

"Yes. We named him Stefano, after Dad, as well as Draco's maternal grandfather."

Leticia's spine snapped to attention. "Your father's name was Stefan, not Stefano."

"But he's named in honor of Dad," Shayla said gently.

Leticia relented enough to peer down at the baby. "He... he looks more like you than Draco. I don't suppose he could be Derek Algier's son?"

Draco saw red. "Son of a—"

Shayla cut him off with a quick shake of her head. "I insisted on a paternity test right after Stefano was born. Even though Draco knows he's the father, I heard there were rumors floating around Europe that Derek and I had an affair and I was pregnant with his child. I wanted the facts set straight for everyone's benefit."

Leticia chewed on that for a long minute. Based on her expression it must have tasted bitter. "How altruistic of you."

"You never give up, do you?" Draco strove to keep calm.

She whipped around. "Would I rather the boy be Derek's? In a heartbeat. You Dantes have stolen everything from me. My business. My son. My granddaughter. Now you've even hijacked the Charleston lineage, stamping your Dante genes into our pool."

"Grandmother!"

"Muddying the waters?" Draco suggested coolly.

"Yes! That's exactly right. It wasn't enough that you killed my only child." It was the most passion he'd ever heard from her, her breath sobbing from her lungs. "Now you've robbed me of my granddaughter and my great-grandson."

"The Dantes aren't responsible for your son's death," Draco stated. "Shayla's parents died in a car wreck."

"Because they'd just found out we were bankrupt, bankrupt because of the Dantes."

"First, the Dantes were only partly responsible for the bankruptcy. Granted, you couldn't compete against our fire diamonds. Not back then. But it was your mines drying up that ultimately ruined your business."

Leticia swept that aside as of no account. "The bottom line is you destroyed my son!"

He wouldn't let her get away with it. "No, Shayla's parents died returning home from a night out celebrating," he corrected. Reluctant compassion flooded through him. "I looked it up, Leticia. I looked it up after I learned that you blamed us for their deaths. I read the newspaper account. It was raining. They'd been drinking and took a cab home because neither were willing to drive."

Leticia's chin quivered. "No. They had nothing to celebrate and every reason to despair."

"He wasn't upset about the bankruptcy. They were celebrating his new job. A job with Dantes' New York office."

Shayla stiffened. "Grandmother, is that true? All this time you told me the Dantes were responsible for my parents' death. But they weren't, were they?"

Her face crumpled. "Yes! It *is* their fault. Stefan would never have gone over to the enemy."

"But he did," Draco replied. "And that's what you can't forgive. His betrayal."

Tears rained unchecked down her cheeks. For the first time since he'd known her, she looked her age. "He'd never have accepted a job with you people if Primo hadn't tempted him."

Despite the "you people" dig, empathy underscored Draco's comments. All things considered, he could afford to be generous. "After your husband died, you hoped Stefan could pick up the reins and run Charlestons. But he wasn't management material anymore than Shayla was. He was a designer. An artist. He didn't have the necessary skills for business." He dared to take her hand in his. "But you did. Why didn't you step in, Leticia? You have everything it takes to go head to head with Dantes. You could have given us a real run for our money."

For an instant, he thought he had her. Then she snatched her hand free and her chin assumed a proud tilt. "That would have been inappropriate for a woman in my position, with my upbringing."

"Why? You expected Shayla to do it. Why not you?"

Her chin quivered ever so slightly. "Times have changed," she whispered. There was a painful honesty underscoring her words. "By the time they did, I was too old to handle the reins."

Before Draco could say anything further, his cell phone buzzed. He checked it swiftly and read the text message from Juice. *Found #5. Come now.* He returned his attention to Leticia, but she'd closed down. Worse, she fixed him with a "the South will rise again!" look of defiance, no doubt because he'd managed to slip beneath her guard.

"I'm sorry, Shayla. I have a meeting I need to take." He shot an uneasy glance in Leticia's direction before returning his attention to his wife. "Will you be all right?"

"Just fine." She smiled brightly. "I can spend the morning with my grandmother and the baby. We'll have tea."

"Hmm. I don't think the baby can handle tea, yet." Or his great-grandmother.

She laughed as he hoped she would. Leticia rolled her eyes. Reluctantly, he gave his wife a swift kiss and left. But he had an itch in the middle of his back, no doubt at the exact spot where Leticia wanted to plant a knife. And he couldn't help but wonder if he was making a terrible mistake by leaving.

"He only seduced you in order to get a better deal on leasing our mines, you know."

"Dante mines," Shayla corrected mildly.

It was an accusation she'd heard more than once. In the beginning, she'd gone for the bait every time. Now she just shrugged it off. Her grandmother didn't understand how it had been the night Shayla and Draco first met. As for which of them seduced the other... There were only two people who knew for certain what went on that night, only two people in the bed where Stefano had been conceived, which meant that only she and her husband knew how and why they'd ended up there. She could state for a fact that it had nothing to do with the Charleston mines or fire diamonds or Dantes, and everything to do with simple, irresistible passion.

"They're not Dante mines, yet. Not until I sign the final papers." Leticia folded her arms across her narrow chest. "Maybe I won't sign. What do you have to say about that?"

"Think of all the money you'll be out if you don't sell. Money that will restore the mansion. Wouldn't you like to see it looking like it did in its heyday?"

"Of course I want to restore my home." She paused, fussed with her collar. "But what's the point?"

"The point?" Shayla dropped a kiss on the top of Stefano's head, feeling a gentle warmth radiating from the baby. She filled her lungs with his distinct baby scent and sighed in pleasure. How had she gotten so lucky? "I don't understand, Grandmother. Why wouldn't you want to restore the mansion?"

"Your father is gone. You're gone. My great-grandson is gone. What's the point of restoring something that will never be used by my family once I'm dead and buried?"

"Oh."

Shayla looked at her grandmother. Really looked this time. Unhappiness glittered in Leticia's striking blue eyes and deepened the lines around her mouth, aging her. She played restlessly with the wedding ring strung on her necklace, the fire diamond winking slyly. Why she refused to wear it on her finger, Shayla had never understood, but then, there was a lot about her grandmother she didn't understand.

She'd never been a particularly cheerful woman, more inclined toward an autocratic nature, which was the exact opposite of how Shayla preferred to live life. But she'd always exuded a fierce determination and purpose. Drive and ambition. Until today.

Understanding slowly dawned. "If you sell the mines," Shayla said slowly, "then your fight with the Dantes will be over. You won't have any new battles, will you? No more dragons to slay."

"What the dickens are you talking about?" Leticia demanded testily. "My fight with them will never be over."

"Even after everything Draco said?"

Her grandmother shot to her feet, fury igniting and driving her to pace the kitchen in her agitation. "You think I believe a word of what that man has to say? A man who only married you to get his hands on the Charleston mines?"

"Now you're not even being logical. How in the world would marrying me help the Dantes get their hands on our mines? Just because I'm married to Draco doesn't mean you're required to sell them to his family."

Before Leticia could respond, Stefano stretched, his little mouth popping open in a wide yawn. His ink-dark eyes fluttered, blinking up at her. Then he grinned, showing off his cute pink gums. Shayla refused to believe it was gas. Her baby saw her, tracked her with his gaze and responded every time he looked at her with that same happy smile. Or at least it started out happy. Then he spat up the little bit of milk she'd coaxed him into swallowing before his nap. His little face puckered and he let out a bellow that threatened to shatter glass.

"Lord have mercy," Leticia said while Shayla mopped him up. "That boy has a set of lungs on him."

"He has from the start." Shayla checked his diaper and stood. "Okay, I think I've found the problem. I'll be right back, Grandmother. Then we'll finish our discussion about the Dantes and our mines."

By the time she returned, though, her grandmother had left. A note sat on the kitchen table: *Must run. Time for my meeting with those vultures.* Shayla shook her head. She had a fair idea how much the Dantes were paying for the Charleston mines and the amount staggered her. Far from being vultures taking advantage of the Charlestons' misfortunes, they'd given her grandmother an excellent price. In fact, it made her uneasy wondering if her marriage to Draco hadn't added a zero or two to the back end of the check. Not that anyone would admit to such a thing.

She'd just finished feeding Stefano, concerned that he continued to fuss on and off while he suckled, when Draco returned from his meeting. She slipped their baby into his carrier. His little eyelids drifted closed and his face, a miniature of his father's, despite what her grandmother claimed, relaxed into sleep, innocence personified. She rested her hand on his head, feeling the same warmth she'd detected earlier. Before she could comment on it, Draco strode into the kitchen.

She caught a fierceness in his expression, a restlessness in his graceful movements. A predator on the hunt, came the nerve-racking thought. His eyes flashed a sharp gold while a ruthless smile slashed across his face.

"We're close this time," he informed her. "Really close."

She stared at him in bewilderment. "Close to what?"

He blinked as though seeing her for the first time. "Close to uncovering the person responsible for stealing our diamonds. Juice thinks he can track the sale back to the source this time."

Her breath caught in disbelief. "Some of your diamonds were *stolen?* How? When? How many?"

He answered her questions in reverse. "Six. Ten years ago. And they weren't exactly stolen. I suppose it would be more accurate to say I was swindled out of them." He reached into his pocket and retrieved a folded piece of diamond parcel paper, marked with a set of numbers. He unfolded it and set the paper on the table, the diamond neatly centered in the middle of the thin blue inner liner. Flame flashed from the center of the stone. "This was one of them."

She leaned in, studying it. "I can tell it's a fire diamond, and a good one, too. It's stunning."

"One of the best to ever be pulled from a Dante mine," he confirmed. "Equal to the ones you showed us."

Her gaze shifted from the stone to her husband. "How were you swindled out of them?"

"I'd just turned twenty. Even then I had an eye for stones. Could tell a fake from the real thing, oftentimes without even using a loupe." He thrust a hand through his hair and his mouth compressed into a hard line. "I was young and cocky and full of myself."

"Not unusual at that age," she offered gently.

"I had the stones out so I could prove just how good I was. I wanted to grade them. See how close I came to the expert assessment."

"With or without permission?" she guessed shrewdly.

His smile of acknowledgment contained a bitter edge. "Without. One of our staff gemologists caught me and demanded that I turn them over so he could check them before I returned them to the vault." Draco shrugged. "So, I did. He examined them at great length before he satisfied himself that I hadn't damaged them or switched them for other, lower-grade diamonds. My mistake was not watching him during his analysis. He returned all six to their containers and told me to put them back. Several months later it was discovered that they'd been exchanged for inferior stones. I was the last one on record for handling them."

"And the gemologist?"

"Long gone." He turned to look at her, his eyes empty of emotion. "I'm not sure anyone really believed me when I told them what happened."

"Oh, Draco, no!"

"I'd always been the troublemaker in the family," he persisted. "If I'd stolen them, the family preferred to turn a blind eye to my shame. If I'd been careless and allowed someone else to take them, then I was a fool. Of course, it didn't help that I had no business sneaking into the vaults in the first place."

"How did you get in?"

Draco shrugged. "I lifted Primo's passkey."

She winced. "Ah. I guess that didn't help matters, either."

"Not at all."

"And you've been searching for them ever since?"

He didn't need to answer. She could see it in his face, a

drive and determination every bit as ingrained as it had been in her grandmother. "There's only one left. But if we trace this latest stone back, I'll have the gemologist."

"Will you be able to prove he's the one who took them?"

"Juice will." Draco's expression hardened, became as ferocious as a dragon who'd just discovered his treasure had been stolen out from under him. "It would probably be best for all concerned if I stay well away from the man until after we've proven his guilt."

Shayla studied the diamond again, wishing she had a pair of tweezers so she could get a better look. "This really is a beautiful stone. What's the clarity?"

"Flawless."

"Really?" she asked, impressed. "Were they all like this one?"

Draco nodded. "All rounds. Ideal cut. All five carats or larger. All fire diamonds."

She'd received enough training to know her way around gemstones, and come close to guessing the value of what he'd lost. "Dear heaven, Draco," she murmured.

"Someone lived in style off them. One appears on the market every couple of years, though it takes several months before we find out about it. By then it's changed hands several times and is being offered as a legitimate sale item. This latest one was dumped within the last six to nine months." He fished a loupe from his pocket, along with a diamond holder. "Would you like to have a look?"

"Thanks, I'd love to." She carefully picked up the stone and studied it. Something about it nagged at her but before she could make the connection, Stefano began to fuss again. She frowned as she folded the diamond back into its paper liner, then lifted the baby from his carrier. "He's been doing this on and off all day."

"Let me take him." Draco eased Stefano into his arms and gave him an expert bounce. "Is he hungry?"

"I just fed him." She ran her hand over his head. The instant she did, her breath caught in her throat. "Oh, God. He's burning up, Draco. Feel him."

Draco's hand joined with hers and tension leaped into the muscles along his jaw. "Call Dr. Henderly." He gave every appearance of calm, except for his eyes. She could see a bone-deep fear lurking in the depths, a fear that warned that she wasn't being a nervous new mother. Something was seriously wrong with their child. "Tell her we're on the way to the emergency room. I'll get the baby strapped into his car seat and pull the car around."

The next several hours took on a nightmarish quality. The wait to see a physician seemed to take forever. Finally Dr. Henderly appeared and the pace kicked into high gear, speeding by so fast that Shayla had trouble keeping up. The medical staff checked Stefano from head to toe, then stuck an IV in his tiny arm while he screamed his objection.

More than anything she wanted to go to him, to hold him and protect him. Instead, she turned into Draco's arms. She could feel his tension and knew he felt every bit as helpless, holding himself in check through sheer raw nerve. The medical personnel ushered them out of the examination room while they ran a series of tests. Having to walk away from her baby was the most difficult thing she'd ever done. If it hadn't been for her husband, she'd have gone insane.

But he held her. Held her and gave her his strength. Murmured encouragement that gave her hope. Kissed her with a bone-deep passion that told her she wasn't alone and never would be. When they arrived at the waiting room, Shayla discovered that Draco had called the family. One by one they filtered into the area, lending their emotional support, wrapping father and mother in a protective cocoon of solidarity.

At long last the doctor joined them. Her brows shot up when dozens of Dante eyes fastened on her, all filled with nervous dread. Draco's hold on Shayla tightened, a stalwart buffer, and she had a crazy image of a ferocious dragon planting himself between her and danger, determined to protect her from whatever came next.

Dr. Henderly shot them an encouraging smile. "It's strep throat. Very rare in babies his age, but we've been seeing a lot of it this month and considering how contagious it is.... Fortunately, you discovered it early, so try not to be too alarmed. We'd like to keep him overnight for observation and to give him fluids and antibiotics." She focused on Shayla and Draco. "The bottom line is, he's going to be fine. Good catch, Mom and Dad."

Shayla wanted to howl like her baby. Tears she'd fought to suppress rained down her cheeks. Beside her, Draco rocked her in place. "Shh. It's okay now. He's safe."

She lifted her head, clinging to Draco while she struggled for sufficient control to address the doctor. "When can we see him?" she asked.

"Just give us a minute to get him up to isolation. He'll have to stay there instead of in the nursery since we can't risk his infecting any of the other babies. I'll send a nurse for you. She'll take you straight to your son."

The instant she left, conversation exploded around Shayla, relief the predominant emotion. All the while, Draco held her and continued to whisper reassurances to her. She'd never have made it through the trauma of the past few hours if it hadn't been for him. He'd been an absolute pillar of strength.

And more, his family had come storming to the rescue, as well. She'd never experienced that before, never had an extended family to help out in her moment of need. Well, other than her grandmother.

She realized something else, too. Something that shocked her to the core. She wanted Draco beside her. Needed him. She tried to picture what would have happened if she'd been living in Atlanta when Stefano became ill. She wrapped her arms around her husband's waist and clung. She'd have managed. For her child, she'd have done whatever it took.

But she'd have done it alone.

Stefano remained in isolation for two endless days before the doctor released him to return home. Though Shayla tried not to fuss throughout the ensuing days and nights, she couldn't seem to help herself, rushing to check on him every time he so much as squeaked. A week after the crisis, Draco caught her hand when she ran upstairs to the nursery for the umpteenth time.

"Enough," he said, steering her into the master bedroom, a room and a bed they'd shared ever since she gave birth to Stefano.

"But I thought I heard—"

"You heard the same thing I did. A baby sighing in his sleep."

"I need to check, Draco."

"Look at me, sweetheart." He waited until her gaze was fixed on his. "Would I willingly allow anything bad to happen to our son? For that matter, would I allow anything bad to happen to you?"

"No. Never."

"Then stop. You've been a bundle of nerves this past week and I won't allow it to continue any longer."

Her eyebrows shot upward. "Won't *allow*?"

He didn't back away from the word. "No. It's not good for you or the baby. Listen to me, Shayla. I grew up with four male cousins and two brothers, not to mention a sister with a tomboy streak a mile wide. Accidents happen. I should know considering I broke my leg falling out of a tree."

"Draco." It clicked then. "The scars on your leg?"

"It was a bad break. It could have turned life-threatening. My parents stood right where we did, terrified, helpless. But afterward they found a way to let go. You can't protect Stefano from every bump and bruise that will come his way. And they will come. Worrying about the what-ifs in life won't help."

"I know, I know. It's just—" She spared a swift glance toward the bedroom door…and Stefano.

"Will you smother him with worry? Will you clip his wings each time he tries to fly?"

His question hit home and hit hard. Take away Stefano's freedom, the way her grandmother had tried to do with her? Never! "It's just that he's so tiny and helpless."

Draco smiled gently. "He'll always seem small and helpless. When he's one and wants to walk without you helping him. When he's three and wants to climb the slide by himself. When he's six and goes off to school without you. When he has his first sleepover with friends. When he goes on his first camping trip. When he leaves for college." Draco gripped her shoulders. "Of course you want to protect him and make sure he takes those steps without putting himself in danger. But you have to let him take them. Do for our son what your grandmother refused to do for you."

She saw it so clearly, understood it so painfully. "You're right." She didn't want him to be. But he was.

"The past is over." Draco gathered her into his arms, his voice lowering. "Focus on right here and now. Stefano is safe and sleeping in his crib, dreaming whatever delightful fantasies babies dream. He saw the doctor only yesterday and she said the infection was gone. Let go now. Take time for yourself."

Time for herself. It sounded wonderful. She released a gusty sigh. "What do you suggest I do with all this time for myself?"

He paused, his gaze filling with unmistakable passion. "Be a wife instead of a mother."

Nine

Shayla knew what Draco wanted. If she were honest with herself, she wanted the same thing every bit as much. Unable to resist, she surrendered to her need. Utterly.

He must have read the hunger in her eyes, the acceptance in the sway of her body. Blatant desire burned in his eyes, fast and desperate. She heard the rumble in his throat, low and powerful, and knew when he made love to her this time it would be unlike any other. And she was right.

A quick tug and he had her. A quick rip and he yanked her blouse open and off her shoulders. Shock held her in place while a liquid heat exploded deep in her belly.

"I want you. Not slow, but fast." He stripped away her bra. "Not gentle, but rough." Her slacks and panties were hauled down her legs. "And hot. And thorough. And all night long."

He swept her up and tossed her onto the bed. She bounced once, naked and tousled and more aroused than she could ever remember being. He peeled off his own clothes, shredded them in his haste, tossed them aside. She couldn't think straight, didn't want to think. Just feel. Yield. Allow herself to spin helpless and free along whatever path he chose to take them.

He was on top of her before she could draw breath, snatching a kiss full of pent-up fire and demand. His mouth devoured her, but she wanted to be devoured. To be taken. To have his hands on her and his body in her and The Inferno burning, burning, burning until there was nothing left of either of them but the fire.

"Do it now," she demanded, practically weeping in her desperation to have him. "I've waited for you. Waited for nearly a year."

"Forty-seven weeks and two days." His eyes glittered down at her like liquid gold. "But not another minute longer."

She parted her legs for him while he gathered up her hips, lifting, opening. Then he mated their bodies in one swift act. She closed around him, wrapped him up with arms and legs, and moved. Oh, how she moved, catching his rhythm and driving him higher and harder.

The blood pounded from head to heart to the very core of her and she trembled, felt the earthquake grab her. Shake her. Grab at him. The scalding, turbulent pressure building with only one place to go. It sent her rocketing to a shimmering, glittering place where stars exploded and the heavens wept. She bowed back, tight, then tighter, while he took her over and over. And she reached, found that unbelievable delight and seized it, knowing all the while that she'd never, ever be able to find it anyplace else but with this man.

Shayla muffled her shriek against his shoulder, clinging to that moment of wonder with all her strength, while Draco followed her up and over, roaring his pleasure. She glided then, slid into the aftershocks that pulsated through her in a glorious, endless stream. It took long, endless moments before she could gather enough breath to speak.

"Now *that's* what I call a hallelujah moment," she informed him in a dreamy voice. "Please tell me you have an entire chorus of them."

He choked on a laugh. "Oh, yeah. All saved up and ready to go."

"How soon?"

"Just let me catch my—"

She rolled over on top of him, captured the last of his words with a demanding kiss. She couldn't seem to help herself. This need, this overpowering want, was still so new to her. She didn't think she'd ever tire of it. But tonight she'd give it her best effort. She trailed downward, exploring freely, delighted with his response to her efforts. Peering up at him, she grinned.

"I see you have the second chorus ready to sing. Why don't you hum a few bars and I'll follow along."

He glanced down. "That isn't a chorus, sweetheart. It's a whole damned symphony. And I plan to have you play every last note."

And she did.

Draco woke in the dark of night, Shayla held safe and secure within his arms. *Great speech, Dante.* No question that his darling wife needed to hear every word of it—the importance of letting go. But the time had come to heed his own advice. He'd held on to Shayla for weeks, finding excuse after excuse to keep her caged, even though he'd filled her cage with every manner of temptation.

How could he demand she allow their son to fly when he kept her wings so carefully clipped?

She stirred in his arms, snuggling closer to his warmth,

and he gritted his teeth. Just the mere idea of losing her, of having her live apart from him, just about gutted him.

He wanted her. Needed her. Adored her. Would move heaven and earth if it meant giving her happiness. He closed his eyes, feeling the unrelenting pull of The Inferno. The last tiny barrier fell.

He loved her, loved her beyond measure.

And because he loved her, he'd set her free.

Shayla awoke to Stefano's predawn squall, signaling his need for breakfast. He'd actually lasted an hour longer than usual. Cautiously, she eased from Draco's embrace, hoping he'd sleep through his son's impatient cries.

Entering the nursery, she lifted Stefano from his crib and nestled him close. She carried him to the rocking chair and gently rocked while he fed. As always, her gaze traveled around the room and she couldn't help but smile. Every time she sat here she saw some new bit of whimsy, either something she'd overlooked until then, or some little detail that Draco had slipped in without her noticing.

She loved these moments with her son. Sweet, fleeting occasions that would be over before she knew it. It gave her time to think. To quiet her thoughts and slow life's rhythm. To enjoy the now and simply feel. And while she sat and rocked, she considered what Draco had told her the night before—the importance of letting go.

It had struck a serious nerve with her, not just because of her son but because of herself. Until last night she'd thought if she were released—let go—it meant she'd be free. Back on that fateful night when she met Draco, she believed that if she fulfilled her obligations to her grandmother, she would take the job with Derek and experience that freedom. And yet… All during those first months overseas, Draco consumed her every waking thought. And as soon as something had gone wrong, where had she gone? Back to her roots. Back to her family ties.

"Back home," she murmured.

She'd never been free of those ties and never would. How foolish to think otherwise. There might be many things about Grandmother Charleston that bothered her. But when push came to shove, that's the person she'd turned to in her moment of crisis. And she realized something else, as well. It would have been Draco if she hadn't been told he was already married. Because she was tied to him not just through their child, but with body and heart and soul.

She closed her eyes and faced facts. She didn't want to be free, not if it meant living without Draco. Oh, she could find a certain level of contentment if she lived in some small, cozy apartment with Stefano. But she wouldn't be happy. Because the truth was she loved Draco, loved him beyond measure and for all of time.

She opened her eyes and looked around the nursery he'd created. Thought about all that he'd done over the past two months. Her gaze landed on the bare stretch of wall behind the crib and an idea occurred to her. An idea that might express her heart's desire and prove to Draco that she'd only know true freedom if it was in his arms.

"You heard me, Sev. I want the suite for Shayla and the baby."

"I heard you. I just don't like what I'm hearing. How long will they be staying at the suite?"

"I don't know. As long as it takes."

"Look, whatever you did, just apologize. It's not worth having her move out."

"I didn't do anything," Draco snarled. "And before you ask, no, we're not having marital problems."

"Sounds like marital problems to me. Wives don't just up

and move out of their home and away from their husband without a damn good reason. And they especially don't do it a few short weeks after giving birth. The way I see it, *you* must be the reason."

Draco gritted his teeth. "Look. I made a promise to her when we married, okay? And I intend to keep it no matter how much I'd rather— No matter how much it—" Hurts. Kills him. Rips him to shreds. He closed his eyes and swore. "Can they use the suite while I find them a suitable house or not?"

Sev's sigh came long and rough. "Sure. If there's anything I can do, let me know, will you?"

"You'll be the first one I call."

Shayla rested the phone between shoulder and ear while she wrestled a diaper around Stefano's pumping legs. "Actually, I called to ask for a favor."

"Anything," Ariana answered promptly, her voice carrying a hint of her Italian origins. "Name it and it's yours."

Stefano's onesie came next, something her son was intent on keeping off his little squirming body at all costs. Shayla smothered a laugh as she struggled to dress her son and speak at the same time. "The mural," she managed to say. "You painted it, didn't you? I recognize your style from the Mrs. Pennywinkle books you write and illustrate. It's absolutely stunning and I can't thank you enough for all your hard work."

"It is kind of you to say." Warmth filled Ariana's voice. "When I stepped into my grandmother's shoes, my publisher was not sure readers would enjoy my more whimsical style."

"Personally, I love it. But…I wonder if I could hire you to add to the mural for me as a wedding gift for Draco. I'd like a final scene painted on the wall behind the crib, a personalized scene. With Stefano arriving so soon after the ceremony I never had the opportunity to give him anything."

"This mural, it is for love?" Ariana asked.

Shayla lifted her son off the changing table and carried him to the rocking chair. Collapsing into it, she couldn't help grinning and allowed her happiness to radiate into her voice. "Very much so."

"Then consider it done. Now tell me what you want." When Shayla finished describing her idea, Ariana sighed. "I am so sorry, but I am not the one you need for this project."

Shayla hesitated, fighting to conceal the extent of her disappointment. "Are you sure?"

"Positive. However, I do know someone else who would be the perfect artist. Tell me, have you ever heard of Jacqueline Randell Blackstone?"

"The name sounds familiar...." If only she could remember where she had heard it before.

"Perhaps you would recognize her other name. Jack Rabbitt."

"Jack *Rabbitt?*" Shayla flat-out adored her storybooks. And the glass desktop Jacq had painted for her husband, Mathias, one featuring the fairy-tale creatures from her stories, was downright famous. "You *know* her?"

Ariana laughed. "Know her? She and Mathias will be flying in from Seattle this weekend. They stay with us whenever they visit. We are all the best of friends. I am sure she would be delighted to finish the mural."

It took Shayla a second to control the wobble in her voice and she hugged Stefano close, drawing comfort from his warm little body. "Thank you, Ariana. It would mean the world to me."

"My pleasure. After all, we are family, yes?"

"Why, yes." Now it was her chin wobbling. "Yes, we are." And that said it all.

* * *

Shayla glanced over at her husband and smiled. "So, where are we going?" she asked.

"To Dantes'."

His hands tightened around the steering wheel as he said it and he spared her a swift glance. For some reason that look bothered her. Perhaps it was the tarnish that darkened his hazel-gold eyes. Or the taut set of his mouth and jaw. She couldn't begin to imagine the problem, just that there clearly was one.

"Oh, okay," she replied calmly, deciding to hold fire.

Hadn't she decided to live in the "now"? To not worry about tomorrow, but focus on today? She spared her husband another swift glance. Unfortunately "now" didn't look all that great.

He parked in the underground garage in a spot with his name stenciled on the wall in front of it. After Draco unbuckled Stefano, they crossed to the elevators. Listening to their footsteps echo against the cement brought back vivid memories of the morning after the Eternity reception when she'd made a similar walk in this exact same garage. It also reminded her of the night they'd spent together—the results of which were in the portable car seat Draco carried. For some reason she found the memory disturbing.

"Why are we here?" she couldn't help but ask.

"I want to show you something."

She could tell she wouldn't get more out of him until he was good and ready. They arrived at the bank of elevators and just like the night of the reception, he ushered her into the car and keyed the panel for the penthouse level. And just like the night of the reception, he escorted her to the suite they'd shared nearly a year before. Only this time he didn't carry *her* over the threshold, but their son. How odd to recall that long-ago self and her plans for the future, a future far different from the one fate had determined for her.

"Okay, Draco. Enough with the surprises." She folded her arms across her chest. "I want to know what's going on."

He carefully placed the baby out of harm's way, then turned to face her. With the windows at his back she didn't have a hope of reading his expression. "We made a pact before we married. Do you remember?"

She stiffened. "What are you talking about?"

"You asked for your own place as part of our agreement. I'm simply fulfilling the terms of that agreement. You can stay here for the time being while we find you a suitable house or condo. I have the name of a realtor who'd be happy to work with us." He shot a hand through his hair, the only outward sign that he wasn't as cool and collected as his voice suggested. "Work with *you,*" he corrected.

She took a moment to absorb the hit and found she couldn't. The impact had caught her completely off guard and it hurt. Dear heaven, but it hurt. Anger came to her rescue. "Let me get this straight. You want me to move out? You want me and your son to move out of your home? That's what you're telling me?"

"No! Yes." He swore in Italian, though she could have told him that if it was to protect her poor, delicate ears, he failed miserably. She understood every word. "You asked—demanded—to have your own place before you'd agree to marry me. I'm simply giving you what you want."

If only she could see his eyes, read his expression. Taking matters into her own hands, she circled the couch so the sunlight struck him in profile. "What about what you want, Draco?"

"That doesn't matter. It isn't important. You'll be in the city, nearby. Our son will be where I can see him every day."

She saw it then. The stoicism. The tamped-down pain. The grit and determination to tough it out. Relief flooded through her. He was honoring his commitment not because he wanted to, but because he'd made a promise. One he took every bit as seriously as their wedding vows.

She smiled, taking a swift, eager step in his direction. "What if I told you I don't want to move? That I want to stay with you. Would you force us to go?"

His mouth opened and closed and he sucked in air as though he'd just taken a hit to the solar plexus. "Force…?"

Before he could say anything else, his cell phone rang. He glanced at it impatiently before swearing again, this time in English. He flipped open the phone and barked into it, "Damn it, Sev, I'm right in the middle of something vital here.…" Dead silence, then, "*What?* You must be joking." He froze, his gaze sweeping toward her, pinning her in place. "Are you positive? There's no mistake? No, I guess there wouldn't be. Let me get back to you."

She'd only seen that expression on his face once before, when he'd been talking about the gemologist who'd swindled him. A fierce look, one filled with threat and vengeance and an unholy fury. It had never before been aimed at her.

Until now.

"What's wrong?" she asked uneasily, falling back a step.

He stalked after her. "That was Sev. It would seem that the initial reports about the Charleston mines were inaccurate."

She stared in confusion. "What do you mean? What are you talking about?"

"Your mines, Shayla. Or rather Dante mines now that the final contracts have been signed. They're played out—*still* played out. And I just want to know…" He took another step in her direction, moving with predatory grace. "Were you in on the scam?"

Shayla paled. "Why are you assuming there's some sort of scam?"

"Because there aren't any more diamonds. Just those few Leticia removed and enough others to convince us the mines were viable. The reports claiming otherwise are forgeries. Very clever, very convincing forgeries. But you already know that, don't you?"

She shook her head. "No. No, I didn't know that. How can you even think such a thing?"

"I just want to know if it was a setup right from the start."

Tears glittered in her eyes, turning them to jet. "There was no setup."

"No?" He smiled, a humorless flash of teeth that caused her to fall back another pace. "And yet, you ended up in my bed. Played your role brilliantly, I might add. Your shock and outrage when you discovered I was a Dante. Dropping the information that you had a meeting with my relatives before rushing off, knowing full well I'd crash the party. The stones hidden in your purse—a purse with a broken catch. The list. All tantalizing tidbits meant for me to find. Meant to whet my appetite."

A hint of anger flashed across her expression. "Stop and think, Draco. I was just there for the initial lease negotiations. Why would your name be on my list? Why would I involve you?"

"Because I grade the gemstones. Because I'd be the one who would have pushed to go forward with the lease, and later the sale."

"You're also the one who kept his name out of all the Dante literature, who kept the lowest profile of all."

He waved that aside. "I'm sure you had ways of uncovering

my identity. Granted, the pregnancy probably came as a bit of a shock. But then, why not use that, too?"

She darted toward the carrier and snatched up Stefano. "Don't you dare bring him into this. He's your son! He's an innocent."

"But his mother isn't, is she?" He circled her. "You could have approached me at any point once you realized you were pregnant. But I didn't find out until you were days away from giving birth. Convenient, wouldn't you say?"

"There was nothing convenient about my pregnancy," she snapped.

Not that he paid the least attention. "By the time I discovered your whereabouts there was no time to think. To consider. You knew I'd rush you to the altar in order to give our son the Dante name. And you were right. Our marriage was your safety net. After all, once we bought the mines and discovered it was all an elaborate con job, you and I would be married."

"What difference would that make?" she asked tightly.

"You know damn well that my family would never go after my wife. And they sure as hell wouldn't go after the mother of my son."

It was the last straw. Shayla gently returned Stefano to his carrier. Then she approached, got right up in her husband's face. "I'm going to say this once and only once. I knew nothing about the mines. I'm not interested in the mines. I never have been, nor will I ever be. I don't swindle people, as you damn well should know...or would if you took two minutes to stop and consider the situation logically. If there's a problem, look elsewhere for the cause."

"Even if your grandmother is responsible, how the hell could you not at least have suspected?"

"How about you?" she shot right back. "You've even had

experience being swindled. Or haven't you ever heard the expression, 'fool me once'?"

He winced. "So I should have seen the swindle coming?"

"Yes. At the very least one of you clever Dantes should have suspected my grandmother was up to something and dug in to the possibility. Which, in case it has escaped your notice, is not my job." She drilled her finger into his chest. "It's yours."

"She's *your* grandmother!" How the hell had she managed to shift the dynamics, putting him on the defensive?

"And yet…I'm not the one doing business with her." She unplugged her finger from his chest and aimed it at the door. "I'm done discussing this. You may leave."

"Leave?"

"That's right. You offered me the suite and I'm taking you up on your kind offer. Now go."

"I'm not finished with our discussion."

"Well, I am." She stalked to the door, yanked it open and jerked her head toward the hallway. "You can call tomorrow once you've had time to cool off and smarten up. Until then, I have nothing further to say to you. And FYI, *you* have nothing further to say to *me*. At least, nothing worth listening to."

He visibly considered his options, and she watched, barely clinging to anger over tears, while he weighed the advantage of pursuing a fruitless argument versus gathering more information to damn her with. She saw his decision a second before the tears won out.

"Fine," he announced. "I'll leave. But when I come by, I expect answers. Real answers."

Draco stalked past her and she slammed the door behind him. Then he stood in the plush hallway for a full minute wondering how the hell he'd come to be on the wrong side of the door, feeling as though he'd also been on the wrong side of their argument.

More than anything he wanted to bang on the door and demand she let him in. After all, it was his family's suite. His wife. His child. His life unraveling at the seams. But until he met with Sev and heard the entire story, what would be the point?

Swearing long and bitterly, he left, telling himself he was doing the right thing. They both needed time to cool off and he wanted to get his facts straight before he confronted her again. Of course, when he returned late that afternoon it was to discover that history had repeated itself. Shayla was gone.

And so was his son.

Leticia Charleston greeted her granddaughter with a smile of satisfaction and a snap of tartness. "About time you returned home where you belong. Now make my day and tell me you've left that despicable Dante husband of yours."

Shayla hid her sigh by placing Stefano's carrier on the floor beside her chair and across from the settee where her grandmother sat. Since his belly was full and his diaper pristine, he'd fallen sound asleep. Perfect, considering the upcoming conversation would take a while. A long while.

"Actually, I'm here to discuss something with you, Grandmother."

Leticia sniffed. "I'm not sure I like the sound of that."

"I'm sure you're not going to like the sound of most of what we'll be discussing," Shayla responded smoothly. "I asked Bess to bring in tea and snacks since we're going to be here for the next few hours."

Leticia took immediate umbrage. "That's rather highhanded of you, coming into my house and ordering my housekeeper around."

"You're right." Shayla offered her most sunny smile. "I only get more highhanded from here."

Leticia folded her arms across her chest and fixed her granddaughter with her most intimidating glare. Once upon a time it would have worked like a charm. But not any longer. Any one of the Dantes' glares could easily trump it. Especially Primo's. Though, now that Shayla considered the matter, the one Draco turned on her the previous day had been the most impressive she'd ever seen.

Bess appeared with a loaded tray and set it in front of Shayla before scuttling out again. "Tea?" Shayla offered.

Leticia's mouth fell open at the effrontery of being offered tea as though she were a guest in her own home. After a few seconds her mouth buttoned up tight and her eyes narrowed to calculating slits. Shayla could practically see her weighing and considering, plotting and planning. "I'll take my tea with lemon," she ordered at long last. "One lump of sugar instead of two. I'm cutting back."

"I can understand." Shayla poured and served with the ease of long practice. "You wouldn't want to risk becoming too sweet."

There was stony silence for an endless minute before a sound escaped her grandmother, one Shayla had never heard before. A snort of laughter. Then she tipped her head back and let it rip. When she finally gathered herself again, she took one of the dainty napkins from the tray and dabbed her eyes with it. "Oh, Shayla, you are so good for me. I've missed you."

"I've missed you, too." And surprisingly, she had. She considered how to ask her next question. She could use delicacy and tact, but considering it was her grandmother, decided to go for broke. "Why did you do it?"

To her credit, Leticia didn't feign ignorance. "Oh, honey, you know why."

Shayla leaned back against her chair and sipped her tea while she contemplated her grandmother. "I have to admit…I really don't know. I understand you being angry with the Dantes for contributing to Charlestons going under. I can even understand you blaming the Dantes immediately after Dad's death. But that was more than a decade ago. Why swindle them now, after all this time? You must have been able to put emotion aside and look at the facts logically after so many years?"

Leticia played with the ring on her necklace, her restless movements causing the diamond to flash and burn. "It's a long story."

"I'm not going anywhere."

"No, I suppose you aren't."

And so she told her tale. She even told nearly all of it, and mostly stuck to the truth. When she finished, she regarded Shayla with affectionate relief. "There's only one other thing I'd like to say, though it has nothing to do with—" She waved a dismissive hand to indicate their conversation up to this point. "It's about your father."

Shayla perked up. "Dad?"

"I don't think I ever told you this about Stefan, but he was the kindest man I've ever known. Gentle. Generous. Easygoing." She sighed. "Too easygoing to have successfully run Charlestons. I loved that man to pieces, but he didn't inherit any of my steel. You, on the other hand…" She tilted her head to one side and gave her granddaughter a long, hard look. "I always thought you were just like him. But you aren't, are you? You have his kind nature, but it hides my steel. I'm right, aren't I?"

"Yes." Shayla lowered her voice to a stage whisper. "But do me a favor. Don't tell Draco. I don't think he'd take it well."

Her grandmother actually smiled, a wide, natural smile,

revealing a beauty Shayla had never noticed before. "We'll consider it our secret." She placed her delicate porcelain cup and saucer onto the tray with a gesture of finality. "You're going back to him, aren't you? You and little Stefan are leaving Atlanta and returning to San Francisco."

"Stefano."

Leticia rolled her eyes, but her heart wasn't in it. "He'll always be Stefan to me."

Shayla let it go. "And yes, to answer your question, we're going back. Though where I live depends on any number of factors."

Since the information Leticia had imparted was one of those factors she nodded in understanding. "What do you think your Dantes will do to me?"

Shayla answered with complete honesty. "I don't know. We'll find out when we get there."

"We?" Leticia drew back in alarm. "I'm not going to San Francisco."

Shayla fixed her grandmother with a cool, unrelenting stare, leaning on each and every crisply spoken word. "Just so you know, this is where I show some of that spine I inherited. So, yes, you are coming with me. And when you get there, you'll have a lot of explaining to do. You'll manage. You always do."

"But I don't want to."

Ignoring the petulant retort, Shayla stood, pulled her grandmother to her feet and hugged her. To her surprise the hug was returned, long and hard and tight. "*And* when you get there, you're staying. I need my family close by."

"No, I couldn't," she protested. "My home—"

"Is near me and Stefano." Shayla pulled back and grinned at her. "Besides, think of how much it'll annoy Draco."

Leticia hesitated, gave it some thought, then chuckled. "I do believe you just sold me on the idea."

Ten

"What are you doing here, Sev?" Draco demanded, scrubbing sleep from his eyes.

His cousin shoved past him into the suite. "I might ask you the same question. I've been to the house. You weren't there. Your wife wasn't there. Is Stefano with you or her?"

"I don't much care for the way you said 'her,'" Draco growled.

"Too bad. I don't much care for the fact that your wife swindled the Dantes out of millions of dollars."

As though from a distance Draco heard himself roar. Saw his fist fly through the air and connect with Sev's chin. Watched his cousin crash to the floor. He swore, long and loud, more angry with himself than with Sev. "She didn't swindle us."

Sev jiggled his jaw in order to determine whether or not it still worked. Once he satisfied himself on that count, he said, "Well, someone sure as hell did. You gonna hit me again if I get up?"

"That depends. Are you gonna say something I'll have to hit you for?"

Sev climbed to his feet. "Where is she, Draco?"

"Atlanta."

And that's all he knew. While he'd been busy hammering on the suite door late in the afternoon after their fight, Shayla had called the house and left a painfully brief message on the answering machine. "I'm in Atlanta." Her voice had come across cool and remote, the sugar in her Southern accent tart with vinegar. "I'll be in touch soon."

That was it. *Soon.* What the hell did soon mean? Tomorrow? Next week? Next year? When she was eight and a half months pregnant with their next child? He returned to their house in Sausalito, but it took him all of a single hour to realize he couldn't handle living in his own home. Not without Shayla. Not with her ghost and the ghost of his son haunting every damn room.

So he'd thrown some clothes in a duffel and moved back into the suite. Not that this place had been much better, though a good part of a fifth of Scotch had gone a long way toward easing his pain. Or it did until Sev's arrival in the wee hours of the morning.

Draco checked his watch and saw a blurry 10:02 a.m. The hell with it. Considering the night he'd had, ten was the wee hours of the morning for him. And he sure as hell didn't appreciate waking to someone pounding on the door, especially when it was an unwelcome echo to the pounding in his head.

"Atlanta," Sev repeated. "Your wife flies off to Atlanta with your son right after we discover the Charleston mines are depleted and you don't find anything odd about it?"

"Right now the Starship *Enterprise* could have landed in the middle of Union Square and I wouldn't find anything odd about it," he snarled.

"Son of a— You're *drunk!*"

"Not anymore. I'd *like* to be drunk. Right now I'm somewhere between hungover and unconscious. Maybe a couple more shots and I can tip the scales in the appropriate direction."

"Screw that. You need to sober up and deal with this."

"Yeah? Good luck making me."

Draco barely got the words out of his mouth before Sev grabbed him by the shirtfront and wrestled him in the direction of the master suite. Maybe if he hadn't used up what little energy reserves he had landing that punch on Sev he'd have put up a better fight. It wasn't until he found himself on the tile floor of the shower with icy cold water pouring down on him that he fully woke—and awoke with a roar of fury. By the time he dragged his sorry backside out of the stall and into dry clothes, Sev had a steaming cup of coffee ready to go. He shoved it into Draco's hands. To his utter humiliation all he could do was whimper pitifully while he poured the scalding liquid down his throat.

"Some dragon you are," Sev sneered. "You were always the most ferocious when we were kids, the toughest of us. There wasn't any dare you wouldn't take. You weren't afraid of anything, ever. Now look at you."

"Who says I'm afraid?" he shot back, relieved to hear the power return to his voice.

"Then why aren't you fighting for what's yours? Why haven't you flown out to Atlanta and taken back what belongs to you? Or have you given up?"

"Never!"

"Then, damn it, Draco, go get her."

Draco shot his cousin a grim look. "So she can explain about the mines, or because she's my wife?"

Sev shrugged. "Does it really matter? One way or the other this all has to be straightened out."

As much as Draco hated conceding the fact that his cousin was right, he didn't waste any more time. He downed another cup of coffee, along with a half-dozen aspirin, and headed home. Once there, he arranged for one of the Dante jets to be fueled and prepared for takeoff. He didn't bother packing an overnight bag. He didn't intend to be gone that long. Just long enough to retrieve his bride and his son, and possibly take a few shots at the Wicked Witch.

All the while the question nagged at him. Was his wife complicit in the swindle, or another innocent victim of her grandmother? Had she planned all along to return to Atlanta once the Dantes discovered the Charleston mines were depleted? Or was there another explanation for her vanishing act?

Unable to help himself, he stared at the detritus of his wife's presence in his life, the feminine bits and pieces she'd left behind. A bottle of perfume, its familiar fragrance lingering in the air, a fragrance that twined through his senses and elicited memories of their passionate lovemaking. He ran a finger over the jeweled hair clips clustered on the dresser, clips that attempted to confine the mass of her dark hair. Clips that he'd taken great delight in removing so he could watch that glorious length rain down her shoulders and back. He picked up a pair of heels kicked hastily in the direction of the closet and tucked them away. No doubt she hadn't because the baby started fussing and she'd gone running to his rescue.

Draco flinched. *Stefano.* Dear God, how he missed his son. Missed those deep, dark brilliant eyes that were so much like his mother's. Missed that crazy little infant giggle he gave whenever Draco tickled his round little belly. Missed the energetic kick and squeal each time he walked into Stefano's nursery.

Snatching a deep breath, Draco started for the steps, intent on heading to the airport, when something stopped him, turned him in the direction of his son's room. He didn't question, just surrendered to his gut instinct.

He opened the door, wondering what had drawn him here. Everything was in place—more or less. The hamper half-full of discarded baby clothes, the closet slightly ajar, no doubt from the last time he'd pillaged the toy boxes, looking for a new treat for his son. One of the dresser drawers gaped ever so slightly. And the crib... He closed his eyes. The crib, so empty and silent. He gathered himself, started to turn.

And saw it.

The wall behind the crib was no longer empty. At some point during the past twenty-four hours, the mural had been completed. A huge dragon occupied most of the formerly vacant space. Draco stared in amazement. One look and he could tell the creature was meant to be him, or a dragon version of him. Fierce, hazel-gold eyes glittered a warning, one echoed by the intimidating stance and defiant expression on the dragon's face. It said, "I protect all who dwell here."

Curled within his dragon arms was a beautiful princess with flowing hair of richest ebony. A princess whose jet-dark eyes mirrored love and adoration for the creature who held her. A princess who looked exactly like his wife. The dragon's tail wrapped around her, and clinging from his tail was an adorable hatchling. The babe dangled from the very tip by his sharp teeth, a mischievous expression painted across his tiny dragon face.

Stefano.

A memory stirred, something Shayla had said at the suite before they'd been interrupted by the phone call about the mine. He'd just finished offering her the apartment, or a house or a condo, offering her the freedom he'd have given anything to withhold from her. And she'd said... His brow wrinkled in concentration.

She'd said, "What if I told you I don't want to move? That

I want to stay with you. Would you force us to go?" There had been a tremulous smile on her mouth and a look in her eyes....

That's when he knew, knew without hesitation or doubt. And he also knew what he had to do about it.

"What are we all doing here, Draco?" Sev demanded. He poured two cups of coffee before returning to his seat at the Dantes' conference table. He handed one of the cups to his wife and took a long swallow from the other. "You have the entire family gathered and we've been sitting twiddling our thumbs for the past twenty minutes waiting for you to get to it."

As it turned out, Draco hadn't flown to Atlanta as planned. It hadn't been necessary, not with Shayla and Stefano on their way home. Instead, he'd called an emergency meeting of the family. "Then you've answered your own question, haven't you, Sev?" he responded coolly. "You're twiddling your thumbs."

"Listen up, smart guy. I have better things to do with my time—"

"No, you don't." Draco's gaze landed on each of them in turn—brothers, sister, cousins, wives, parents, grandparents, before settling on Primo. "There are a lot of issues to resolve, both old and new. And by God, every last one of them is going to be resolved today."

His brother, Rafe, grinned at his wife, Larkin. "I get chills when he turns all tough and domineering, don't you?"

"Stuff it," Draco snapped, but his smile stole some of the sting from his words. He checked his watch, his cell phone, then shot off a quick text message. Behind him the door opened and Juice stepped in.

"They landed almost an hour ago," he announced in his

rumbling basso profundo voice. "Should be here any minute."

"Thanks," Draco said. "Help yourself to coffee and take a seat wherever you can find one."

"Hey, Juice." Luc greeted his former employee with a huge grin. "What are you doing here?"

The tank-size man swallowed Luc's hand in his. "Have some information your brother would like me to share with you all."

No sooner had he helped himself to coffee than the door opened again. Finally. Finally, she'd arrived. Shayla swept into the conference room, her chin set to combat mode. To Draco's amusement it perfectly matched the tilt of Leticia's chin.

"Welcome home," he murmured for her ears alone. He scooped up his son, who pumped his little legs and burbled in baby pleasure. "I've missed you." His gaze fell on Shayla's grandmother. "Or most of you."

Leticia sniffed, took one of the empty chairs near his and glared at him. "Well? The least you can do is offer me some tea. It's been a long flight and though I may not look it, I'm not a young woman."

"I'll get it," Shayla said.

She hadn't responded to his greeting and he took that to mean there were still a lot of roadblocks between them. Well, he'd see what he could do about knocking a few of them down. As soon as his wife and—heaven help him—grandmother-in-law were seated and supplied with drinks, he began.

"We're going to start with Leticia Charleston, since most of this is her story." He fixed his gaze on her and went straight for the jugular. "You've had it in for the Dantes since day one. I can understand why you blame us for your bankruptcy, although you and I both know the depletion of your mines was the true culprit. But there's more, isn't there? More to your wanting revenge."

She didn't bother arguing the point. She simply inclined her head in agreement and said, "It was because of Dominic Dante."

"Dad?" Sev said, surging to his feet. Anger ripped through that single word and Draco could tell it took every ounce of restraint to keep his cousin from calling Leticia an unforgivable name. Beside him, Primo and Nonna joined hands and shifted closer to one another. "What the hell are you talking about? How could Dad have anything to do with this mess?"

"Sev, please," Francesca murmured, tugging her husband back into his seat. "Let's hear her out."

Leticia waited until the room fell silent again. "He flew out to meet with my husband, oh, decades ago it must have been. But William wouldn't receive him. Told him to go away. He didn't, of course. None of you Dantes ever did what you were told and he was no different."

"Grandmother," Shayla said with a sigh. "You do notice we're a bit outnumbered here. Please try for just a shred of tact."

"Let them do their worst," she snapped. Her eyes swept the assembled group and she returned hostile look for hostile look. "Dominic had the unmitigated gall to approach me. He claimed we stole away one of his top designers, a woman named Cara Moretti. He demanded I return her." Leticia's eyes flashed. "As if she were a piece of furniture or a ring he'd misplaced. I told him to go straight to the devil. If he couldn't keep good help, how was that my problem?"

The name dropped like a stone among the Dantes. "There must be more to the story than that, Leticia," Draco insisted. "You don't swindle an international company out of millions of dollars because of unmitigated gall."

She gave an elegant shrug. "Dominic swore he'd get even with us. I simply laughed at him. Charlestons was in its heyday back then. Our two businesses were locked in fierce competition. Why would I give you Dantes anything or anyone who might tip the scales in your favor?"

"Did you tell your husband about Dominic's demand?" Primo asked heavily.

"Good gracious, no. Why would I do that? William had a hair-trigger temper. I felt it best to simply let the matter rest." She took a dainty sip of her tea, added a second packet of sugar and slowly stirred. "We liked Cara, even though she came to us pregnant and unmarried. She worked for us for a number of years and then moved on."

Nonna pushed back her chair and stood, her face a mask of grief. "I will wait elsewhere," she announced, her accent heavier than Draco had ever heard it. Then it failed her altogether and she switched to Italian. "The baby. He is an innocent. He has no place here. I will take him in the other room with me so this does not touch him."

The instant the door closed behind Nonna and Stefano, Draco demanded, "What happened after that?"

Leticia sighed. "The years slid by and you Dantes grew more powerful, thanks to your lock on the fire diamonds. When you entered the international market, I could see the end, even though William remained blind to it. We struggled on. And then…"

When it was clear her grandmother couldn't go on, Shayla supplied the next piece of information to the group. "Grandpa had his heart attack," she said. "It was fatal."

"Yes," Leticia whispered. "It was right after we discovered the mines were depleted. The discovery came as a terrible shock. I'm sure the news caused his heart to fail. His death, combined with the issue with the mines, threw Charlestons into chaos." She spared Draco a brief look. "I begged my son to take over, but you were correct in your analysis. Stefan didn't possess what it took. He simply didn't have the drive or ambition necessary to run Charlestons. We were teetering on the edge of bankruptcy. If we went under it would all be gone. The business, the beautiful jewelry, the cars and parties and lifestyle. We'd even lose the mansion."

"What did you do?" Draco asked, though he suspected he knew and threw a look of sympathy in Sev's direction.

Her chin wobbled and it took her a moment to continue. "I swallowed my pride and approached Dantes. I had my family to consider, to put ahead of my own dignity or embarrassment." She clenched her fingers around her napkin. "So, I made an appointment with Primo."

"I never met with you, Letty," Primo instantly denied. "You know I would have helped you if I had."

"Perhaps if your son hadn't taken the appointment in your place this would have all gone down far differently." She closed her eyes briefly, aging before their eyes. "But Dominic did take the meeting, claiming it was at your insistence. It must have been just weeks before his death, near the time of my own son's death."

"What happened at the meeting?" Draco asked gently.

Tears trickled down Leticia's cheeks. "I begged for mercy. Begged for time to reorganize. I had the crazy idea that maybe I could turn Charlestons around."

"So you were going to try and run the company, after all?"

Her cup rattled against the saucer. "All right, yes. You were right, Draco. *Again.* I decided to take the reins. But I needed time, time Dominic wouldn't give me. He told me it was because I wouldn't help him with the Moretti matter, even though that was long past. For him, it might as well have been yesterday. He was cruel. Terribly cruel. He laughed at our plight. He said…" She set her tea down on the conference table with such force the porcelain sang in protest and buried her face in her hands. "He said that if I couldn't afford to feed my family that perhaps I should apply for welfare and put Shayla in foster care."

For a proud woman that must have been the ultimate slap in the face. Draco spared his grandfather and his cousins a swift look. They weren't taking the information well. He could see anger and resentment in some faces, a flat-out refusal to accept the story in Marco's. But Primo's expression proved the most telling. Not only did he accept Leticia's version of events, but he also felt compassion for her plight.

Draco pushed on. "I don't understand something, Leticia. Surely my uncle knew that someone at Dantes had hired your son, Stefan, to run the design department at our New York office?"

She lifted her head and fought for control. "I have no idea. If I had learned of my son's defection from Dominic, it would have crushed me. If he'd known, I guarantee he would have rubbed it in my face, so I suspect he hadn't been told at that point. After my meeting with him, I salvaged what I could. Then Stefan was killed and—"

She broke off, but everyone sitting at the table could see the emptiness and despair. And maybe, just maybe, they began to understand why she'd sought revenge.

Shayla broke the silence. "My grandmother's here to return the money you paid for the mines."

Her grandmother released a slow sigh. "I always knew I'd have to."

"You did." Sev drawled out the words, a caustic edge to his voice. "Really."

Leticia shot to her feet. "Don't you dare look at me with your father's eyes, Severo Dante, and presume to know what happened or what I would or would not have done. Of course

I'm returning the money. Taking it was no more than a coup, an act of defiance."

Draco lifted an eyebrow, impressed despite himself. "Like when American Plains Indians would touch their enemy during battle to prove their bravery."

Leticia nodded. "Exactly. I knew you'd eventually realize that the shaft containing the fire diamonds was an aberration. Not that it matters." She swept a hand through the air as though brushing aside a pesky mosquito and resumed her seat. "You'd have discovered soon enough that the sale wasn't even legal. How could it be when I don't own the mines?"

Shocked silence greeted that statement. "If you do not own the mines, then who does?" Primo demanded.

"Shayla does." Draco dropped the information like a stone into a puddle. Varying reactions splashed from face to face, from unholy amusement to stunned disbelief, Shayla's the most stunned of all. He took her hand in his, lending her his strength. And he took heart in the fact that she let him. "Juice?" he prompted.

Juice regarded Shayla with sympathetic kindness. "The minute you married Draco, the mines became yours. You would have been informed as soon as the lawyer notified you." He shot Leticia a look that contained a grudging hint of respect and, possibly, admiration. "Would it be an accurate statement to say you may have been a trifle lax about informing the lawyer of your granddaughter's marriage?"

"Grandmother, is this true?" Shayla whispered. Hurt and confusion vied for supremacy.

"I would have notified him. Eventually." Irritation sounded in Leticia's voice. "Needless to say I wasn't in any great hurry to bother with such a trifling detail when I had more immediate concerns in need of my attention."

Draco shot her an ironic look. "In other words, you didn't want the news to leak too soon or you wouldn't have had the pleasure of watching the ants scurrying around when you kicked over the anthill."

"See? You understand perfectly."

"The scary part is…I do." He allowed honed steel to gather in his words. "But what I find unforgivable is that you kept Shayla and me apart in order to prevent us from marrying. And all to carry on the Charleston name. All so that my wife wouldn't come into her inheritance too soon. If that happened the hand wouldn't have had time to play out, would it?"

A fierceness burned in Leticia's eyes, drying her tears and turning the irises an iridescent blue. "I didn't want you to just lease the mines, but to buy them. To be desperate to buy them. Careless. Hasty in your assessment. To be distracted enough to believe the reports—or rather forgeries—that hit your desk about the viability of the mines."

"I'm curious. How did you manage that?"

Her mouth snapped closed, warning that she'd never reveal the name of those responsible. "Let's just say I still have contacts in the business," she finally told him. "And it worked. The reports reassured you while the suspicion gnawed at you that I might decide to sell the fire diamonds to your competitors—once I'd bled you as dry as possible, of course. It forced you to buy the mines outright, and quickly." She smiled, a cat-dining-on-canary type of smile. "The bottom line is…I finally beat the Dantes. That's all I ever wanted. To win."

Fury exploded over Sev's face and only his grandfather's restraining hand held him in place. "And now?" Primo asked.

She shrugged carelessly. "Now that the game is finished, you can have your precious money back, less a small brokerage fee."

"Grandmother!"

"What? I need a new car. It's not like they're going to miss thirty thousand or so."

"Thirty!" Shayla choked.

"That's quite some car," Draco said.

Leticia lifted an eyebrow. "Darling, I only travel in style."

He let it go and focused on more important matters. "Now for the final piece of business."

Leticia frowned. "I don't know what's left to be said. I've told you everything," she insisted. "At least, everything I intend to."

He didn't argue. He simply held out his hand. "Your wedding ring, please."

For an instant, he thought she'd refuse. Then she slipped the necklace from around her neck and set it gently on the table. The diamond flashed with unmistakable fire.

Beside him, Shayla stiffened, then jerked as understanding struck. "Oh, Grandmother. What have you done?"

Leticia bowed her head. "I'm sorry, sweetheart. I'm so sorry."

Shayla's chin quivered. "I should have made the connection sooner. It's a fire diamond, but it can't possibly be a Charleston stone because ours were only recently discovered." She stared at her grandmother in utter disillusionment. "I always wondered why you stopped wearing Grandpa's ring. It's because it's not his ring. You arranged the theft of Draco's fire diamonds, didn't you?"

"I swear I didn't. Please, Shayla, you must believe me." She reached for her granddaughter's hand, but Shayla pulled back and Leticia's face crumpled. "But I am culpable because I know who stole them. He was a former employee of Charlestons, Clint Bodine, and I'll always regret that I didn't report him to the authorities when he told me what he'd done."

"Why didn't you?" Draco demanded.

Her hands clenched. "Because he gave me one of the fire diamonds he'd taken, already set in that ring."

"It is a wedding ring. Why would he give you a wedding ring, Letty?" Primo interrupted. "What happened to the one William gave you?"

"I sold it," she whispered. "To help pay off our debts. Clint knew what I'd done and gave me this to replace it. I was going to return the diamond, but in the end I didn't. And for that, I'm truly sorry. And ashamed."

What a strange woman. She didn't turn a hair at the idea of swindling Dantes out of millions of dollars. She saw that as justifiable. But keeping a stolen diamond was wrong. Shameful. Draco's eyes narrowed in thought. "You didn't return it because it was your safety net, wasn't it?"

She nodded, exhaustion lining her face. "In case of an emergency." She reached again for Shayla's hand in a gesture part plea, part apology. When Shayla took the offered hand, she closed her eyes in blatant relief. "And I suppose, if I'm being brutally honest, it also provided a reminder of all the Charlestons had been through at the hands of the Dantes."

The meeting broke up then. Primo insisted on speaking to Leticia privately, while the rest of the family went off to discuss what they'd learned. Juice approached Draco on his way out of the room. "I hope I helped, but somehow I suspect I've only made matters worse for your family, especially Sev."

"My cousin and his brothers just need time to come to terms with what they've heard. We'll all help with that." Draco offered his hand. "Thank you again, Juice. As far as we're concerned, you're family and your help is always appreciated."

"Anytime."

The instant the door closed behind Juice, Draco leaned

against the table and studied his wife. She continued to stand with her back to him. If she stood any stiffer he suspected her spine would crack. "Who goes first?" he asked mildly.

Shayla turned, holding her cup and saucer in front of her like a shield. "I'm so sorry, Draco," she said with painful formality. "My grandmother has caused a great deal of damage."

"You're not the one who owes me an apology. In fact, of all the people here, you owe me one least of all," he informed her roughly. His mouth curved into a smile that held only a trace of old bitterness, a bitterness that faded with each passing second. "And somehow I suspect I won't be getting one from Leticia."

Shayla hesitated. "So, what now?"

"First and foremost, you get the apology you deserve." He looked her straight in the eye. "I am so sorry for everything I said yesterday at the suite. I was wrong to suspect you of any involvement in this mess. Dead wrong. It was a knee-jerk reaction based on past experience and a bad one. I should have known better. I should have known *you* better."

He couldn't tell from her expression whether she accepted his apology or not. "How long did it take you to come to that realization?" she asked. She continued to hold her tea in front of her as though desperate to maintain a buffer between them.

Gently, he removed the cup and saucer from her hands and set it aside. "My heart knew the second you slammed the door in my face. It might have taken my head a little longer," he confessed. "But I got there. Eventually."

"You can be unbelievably stubborn." A hint of her grandmother's tartness slid through the observation. "And now that you know I wasn't trying to swindle you?"

He took a step back and fought to keep his voice even and unemotional. "Now you have a choice," he said carefully.

"I've been in touch with your old boss, Derek Algier. He's a tough man to track down because he's such a recluse, but Juice helped out."

Her eyes widened in surprise. "Derek? Why would you contact him?"

"To see if he needed a translator. I explained your situation. Told him that once Stefano was a little older I would hire a nanny to accompany you abroad while you worked."

"You...you want me to leave?" An odd quality entered her voice, hitched in her throat. "You want a divorce?"

"No!" The word was ripped from him before he could prevent it. He fought to steady it. His hands folded into fists as he struggled for control, struggled to present his case dispassionately. "We made a marriage pact, remember? I'm offering you your freedom, Shayla, just like I promised. Or..."

"Or?"

"There's option number two." No matter how hard he tried to remain detached, a whisper of hope colored his statement.

She must have caught it because she stared, considered, then slowly smiled. "What's option number two?"

"Answer a question first. The mural in Stefano's room." He gazed at her with burning eyes, eyes he suspected reflected the hope in his voice. "Did you mean it?"

She didn't hesitate. "With all my heart."

"Then stay." He went to her, gathered her up and held on so tight that he couldn't tell where he ended and she began. "I love you, Shayla. From the moment you first walked into the Eternity reception no other woman existed but you. I've wanted you since the moment we touched and The Inferno bound us together. I fell in love with you the first time we kissed. I don't think I could stand it if you walked away again."

"Oh, Draco."

She flung her arms around his neck and inhaled him as though his scent was as necessary as the very air she breathed. Then she kissed him, a hard, deep, thorough kiss. He crushed her to him, devouring her, putting every ounce of love and passion, hope and promise, into that one kiss. He ran a hand down her spine so that her curves mated with his angles, a lock to his key. They belonged together, but no matter what it took or how difficult, he'd give her the freedom she craved and the love she deserved.

"Tell me what you need and it's yours," he told her. "I don't want our marriage to trap you. Not ever."

"Our marriage isn't a trap and never could be." She pulled back and cupped his face, tracing his mouth with her thumbs. "I love you, Draco Dante. I've loved you from Inferno to motherhood. And I'll love you from motherhood until you're Primo and I'm Nonna to our great-grandchildren. I don't want to leave. How could I when being bound to you is what set me free?"

He touched her wedding ring. "Eternally Bound?"

Her fingers rested on his so they traced the fire diamonds together. She smiled softly. "I knew it even then, when you told me the meaning of my wedding ring. I was just too afraid to believe. To trust."

"What about our marriage pact?" he asked.

"I suggest we forget all about it."

He shook his head. "Or maybe we just choose to honor a different pact. One we made when I put this ring on your finger."

She closed her eyes, fighting back tears. "I'd like that very much." She hesitated, then rushed to confess, "Maybe this would be a good time to warn you that my grandmother is moving to San Francisco."

"God help us all," he muttered. But he accepted the

inevitable. As much as he might wish it otherwise, Leticia was the last Charleston relative Shayla possessed. He tilted his head to one side. "You know...Dantes is often in need of a translator. Sometimes it requires trips abroad."

She laughed. "Are you asking me to be your wife or trying to get rid of me in the hopes that I'll take my grandmother with me?"

"Tempting. Very tempting." Then he replied, with bone-deep honesty, "I'm trying to make your dreams come true."

She slipped back into his arms and wrapped herself around him. "Stop trying," she whispered against his mouth. "You already have. Now let me take a turn at making yours come true."

"You just did, my love." He held her close and linked his hand with hers, feeling The Inferno well up, solidifying the bond between them. "You just did." Then he lost himself in her kiss. In her embrace.

The dragon had finally found his mate. And as soon as possible he intended to carry her back to his lair and keep her there for a long, long time to come.

* * * * *

A sneaky peek at next month...

Desire

PASSIONATE AND DRAMATIC LOVE STORIES

My wish list for next month's titles...

2 stories in each book - only £5.30!

In stores from 18th November 2011:

☐ The Tycoon's Paternity Agenda – Michelle Celmer

& High-Society Seduction – Maxine Sullivan

☐ To Tame a Sheikh – Olivia Gates

& His Thirty-Day Fiancée – Catherine Mann

☐ Taming the VIP Playboy – Katherine Garbera

& Promoted to Wife? – Paula Roe

☐ A Wife for a Westmoreland – Brenda Jackson

& Claiming His Royal Heir – Jennifer Lewis

Available at WHSmith, Tesco, Asda, Eason, Amazon and Apple

Just can't wait?

Visit us Online

You can buy our books online a month before they hit the shops! **www.millsandboon.co.uk**

1111/51

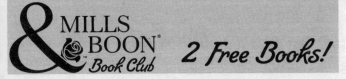

www.millsandboon.co.uk/freebookoffer

Or fill in the form below and post it back to us

THE MILLS & BOON® BOOK CLUB™—HERE'S HOW IT WORKS: Accepting your free books places you under no obligation to buy anything. You may keep the books and return the despatch note marked 'Cancel'. If we do not hear from you, about a month later we'll send you 4 brand-new stories from the Desire™ 2-in-1 series priced at £5.30* each. There is no extra charge for post and packaging. You may cancel at any time, otherwise we will send you 4 stories a month which you may purchase or return to us—the choice is yours. *Terms and prices subject to change without notice. Offer valid in UK only. Applicants must be 18 or over. Offer expires 28th February 2012. **For full terms and conditions, please go to www.millsandboon.co.uk/termsandconditions**

Mrs/Miss/Ms/Mr (please circle) _____

First Name _____

Surname _____

Address _____

_____

_____ Postcode _____

E-mail _____

Send this completed page to: Mills & Boon Book Club, Free Book Offer, FREEPOST NAT 10298, Richmond, Surrey, TW9 1BR

Find out more at
www.millsandboon.co.uk/freebookoffer

Visit us Online

0611/D1ZEE

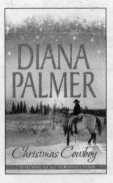

Have Your Say

You've just finished your book.
So what did you think?

We'd love to hear your thoughts on our 'Have your say' online panel
www.millsandboon.co.uk/haveyoursay

- Easy to use
- Short questionnaire
- Chance to win Mills & Boon® goodies

Visit us Online | Tell us what you thought of this book now at **www.millsandboon.co.uk/haveyoursay**

YOUR_SAY